PR

FOREVER THIS TIME

"McGinnis weaves an engrossing and uplifting tale of enduring love."
—*Publishers Weekly*

"Maggie McGinnis really outshines herself with this well written story."
—*Night Owl Reviews* (5 stars! Top Pick!)

"Finely crafted, well-rounded characters, and the delightful plot make this a must-read."
—*Reader to Reader Reviews*

"Such a heartrending story of growing up, running away, then coming back to find where you left your heart."
—*Romance Junkies*

HEART LIKE MINE

"An engaging plot, genuine, relatable characters, and a sweet yet sexy romance will keep readers turning the pages."
—*RT Book Reviews*

"A book that can [make you] laugh and cry while reading. Read it in one sitting, just couldn't put it down."
—*Fresh Fiction*

Also by
Maggie McGinnis

Forever This Time

Heart Like Mine

Snowflake Wishes (novella)

She's Got a Way

Maggie McGinnis

St. Martin's Paperbacks

This is a work of fiction. All of the characters, organizations, and events portrayed in this novel are either products of the author's imagination or are used fictitiously.

SHE'S GOT A WAY

Copyright © 2016 by Maggie McGinnis.

For information address St. Martin's Press, 175 Fifth Avenue, New York, NY 10010.

ISBN: 978-1-250-06909-2

Our books may be purchased in bulk for promotional, educational, or business use. Please contact your local bookseller or the Macmillan Corporate and Premium Sales Department at 1-800-221-7945, ext. 5442, or by e-mail at MacmillanSpecialMarkets@macmillan.com.

Printed in the United States of America

St. Martin's Paperbacks edition / September 2016

St. Martin's Paperbacks are published by St. Martin's Press, 175 Fifth Avenue, New York, NY 10010.

10 9 8 7 6 5 4 3 2 1

To Aunt Judy

For her courage, her grace, her laughter . . .

. . . her love

Acknowledgments

In a busy year full of excitement and possibility, I'm incredibly honored and humbled to thank the following people for their assistance with this book:

My editor, Holly Ingraham—for her kindness, her humor, and her keen editorial eye. It's been so fun bringing Echo Lake to life with you.

My agent, Courtney Miller-Callihan—I'm so lucky and excited to be part of Team Courtney's new venture.

The entire St. Martin's team, for the gorgeous cover, the fabulous book-love, and for making me feel so welcome.

My critique partner and cheerleader extraordinaire, Jennifer Brodie—for just being indescribably awesome. Always.

My bunnies—for five amazing years of *what ifs*.

Markus B—for generously sharing his expertise on at-risk teens and outdoor education. And for taking me rock-climbing and not dropping me, even if I made it tempting.

The men in my family, who inspire my book-heroes. You, every day, are the real heroes.

Most importantly, to my girls, because truly, there's no greater gift than you.

Chapter 1

"First offense—itching powder on the headmaster's toilet paper." Gabriela sighed as she let her eyes land on the four teenaged girls seated in the lounge area of the dorm. She loved them like they were her own, but right now, she'd happily rent any one of them out as birth control. They'd make even the most anxious parent-to-be think twice.

"Second offense—baby powder in her blow dryer." She took a deep breath. "Third offense—the crickets in her bedroom. I *still* don't think she's found them all."

Madison—blond, beautiful, ringleader Madison—snickered. "Pritchard deserved it, and you know it. She's a bi—"

"Madison." Gabi's voice was firm, her eyebrows hiked. "That'll be enough. None of those things even comes *close* to what you guys did last night. You have no idea how much trouble you're in right now."

"Is this when you say, 'Fourth offense: sneaking off to a boys' school in a stolen vehicle'?" She rolled her eyes. "Because we're going to be all overdramatic here?"

Gabi lifted her eyebrows even further, but Madison just shrugged in response. "I just don't think it's as big a deal as you and Pritch-bitch are going to make it. As usual."

"Wrong. It's a *huge* flipping deal. You hotwired the school van, for God's sake."

"But Gabi—" Waverly started to plead, but Gabi put up a hand.

"Sorry, girls. Briarwood Academy has an ironclad code of conduct, and you smashed it to smithereens. The board called an emergency meeting this morning, and the headmaster has been in touch with all of your parents. You will be *very* lucky if they don't expel you."

Gabi paused, letting that sink in. She noticed Waverly's arms dropping a bit, Eve's eyes darting around the room, Madison biting her lip. Good. These four suitemates had been at each other's throats all year, and in an irony of ironies, the first time they'd actually collaborated on *anything,* they'd chosen something that could get them all thrown out on their snarky little butts.

Sam—short for Alexandra-don't-ask—narrowed her eyes. "She seriously called our—parents?" Her voice caught on the last word, but only she and Gabi knew why.

"Well, if the police get involved, there's no way we can have your families hearing about this from *them* first."

"The *police*? But Gabi"—Waverly's hand moved to her throat—"didn't you defend us? It was just a prank sort of a thing. Not, like, a criminal thing. Jeez."

Gabi shook her head. Waverly had probably been dragged along against her will, as usual. The girl needed a serious spine transplant. "Don't make me list the criminal offenses here."

Madison rolled her eyes. "Not that we're going to be dramatic. Again."

Waverly looked up, eyes starting to water. "But you're

our housemother. Don't you have leverage here? Can't you help us?"

Gabi bristled at the title, just like she always did when it was spoken out loud. She was, in essence, the residential director for the entire boarding school, but Headmaster Pritchard preferred the antiquated term. Pritchard also preferred a school where everyone knew her place in the pecking order, and she liked that Gabi's was firmly below hers, despite her master's degree and eight years of employment.

Gabi shook her head. "My leverage—such as it is— ended the minute you all stepped your pretty little heads off campus. You took it too far this time, and you're going to have to deal with the consequences."

Just then, the lounge door opened, and Priscilla Pritchard stepped through, the picture of composure . . . and a cat-ate-canary smile that made butterflies take flight low in Gabi's stomach. Priscilla was dressed in her customary navy skirt, navy blazer, and Hermès scarf— the green one, because it was Friday. Not a hair escaped her fashionable bun, and though she was pushing sixty, Gabi suspected her Boston colorist was paid extremely well to make sure not one silver sparkle ever peeked through her blond strands.

Priscilla crossed her arms and leaned against the wall. "Ladies."

Silence greeted her, which—strangely—made her smile grow even bigger. Gabi swallowed. She had a bad feeling about this—worse than the one she'd had as she'd climbed the fire escape of the Pendleton dorm and rounded up the girls twelve hours ago.

Finally, she spoke. "I assume you expect I'm here to expel the whole lot of you. And fortunately for me, your parents all agree that expulsion is a punishment that would match the crime."

Dammit. She *was* going to expel them. And maybe they deserved it, but Gabi had way too much skin in this particular game to be happy about it.

As if by silent signal, the girls transitioned out of their defensive postures, apparently believing there might be more power in pretending they didn't care. Madison and Waverly probably *didn't,* actually. They'd just transfer to another boarding school, decorate their new rooms in next year's designer colors, and stir up trouble once again.

But Sam and Eve wouldn't know a designer color if it landed on their heads. If they lost their scholarships at Briarwood, they'd be headed back to Boston—back to foster homes that would hardly notice they were back . . . if they even landed in the same ones they'd come from.

"Have any of you ever heard of Camp Echo?" Priscilla raised her eyebrows, that snarky little smile lurking at the corners of her lips. At her question, Gabi's butterflies started banging on the walls of her stomach.

Priscilla took a couple more steps into the room, then sat down in a hard-backed chair facing them. "It's a lovely little place on the shores of Echo Lake, Vermont, just three hours from here. Briarwood recently bought the property, and the board is anxious to get started using it. Luckily for us, it seems we have suddenly been presented with the perfect opportunity."

Gabi sat down hard. Oh, holy hell. Priscilla was sending the girls to . . . camp?

"So." Priscilla put her hands together like a delighted grandma on the verge of giving her grandchildren a new car. "With the permission of all of your parents . . . or guardians, we have come up with an alternative to expulsion. The four of you will leave your rooms next week only to take your exams and eat your meals, and on Friday, you'll pack your bags for a four-week stay at Camp Echo."

Madison narrowed her eyes. "Not possible. My father would never have agreed to this."

"He did." Priscilla pointed to each girl in turn. "As did everyone else's. You're lucky this is the consequence we came up with. You're *extremely* lucky the board didn't elect to send you to my first choice of camps, where you would have to make your own clothing, your own soap, and your own shelters."

Gabi felt her teeth almost bite through her bottom lip. As much as she was relieved that someone had taken expulsion off the table, Priscilla was far too delighted about this consequence to have Gabi believing the girls were headed to some sort of pristine lakeside paradise for half the summer.

There had to be a catch.

Eve adjusted her arms so they were tighter to her chest. "This Camp Echo—does it have, like, cabins?"

Priscilla shrugged her shoulders delicately. "I haven't been there, but I was assured by the director just now that the facilities would be appropriate for the situation."

Gabi darted her eyes toward her. Right now, "appropriate for the situation" would be pup tents in bear country, with loaves of bread for pillows.

Waverly blinked hard. "But I'm supposed to go to Paris."

Gabi pictured her own flight reservation, currently tacked to the bulletin board above her desk. Next Friday night—apparently now after she'd seen this little crew off to Camp Echo—she'd be boarding a flight to Barbados for a well-deserved trip to paradise. Ideally, it would have been a honeymoon—say, with her favorite romcom hero—but with her thirtieth birthday looming, she'd yet to find a guy she could imagine lasting much *past* the honeymoon.

It wasn't that her expectations were unrealistic, of course, even if the girls did accuse her of living in some sort of Hollywood-induced romancelandia. And it wasn't her fault that she firmly believed a guy, with the right influence, could actually turn out to be perfect. It was just . . . well, she had no idea what it was, really. But here she was, twenty-nine years old, living in a tiny apartment at a girls' boarding school, and oddly enough, Prince Charming hadn't yet found his way to her door.

So she was taking her own damn self to the Caribbean. Maybe, among the lovestruck honeymooners at the tiki bar, she'd find a kindred soul looking for *his* happily-ever-after.

Right.

Sam drew her knees up to her chest, settling into the corner of the couch in a defensive move Gabi recognized from when she'd first arrived at Briarwood. The girl could hotwire a school van, drive across state lines without a license, and probably drink a twenty-one-year-old under the table, but right now, she actually looked scared. Gabi almost felt sympathetic, until she remembered the hours she'd spent on the road last night, praying that the girls were alive.

"How are we getting to this camp?" Eve asked.

"You will be driven there in the school van—using the ignition key this time." Priscilla smiled, pleased with her little attempt at humor. Then she looked straight at Gabi. "Ms. O'Brien will be taking you."

Gabi felt her eyes go wide.

Wait just one flipping Barbados minute. Oh, no, she wouldn't be.

"I'm sorry, Pris—Ms. Pritchard. I have a flight that evening. We'll need to find someone else to drive the girls." Gabi knew damn well that Priscilla was aware of her trip. It had taken the woman a full month to hem and haw over whether Gabi could be allowed to *take* the two-week unpaid vacation, but maybe in the chaos of the morning, she'd forgotten.

Gabi felt her stomach clench as her lips tightened. The girls' heads all swiveled to look at her. *They* knew how much she was looking forward to this trip. They'd been cutting out tropical pictures for her bulletin board all spring. They'd planned her sightseeing itinerary down to the minute for her, and they'd loaded up her tablet with ten of her favorite movies to watch on the beach.

Priscilla cleared her throat. "Actually, Ms. O'Brien, we need to talk about your trip."

Gabi's stomach fell.

Or . . . maybe she hadn't forgotten at all.

"Boarding-school girls?" Luke Magellan shook his head in confusion later that afternoon. *"Here?"*

Oliver nodded, rocking back in his rickety lawn chair as he sent a hand through his shock of gunmetal-gray hair. "Nothing I could do. Briarwood bought the property in April. They own us now. And I guess they're getting started on the 'using us' part."

Luke looked out at Echo Lake, glistening in the early summer sun. The beach was quiet, the dock was quiet, the dining hall was empty . . . just like he'd thought it was going to be all summer. No boys on the tire swings, no boys paddling the lake, no boys whooping and hollering from the diving raft.

Utter, awful silence.

He put his hands on his hips, completely mystified. "I don't get it. First, they buy the place as a completely transparent tax write-off. Then, despite their promises to keep it operating as you've run it for three decades now, they close us down for the summer and hand us a project list that makes it very clear they actually have *no* such intentions. And now they're sending us a group of little rich girls who are *this* close to expulsion? What the hell are we supposed to do with them?"

Oliver blew out a pained breath. "I don't know."

Luke paced the dock, automatically stepping over the three loose boards he hadn't had time to fix. Then a thought occurred to him. There was no way this Briarwood headmaster would send her students if she knew the true shape of the facilities right now. The girls' parents would shit bricks.

He turned back to Oliver. "They know we don't have anywhere for them to sleep, right?"

"We have tents." Oliver shrugged slowly.

Luke snorted. "Right. You're thinking a limo full of Briarwood girls are going to roll in here and be okay with us showing them to their army canvas?"

"I'm thinking these particular girls have reached the end of the Briarwood rope, if the alternative was to send them home for good. Tents might be the least of their problems."

Luke rolled his eyes. "Why didn't they just expel them, if that's what the girls deserved?"

"Two words: rich parents. You piss them off, you kiss your future endowment money good-bye. Briarwood wants the money, so Briarwood has to keep the kids." Oliver shook his head. "But it sounds like the board insisted on a consequence that matched the crime. Maybe they're using the girls as an example to their other wannabe-miscreants. I don't know."

"So they chose Camp Echo." Luke sighed. "They

know that besides the dining hall, every last thing here is on its last legs, right? They know you and I are the only staff members left?"

As he said the words, he swore silently. How could they *not* know? They owned the place now, damn it all.

"They know. And it might just be me, but it seemed like the headmaster was actually happy to hear it."

"Then she must be extremely pissed at this crew. We've got no programs, no counselors, no nothing. And they wasted no time demoting me right down from director to camp handyman. Who's supposed to supervise them all summer? Who's going to keep them from running wild all over *this* property?"

Oliver looked down at his notepad. "Gabriela O'Brien. The housemother. Apparently she drew the short straw."

Luke felt his eyebrows go skyward as he pictured steel-wool hair and flowered muumuus. A *housemother*? "And is this . . . housemother responsible for entertaining them?"

"Apparently."

"Well, this is just. *Shit.* What are we supposed to do with an elderly woman here? We can't make *her* sleep in a frigging tent, Oliver."

"You want to give up your cabin?"

"Hell, no. It's all I've got left." Luke rubbed his forehead with both hands. "But I'm not going to put her in a tent, for Christ's sake."

"Well, not sure we've got other options. I can't put her in the back room of the admin cottage with me. People would talk."

Luke smiled for the first time as he pictured Oliver's living quarters, which were just about big enough to turn around in, as long as you held your breath so your stomach caved inward.

"We don't have time to build them a cabin, not with our other priorities here. They'll be here in a week."

Oliver nodded. "Let's play it by ear. Maybe she's not elderly. Or maybe, if she is, she's the type that loves a good summer of roughing it in the wild."

"She works at Briarwood. The roughest thing they have there is the oatmeal, and even that's probably organic and steel cut and gluten-free." Luke felt his eyebrows pull together. "We've got a project list a mile long. What we *need* is a work crew, not a bunch of rich girls sunning on the beach."

"Unless you turn them *into* your work crew." Oliver bounced his eyebrows.

Luke leveled a look his way. "This is just the first step, Oliver. You see that, right?"

"What do you mean?"

"I mean—first they send a group like this, and they frame it as a desperation move, nowhere else to send them, yadda yadda. Next, we hear about how maybe they were a little hasty in their decision to keep Echo running as a boys' camp, because look how well suited it was for their girls. And then we get a bunch of mumbo-jumbo paperwork that excuses us from our positions because their original mission has changed, but best of luck in the future—"

"Yadda yadda?"

"Exactly." Luke nodded. "I'm just saying. This smacks of a plan, not an emergency at all."

"Well, it sure *sounded* like an emergency."

"I don't buy it. They never intended to run this place as a boys' camp, and this is their first step toward re-neging on that promise. I'd bet my new handyman salary on it."

Oliver rolled his eyes. "You're the only one calling yourself that, Luke."

Luke laughed, short and bitter. "Well, I went from running programs for a hundred needy kids every summer to working my way through an endless project list in an empty camp. It's not much of a stretch."

He sighed. He'd designed challenge-based programs for at-risk kids for ten years now under Oliver's tutelage, and he was damn good at it, because he'd worked his ass off to get there. His own history gave him an auto-in with a lot of the boys, and helping them learn to give a shit about themselves and their futures was a job he took very, very seriously.

It was the best lesson Oliver had ever imparted, and it had started the moment Luke had walked onto Camp Echo property as an angry foster kid determined to make everyone hate him, because it was easier. You knew where you stood.

He knew exactly where these kids could end up without his help, and he didn't want that for anyone. Been there, done that, had the scars to prove it.

He looked out at the lake, where a couple of little sailboats struggled to find a wisp of a breeze. "So what do we do?"

"We welcome them when they get here, we show them where everything is, and then we go on about our merry ways, doing the jobs we're *supposed* to be doing for the summer. The fact that four Briarwood girls snuck off campus and got themselves into this situation isn't our problem."

"You're going to stick to that?" Luke raised his eyebrows. "You're not going to go all sympathetic when it's clear that this housemother person is completely out of her Briarwood element here?"

"We don't know that she will be."

"Seriously."

"Fine. She'll be *completely* out of her element." Oliver

put up his hands. "But she can figure it out. I'm sure she'll have a plan by the time she gets here."

"And if she doesn't?"

"Then we give her a week to flounder, and we send them home."

Luke sighed. "You sure we're not being pranked? Not about to be the victims of some new reality show where they send mini-princesses into the wilderness to see who lives through the summer?"

"At this point, I'd believe just about anything."

"Well, I'll tell you this—if that Briarwood limo pulls in here with a camera van in tow, I'm outta here."

"Fair enough." Oliver shook his head. "But you're gonna have to move pretty fast to beat *me* out the gate."

Chapter 2

A week later, Luke strode into the dining hall, two fur balls at his heels, annoyance speeding his steps.

Piper Bellini, temporary camp cook, popped her head up from among a pile of boxes in the kitchen, took one look at his face, and slid back down behind them.

He rolled his eyes. "Shut up, Piper."

She popped back up. "I didn't say anything!"

"You didn't have to."

"So you already know you look like you're about to kill somebody?" She pointed at the dogs. "Health department will freak if they know you let them in here, you know."

Luke looked down at the pups circling his feet, still not quite sure how he'd ended up with them. Six months ago, he'd had an old black Lab who'd followed him everywhere, but a month after Duke had died in his sleep, these little puffballs posing as dogs had shown up on his porch.

Piper reached down to pick up one of them, motioning Luke and the other one out of the kitchen area. "Is this Thing 1? Or Thing 2? And also, when do they get their real names?"

"I've been thinking, okay? How about Ding and Dong?"

She laughed as she covered the dog's little ears. "Not nice."

"Ping and Pong? Riff and Raff?"

"Wow. You really *are* in a mood." Piper set the dog down and motioned for Luke to sit down at one of the long indoor picnic tables she'd painted last weekend. She was an art therapist by day, waitress in her family's restaurant by night, and wielded a mean paintbrush when she wasn't doing the other things. When Luke had called her last Friday about doing some emergency spiff-ups, she'd arrived within an hour, her fiancé Noah's truck loaded with a rainbow of paint cans.

She picked up the other dog and cuddled it under her chin. "So when are the preppy chicks arriving?"

He rolled his eyes. "Four hours."

"You have tents ready?"

"I've got *a* tent ready. But they're going to have to put it up."

Piper smiled widely. "That ought to be fun to watch. How about a bathroom and shower?"

"We have a perfectly good outhouse. And a lake. If they want a bathroom, then they can *build* a damn bathroom. It's on the project list, anyway."

Piper stopped petting the dog. "It's good that you're not at all bitter here."

"Oh, I passed bitter just about the time Oliver had to sign the sale papers, Piper. This place should be busting at the seams with obnoxious boys right now."

"Is there any hope that you're—you know—wrong? That maybe Briarwood really is planning to keep this place running as a boys' camp after it's brought back up to code?"

Luke pulled a folded-up piece of paper out of his back

pocket and spread it out. "I'll let the project list answer that for me."

Piper took the piece of paper and scanned it quickly. He knew she was seeing shower stalls, a TV lounge, and cabins with central air. Camp Echo would no longer be a rustic camp on the shores of a quiet, beautiful lake. No—it was going to join the ranks of a million other lakefront properties that called themselves camps . . . but were really just glorified boarding schools. Hundreds of girls who needed . . . well, nothing . . . would cycle through here starting next summer, he'd bet his left foot.

Meanwhile, hundreds of boys who needed *everything* would be out of luck.

"Fine." She pushed the list back toward him. "I see what you mean. So what are you going to do with the little princesses? Got your programs all worked out?"

Luke shook his head. "No programs. Oliver wants to let them figure things out themselves, and I wholeheartedly agree."

"Really."

"Don't roll your eyes at me, Piper. Yes, really."

"And you're not at all concerned about how that might work out?"

"Oh, I'm completely concerned." Luke sighed. "Oliver's plan, as of this morning, is to give them a week and send them home. *My* plan is to make like a lynx and disappear as soon as they arrive."

"Now that's the big, brave Luke I know." Piper patted his sleeve.

"Piper?" he growled.

"I know." She laughed. "Shut up. But before I do, I can't help but warn you."

"About what?"

"About the fact that you generally pretty much suck

at letting other people loose in your space. Especially strangers."

"Well, lucky for us all, I'm too busy to care."

"Okay." She sighed. "You go with that. But I'll bet you a Bellinis special that you cave by day three. There's no way you're going to let some hoity-toity housemother from some hoity-toity school take over your camp." She shook her head. "Not. Gonna. Happen."

"We'll see, Pipes. We'll see." He looked out at the lake, feeling his shoulders drop. "Not really my camp anymore, though, is it?"

Four hours later, Luke heard the van before he saw it, but still hadn't managed to quite extricate himself from the climbing ropes he was untangling by the time it pulled to a stop in front of the administration cottage. It was exactly what he'd expected—a shiny BMW with the Briarwood logo emblazoned on the side, and he tried to compose his features into a welcoming, tolerant smile as he waited on the lawn.

The sooner they started, the sooner it'd be done, after all.

And at least there wasn't a network van behind it.

"Be nice." Piper growled in his ear as she joined him. "Even if it kills you."

"Oh, it's definitely going to kill me."

"Do it anyway." She pasted a huge smile on her face as the double doors opened in the back. "I'll take the girls into the dining hall. You deal with the housemother. I guarantee you she doesn't want to be here, either."

Whatever, he muttered inside his head. But for the sake of pretending to be an adult about the whole thing, he conjured up his best smile and walked around to the driver's side of the van. When he caught sight of the woman stepping out, though, he stopped short. This was no steely-haired old bird in a flowered dress. No. She had sleek, dark hair, a wrist full of gold bangles, and curves in all the right places. He blinked, then peered into the backseat, searching for the housemother. Had Briarwood sent them with a hottie driver?

"Mr. Magellan?" The woman raised her eyebrows, her hand outstretched, and he realized she'd probably said that once already. Crap.

He shook her hand quickly. "It's Luke."

"Gabriela." She pointed a finger toward her chest, and he blinked hard.

"Wait. *You're* Gabriela?"

"Yes. I promise."

"Sorry." He smiled. "You're just . . . not exactly what I was expecting, from your title."

No, she was *nothing* like he'd expected, and damn, she was holy-shit gorgeous. If she was a day over thirty, he'd be shocked. She had on a lavender-colored sleeveless shirt that probably cost more than his groceries, and jeans that came to just below her knees. Strappy leather sandals with pink-painted toenails completed her look, and if ever there was a woman who'd set foot on Echo property and looked less like she belonged, it was her.

"I left my housemother curlers and bathrobe back at the dorm, since I wasn't sure what your facilities would be like. Brought my fuzzy slippers, though."

"Touché. I apologize."

"It's okay." She winked. "I'm not a big fan of my job title, but the headmaster is *very* attached to it. I'm kind of stuck."

"What do the girls call you?"

"Gabi."

"Well, welcome to Camp Echo, Gabi." He pointed to Piper. "This is Piper. She'll be handling the kitchen this summer for us."

Gabi reached her hand out to Piper, smile still in place, then motioned for the girls to join her. "This is Sam, Eve, Madison, and Waverly." Her bracelets clinked softly as she pointed to each of them.

Piper clapped her hands. "I just made cookies. How about I take the girls in for a snack while you two get acquainted?"

Luke heard a snicker from the little herd of teens, then saw Gabi's smile break for a brief second as she shot the offender a death ray.

"I think a snack would be lovely. Thank you, Piper." She tipped her head graciously. "Girls, why don't you head in with Piper, and I'll catch up to you?"

A chorus of mumbles served as their reply, and Luke fought not to sigh. After they'd disappeared up the pathway behind the admin building, Gabi closed the van door, sliding her hands into her pockets.

"Thank you for making space for us for the summer. I imagine you've got a full camp already."

He blinked. She imagined *what*?

"Um, no. We don't actually have *any* campers this summer."

"What?" Her eyebrows pulled together. "What do you mean, you don't have any campers?"

"Camp's closed, Ms. O'Brien. Briarwood shut us down. We're scheduled to open back up *next* June. Maybe."

"But . . . why would they shut down the camp?"

"They want some changes made before we open under their umbrella. This summer's all about making those changes happen. So . . ."—he waved an arm around the empty beach—"we're closed."

"I don't underst—" She looked around nervously, probably taking in the lack of activity for the first time. He followed the path of her eyes, seeing the empty dock, the canoes tied up in rows, the gaping holes in the trees where sleeping tents had stood in years past. "There's really no one here?"

"Just me and the camp director, and now you guys."

"So . . ." Her eyes returned to his. "I'm confused. Priscilla Pritchard sentenced the girls to . . . *camp*. There *is* no camp. Does she—she can't possibly know this . . . right?"

The last word was quiet, and for a moment, Luke actually felt a pang of sympathy for her. Here she'd been sent to the boonies with her rule-breaking cretins for the month, and she'd probably pictured a pristine camp on the shores of a pristine lake, with pristine cabins and a full-service dining room.

His pang faded quickly. Of course that's what she would have expected. It's what Briarwood types *always* expected. He sighed. It's probably what she *could* realistically expect next year, if all went as Briarwood planned for it to.

But for now, she was going to have to deal with what they had. Which was not much.

He cleared his throat. "Not sure about your use of the word 'sentenced.' And I don't know what your headmaster knew. I didn't have those conversations with her."

"She knows." Oliver's deep voice came from behind him as he reached out a beefy hand toward Gabi. "Hi. Oliver Black. Camp director, past tense. She didn't tell you the camp's officially closed?"

"No." Gabi shook her head, looking a little bit like a deer in the headlights. "No, she didn't. I don't understand. This is never going to work. You guys aren't even an operational camp. I—I need to make a call." Gabi reached back into the van for her phone, but when she pulled it out, she frowned. "There's no cell service here, is there?"

"Nope."

"Is there a phone I could use?"

Oliver grimaced. "If you're calling the headmaster, I'm afraid she isn't going to answer."

"Why not?"

"Well . . ." He looked from her to Luke, like he was debating whether to continue. "Seems she had a four o'clock flight."

"A four o'clock *what*?" Luke heard the growl in Gabi's voice, and he almost laughed. Closing her eyes, she took a deep breath, then looked at both of them. "There must be a mistake."

"Sorry, honey. No mistake." Oliver pointed at the pathway where Piper'd led the girls. "We've hired a part-time cook to help you out, but it looks like you're stuck with us for the month. Let's get the girls settled in, and in the morning, we can figure things out."

She took another deep breath, glancing at her watch. "I can't even . . . there's no way . . . we can't stay here." She looked around at the surrounding woods, which were practically silent, save for the birds and squirrels chattering away in the trees. "So you really have no counselors?"

"Nope."

"No programs? No schedule?" She put up her fingers as she listed. "No nature hikes and origami and swim lessons?"

"None of the above."

"So what are *you* doing this summer, if the camp's closed?"

Luke smiled tightly. "I'm the . . . camp handyman. Oliver's the previous director. And right now, our job is to get the place shipshape for next year. So we'll stay out of your way, but you'll be on your own with your girls."

Her face fell, and again, he felt guilty, but for Christ's sake, it wasn't his fault she'd been sent up here. Not his fault she was stuck here for the summer with four little rich girls to entertain. He had a job to do, and as much as he hated it, it did *not* involve helping this gorgeous stranger out of her own mess.

"Well." She stiffened her shoulders and raised her chin a notch. "I will do my best to stay out of your way, as well."

Luke nodded. "I'm sorry to be blunt. Just trying to be clear about where things are at. Briarwood bought us, but Briarwood hasn't staffed us at this point. We've got a property to bring back up to code, and we've got only two employees. Piper Bellini's offered to help us out on the food end as much as she can, but that's it. You're looking at Camp Echo as it stands right now. We just don't have the manpower to create a surprise four-week program."

"Understood." She nodded, but the mad-spots on her cheeks hadn't faded a bit. "I'm not entirely sure *what* I understand, but it's too late to turn around, at least to-night. Maybe you could show us to our cabins, then? So we can be out of your way?" Gabi got her keys ready, like she was about to drive down some sort of flower-strewn pathway to her two-story cottage with its maid service and full bath.

"We don't have camper cabins, Gabi."

"What do you mean—you don't have cabins?" She peered around him, and he knew she could see the admin cottage and the dining hall, but no other structures, since his own cabin was up over the hill. He could practically feel the fear, not to mention the barely bridled anger, radiating from her skin.

He crossed his arms again. "We have tents."

"Tents?" She narrowed her eyes. "You're not serious."

"Dead serious." He pushed away from the van, motioning for her to follow. "But I'll be happy to show you to yours."

She reached for his elbow, touching it lightly, then pulling back quickly like she hadn't meant to actually do so.

"Please tell me you're joking."

He turned around. "Look, this isn't Camp Ritz. We have tents."

"Oka-ay?" Her eyes darted left and right. "But what about . . . wildlife? I mean—because the girls will ask. What kinds of creatures do you tend to have . . . here?"

"You mean, which kind can get into tents? Or which kind doesn't generally bother?"

"Not funny, Mr. Magellan."

"It's Luke."

"It's not funny, *Luke*."

He put up his hands in a placating motion. "We have a lot of wildlife. But as long as the girls follow the rules, they shouldn't have a problem."

"Okay." She took a shaky breath. "And you'll tell us those rules before dusk?"

"If we have time." Then he put up a hand. "I know. Not funny. Come on. Follow me. I saved you a special bearproof tent."

"They make those?"

He stopped and turned, almost making her crash into him. The smell of her perfume *did* crash into him, and the sweet spiciness of it wasn't at *all* what he expected. Dammit. He did not want to like anything about this woman, including how she smelled.

"Gabi, have you ever *seen* a bear?"

"No."

"Have you ever seen a *picture* of a bear?"

"Of course." She rolled her eyes.

"How about their teeth?"

"Um . . ."

He smiled, then turned back down the pathway. "There's no such thing as a bearproof tent."

Chapter 3

"You said we had a tent." Five minutes later, Gabi stared at a twelve-by-twelve-foot plywood platform surrounded by pines. She'd grudgingly admit that the clearing was gorgeous—tall, tall trees, pine needles carpeting the ground, and a cacophony of bird sounds coming from every direction.

But there was no tent.

"It's in the storage shed." Luke pointed at the boards, right now covered with pale orange needles. "But it'll go right here."

"Who's going to put it up?" She hated the words as they came out of her mouth, already having a pretty good idea what his answer was going to be.

"The girls should."

Gabi laughed nervously, picturing her four girls having to figure out how to put up a tent. It was so not going to happen, even with her help. She'd never put one up in her life, either.

"Does it come with directions?"

"Nope. Just a lot of parts. But I'm sure they'll figure it out. Tents aren't all that complicated."

"So you're thinking that on day one of arriving here

at Camp Echo, these girls should have to figure out how to build their own sleeping structure?"

He rolled his eyes. "They're not *building a sleeping structure*. They're putting up a tent."

Then another thought struck Gabi. If there were no cabins, then what about bathrooms? "Just out of curiosity, where are the restrooms?"

She saw a tiny smile sneak over Luke's face as he pointed a little farther down the trail. "Follow me."

They walked for about thirty steps over a small rise, and Gabi almost tripped when Luke stopped and pointed.

"There you go."

Gabi took a quick, appalled breath when she saw the three-by-six-foot wooden hut set just off the path. It looked like someone had gone a little wild with a paintbrush not long ago on its sides, so it was fresh and colorful, but good Lord, it was an outhouse. An *outhouse*.

"That's. Not. A restroom."

"Oh, but it is."

"We were told—"

"Look." Luke put up both hands. "I don't know the person who made these arrangements, and I don't know what you all did to end up here, but what we've got is what we've got. Nobody at Briarwood would have been told there were cabins *or* restrooms. We've got tents and outhouses. The only reason the dining hall is an actual building is because the health department requires floors and windows where you serve food."

"Charming."

"Piper said she made some—what did she call them?—female adjustments inside. I don't know what that means, and I don't want to, but they should be fine for your girls. There are two stalls, two doors, and five of you. This is what camping's all about, Gabi. You're lucky you don't have to teach them how to go out to the woods to deal with things."

"Even *more* charming, thank you." Gabi put her hands on her hips, looking around in consternation. She *did* know the person who'd made these arrangements—knew her very well—and she could imagine the abject glee Priscilla was feeling right now as she sat in her first-class seat sipping white wine, picturing Gabi arriving at this camp where there were no cabins, no real bathrooms, and no—

"Wait a minute. Where will we shower?"

Luke hooked a thumb toward the lake. "In there."

"Not funny."

"Not lying."

She narrowed her eyes. "You know what? If the construction crew hadn't rolled up to our dorm the moment we pulled out, I'd be tempted to load the girls right back in the van and head back tonight."

He shrugged, like he couldn't care less what she did, and somehow that made her even angrier. "Your call."

She sighed, picturing the hard-hat signs tacked up on the doorways. *Dammit.* She was so stuck.

Gabi eyed him for a long moment, knowing he was hoping she'd do exactly that—give up on this stupid camp before she'd been here a whole hour. He was obviously pissed that she and the girls were crashing his summer, and probably there'd be nothing he'd like better than to see them turn around and head right back to Briarwood. He'd obviously pegged them as prissy rich chicks who couldn't handle his camp, anyway, so their departure would just prove it.

For some reason, that ticked her off more than the

rest of the situation, which was really saying something at this point.

"We'll be staying, thank you." She felt her chin rise. The girls would build the damn tent. And she would help them. They'd figure out the bathroom situation later. "If you could show me to the storage shed and point me to the tent pieces, we'll get started."

"Gladly." He paused, then turned to head back up the pathway. As she followed him, Gabi looked around, seeing nothing but trees.

"So where's *your* tent?"

He smiled, turning toward her with a wink. "I have a cabin."

"Okay, let's lay out all of the pieces and see if we can make sense of this." Gabi pointed to a pile of poles twenty minutes later. "Waverly and Sam, how about you group the poles by size, and Madison and Eve, you spread out the canvas?"

"I'm not touching that." Madison shook her head and crossed her arms. "Who knows where it's been?"

"It's been in a storage shed. That's where it's been." Gabi pointed. "Now spread it out."

Madison let out a disgusted sigh. "Do we have gloves or anything? Eww. My father will be furious if he hears about this."

"You really think so?" Gabi raised her eyebrows. "Madison, want to know something *I* know about this current situation?"

"No. Not really." Madison pointed at the pile of canvas. "Because clearly, you knew shit about this *entire* situation."

Gabi nodded, seeing Eve's eyes go wide at Madison's words. "I'll give you that, actually. And I'll excuse the language and attitude this one time because we're all exhausted and out of our element. But here's the thing. Guess who *did* know exactly what we were in for here?"

Sam snorted. "Pritch-bitch, that's who."

"Exactly. And stop calling her that. But guess who else knew?" Gabi let her eyes land on each of the girls. "Every single one of your parents or guardians. Priscilla would have had to be honest with them, and would have needed their approval."

She let the words sink in for a moment. Then she smiled tightly. "They all gave it, or we wouldn't be here right now."

"Impossible." Waverly's voice was small. "My mother was completely freaked about the whole thing. She said she didn't approve it at all."

"Sorry, Waverly. She did." Gabi pointed toward the parking lot. "I've got the permission forms in the van, if anyone needs to see proof."

For a long moment, the muttering ceased as all of the girls took in what Gabi was saying. Yes, it appeared that Priscilla had known exactly what she was getting them into. The parents had known, and Luke and Oliver had known. The only five people who *hadn't* known they were spending a month in outhouse-hell were Gabi and her girls.

"All right. Let's get moving." She finally spoke, motioning to the tent pieces. "If we're going to get this thing built before dark, we'd better get to it."

The girls grumbled, but a few minutes later, they'd assembled the pieces into some semblance of order, and were trying to figure out which poles to slide into which flaps when Luke appeared.

He crossed his arms, studying them with a half-smile on his face. "How's it going, ladies?"

"Well." Madison winked. "We could use some help, actually. None of us have ever really done the tent thing."

"Huh." Luke didn't move. "Well, I'd say it's high time all of you learned, then." He turned to Gabi. "May I have a word?"

She followed him up the pathway, and when they were out of sight of the girls, but could still hear them, Luke turned, crossing his arms. She wondered if he always spent so much time in that position, or if she was bringing it out in him.

He raised his eyebrows. "Think it'll be up by nightfall?"

She raised her eyebrows to match his. "It might, if we could get some help."

He looked at her for a long moment, then finally spoke. "Here's a question for you. What exactly are your hopes for this summer?"

"What?" Gabi blinked, shaking her head. "That's a pretty broad question."

"Yep."

She sighed quietly. "My goal right now, quite frankly, is to survive the night without being eaten alive by whatever creatures are lurking at the forest edges. Beyond that, I don't yet know."

He smiled, and she wished it didn't look so good on him. "You want some advice?"

"If it's about putting up the tent, yes."

"It is. And it's simple. You really need to make the girls do the work."

"Why?" She fought not to bristle. Who was he, to tell her how to treat her own students? He didn't know her *or* them.

He shrugged. "Listen, it's not my place to judge, but it looks to me like whatever got them sent here was bad enough that somebody thinks they deserve four weeks in hell—because that's what this'll be to them. And we both know you can't leave, because you've got nowhere else to take them. You coddle these girls while they're here, you'll bring the same girls back home in four weeks. But you ease off the princess-glove treatment, and maybe you'll actually bring back better ones. And it's bound to work better if you start on day one. That's all I'm saying."

Gabi stared at him for a long moment, crossing her own arms this time. The *nerve*.

"With all due respect, you don't know these girls, and you don't know me. I appreciate your advice, but if it's all the same to you, I'll make the decisions. We'll get the tent up."

"Your call." He put up his hands in a classic just-trying-to-save-you-here pose, which just irritated her more. "Good luck," he said, then turned, but not before she saw his incessantly irritating half-smile.

She'd show *him,* dammit.

"Princess gloves, my butt," Gabi muttered as she headed back to the tent platform. "I'll show *him* some princess gloves."

As she came back over the little rise, she could see the girls sitting on the platform, not one of them moving a muscle to get the tent put together.

Dammit.

She was used to their complacency. She saw it every day. She *fought* it every day. But right now, in the middle of the woods, with darkness and critters creeping in within the next two hours, that complacency ticked her off like nothing had since . . . well, since *last* Friday when she'd found out her entire summer had gone down in flames.

She hated to admit Luke could be right, but looking at them all sitting on their butts waiting for her to do their thinking for them suddenly made her downright furious. They'd gotten themselves into this mess. They needed to deal with the consequences.

Consequence number one? Putting up the damn tent.

"Jeez, Gabi. Nice of you to come back." Madison put up her hands as Gabi walked back into the clearing. "It's getting dark."

Gabi raised her eyebrows, nodding slowly. "So why aren't you putting up the tent?"

"We can't figure it out," Waverly whined.

"Well"—Gabi took a deep breath—"if you want somewhere to sleep tonight, it looks like you're going to have to. I need to go make some phone calls in Oliver's office. While I do that, *you* put up the tent. Questions?"

"You're *leaving*?" Eve gasped, looking around at the poles and canvas strewn all over the platform. "You can't just *leave* us here."

"Can. Will. Am. Luke said the bears don't generally start roaming around until dusk, but I guess I wouldn't want to test that theory if he's wrong. The sooner you have a place to sleep, the better, right?"

Luke had said no such thing. For all she knew, bears slept in their cozy caves all night. But the girls didn't know that. Leaving them with their mouths hanging open, Gabi turned around and headed resolutely up the hill, not glancing backward once.

She had no phone calls to make, but the girls didn't know *that,* either. Her two best friends from Briarwood were on a kayaking expedition off the coast of Maine, or she'd have called *them*. She'd have pressed her speed-dial button and told them about her hellish first hour at Camp Echo . . . about a camp that probably should have been closed down years ago . . . about tents whose holes were so big that she was bound to qualify for her one-gallon blood donor pin within a week . . . about a tall, dead-sexy camp handyman so full of himself that he was already trying to tell her how to do her job.

She slapped at her arm as a mosquito landed, then eyed the van. Fine. She'd wait out the girls in the BMW. It was going to take every ounce of effort not to drive the thing right back down the driveway without them, though.

As she got to the parking lot and slid into the driver's seat, Luke's voice made her jump.

"Leaving already?" He walked out of the admin cottage and toward the van. The same amused smile was still on his face, and she hated that her eyes were so appreciative of the way his five o'clock shadow outlined a sculpted jawline. Thick, dark brown hair completed the package—the kind that begged for a woman to run her fingers through it.

She swallowed, ripping her eyes away. Then she held up the keys. "You caught me."

"I really thought you'd last at least one more hour."

"Nope." She shook her head. "I'm outta here. They're all yours. You're not afraid of a few teenaged girls, are you?"

"Deathly. Any man in his right mind would be."

"Well, I'm sure you'll figure it out." She put the key in the ignition, and he immediately strode to the window, placing his arms on the frame.

"You're not really leaving."

"Try me, mister."

He smiled. "You *can't* leave."

"Why not?"

"Because you'd feel too guilty, for one."

Gabi shook her head. "At the moment, no."

"Maybe." He tipped his head. "But about ten miles down the road, you'd reconsider. You know you would."

"Not so sure about that. Did I mention *I* was the one

who was supposed to be flying out on vacation tonight, not the headmaster?"

He pulled his arms off the van, like he was mildly disgusted, but trying to hide it. "Such problems."

"I'm just saying."

"I heard you. And I imagine the princess posse had other plans, as well."

"They'll recover." She put on her seat belt like she really *was* planning to take off. "So will you. I've changed my mind about staying. I was told to deliver them to camp. You're camp. So have fun, keep them alive, and I'll be back to get them in four weeks."

He smiled, and her stomach did a weird jumpy thing she hadn't felt in a long, long time. "Right. Well, you have a good trip home, then."

Gabi felt her eyebrows pull together. He was calling her bluff. Well, she'd show him. She'd call his right back. She'd head on down the road, and she wouldn't come back till dark. See what he and the girls thought of *that*.

"Okay." She put the key in the ignition. "Good luck. You'll need it."

"Gotcha." He slapped the side of the van, then turned to head toward the admin building. "Don't get lost."

Gabi turned the key. Oh, she'd get lost, all right. She'd take this van right to a hotel with power and Wi-Fi and food, and she'd stay *there,* dammit.

Except that the van wasn't starting.

She was only bluffing, but the damn van was not *starting.*

She turned the key, turned it back . . . turned it again. An ominous click-click-click was the only sound she heard. Where was the beautiful purr of the engine?

"Problem?" Luke emerged from the doorway, and was it her imagination, or was he biting his cheek?

Gabi popped the hood and got out, like she had a clue

what she'd do once she got to the front of the van. She propped the hood up on its lever, then scanned the engine compartment.

Then she closed her eyes in abject frustration.

"Where's the battery, Luke?"

"In the camp safe."

"What?"

"Oliver said we had strict instructions not to let your little hotwiring artist take off with the school van. Again. So I disabled it."

Gabi crossed her arms. "You disabled *me.*"

He shrugged. "Side benefit."

"Luke, seriously. You can't hold us hostage here."

"Not hostage. Just helping. Running these roads at night looking for runaway teens is nobody's idea of fun. If you need the battery, just ask. We'll put it back in."

"I need the battery."

"Nah. You don't, really." He smiled, locking the admin cottage door. "Nothing's open in town after six. There's nowhere to go." He turned toward the pathway. "Have a nice night, Gabi. Make sure those girls don't have anything edible in that tent when you're done, or I guarantee you'll have visitors."

Gabi shivered as he walked away, then crossed her arms over her stomach.

If the girls had any food in that tent, she'd leave *them* out as bear bait.

Chapter 4

"Gabi, what's that noise?" Waverly's panicked voice came from somewhere near Gabi's feet. It was two in the morning, and not one of them had fallen asleep yet. Gabi'd spent a full four hours fuming over Priscilla's directive to have Luke and Oliver disable the van once they'd arrived, and by the time the girls had finally constructed a canvas and pole structure that resembled a tent, it'd been well after dark.

By the time they'd pulled the sleeping bags out of the van, the moon had been high in the sky. And by the time they'd put their elementary spatial reasoning skills to work and figured out how to *fit* five sleeping bags in the space, Gabi had been ready to go sleep in the van.

It had practically killed her to sit there and watch the girls struggle to figure out the tent. As they'd argued and clanked poles and screeched when the whole thing came crashing down—multiple times—she'd checked her watch, checked the sky, checked the perimeter of the clearing for glowing eyes, sure that a message had to have gone out into the wilderness by now announcing the arrival of fresh meat.

After five long tries, though, the girls had finally pushed up the poles and braced themselves for the tent to come falling down again . . . but it hadn't. Gabi's eyes had widened as she'd watched the four of them, all with their hands out in front of them, ready to catch poles and canvas. And when Sam had given her pole a gentle push and nothing bad had happened, a whoop had gone up, and Gabi'd smiled in relief.

But now it was dead-dark, the mosquitoes had discovered every single hole in this godforsaken tent, and it sounded like the entire wild kingdom had gathered just outside the platform to investigate.

"I'm sure it's nothing, Waverly. Go to sleep."

Suddenly Waverly leaped out of her sleeping bag and crawled over Sam, making Sam curse loudly.

"Well, it might be nothing, but it's got a nose, and it just poked right through that hole." Her voice was half whisper, half screech, and Gabi pulled out her flashlight to shine it in the direction of Waverly's pillow.

Two brown eyes and a masked face froze in the light, and crafty black paws closed around a chocolate bar.

The next thirty seconds were a blur of screeches and confusion as Gabi and the four girls slithered out of their sleeping bags and made for the tent flaps, running out into the clearing. They'd almost made it when Waverly accidentally tripped Eve, who went flying into a tent pole. As Gabi closed her eyes and cringed, the entire tent crashed to the ground, and five little raccoons skittered back into the woods.

Gabi scanned the clearing with her flashlight, hoping her heart rate wasn't going to send her to the nearest ER. After she'd assured herself that there weren't any more four-legged creatures lurking, she turned the light on the girls, who were huddled near the collapsed tent, their eyes wide as they slapped mosquitoes.

"Who. Had. Chocolate. In the tent?" Gabi ground the words out between clenched teeth.

No one raised a hand. Shocking.

She pointed to the tent. "Waverly and Eve, hold up the edges. Sam and Madison, go get the backpacks."

"Are you going to search us?" Madison crossed her arms. "At two o'clock in the morning?"

"Are you concerned that I might?"

She tightened her arms. "No."

"Then go get the backpacks." Gabi pointed with the flashlight, then jumped when she saw another light appear on the pathway.

Great. This would be Luke.

"Everything all right down here?" He came closer, and in the flashlight-lit darkness, his hair looked rumpled, his eyes sleepy, his T-shirt just thrown on. Gabi swallowed hard, not wanting to like the sight even half as much as she did.

"We're fine, thank you," Gabi answered.

"Engineering flaw?" He raised his eyebrows as his flashlight swept the pile of canvas.

"No," Madison growled. "The tent was fine until Eve knocked it over."

"Waverly tripped me!" Eve shot back.

"I was trying to get away from the raccoons!" Waverly screeched. "I'm sorry!"

Gabi saw Luke smile as he turned to her. "Got a visit from the welcome wagon, did you?"

"Something like that."

He turned back to the girls. "Somebody forget what I told you about coons and food?" Nobody answered, and Gabi could tell he expected just that. "Well, now you know I wasn't joking. Gonna be tough putting this tent back up in the pitch-dark." He clicked off his flashlight and turned toward the path. "Good night, then."

"He's not going to help us?" Madison glared at Luke's retreating form.

"Obviously not," Gabi answered. "Why should he? Is *he* the one who brought chocolate into the tent? Did you guys think he was kidding about that? Did you think *I* was?"

The girls were silent, Gabi was dead tired and sick of slapping mosquitoes, and there was no way she had the energy to supervise putting up this damn tent again right now.

"Get your bags, girls." She sighed, wishing she had a voodoo doll of Priscilla Pritchard. Right now she'd poke it square in the eyes. "Looks like we're sleeping in the van."

Sam eyed Madison, glaring, and suddenly Gabi knew exactly who'd brought chocolate into the tent.

Maybe, in the light of morning, she'd have a remote clue what to do about it.

"I see you survived the night." Luke smiled over his coffee mug as Gabi stumbled into the dining hall the next morning, four grumbling girls at her heels. He was leaning against the service counter in a soft gray T-shirt and dark charcoal khaki shorts, and Gabi fought not to compare him to the guy on that coffee commercial she loved. "How'd everybody sleep?"

She reached deep to pull out a fake smile. "Just fine, thank you."

"Comfortable van?"

"Not a bit, but at least we were safe from the stinging hovercrafts you people call mosquitoes."

"Yeah, they're bad this year."

"You think? How much blood does the average child *lose* here at Camp Echo?"

"They generally pack bug spray."

"Ah." She nodded, kicking herself for forgetting it.

"Maybe you could give me back my battery today so I could go buy some?"

"Maybe." He picked up his coffee mug and took a sip. Gabi found herself uncomfortably drawn to this early-morning version of Luke, all freshly showered and relaxed.

Showered.

He obviously had running water.

"Luke, seriously. You can't hold the van hostage."

He shrugged, smiling. "Can if I have orders from your boss, who is now—apparently—somehow also *my* boss. And you know her far better than I do, so I would imagine the orders don't really surprise you, as much as they're probably pissing you off."

"It might be the glee with which you are *holding* the van that makes me *more* angry."

"Oh, believe me, Gabi. There's no glee here." He handed her a mug. "Little grouchy before your morning coffee?"

She glared at him. "Yes. That's what this is—a coffee issue."

He handed her a jug of creamer, amusement making the edges of his eyes crinkle. They were like dark, sooty emeralds—a color he'd probably hated as a kid, but girls had probably loved.

Gabi tamped down her irritation. He'd made her coffee, for goodness' sake. She could at least try to be civil.

"Thank you for the coffee."

"Ladies?" Luke turned to Gabi's charges, who were milling uncomfortably near the door. "Piper's got pancakes and bacon ready. Juice and milk are here on the service counter. Grab a plate, fill 'er up, and eat. Kitchen's only open for a half hour, then closed till noon."

Sam and Eve came toward the counter, but Madison

hung back, which meant Waverly did, too. Gabi raised her eyebrows in their direction.

"Girls? Did you hear him?"

"I heard him." Madison crossed her arms delicately. "Just not a fan of pancakes and bacon."

"No problem." Luke shrugged. "Don't eat."

"But—don't you have other options? Yogurt? Fruit?"

"Nope."

Madison huffed dramatically. "I can feel my arteries screaming already."

"Your arteries are fifteen. They'll survive a slice of bacon." Luke raised his eyebrows at Gabi and motioned to the counter. "You going to eat?"

Gabi wasn't the least bit hungry, but well-drilled manners prevented her from saying so. The last thing she wanted to do was insult Piper's cooking on the second day here. After all, the woman could turn out to be the only ally Gabi might *have* this summer.

"Coffee first." She took a sip as she sat down on a rickety wooden stool propped near the counter, then sighed without meaning to. "Oh, God. This is good."

Gabi studied Luke over the top of her mug, noticing that his stubble was a little lighter than yesterday, but not fully gone. Either he needed a new razor, or he preferred the shadowy look. Her eyes locked onto his biceps, then slid to his pecs, outlined under the soft T-shirt.

She wondered if he was married. Then she closed her eyes.

Seriously.

When she opened them, he was looking straight at her, an amused expression on his face. She felt her cheeks flush as he raised his eyebrows again.

"Going forward, as long as you don't have any food in that tent, the coons shouldn't bother you. You'll get used to them sniffing and scratching around. Skunks, too."

Gabi pictured the girls' backpacks, currently sitting in the van. She knew darn well that most of them were probably brimming with whatever they'd been able to collect from the dining hall and vending machine before the van had left Briarwood yesterday.

"And by food, I mean anything that can be eaten. One granola bar could send a family of raccoons on a search-and-destroy mission through your entire tent. And anything a bear can smell, a bear could decide to eat."

Gabi shivered, despite herself. "Of course. Obviously. Right."

"Happy to use my voice of doom to remind the girls of this, if you want."

"I have a perfectly good voice of doom, but thank you."

He smiled. "Has *your* voice of doom ever cleaned up after a raccoon raid? What they did to the tent last night was nothing."

"No." She tipped her head, conceding. "Mine has not."

"Then mine will be scarier."

"Fine." Gabi waved a careless, exhausted hand. "You be doom." Then she sighed, leaning her chin on her hand.

"Hey, Gabi?"

She lifted her eyes to his. "What?"

"I'm not kidding about the bears."

Chapter 5

"Craft project?" Eve's eyebrows almost touched her purple-streaked hair an hour later. "You can't be serious."

"I'm dead serious." Gabi handed out plastic bags. "We're at camp. We're going to do camp . . . stuff."

Madison sighed. "We're going to die of boredom."

"Maybe, maybe not." Gabi tossed a bag her way. "But you never know. This craft project could be epic."

All four of them groaned and rolled their eyes.

If she'd known ahead of time that Camp Echo was completely devoid of both staff and programs, she would have at least headed to the library to check out a stack of books that could have helped her survive being a pretend camp counselor. As it was, she was limited to what she could remember from her own summer camp days . . . and they'd been a scary-long time ago.

As she doled out paper and crayons, her eye caught on Luke as he came down the pathway hauling a small pine tree he'd just cut down. He moved with a smooth grace that belied his muscular build, and *God,* those muscles. They were the kind that came from good, honest work, not a set of barbells, and in a moment of sleep-deprived insanity last night, she'd wondered what it would be like to touch them . . . him.

Gabi shook her head. The handyman's body was *not* what she needed to be focused on right now. The sun was out, the lake was beautiful, and she'd arbitrarily decided it was arts-and-crafts hour. She already knew the girls would hate it, and honestly, she didn't care. They'd gotten themselves sentenced here. They'd have to deal with . . . here.

She pointed up the pathway from the beach. "Here's your job: without losing sight of the admin cottage, head out into the woods and find some leaves, ferns, flowers—anything that can lie almost flat. Put them in your bag, and once you have ten different items, come back to the picnic table and I'll show you a project."

Madison did her patented eye roll. "This is so stupid."

"You want to head for the other camp? Catch your own food? Because that can be arranged."

Madison grumbled and snatched her bag. As she turned, Gabi was pretty sure she heard her mumble "bitch," but she was honestly too tired to call her on it.

Waverly called up her best sneer as she took her own bag, anxious to show Madison that she, too, thought the project was lame. Too bad her efforts were wasted, as Madison was already halfway across the lawn.

Eve sighed and held out her hand. "Ten different things?"

"Ten different things."

Sam raised her eyebrows. "You hoping this will take forever? Because guess what? There are a lot of plants out there. We'll be back in, like, five minutes."

Gabi shook her head as she handed Sam her bag, but she couldn't help smiling. She was probably right.

"Walk slowly, okay?"

Ten minutes later, long before Gabi was ready for them, three of the four girls were back at the picnic table, their bags full of leafy plants. She showed them how to take the paper she'd found in a supply closet Oliver had shown her in the admin cottage, flip the leaves so their veins were showing, and rub crayons over them to trace the shapes. It was a project she remembered doing way back when she was a kid, but as she demonstrated, she didn't remember it seeming nearly so lame when *she'd* done it.

With a minimum of grumbling, the girls started arranging their plants, and when they'd been at it for almost half an hour, Gabi looked toward the edge of the woods where Madison had been sitting since leaving the picnic table.

"You going to join us, Madison?"

Madison rolled her eyes again, and for a moment Gabi wished the old wives' tale about eyeballs getting stuck that way actually held true.

Sam looked over. "It's better than sitting on your ass in poison ivy."

Madison jumped up like a marionette, then looked down at the ground. "Shut up, Sam. It's just grass and weeds."

Sam laughed, not looking at her. "Do you even know what poison ivy looks like?"

Madison gave her the finger, but made her way reluctantly to the table, dumping her bag of leaves at the end. Gabi handed her paper and crayons, but didn't bother to give directions again. After all, as Madison had so kindly pointed out, it was something fourth-graders could do. Or kindergarteners, really.

"So what *does* poison ivy look like, anyway?" Gabi paused her own rubbing, figuring it was something they should probably know, since they were here in the boonies.

Sam looked up at her. "You don't know?"

"No. No idea."

"Huh." Sam bit her lip, looking down at her paper for a moment, then at the little pile of leaves in the middle of the table. "Looks pretty much like that." She used her eraser to point at a couple of shiny plants at the center of the pile. Then she turned toward Madison, who held a similar one in her hands. "And that."

She looked down again, not even bothering to contain her smile this time. "And you *were* sitting in it, princess."

"Poison ivy? You had them do a project . . . with poison ivy?" Luke's eyes were wide when Gabi tracked him down in the admin cottage a few minutes later.

"I obviously didn't *know* it was poison ivy. And I didn't pick it—the girls did."

He shook his head. "Do you have any idea how much that stuff itches?"

"Yes, Luke." She tried to subtly scratch her palms, even though she was pretty sure she couldn't possibly be having a reaction yet. "What do we do about it?"

"Is it just on your hands?" He walked to a cupboard over the copier, opening it as he talked.

"I think so. Except for Madison. She—um—she apparently sat in it."

Luke paused, his hand on the cupboard. Then he turned to her. "I won't even ask."

"I appreciate that."

"Here." He handed her a bottle. "It's safe for the lake. Get them in the water and use this. And you might want to get your hands on an industrial-sized bottle of calamine lotion for later. Sounds like you're all going to need it."

"This isn't funny." She took the bottle, wishing she could wipe the grin from his face.

"No. You're right. It's definitely not."

"Stop smiling."

He laughed. "I'm sorry. I just—can't."

"Let me ask you this—are there *other* plants that might attack us in the area?"

"Eh." He shrugged. "Depends whether you give them a reason to."

"Luke."

He put up his hands. "Sure. There are plants that'll make you itch, plants that'll make you bleed, plants that'll kill you if you eat 'em. So just don't mess with anything if you don't know what it is."

"I don't know what *anything* is."

He nodded sagely, turning back to the ancient computer on the desk. "Guess you'd better stick close to camp, then. That's just the plants that can do you in. There are four-legged critters out there who can smell fear. And they like it."

Fifteen minutes later, Gabi and the girls were gathered on the sandy beach, all of them stripped down to their bathing suits except Sam. *She* still sat at the table, running her pencil over sheets of paper, grinning when she looked at them.

Gabi was not amused.

"We're not seriously going to bathe in there." Madison's eyebrows slid so high Gabi feared they might get caught in her hair.

Gabi handed her the bottle of organic soap-shampoo. "Would you prefer to scratch yourself insane? Your choice."

"I'd prefer to take an actual *shower.*"

"Well, that's not an option." Gabi tried to keep the growl out of her voice.

Eve piped up. "Luke must have a real bathroom in his cabin. Why don't you go distract him and we'll sneak in and take showers?"

"No. Not going to happen."

Madison crossed her arms. "Come on, Gabi. He can't possibly think we're going to bathe in this disgusting lake. This is inhumane."

"The lake is as clear as can be, and nobody's making you do anything, Madison. It's your choice."

Gabi tried to make her voice sound firm, but oh, what she wouldn't give for a hot shower herself right now. Once again she pictured her imaginary Priscilla Pritchard voodoo doll—imagined sprinkling itching powder all over its hands, just to share the pain.

She smiled tightly. "Just think of it as an adventure, girls. When's the last time you shampooed your hair in a lake, right?"

Nobody uncrossed arms.

"Okay. Suit yourselves. I'm going in."

She walked to the end of the dock, and knowing it was the only way she'd actually convince herself to get into the freezing water, she held her breath and did a shallow dive. When her body hit the water, it felt like a thousand ice picks were stabbing her, and she almost inhaled a lungful of water by gasping.

Holy. Shit. The water was flipping arctic.

She popped her head out of the water, but knowing the girls were gauging her reaction, she bit down on the shriek that was aching to come out of her throat.

"Who's next?" she called as she treaded water like it was a balmy seventy-five degrees here in Echo Lake. Meanwhile, she'd lost feeling in her feet already.

Madison dropped her arms and sighed. "I'm only doing this because I'm desperate. Come on, Waverly."

She grabbed Waverly, who shrieked, but let herself get pulled to the end of the dock. Eve finally joined them, and on three, they jumped into the lake.

When they emerged, Gabi was pretty sure the entire town of Echo Lake heard them.

"What in God's name is going on down there?" Luke's friend Noah peered out the window of the dining hall. "If they keep yelling like that, somebody's going to call 911."

Luke rolled his eyes from where he sat at a table, trying to fix a fan. It was going to hit eighty-five today, and Piper had made no bones about saying she wasn't cooking them *anything* for dinner unless he got the fan running.

"They're taking their first lake bath. Got themselves into poison ivy."

"Already? How'd they manage that?"

Luke jerked his chin sideways. "Got into that patch I've been battling for two years now."

"I can't believe you're making them bathe in the lake. It's fifty-five freaking degrees."

"We don't have any other options. We don't have showers."

"*You* do."

"Well, I'm not sharing."

Noah raised his eyebrows. "You could at least maybe offer it to Gabi."

"No way." The thought of Gabi's silky, curvy body all sudsy in his bathroom was a vision he didn't need in his head right now. "It builds character. I'm not *making* them do anything. They're jumping in of their own free will."

Noah turned back to him. "You have a defibrillator on-site in case one of them has a heart attack?"

"Eh, they're young and healthy. A little lake water never killed anybody."

"A little hypothermia could."

"I told Gabi if they start to feel warm, they need to get out. And by the way, before you get all sympathetic, these girls wrote their own ticket here. Hot showers were never part of the deal."

Luke looked down at the fan and swore, realizing he'd just put an entire piece of it back in upside down. If Gabi didn't cover up that swimsuit—and soon, dammit—he'd never get anything done today.

"You don't have *any* sympathy for Gabi, at least?"

"Not right now, no. Oliver and I were begging for a work crew for the summer, once we saw the never-ending project list from hell. What did Briarwood send?" He waved a hand at the window. "A bunch of prep school kids and their preppy little housemother, or whatever she's called. How am I supposed to work with them around, getting in the way?"

Noah looked out the window again, and Luke realized the shrieking had finally died down.

"Are they out? Or are they dead?"

"They're not dead." Noah tipped his head. "Hey—any chance you've seen Gabriela in her bathing suit?"

"Yes, and stop looking."

Noah grinned. "Why?"

"One—Piper would kill you. And two—just . . . don't."

Shit. He closed his eyes, knowing damn well that Noah heard the territorial directive he hadn't meant to give. Heard it loud and clear.

"Gotcha." Noah nodded slowly, his smile still in place. "Is somebody crushing on the hot housemom?"

Luke raised his eyebrows. "Is somebody twelve? No. Nobody's crushing on anybody."

Noah shrugged. "Hey, four weeks is a long time. You're stuck here, she's stuck here . . . you never know, right?"

"I do know. And no. Not my type. Not my lifestyle. Not happening."

"Whatever you say." He looked out the window again. "Little piece of advice, though—definitely don't look at her when she gets out of the water. You might decide her type might be *exactly* your type."

"Noah?"

"Fine. Not talking about a hot girl in a hot bathing suit."

"Thank you." Luke looked out the window, then forced his eyes back to the fan. They only stuck there for a brief second before returning to the window, though. It looked like Gabi was thinking about trying to teach the girls how to—fish? Seriously? Where had she found those old poles?

Noah tipped his chin toward the admin cottage. "How's Oliver feeling about having them here?"

Luke dropped a screw and swore when it rolled so far under the table that he couldn't reach it. The man who'd spent his life pouring his every minute and every penny into young men everybody else had given up on was now looking at his entire mission going down the drain. He'd finally admitted that his age was getting the better of him, and it was killing Luke every time Oliver sat down, because for as long as he'd known him, Oliver had *never* sat still.

"I don't know," he finally answered Noah. "But the only thing that'll kill him faster than retirement will be to see this place turn into some rich girls' summer boarding school."

"So what are you doing about it?"

"Going through my list of incredibly wealthy contacts, trying to convince one of them to buy the place."

"Well, obviously, yes. But say that doesn't pan out? Given that you *have* no incredibly wealthy contacts?"

"I'm toying with going straight to the Briarwood board, actually."

Noah's eyes widened. "And saying what?"

"I haven't figured that out yet." Luke shook his head. "But there has to be at least one sympathetic person on that board—one soul who would be willing to try to understand what we'd be losing if this plan goes through. And then maybe that person could somehow convince the others."

"You don't sound very optimistic."

"I'm not, but I have to try. I can't just sit around here all summer and turn this camp into something it was never supposed to be, then pack up my stuff in September and try not to let the proverbial door hit me in the ass."

Noah returned his gaze to the beach. "You have a med kit handy for the first hook that lands in somebody's cheek?"

Luke looked up, watching Gabi spread the girls out on shore, then try to demonstrate how to cast. He shook his head, but found himself smiling. She had absolutely no idea what she was doing, but damn, she was earnest about it. If she kept this up all day long, he suspected the girls would all go to bed willingly tonight, if only to get free of her chirpy little camp-activities list.

"What'd you do to your thumb?" Noah pointed to Luke's hand, which he'd whacked with the hammer an hour ago. "Get busy looking at Gabi and forget where you were aiming?"

Luke gave him the finger, which only made Noah laugh.

"Eh, if it was me, and I was single, and this gorgeous woman showed up at *my* camp for the summer, I'd probably have bruises, too."

"Well, you're not single, she's at *my* camp, and Piper would *give* you bruises if she knew you were looking. She's here for four weeks, and then she'll be headed back to Briarwood paradise, where everyone's from the same social stratum, and posers are turned away at the gate."

"Not that you have some hidden issues here."

Luke shrugged. "Nothing hidden about my issues. She and I are from completely different worlds. Never the twain shall meet, and all that."

"Gotcha." Noah nodded as he looked back out the window. "So take care with the bathing suit, then. Your *twain* might have other ideas."

Chapter 6

"A scavenger hunt? Ooh, I can't wait." The next morning, Madison sighed as Gabi handed out the lists she'd made an hour ago.

"Keep it up, and I'll put a bear cub on yours."

"Now, now, Gabi," Sam muttered. "Pretty sure you're not allowed to feed us to the bears."

"You show me the line that says that, and I'll take the option off the table. Otherwise, I can totally frame it as an accident." Gabi handed Sam her list, then sat down at the picnic table with them. "You're in teams today. Madison and Sam on one side, Eve and Waverly on the other. You've got two hours. Keep the camp in sight at all times. First team back with all of the items wins."

"What do we win?" Sam asked.

Gabi thought for a moment. She had no flipping idea. Finally, an idea popped into her head. "Dessert. If you can do this activity without killing each other, falling in the lake, or getting lost, I will make you something delicious for dessert."

"More delicious than Luke's granola?" Eve made a face, quickly joined by the others. Even Gabi shivered involuntarily. Luke had foisted it on them at breakfast, claiming he'd made it from everything including the kitchen sink. Unfortunately, that's exactly how it had tasted. Gabi was all in favor of a little fiber in one's diet, but taste was a nice feature, as well.

"Better than Luke's granola, yes. I'll even use sugar." She motioned them away from the table. "Go. Find stuff. Bring it back. Win dessert."

Ten seconds after the girls had headed up the pathway, Luke's voice behind her made Gabi jump. "Find stuff, bring it back, win dessert? Today's epic activity?"

She could hear the humor in his voice—or maybe it was a sneer—but she was almost too tired to respond as he strolled around to the other side of the picnic table.

"If you have better ideas, you may happily adopt the girls as your own, and I will leave for the rest of the summer."

"After only two days? Wow." He sat down on the opposite bench. "Nope. Couldn't pay me enough. Plus, you don't let them out of your sight for more than five minutes. You'd never leave them here with me."

"Don't call my bluff again, mister. You might be surprised this time."

He looked into her eyes. "You hanging in?"

She felt her eyebrows furrow. What was this tone that bordered on . . . nice? He'd been avoiding her and the girls as much as possible since they'd arrived, but right now he actually sounded sympathetic. She wasn't quite sure what to do with it.

"I'm hanging in fine, thanks."

"Have you actually slept through the night since you got here?"

She rubbed her eyes. "Is it that obvious?"

"Depends what shade of purple your eyes *usually* are, I guess."

"I'm actually a really good sleeper . . . usually."

He smiled. "Haven't gotten used to the night noises yet?"

"It's more that I haven't gotten used to sleeping on plywood yet."

"What do you mean? You're not using a cot?"

Gabi felt her eyes widen. "There are *cots*?"

"Of course there are cots. They're in the shed, right beside the tents."

"And the reason you neglected to mention them was . . ."

"I didn't?" He actually looked mortified. "I must have."

"You didn't."

Luke shook his head. "I know I haven't exactly been a welcoming committee here. But seriously, I wouldn't have purposely made you sleep on the tent platform. I'll show you where they are later."

"Thank you. Could you also show me where you keep the sugar? Looks like I just signed up to bake."

"After the attitudes I just heard, you're going to reward them with a special dessert?" His eyebrows were up, challenging her.

"I'm not rewarding the behavior you just witnessed. I'm rewarding the successful scavenger hunt they've just set out to do."

"Right. Gotcha."

She tipped her head. "What are you saying?"

"Nothing." He shrugged. "They're your kids, not mine."

"And yet you're clearly choking on your opinions."

"I'm not. I'm sure you know exactly what you're doing."

She sighed. "I think it's pretty clear to both of us that I have no *idea* what I'm doing. I'm a little out of my element here."

"Actually, I've been pretty impressed with your activities so far. If they're not regretting whatever escapades got them sent here yet, they certainly will soon."

"Wait." Gabi felt her eyebrows furrow. "Are you telling me my activities reek of . . . punishment?"

"Seriously? The leaf collecting and rock painting? The bogus fishing? The scavenger hunt? They *aren't* . . . punishment?"

Gabi crossed her arms, stung. "It's camp. I'm trying to do . . . camp."

"Have you ever *been* to camp, Gabi?"

"Of course I have."

"How old were you?"

She sighed. "Ten. But three days ago, I thought I'd be sitting in a chair on the beach while certified, trained counselors put my students through their camp paces. I had no idea it was going to fall to me. This—camp thing—really isn't my forte."

Luke was silent, like he was weighing whether to say something that was clearly on his mind. Finally, he uncrossed his arms and set his elbows on the table. He looked relaxed, yet tense, and Gabi's eyes were drawn to his hands, much to her consternation. They were strong, tanned, nimble. She closed her eyes, lest she start picturing those hands doing things she really shouldn't be thinking about.

He tapped one fist on the table. "You know, I *have* been doing . . . have been around camp for a while now. I might have picked up a few ideas along the way if you need help—"

She shook her head. Dammit, her self-confidence was already struggling to stay afloat here. Accepting a rescue on day three wasn't likely to do a whole lot to help that, even if she was already desperate. She couldn't.

"Thank you. I appreciate the offer. But you have a lot to do, and I don't want to take you away from it. We'll be fine."

He smiled, but it didn't reach his eyes. "Okay. Your call." He pushed himself up from the table and strode back up the pathway toward the dining hall. She waited till she knew he was well out of range before she sank her head into her hands and did her best not to give way to the tears threatening just behind her eyes.

She was supposed to be well into her third piña colada of the day right now, a Caribbean breeze tickling her toes as she solved a whodunit before the detective did. She was supposed to be sidling up to a tiki bar later tonight with her new sundress on, irresistible with her sun-kissed shoulders and coconut-shampooed hair.

She was *not* supposed to be playing camp counselor to a bunch of teenaged twits who'd ruined her entire summer.

And she was *definitely* not supposed to be melting into a stranger's smoky green eyes while she imagined his hands making her forget all of it.

"What did you say to her?" Piper's voice was sharp as Luke came around the corner into the kitchen.

"What? Who?" He shook his head as he plucked a bottled water out of the fridge. "What are you talking about?"

"Gabi. Who do you think?" Piper hooked a thumb toward the window. "She looks like you just stole her puppy."

Luke glanced out the window, and felt his stomach clench as he watched Gabi rub her temples, then close her eyes as she raised her face to the sun and took a long, deep breath. Even from here, he could see the tension in her shoulders, could see the tightness in her jaw . . . could see the frustration in her posture.

She was so out of her element that she might as well be on Mars, but apparently, she was too proud to accept help. Yet, anyway.

"I offered to give her a hand, if you must know."

"Wow." Piper raised her eyebrows. "Only took you till day three to freak out about strangers taking over?"

"Shut up, Piper."

She laughed. "Just saying. I knew you couldn't stand back and watch."

"Don't really have a choice, do I? She's in charge of them, whether she's got the least clue or not."

"*Does* she have a clue?"

Pictures of the past forty-eight hours flashed through his head—the raccoons, the poison ivy, the fish hook that had, as predicted, ended up embedded in Eve's cheek.

"I'm sure she knows what works in her normal setting. But this is decidedly *not* her normal setting."

"Obviously. But why do you want to help?"

Luke sighed. "Because it occurred to me sometime in the past twenty-four hours that maybe the best way to convince Briarwood not to decimate our existence is to show someone *from* Briarwood how we do things here."

"Ah." Piper nodded. "But she's not biting. So what are you going to do?"

"What *can* I do?" He put up his hands. "She's determined to do it on her own, and I've got a project list fit for ten men. I guess for now, if she and the girls leave *me* alone, I'll give them the same wide berth."

"Mm-hm." Piper poured ingredients into a mixing bowl, but kept her eyes carefully averted.

"Piper?"

She rolled her eyes. "I know. Shut up."

"Gabi?" A little while later, Oliver swung out of the doorway of the admin cottage. "I have a thought."

"Okay?"

"C'mere. I want to show you something." He motioned for her to follow him up a pathway she hadn't yet taken. It headed uphill from the beach area, toward a thick stand of pines, and it was cool as Oliver led her through the trees and up some stone steps that looked like they'd been placed in the hill a long time ago.

He paused halfway up, pointing out at the lake. "Best view on the property right here, don't you think?"

She followed his finger, nodding at the view of tiny, colorful sailboats hopping along the whitecaps, but suspected his reason for stopping had more to do with catching his breath than showing her the scenery.

After a moment, he turned to climb the remainder of the hill, and it pained Gabi to admit she was huffing like an asthmatic by the time they crested the top. Before her was a large, flat expanse that looked like a former garden. To her left, over a split-rail fence, the view of the lake was incredible.

"Wow." She tried to wipe her forehead subtly. "It's gorgeous up here."

"Yup. Maybe *this* is the best view on the property." He nodded, then turned toward the grassy area. "Ever had a garden?"

"I tried doing herbs in a pot last year." She shook her head. "It didn't go well."

He laughed. "Well, we plant this every spring, and whatever we don't eat goes to the food bank in town. We haven't had time to get to it this year, but I was thinking maybe you and the girls could use a little project. I hate to think of good growing land going fallow."

"Really?" Gabi stared at the expanse of weeds and dirt. This looked like more than a little project.

"Really." He shrugged. "It's a little late to plant, but we could still get some good stuff out of it. Girls could pick out the seeds, and I'd be happy to show you how to make it all work."

Gabi nodded slowly, picturing her four girls industriously hoeing and shoveling and exclaiming in delight as their little green sprouts appeared.

She rolled her eyes internally. Because yes, that's exactly how it would go.

But still. It *was* a good idea.

"You know what? I think this is an excellent idea. Thank you, Oliver."

Oliver laughed quietly. "Now, don't go getting all starry-eyed about it. Gardens are a serious project. There's a lot to it, but I'll teach you, if you think your girls could benefit from the work."

"Oh, they could *definitely* benefit from the work. Thanks, Oliver. This is great."

He nodded, looking out over the lake. "Y'know, it might not be my place to say this, but if you're willing, Luke's been dealing with teenagers for a long time, and he's been doing camp even longer. Boys, mostly, but the skills are pretty transferable. He might be able to help you, if you find yourself wishing you had some extra hands around here."

Gabi frowned. "Am I giving off some sort of desperation vibe today?"

"Nope." He shrugged. "We're just used to working as a team here at Echo. We help each other out. Seems you're now part of the team, whether you intended it or not, so we're here if you need us. We can't all be experts at everything. There's no shame in asking for help, is all I'm saying."

Gabi took a deep breath, her eyes catching on the sailboats. Oliver had no way of knowing her independent streak had already been six miles wide before she'd ditched her family, her home, and her trust fund ten years ago. Since then, she'd had exactly one person in her life that she could fully trust . . . one person she could rely on, no matter what the circumstance, and that was the *only* person she *ever* wanted help from.

Herself.

Yes, she watched rom-coms every weekend. Yes, she loved the whole knight-in-shining-armor shtick, just like the rest of Hollywood's target audience. But she didn't need one. She'd figure this out.

Because if she didn't, she had a feeling Luke was going to step in and figure it out *for* her.

Chapter 7

"Luke! Luke!" Trina screamed. "Help!"

Luke ran toward the sound, his sneakers pounding down a hallway lined with gray metal lockers. Fluorescent lights buzzed above his head, and he started counting doors, trying to catch up to her.

He rounded a corner, caught a glimpse of her as Randall paused long enough to tighten his grip. Then Randall sprinted, Trina flung over his shoulder, her blond head bouncing as she struggled to get loose.

"Help me, Luke! Don't let him take me!"

Luke ran faster, then felt the hallway lengthen before him. He turned right, turned left, turned right again, always just enough behind them to catch a quick glimpse of her hair before they disappeared. But he never got closer. He reached out like he could almost touch her, but she was too far away.

"Luke! Save me!" Trina pounded her tiny fists on Randall's back, trying to break free of his iron grip as she screamed. "Help!"

Luke called up every ounce of energy, pumping his arms to catch up, but the hallway got longer, her voice grew fainter, Randall's footsteps faded to a rhythmic, dull staccato as the sound of his own harsh breathing drowned everything else out. He was sweating, cursing himself, shouting for her, the sound of his own voice bouncing off cement-block walls.

"Trina! Trina! Triiiiina!"

"Luke. *Luke.* Wake up." Piper's voice startled Luke out of his nightmare the next afternoon, and he blinked rapidly, trying to center himself. Gone was the long hallway with endless corners, gone were the ugly metal lockers, gone were the buzzing lights.

Gone was Katrina.

"You okay?" Her eyes were troubled as she handed him a water bottle. Luke nodded as he closed his eyes, trying to bring his breathing back to normal. "Same dream?"

"Yeah." He sighed, trying to focus on the chickadees twittering above his head, rather than the screaming from inside it. He was used to the damn dream attacking him in the middle of the night, but Jesus, the middle-of-the-day approach was new. He hadn't slept for shit last night, so he'd decided to grab fifteen minutes in the hammock out in back of the cabin before facing the girls. Apparently that's all it had taken for the demons to take hold.

"What was it this time?"

"Hallways. I couldn't get to her." Luke scrubbed both hands over his face. "I can *never* get to her."

Piper put a tentative hand on his shoulder, like she wasn't quite sure if he was far enough out of the dream to handle being touched.

"I'm worried about you, Luke."

"Don't be. I'm fine. It's just a dream."

"It's a dream that won't leave you *alone*. You should see yourself, Luke. When it's happening, you're terrified."

"I'm not . . . terrified."

Oh, who was he bullshitting? He woke up in a cold sweat once a week. Sometimes he could remember the dream, and sometimes he could only remember the fear.

"Fine. You're not terrified, because you're a big, strong he-man who doesn't *do* terrified. I get it. But your dreams are telling you something, and I'm not sure it's healthy to ignore them like you're trying to do."

Luke sighed, pushing himself out of the hammock. "I have way too many meddling therapists for friends. Have I ever mentioned that?"

"At least twice a week, yes." Piper smiled, but it didn't reach her eyes. "We just care about you. And this thing is eating at you, little by little. I just think maybe it'd be good to talk to somebody about it, you know?"

He shook his head and picked up the Red Sox hat that had fallen to the grass. "I don't *want* to talk to anybody, Piper. These dreams are my penance, okay? I didn't save her. I couldn't. And I'll live with that guilt for the rest of my life."

"Luke—"

He put up a hand. "It's all I have left of her, Piper, okay? I'll take the damn dreams."

The next night, after the girls were asleep, Gabi wandered down to the beach and sat in an Adirondack chair, desperate for some alone time. She'd spent two days trying to stay one step ahead of the girls, but it had taken almost inhuman effort to find things for them to do, while preventing them from killing each other. Luke had kept a wide berth, only joining them for quick lunches, and she hated that her eyes had kept looking for him all day long, despite the fact that he was obviously trying to steer clear of them.

As she listened to the frogs and loons, she felt her breathing slow and her shoulders relax. Water lapped softly against the sandy shore, and the moonlight made a shiny path from the end of the dock to the other shore. It wasn't Barbados, but she had to admit it was peaceful, and pretty.

She took a deep breath and closed her eyes, leaning her head back against the chair, but she snapped back up when she heard soft footsteps in the sand.

"Mind if I join you?" Luke paused beside the other chair. In the darkness, his face was in shadow, which added delicious definition to its planes and hollows.

"Um, okay?" Her fingers flew to her hair, which she knew was already at its wildest and curliest since she'd arrived, thanks to lake water and organic shampoo. She didn't want to care what he thought of how she looked, but she could be forgiven a tiny slice of pride, right?

"Girls asleep?"

"They were when I snuck out."

He nodded. "Hard to resist the pull of a well-made Adirondack chair on a beach."

"It's quiet." She pulled her knees up to her chest. "And as you may have noticed, the rest of my day generally isn't."

"Hard not to notice." He smiled at her. "The lake ought to start warming up at some point, so at least the cold-water squealing might ease. Can't speak to all of the other squawking that goes on."

She sighed. Even though she'd spent the past three days resenting Luke for either giving her unwanted advice or steering clear of her altogether, right now she felt like she owed him an apology. She couldn't imagine it felt like anything but a whiny, screechy typhoon had blown in, but wasn't leaving anytime soon.

"I'm sorry. I know this isn't at all what you expected your summer to look—or sound—like."

They sat in silence for a long moment before he cleared his throat. "So tell me about the girls."

"What do you want to know?"

"Well, I've got them a little bit pegged, having listened to them for the past few days . . ."

"They've not been at their best, just in case it matters."

He shook his head. "Wouldn't expect them to be. But I imagine they're not acting too far out of character, either."

She sighed. "Unfortunately, no."

"Let me see what I can guess. Madison's your ringleader, obviously."

"Classic mean girl." Gabi nodded. "Collects her posse, discards at will, rules by fear of being the discarded one."

"Any redeeming qualities?"

Gabi sighed. "I think, deep inside, she's actually a very kind person. But for some reason, she's afraid it's a weakness." She put up a second finger. "Next— Waverly. Biggest fear is being cast out of the crowd, so she'll pretty much do anything Madison asks, whether she likes it or not." Gabi tipped her head. "And by my estimation, she rarely likes it. Basically, the girl needs to grow a spine, but it's a long process."

"We carry those here, if it's of interest." He winked.

"Good to know." She put up a third finger. "Eve."

Eve was Gabi's second scholarship choice, straight out of another tiny apartment teeming with kids. Bars on the windows, six dead bolts on the door, and a frightening collection of young, sneering men sitting on the stoops up and down the street. After Gabi had gotten her settled at Briarwood, she'd placed a call to social services, since it had been painfully obvious that fifteen-year-old Eve had been more a parent in the household than the adults.

She sighed. "Eve's a pleaser and a caretaker, though she'd be loath to admit either of those things. My suspicion is that she ended up on their little escapade because she figured the other three needed someone to make sure they stayed safe."

"And that brings us to Sam. Is she your resident hot-wiring expert?"

Gabi sighed, picturing the spunky, freakishly intelligent girl who'd come to Briarwood with her clothes in a garbage bag, despite the fact that Gabi had hand-delivered a suitcase to her foster home so Sam could pack her things.

Obviously her foster mother had had different plans for the suitcase.

"Sam's a good kid. She's got a ton of potential. She just got mixed up in the wrong thing this time around."

"She needs a spine, too?"

"No." Gabi shook her head. "She's got more spine than anybody I know. Why would you pin the hotwiring on her?"

Luke leaned back, stretching, and Gabi struggled to keep her eyes from gluing themselves to his chest as his muscles tensed.

"I just pay attention," he finally said. "Whenever that girl walks into a space, she has it cased within ten seconds. She's got her escape routes planned before she commits to hanging out. I guarantee that kid knows three ways to get out of *any* spot, wherever you try to put her." He nodded, but then his face grew serious. "Also suspect something in her history gives her good reason to do it."

Gabi stared at him. For a camp handyman, he had some pretty serious observational skills.

"Sam's a complicated kid," she conceded. "I think there's probably a lot we don't know."

"You know she hoards food? I caught her in the dining hall last night when you guys were swimming."

"That I do know, yes." It was something Gabi'd noticed as soon as Sam had arrived at school. And despite having easy access to as much as she could possibly eat for nine months now, the poor girl still acted as if her next meal wasn't guaranteed. "I'll speak to her. I'm sorry."

Fear suddenly clutched Gabi's gut as she realized if Luke turned Sam in to Priscilla, the headmaster wouldn't hesitate to send her right back to a place where apparently she couldn't even depend on having food . . . or safety.

"I'd appreciate it if you didn't say anything," she said, almost in a whisper. "Priscilla's not the most understanding type. She's also fairly committed to seeing Sam's backside as she heads out the Briarwood gate, so any excuse might be enough of an excuse for her."

"I'm not going to say anything. To anybody."

"I had no idea she was doing it here, too."

"It's all right, Gabi." He looked at her like *she* was out of line for apologizing. "She's got her reasons. And if the girl's hungry, the girl needs to eat. I just showed her where everything is so she can grab food if she needs something."

Gabi swallowed. "Thank you."

"I also gave her a cupboard so she can keep her own stuff in there. It's got a lock on it."

"You did?"

He shrugged like it was no big deal. "I've seen the type. Odd to see in a rich kid like her, but the behavior's similar. I just figured maybe having a locked-up spot where she can hoard her treats might ease her mind a little bit."

Rich kid—ha. If he only knew.

Gabi looked at him for a long moment. Here he sat in a backward baseball cap and a Red Sox T-shirt that had both seen better days, but he spoke like a psychologist. She wasn't sure what to make of it.

She tipped her head, studying him. "You know, it occurs to me that Priscilla never had a chance to fill me in on your . . . history."

"My qualifications, you mean?" He winked.

"Sure." She tipped her head. "We'll go with that."

"I've been working summers here for ten years. During the school year, I do some work at a couple of the local high schools. That's me."

"Handyman stuff?"

He shrugged. "This and that."

"I have a feeling you're a little more complicated than that."

"Nah. I strive to be *un*complicated. World's tricky enough. I don't need to add to it." He turned toward her. "How about you? What's *your* story?"

"My story? Far too long and mesmerizing to tell."

"Ah." He smiled, turning back toward the lake, his hands behind his head. "A woman of mystery."

"Yup, that's me." Gabi rolled her eyes.

"So tell me. This housemother concept is new to me. What do you actually do there?"

"I didn't put you off with the long and mesmerizing thing?"

"Nope. And I'm serious. It's . . . an unusual career choice."

"If it saves my reputation, I didn't actually set out to be a housemother."

"What *did* you set out to be?"

Gabi took a deep breath, picturing her freshman-year classes, back when her trust fund had been intact and her future had seemed solid.

"I started out wanting to teach math, actually."

"So what changed that?"

"My calculus grade." She laughed bitterly. "My professor hinted that perhaps I might be a better fit for the English department."

"Ouch."

"He was right, unfortunately. And then . . . I took a year off, got my bearings, and went back. Bypassed the English department building—thank you—and double-majored in psych and sociology."

No need to talk about *why* she'd taken that year off. No reason Luke needed to know about her older brother, who lived life like he was entitled to whatever he desired, be it money. . . . or women. No reason to talk about how his actions had led to her complete and utter split with her family . . . and consequently, her trust fund.

No need to detail her year of scrabbling to find an apartment, two jobs, and her dignity.

"So you're yet another overeducated, underpaid minion of the American education system."

"Absolutely." She smiled. "But when my charges aren't driving me to drink, I actually almost love my job. I get to be substitute parent, guidance counselor, homework helper, crisis intervention officer, and midnight-snack sneaker, all in one."

"Sounds . . . busy."

"It's twenty-four/seven. These girls don't have parents on-site, obviously, and most of them don't have families who are even reachable, half the time."

"So you're it?"

She shrugged. "I'm not the only *it* on campus, but I'm one of four houseparents. I'm responsible for the fifty kids in my dorm—making sure they're fed, happy, and successful in all of their Briarwood endeavors."

Luke cocked one eyebrow. "That last part sounds straight from a job description."

"Totally is." Gabi laughed.

"So which part's the hardest?"

"The happy." She said it without hesitation. "A lot of these girls have been tossed around to camps and boarding schools for most of their lives. And now the ones in my dorm, at least, are navigating their teen years, with all of the hormonal hell that comes with it. It's a rocky path, even for the most grounded of kids." She cringed. "And we don't necessarily have a lot of those."

"Can I be blunt?" He raised that one eyebrow again. "Your job title doesn't necessarily seem to do justice to the job—or jobs—you're actually doing."

"You mean because it makes me sound like I sit by the fireplace and knit scarves while I wait for my students to come in for fresh cookies before tootling off to do whatever it is boarding school students do?"

He laughed. "Exactly."

"I know." She nodded. "I actually hate my title."

"You can't change it?"

"Have you *met* Priscilla Pritchard? Titles are power, and she likes to make sure all of her staff members know exactly where they sit in the pecking order . . . which is ten to twenty pecks below her."

"She sounds like a peach."

"Rotten peach, maybe." Gabi pressed her lips together. "Sorry. Given the events of the past week, I have some rather strong feelings on the subject of Priscilla Pritchard."

"Hard to blame you." He shrugged. "Seems to me,

unless Briarwood is pandering to an audience of parents that long for the Dark Ages, Priscilla should *want* to show she's got academic deans and counselors and the like—all of which are titles that seem like they'd be a better match for what you're doing."

"You'd think." Gabi looked back out at the lake. "But Priscilla's first priority is Priscilla. She loves her own title, she loves the fact that super-rich families from all over the country kiss her proverbial boots in order to get their girls into Briarwood, and she loves that she gets to be the face of one of the best prep schools in America. What she *doesn't* want is any of her staff members getting ideas about moving up any invisible ladders and taking her job."

"*Do* you want her job?"

Gabi paused, thoughts spinning through her head. "No. And yes. No, because omigod, I'd absolutely die having to deal with the parents she handles. But yes." She nodded. "I'd love the chance to make Briarwood into a different kind of school."

"Really." He turned toward her, full attention on her, and it was both unnerving and zingy. "What would you do to it?"

Oh, that question was easy. "Set aside a huge chunk of endowment money to fund scholarships for kids like Sam and Eve."

"Kids like . . ." He tipped his head, eyebrows scrunching together. "What do you mean?"

Oops. Oh, hell.

"Are the two of them on scholarship?"

She nodded slowly. "Yes, but I never should have said that. The other girls don't know. Please, please don't . . . say anything."

Even as she asked, somehow she knew he'd never dream of it.

He turned away, sitting back in his chair, hands folded behind his head again. "I'll try not to be insulted that you felt you had to ask that."

"I know. I'm sorry. I know you wouldn't say—never mind. Sorry."

"How many scholarship kids do you have in a normal year?"

She swallowed. *Before this year? Zero.* "We have . . . two."

He turned back toward her. "With an endowment like that? Two kids? *Two?*"

"I know." She put up her hands. "It's sickening. And I had to fight for three years to get the board to even do a trial run of two students this year. And now look. Both of them got themselves in enough trouble that we've been sent to camp for the summer. Priscilla would have expelled them, if it had been up to her. Luckily, she has to answer to the board, and this time, I think that board actually saved the girls."

Gabi pictured the board members sitting in their seats at the huge oak table in the main conference room. To a person, she could predict exactly what their responses to the girls' little escapade probably were. She imagined the expulsion votes divided evenly down the center of the table, and then she pictured Laura Beringer sitting in her spot at the end, nodding carefully. At eighty-something years old, she'd been the board chair for ten years now, and she showed no signs of leaving, much to one side of the table's dismay.

Gabi adored her, and she had a strong feeling that the only reason Sam and Eve weren't packing for Boston right now was because of Laura's deciding vote.

"Did they deserve it?" His voice was quiet, but the question was honest.

"It depends how you interpret the school policies, but

I guarantee you, if it had been just Sam and Eve who'd snuck out, Priscilla would have pushed even harder to expel them. The fact that they did their crime with Madison and Waverly probably saved them, as ironic as that seems."

Gabi saw a look pass over Luke's face—a mixture of emotions she couldn't quite identify—before he set his jaw and nodded slowly.

"What if it'd been the other two who'd snuck out?"

"Then I can almost guarantee you and I would have never met. The incident would have been quietly swept under the rug."

"Shocking."

"They're good kids, Luke. All four of them are. But they're so locked into their patterns that you'd never know it. You'd *certainly* never know it, based on what you've seen the past few days." She fisted her hands in her lap. "I've spent the entire year trying to figure out how to get through to them, but wow. Turtles have nothing on the shells these girls wear."

"And I imagine Sam's and Eve's are the toughest of all?"

"Of course they are. They've both been shoved around their entire lives, house to house, family to family, hell to bigger hell. I interviewed fifty girls for these two scholarships, Luke. I would have taken them all, just to get them out of the lives they were trying to survive. It broke my heart."

He was silent for a long, long moment, just staring out at the lake. Then he turned to her. "I have to ask, then. Why would you stick the four of them together in a suite? Madison's as bitchy as they come, and Waverly will do whatever Madison tells her. Why'd you sic them on two innocents?"

Gabi looked down at her lap. "I've asked myself that

a thousand times, believe me." Then she sighed. "Honestly? Beyond my bigger, lofty, impossible goals, I thought, given time, they'd figure out that they're not nearly as different as they think. All four of them have essentially been abandoned by their parents—just in different ways. I thought that somehow, some way, maybe that would bind them."

"But no?"

"God, no. I mean, there have been moments . . . weeks, even, when things were pretty okay. But then Madison will step up her game, or Sam will preempt her by stepping up hers, and Eve and Waverly end up caught in the middle choosing sides, and then . . ."

"Chaos."

"Yup."

He was thoughtful for another long moment, and then he shifted in his chair, turning to look straight at her.

"Hey, Gabi?" His voice was soft, almost tender, as he touched her shoulder. It was just the briefest touch, but it sent swirling, zappy zings straight to her toes. "Would you kill me if I said it sounds like maybe . . . maybe you've actually all ended up exactly where you need to be?"

Chapter 8

Hours later, Gabi lay awake on her cot, desperate for sleep, but unable to close her eyes as she replayed her conversation with Luke. It was almost dawn, and the girls were asleep, the usual scratches and snuffles filtering in from outside the tent as the coons and skunks made their rounds. Funny how after only a few days, the girls were learning to sleep through it.

She didn't dare move, since one squeak of her cot could wake them all up, and really, sleeping was the *only* cooperative thing they'd managed since they'd arrived.

In her more delusional moments in the week before they'd left Briarwood, she'd tried to convince herself that maybe, like Luke had hinted, this summer could be an opportunity to finally draw the four teens together . . . to find some common ground that could bind them for the upcoming year . . . to find *some* way to make sure they wouldn't do something to get themselves booted right *out* of Briarwood as soon as school opened again.

But despite her best efforts over the past couple of days, the girls were more ornery than ever. She could understand hating the craft projects and the scavenger hunt that nobody had won, and she could *totally* buy the outhouse and mosquito hatred going on. But even swimming—which should have been easy and enjoyable—was fraught with screeches and whines as they complained about the water temperature, about the clams in the sand, about how their hair was never-ever-*ever* going to be clean again.

Actually, she'd give them that one. Thanks to the special lake-safe soap-slash-shampoo Luke had given them, her hair already resembled a frizzy dishrag, as did the girls'.

There had to be a way to rig a shower of some sort. She tapped her fingers on the blanket, thinking. Maybe tomorrow they could figure something out. Surely the girls would work together for something like the promise of a hot shower, wouldn't they?

Just then, she heard something scratch loudly over by where Waverly's and Madison's cots met. She sat up, grabbing her flashlight. She'd grown accustomed to the usual scratching noises, and this was not them. Her pulse picked up speed as she listened. Was something bigger out there?

Trying not to wake up the girls, she shined her flashlight toward the sound. For a few seconds, she saw nothing, but then she drew in a quick breath as she spotted dark fur and a thick white stripe.

A skunk.

In their tent.

Two feet from Waverly and Madison's heads.

She sat stock-still, not wanting to startle it. Maybe it'd do its little investigation and be on its way. But thirty long seconds later, it didn't seem to be going anywhere. It snuffled and snorted its way around the underside of their cots, then stopped at a plastic bag someone must have stuffed in the corner of the tent.

"What's that noise?" Eve's sleepy voice came from the other side of the tent.

"Shh." Gabi pointed her flashlight at the skunk.

"Shit." Eve dove into her sleeping bag, making just enough noise to startle the skunk, who turned around and arched his tail threateningly.

Crap-crap-crap. Gabi cringed, bracing herself, not knowing what to do. Should she make a run for it? Would she get to the tent flaps in time to get out before he sprayed? Should she wake up the girls? Would that make it worse?

She stayed silent and still, willing the stupid little critter to go away, but once he apparently decided he wasn't in mortal danger, he turned around and went back to mauling the plastic bag.

What was in that bag? Gabi narrowed her eyes at the other cots. And who had brought it in here?

Just then, Madison stirred and sat up. Then she turned sleepy eyes toward the corner, and before Gabi could warn her not to move, she let out a screech that had Waverly and Sam popping up out of bed.

Oh. Holy. Hell.

Gabi had smelled skunk spray before. Who hadn't? But ten seconds later, as the five of them stumbled out of the tent and gasped for air, she realized she'd never *really* smelled skunk before. There was *nothing* like ground-zero spray, expertly delivered by a panicked creature who'd just been looking for a little chocolate, dammit.

As Gabi and the girls bent over, coughing and gagging, she saw Luke come sprinting over the hill. Then she saw him stop dead and hold his nose.

Then she heard him laugh, and she thought she might just have to throttle him.

"Ladies?" He tried to tamp down his smile. "What happened?"

Gabi glared at him. "Pretty sure the smell gives that away, don't you think?"

"Who ticked off the skunk?"

"Nobody! He got into our tent."

"Wow. That's pretty odd. They don't usually do that unless—uh-oh." Luke tipped his head suspiciously, like he was about to ask a question he damn well already knew the answer to. "Wouldn't happen to be any *food* in that tent, would there?"

"I don't know." Gabi turned to the girls, picturing the skunk with his little skunky nose buried in the plastic bag in the corner. "Girls?"

All four of them shook their heads, but no one did so harder than Sam, who was tops on Gabi's suspect list. But there was no way any of them was going to admit it at this point, so asking was pretty much moot. Plus, the punishment the skunk had doled out on its own was way worse than anything she might have come up with.

"You guys better get yourselves down to the lake. That stuff burns if it's on your skin." Again Gabi saw Luke trying not to smile, but he was pretty much failing.

Gabi held her hands out to her sides. Good God, she stank. "Will it come *off* in the lake?"

"Sort of. Not really. Gonna need to make yourselves a big ole tomato bath. Luckily, I know a girl whose family specializes in tomatoes." He finally lost his battle not to laugh. "I'll give Piper a call and see if she can score some from the restaurant. Maybe she can bring them when she comes out to make breakfast. Till then, you seriously better go take a swim, all of you."

Waverly sobbed, "I. Hate. This. Place." She headed toward the path, Madison close behind . . . and oddly silent. Sam and Eve brought up the rear, and Luke stepped off the path as they passed, his hand over his nose.

Once they'd gone over the hill and down toward the lake, he turned to Gabi. "You okay?"

"Oh, I'm just fabulous, yes. Thanks for asking."

"They had food, didn't they?"

"Yup."

"So my voice of doom apparently wasn't as effective as I thought? Hard lesson. Sorry you had to be a victim."

"Luke?" Gabi clenched her teeth together. "You'd sound a lot more sympathetic if you could stop laughing."

Four hours later, Gabi and the girls had slopped some sort of tomato-based concoction all over their skin and done their best to rinse it off in the lake, but they all still reeked. Gabi was pretty sure the skunk scent was locked into her scalp, as every time a breeze caught her hair, all she could smell was that sickening, horrible scent.

They'd taken down the tent, washed their sleeping bags in the same pungent mixture of tomatoes and who-knew-what-else, and everything was currently laid out in the sun to dry. Whether that would happen before dark was anyone's guess.

Eve pointed at Sam. "I can't believe you had food in the tent."

"It wasn't mine." Sam shook her head. "Swear."

"It's *always* you." Madison glared. "You're like a squirrel, for God's sake. You *always* hide your food. Jesus, it's like you think we're going to steal it or some-thing."

"It wasn't me *this* time." She sent a pleading look at Gabi. "It wasn't."

Only Gabi knew about Sam's locked cupboard in the

kitchen—not the other girls—and if it hadn't been for that knowledge, she totally would have pinned this on Sam, too.

"Honestly, girls, it doesn't matter who it was at this point. The damage is done, we smell like a bunch of skunks, and our tent is probably ruined."

"So can we go home *now*?" Waverly's eyes were wide.

"No. Now we just have to be more miserable—and smelly. Thank you, whoever did leave food in that tent last night." She let her eyes land on each of their faces. "I assume this won't be an issue again?"

They all shook their heads, and for a moment she was struck by the humor of the scene, from anyone *else's* perspective.

Just then, Sam snorted. "Pritch-bitch would *love* to hear about this."

Eve smiled. "Yeah, she would."

"Girls." Gabi rolled her eyes. "You have to stop calling her that."

Sam raised her eyebrows. "You really want to argue right now about whether or not it fits?"

After a long pause, Gabi sighed. "No."

"So what do we do now?" Madison pulled at her long blond strands of hair, frowning as she lifted them to her nose. "We can't possibly stay here under these conditions, Gabi."

"Here's what we're going to do." Gabi stood up from the grass. "You four are going to go find another tent in the shed, you're going to put it up, on a different platform, and you are *not* going to kill each other doing so. We'll figure the rest out later. Clear?"

"Clear as glass," Sam muttered, then put up her hands in mock surrender as Gabi sent a scorching glare her way.

After they'd disappeared inside the equipment shed, Gabi put her fingers to her eyes, trying to stop the frustrated tears that were wanting so badly to break free. She wished she could believe the rest of the summer was going to get better, but her confidence was fading fast.

Oliver's words echoed in her head, and she blew out a long breath, picturing Luke sitting beside her at the lake last night.

Maybe it was time to ask for help.

She watched the girls jostle each other out of the shed, carrying poles and canvas, then dropping the whole pile in a noisy clatter and squawking about who'd let go first.

She put her hands to her ears, closing her eyes as she turned toward the lake and counted ten deep breaths. Once they put up the tent—*if* they put up the tent—she was going to march them up to the garden area and give them each a hoe, a shovel, and a quadrant of dirt to turn into plantable soil.

And tomorrow, after she'd had time to gather her thoughts and figure out how to request assistance without feeling like a dismal failure, she'd talk to Luke.

Chapter 9

The next morning, Gabi jumped when Luke pushed open the door of the dining hall, despite the fact that she'd been waiting for him. She'd tried to get up earlier than he did so she could at least make him coffee before she begged for help, but even though she'd slid out of her sleeping bag at the crack of dawn, she'd still barely beat him to the coffeemaker.

"You're up early. No more skunks?"

She looked at him in his clean T-shirt, hair damp from the shower, a dab of shaving cream near his ear, and tried not to find him adorable. She barely knew him, for God's sake. She shouldn't be using the term "adorable," even casually.

She'd been the queen of fall-fast-fall-hard-fall-stupid for a long time now, even after she'd identified her own ridiculous pattern. It was mortally embarrassing just *how* stupid she'd been a few times, and "adorable" had no place on her vocab list right now.

This looking at him in the morning sunlight and wondering what the planes of his chest might look like without his T-shirt? It was just . . . a bad habit, not attraction. Not *real* attraction, anyway. He was here, he was hot, and he pressed the fall-fast button perfectly. If she let herself get drawn in by his deep green eyes and that damn dimple, she'd head right into fall-hard territory.

And inevitably, the stupid part would follow.

He'd reveal an irresistible sense of humor, he'd be a great kisser . . . he'd have a kitten back at his cabin that revealed his softer side. And she'd be a goner.

"Gabi?"

She shook her head, clearing the vision. What had he asked her? "I'm sorry, what?"

He raised his eyebrows like he'd seen every thought that had just flown through her head. "Skunks. Just asking if you'd seen any more critters last night."

"Um, no. None. Pretty sure the girls swept out every piece of dust that could be mistaken as a crumb."

"Good. Hard lesson to learn, but a good one. Could have been a bear."

Gabi shivered. "Thank you. I need to have *that* on my mind right now."

He filled a coffee mug, then motioned toward the door. "Want to come sit by the lake for a few minutes before the princess posse awakens?"

She paused. Would it be easier to have the conversation she'd practiced down by the water? Or here in the dining hall?

She shook her head internally. It didn't matter. No matter where they were, it wasn't going to be easy. She followed him out the door and down the wooden steps, inhaling the woodsy scent of pines and moss. Even through her anxiety, she already loved this time of the day at Echo Lake.

In the morning light, with wisps of fog lifting off the lake, it looked like they'd stepped into a magical summer wonderland, rather than a run-down, has-been summer camp. As they walked over the dewy grass to the water's edge, she looked around, trying to appreciate the beauty of the setting, even though the distinct scent of skunk still lingered in the air.

Or maybe she was still carrying it with her, despite three lake shampoos yesterday.

Echo Lake stretched for what looked like a mile or so across, and the camp property was nestled in a sandy cove surrounded by the tallest pines Gabi had ever seen. It reminded her of dream-vacation pictures she'd seen online, where water met land met sky . . . and not one building interrupted the sightline.

The moment she sat down, she felt her blood pressure drop, as it did every time she sat here. She didn't know if it was the mist, or the mountain, or just the fresh, clean air, but there was just something about this spot that called up her inner Zen.

The arm of the chair made a perfect landing spot for her coffee mug, and she closed her eyes for a long moment, just drinking in the peace as she called up her courage. She could hear the water lapping softly against the sand and the dock, and somewhere behind her, birds and squirrels were busy in the trees.

"So what are you going to do with the girls today?" Luke's deep voice made her open her eyes.

Gabi sighed. Here was her opening, but for some reason, she couldn't find the words she'd practiced. "I'm not sure yet. Leave them out for the bears? Send them on a hike with bad directions?"

"If I said I had an idea, would you trust me?" He kept his eyes focused on the other side of the lake, not looking at her.

Wait. Was he about to actually make this easier on her?

"It's . . . possible. Tell me why I should."

He tipped his head. "I think the girls could use a little wake-up call."

"Because the skunk wasn't enough of one? What does *that* mean?"

"It means—and you may not want to hear this—it means despite what they did back at Briarwood, in all honesty, their first few days at camp have been a piece of cake."

"I beg your pardon? Did you miss the part about raccoons? Outhouses? Baths in a glacial lake?"

"And scavenger hunts and art projects and swimming every day. Yes, it's been harsh." He raised an eyebrow like she was being obtuse. "I know Camp Echo is hardly their normal lifestyle, but I also know these four girls aren't feeling a whole lot of pain around the decisions they made that got you sent here."

"No offense, Luke, but I actually think they're feeling quite a *bit* of pain."

"Not the lasting kind." He shook his head. "Not the kind that'll really change their behavior in the end."

She sighed, knowing he was right, but not wanting to admit it quite yet. "So what do you propose?"

"I propose we give them the kind of consequences that'll leave them too tired to even think about causing trouble again—the kind that'll make them test their limits and work together."

"You sound like an advertisement for military school or something." She shook her head. "And also, you might be a glutton for punishment, if you think that approach has a chance of flying with this crew."

Luke shrugged. "Give me one day. Trust me for today, and if it doesn't work, we'll reconvene tonight and you can officially un-trust me."

"One question—less than a week ago, you made no bones about the fact that you had a project list a mile long, and no interest in having us bother you. And now you're sitting here offering to . . . well, I'm not sure yet what you're offering, but it's something. Why?"

He nodded. "Good question. And I don't even know how to answer it."

"Is it because you think I'm so inept that someone's going to actually get hurt? Because the fish hook wasn't my fault. Oliver said those poles are ancient. And the poison ivy . . . well, I guess that one could probably be blamed on me, but really, it was just discomfort, not real pain or anything."

She knew she was babbling, and she *also* knew her goal waking up this morning was to get help, so really, she should be feeling grateful that he was offering first, but instead, her initial reaction was to feel defensive.

Was she really this bad at accepting help?

"I'm not offering to bail you out because I fear for the lives of your students, no." Luke smiled. "I'm just offering because—well, maybe because it's what I do. And honestly, I'm only offering you one day. After that, they're all yours."

Gabi stared at the water. *One day.* "Do you truly have any experience with kids like this?"

"I've got experience with a lot of kids, Gabi."

She heard the tone in his voice before she saw his jaw tighten, and she felt guilty. He was offering help, and she *needed* help. She just hated that she did.

She closed her eyes tightly. "One day?"

Some of the tightness left his jaw, and she saw the traces of a smile return. "One day."

Just then, Gabi heard the girls grumbling their way toward the beach, complaining about the heat and the cold and their hair and the food . . . until she lost track of all the things that were already wrong with the morning. It was barely dawn, for God's sake.

She glanced over at Luke, who had his eyebrows raised, an amused expression on his face as he looked at her. It pretty much hit her from head to toe and everywhere in between. She shook her head and picked up her mug, lifting it toward his in a mock cheers.

"Luke? They're all yours."

Chapter 10

Luke stood up, and Gabi did the same. Madison and Waverly immediately sat down in the chairs they'd vacated, but Luke pointed at them, hooking his thumb.

"Sorry, ladies. Sitting's for later. And from here on out, these chairs are adults-only."

Madison rolled her eyes and sighed before she stood up, but Waverly just popped up like she'd been hooked with a crochet needle.

"All right." Luke reached into his back pocket for a piece of paper, unfolding it as he looked at each of them. "Today we launch Operation Echo."

Silence greeted him. Since they hadn't gotten beyond "one day," Gabi had no idea what he was talking about. Obviously the girls didn't, either.

"I've got a list of the projects that need doing, and I've gone ahead and prioritized them, but I wouldn't mind some input before we get started on them."

Madison crossed her arms. "Gabi? What is he talking about? Are you, like, renting us out or something? Because of one little skunk? Seriously?"

Luke shook his head. "No rent. She gave you guys to me for free."

A sharp intake of breath made Gabi laugh, but she

didn't ease their minds by arguing with him. She'd said yes for today, but he was making it sound like she'd okayed them as his work crew for the rest of the summer.

For some reason, she was totally okay with that right now.

"What *kind* of projects?" Sam's pose matched Madison's.

"The work kind of projects. Building, painting, cleaning—you know. Projects. We needed a work crew for the summer. Instead, Briarwood sent you. Maybe there was a mix-up and maybe there wasn't, but that's where we're at. You've had almost a week of vacation here in paradise, but today we get serious. I've got a list of stuff to do, and you four have *nothing* to do. It's a perfect match. *You* can be my work crew."

Five minutes later, the girls were seated at the picnic table outside the administration cottage, their arms crossed, their faces grim as Luke tacked down four copies of the list he'd made. He handed each of them a pencil.

"All right. This is the stuff that needs doing before the end of August, but I'm going to let you help figure out what order we do it in."

"Gosh, thanks." Madison rolled her eyes. "And how did we end up your slaves, anyway?"

"I prefer work crew. And you don't have to vote." Luke shrugged. "But if you don't vote, you don't whine. Got it?"

She narrowed her eyes, but she kept her mouth shut for once. He paused for a long moment, waiting her out, but finally decided she was going to stay quiet, so he continued.

"I figure we'll work out a reward system. We get the work done, we get to play."

"Play?" Sam snorted. "We're not five."

"Just an expression, Snarkasaurus. If we get the stuff

done that needs doing, then we can take a break and do the fun stuff."

Eve sighed, her expression bored. "And what exactly is the fun stuff?"

Luke smiled. "There's a big lake, a big mountain, and a big forest. We'll figure it out as we go. You're in paradise, girls. The fun never ends."

Madison scanned the list, landing her finger on an item halfway down the page. "You can't be serious. You think building a new bathroom is the tenth priority on this list? Behind repairing the dock?"

Luke shrugged. "You disagree?"

"Are you *kidding*? A bathroom—with an actual toilet—is definitely top priority."

"Everybody else agree?" The other three girls nodded as Luke pointed to each of them in turn. "Gabi? How about you?"

Gabi rolled her eyes, trying not to think of how many types of insects she'd seen in the outhouse over the past week. "A bathroom would be nice, yes."

But wait a minute. There was no way they could build an entire bathroom in a day. She narrowed her eyes. That had to be at least a week-long project. Had he snowed her into turning over her girls so he could have free labor?

She tried to feel mad, but was sobered to realize that all she *actually* felt was relief.

"All right. Bathroom it is." Luke gathered the lists and rolled them up, then stuck them in his back pocket. "I'll give you girls fifteen minutes to go do—whatever girls your age need to do in the morning. Report back here at nine sharp. We've got a lot of lumber to haul."

The girls sat still for a long moment, like they couldn't quite believe they'd been hired out—for free—as Luke's personal work crew, but when Gabi didn't intervene, they mumbled and muttered as they unfolded themselves from the picnic table and headed down the pathway toward the tent.

Gabi studied Luke as he leaned over to scribble on another piece of paper. "Did you really think a bathroom was the tenth priority?"

"Nah." He slid his pencil behind his ear as he turned to her. "Just thought it'd help to give them something to agree on for at least the first day. Figured the thought of a toilet and shower would be a good carrot to get them through our first project."

"*First* day? *First* project?"

He smiled. "We'll see how it goes. I might not know squat about girls, but I do know they love a good bathroom. It's a start, right?"

"Sure." She crossed her arms. "Any chance you've thought through exactly how you're going to teach *this* crew how to build a bathroom?"

"Nah. We'll figure it out." He winked, motioning her toward his truck, which she could now see was laden with lumber. "Come on, Gabi. We've got a team to build. By the end of the day, these girls will be too tired to give *any* of us any crap. That's gotta be worth some level of trust, right?"

Gabi took a deep breath, uncrossing her arms. "Okay, I'm going to trust you, but if anybody cuts off a finger or anything, we're both dead."

"Won't happen."

"Have you *met* these girls?"

He leveled her with a look, and this time all traces of humor were gone. In their place was a jaw set against any argument she might come up with.

"Trust me, Gabi."

*   *   *

Four hours later, the girls had hauled an entire truckload worth of lumber to the site of the new bathroom, complaining and whining the entire time. Two hours in, Luke had promised them lemonade at lunch if they would just shut up for ten straight minutes.

He stood on the cement foundation he'd poured last week, watching as the girls slowly stacked the lumber and turned around to get more from the truck. His early assessments of them were spot-on, if he did say so himself.

He was pretty sure the last time any of them had done manual labor was . . . never. They were clumsy, inefficient, and oh-so-angry about the whole thing, save for Eve, who just tried to stay under the radar. If he hadn't been so amused by the efforts of the other three not to cooperate, he would have been really ticked off that it was taking them so long to empty the truck.

He'd known damn well they'd all choose the bathroom project first. Had counted on it when he'd bought the lumber last night and had it ready and waiting in the parking lot this morning. He and Oliver had already finished the pipework to the septic. All that was left was to frame in the building and do the internal plumbing. It was the perfect project, since pretty much anything that needed doing required at least two sets of hands.

Yep. If the girls wanted to pee on a throne or take an actual shower this summer, they were going to have to work together, whether they liked it or not.

He tried to keep his eyes on the teenagers, but to his consternation, his attention kept drifting to Gabriela. When she'd seen the enormous pile of lumber, her eyes had widened, and she'd looked at him like he was crazy.

"They're not heavy," he'd said.

"But there are a gazillion of them," she'd answered.

"So it'll take a while." He'd shrugged, and she'd shaken her head, but she'd buttoned her lip and let him direct the girls. He was pretty sure it was killing her to turn over control, but it was clear she was well out of her element here, so she didn't have a lot of choices.

And now, four hours later, almost the entire pile of lumber had been moved, and after lunch, they'd be able to start the actual building part.

"Will this be ready by tonight?" Eve asked.

"Well, depending on how well you guys do, there may be walls, but you'll still be able to see through them. No plumbing, though. This stuff takes time. Look how long it took you just to unload the truck."

Madison and Waverly arrived with the last two-by-four, collapsing onto the pile as soon as they'd placed the board on top.

"Please tell us we're done for the day." Madison wiped her forehead, then pulled her hand away and looked at it in disgust, like she couldn't fathom how all of that dirt had gotten there.

"Done for the morning, yep." Luke pointed toward the dining hall. "There's a sink right outside the kitchen. Go wash up. Piper left lunch stuff out on the counter for you. We're back here in thirty minutes."

"Half an hour? That's *it*?" Waverly whined.

As the girls stumbled toward the dining hall, Luke heard "slave driver" come out of someone's mouth, but it only made him smile.

"Are you trying to kill them?" Gabi's voice wiped the smile clean.

He turned toward her. "Nope. Why? They look dead to you?"

"I'm never going to hear the end of this, thank you very much." She put her hands on her hips, and he hated the sudden urge that struck him—the one that made him want to kiss the frown right off her gorgeous face.

He smiled, almost reaching out to wipe a smudge of

dirt from her nose, then stopping himself because *what the hell*?

"Gabi, I guarantee you that by the time you're alone with those girls in your tent tonight, they will be too tired to give you any shit at all. Eight hours of manual labor will do them in. Guaranteed." He put down his tool belt and stood back up. "You know, I'd have thought you'd be the first one to want them put through as much hell as possible, given that they got you sent here, instead of Bermuda."

"Barbados."

He shrugged. "B-something."

She paused like she wanted to say something, but wasn't sure if she should. Then she went ahead. "Just to be clear about something, I've let you be in charge this morning because—well—I've never built a bathroom from scratch. But despite what you're telling them, I'm not turning them over to you long-term or anything."

"Good. I don't want 'em. And you only agreed to trust me for the day . . . so far."

He saw a tinge of pink color her cheeks, and for a moment, he didn't know if it was anger, embarrassment, or fear that put it there.

"I'm sorry," she finally said. "I do. Trust you, I mean. I just pretty much suck at it."

He laughed, and this time he did reach out to wipe the dirt from her nose. "We can work on that. But first, we'll spend the afternoon making these girls regret they messed up your vacation, okay?"

She started to speak, but he put up a hand to stop her. "In a perfectly safe, nonthreatening sort of way." Then he winked. "They might even accomplish something, if we're not careful."

Chapter 11

Early the next morning, Gabi settled into one of the Adirondack chairs beside the dock, reveling in the muted beauty of the sunrise, even though her back was screaming in pain from all of the lumber-hauling she'd done yesterday.

"Morning." Luke's voice came from behind her as he strode onto the sand, then sat down in the matching chair. "Sleep well?"

He looked just-showered delicious, not at all like he, too, had suffered through hours of manual labor just yesterday, even though he'd carted far more boards than she had. Meanwhile, she'd made do with a lightning-fast dip in the lake, one that had done nothing to ease the pain she was suffering from yesterday's exertion.

"I slept perfectly, thank you." If she was careful not to shift her weight right now, he'd never see her grimace as every muscle in her body screamed for mercy.

He looked at her, his eyes tracing her face slowly. "Bullshit."

"Yup." She bit her lip as she crossed her legs slowly. "You wouldn't happen to stock Advil here, would you?"

"Oliver might have some. Not sure."

"Speaking of . . . stocking things, I have a group of

teenaged girls. We thought we were coming to a fully functional camp. I'm going to need to go into town and get . . . stuff, sooner than later."

He nodded, putting up a hand. "We definitely don't have *stuff.*"

"Does this mean you'll unlock my battery?"

"Happily. But I'm not sure I'd take a fifteen-passenger luxury van into downtown Echo Lake. Between the hairpin turns and the crap parking, you'd be making a call to your insurance agent when you got back."

"It was the only vehicle Priscilla was willing to spare for the summer. I didn't have other options."

"I suppose I could let you borrow my truck."

Gabi pressed her lips together, picturing the truck that looked held together by no more than duct tape and a prayer. Would the thing even *get* her to town?

He looked over. "She's not pretty, but she runs."

Gabi felt a tiny laugh bubble out at his words, but when his face went suddenly steely, she swallowed her laughter, realizing he thought she was laughing at the truck itself, not the fact that he sounded like a character from *The Beverly Hillbillies.*

"I'm sorry to laugh. You just sounded like—I don't know—a crusty old man sitting on his porch with his ancient hound dog at his feet and a shotgun across his lap."

"Nice." She could see him trying not to smile, and the steel melted a bit from his cheekbones.

"I'd be grateful if you'd let me borrow your truck. Thank you."

Since the tiny town was beyond Camp Echo, Gabi hadn't actually seen it on the way up here the other day. All she knew from checking on her computer back at Briarwood was that its main street wandered along the Abenaki River, which eventually dumped into the lake.

"What kind of stores do you guys have in town?"

"One grocery, one drugstore, one quilt shop, six antiques places that open in the summer, and a few small restaurants. There's a Mexican place on the river, a new pub on Lake Street, and there's Bellinis—Piper's place."

"She owns a restaurant?" How in the world did she have time to work here at camp?

"Doesn't own it. It belongs to her aunt and uncle. She and her cousin Molly do most of the waiting tables, though, when they're not working their other full-time jobs."

Gabi nodded. "Busy."

"Family."

He let the word land like it had all the weight it needed, like there wasn't any question that Molly and Piper *would* spend their off hours racing around a restaurant on tired feet, because . . . family.

She wondered what it would be like to feel like that about her own family.

And then she wondered about his.

"How about you, Luke? Where'd you grow up? Where's your family?"

Like a curtain at the end of an opera, the muscles in Luke's face contracted, then relaxed as if they'd practiced the bland look he passed her way.

"Long story. So . . . we gonna finish up that bathroom today? You going to let me have your heathens again?"

Gabi swallowed. Okay. Not talking about family. "You really want them?"

He shrugged. "That depends on you. You agreed to trust me for one day. That ended last night. But we've got a bathroom partly built, and we've got a bunch of teens who could use some work to do. You're stuck here, and I'm stuck *with* you. We might as well make the best of it, right?"

"Nice. You really think they can do it? Build an actual—building?"

"You saw them yesterday. Once they got done being miserable, they actually started to cooperate. Not on purpose, but they did. They're a quarter of the way done, and they're motivated. If they *do* get it done, then no more outhouse. I say we let them keep working on it. And I'll agree to keep supervising, on one condition."

"If I say yes, you *have* to keep supervising. I have no *idea* how to build a bathroom."

"Exactly."

"But I don't like conditions."

"I know. But I do." He smiled. "And here's mine— you need to work *with* me, not against me."

Gabi spun toward him, trying not to wince when the action tweaked her tender ribs. "How am I working against you? I helped all *day* yesterday."

"I know. But you're still trying to protect the girls from the big, bad handyman, and you really need to let them do what needs doing in order to get this thing built."

"Are we talking about power saws? And their propensity to eat inexperienced fingers? Because I stand by my opinion on that one. The most complicated tool these girls have ever used is a straightening iron, okay?"

He laughed. "Well, how are they going to learn, if you don't let them try? You can't protect them from *every*thing."

"That's my job, Luke. And if I do nothing else this summer, I *do* need to bring them all back in one piece."

"They're not going to lose pieces by picking up a power tool or running some simple wiring."

"Have you *been* to an ER lately? They totally could." She felt her chin jut out stubbornly, and she put a hand up to hide it. Dammit.

"Well, we'll never find out, if you keep stopping them from doing the things I'm asking them to do. You said you'd trust me."

"When I agreed, there was no mention of power tools."

His face grew serious. "They could gain a lot more than they'll lose, Gabi. Let go a little bit and trust me to keep them safe. This is good for them. I guarantee you."

She paused for a long moment, processing what he was saying. *Was* she being overprotective? Then she sighed, blowing out a long breath.

"How far away is the nearest hospital?"

He touched her hand gently, then pulled back quickly, like he hadn't meant to reach out in the first place.

"It's close enough."

"How long do you think it'll take to finish the bathroom?"

"Depends on whether you allow the use of power tools."

She sighed. "Fine. But no saws. Nothing with blades. I mean it."

"Fair enough." He smiled, but she saw him try to swallow it. "So how about you head into town this morning and get what you need, and I'll hang back here with the girls?"

She eyed him suspiciously. "No blades."

"Trust me, Gabi." He put up his hands. "Nobody's going to get hurt here." Then he got up and headed up the pathway, and Gabi tried—but failed miserably—not to follow him with her eyes.

Once he was out of sight, she turned toward the lake, watching the mist rise, hearing a pair of loons calling to each other from the eastern shore. She touched her hand where his fingers had just been, and took a long, shaky breath.

Oh, somebody was going to get hurt here, all right. She was dead afraid it was going to be her.

Luke swore as he closed the screen door of his cabin behind him. Why in God's name had he just touched her? Again?

Thing 1 and Thing 2 jumped up from their dog bed and headed his way, their tails wagging so hard they almost tipped over. He crouched down to pet them, feeling guilty about how much time they spent in his cabin, rather than out roaming. But he'd quickly found out that their curly fur was no match for the brambles that surrounded the open area of the camp, and he'd *also* quickly discovered their propensity for disappearing into the woods. Between the four-legged critters and hawks that also roamed and soared over these woods, he'd decided the dogs were safer staying inside most of the time.

Thing 1 stood up on her hind legs to deliver her version of a kiss to his chin, and he laughed as he pushed her gently back down.

Then he stopped, remembering how much the camp boys had always loved Duke. He'd watched that old Lab nose his way into more than one tent over the years, and he'd watched boys who couldn't trust affection from *any* human hug that dog silly. Could these pups have the same thawing effect on Gabi's girls, maybe?

"Guess what, ladies?" He grabbed their leashes, making them yip and turn circles. "Enough lazing around living the high life. I'm putting you to work."

He headed out the door and down the pathway, not at all sure what he was going to actually do with them, but to his knowledge, there wasn't a woman on earth who could resist a pair of puffball puppies . . . even four teens who played at being far more inaccessible than they really wanted to be.

Yeah, maybe he was having trouble getting Gabi to fully trust him, but with his two mini-team members in tow, he *should* have a chance of getting through to her girls.

"Oh, not possible. He does not have—are you kidding me?" Two hours later, Gabi stopped short on the pathway, then fumbled to rebalance the grocery and drugstore bags that threatened to fall out of her arms.

The man had puppies.

Puppies.

Had they been here all along, and he hadn't let the girls near them? Or were they some sort of new trick he'd devised in order to elicit cooperation?

"Cute, huh?" Piper came up behind her, reaching for one of Gabi's bags.

Gabi turned. "Are they his?"

"Yup."

"Really? Poodles?"

Piper smiled. "They're bichons, actually. He had a black Lab that passed away a while back. And after an appropriate mourning period . . . well, someone decided he could use some puppies." Piper shrugged. "It was inspired, really, if I do say so myself."

Gabi watched Sam pick up one of the dogs and cuddle it under her chin. She wondered if the girl had ever had a dog, in any of the homes she'd lived in.

"Let me guess. You got him the puppies."

Piper widened her eyes. "I know nothing. They appeared on his back porch one morning, he said."

Gabi laughed. "No offense, Piper, but I'm not sure you have a future in the theater."

"Really? Didn't fly?"

"Nope." Gabi shook her head as she watched the little scruffy pups hop around Luke's feet. "Why . . . bichons?"

"It was fate, really. Old Mrs. Devereaux was moving to senior housing, and couldn't take them with her. Young Mr. Magellan was in need of canine therapy. Match made in heaven, I decided."

Gabi laughed as she turned toward the dining hall, Piper on her heels. "I've got ice cream in here. Better get it put away before it melts."

"I see Luke let you drive his truck?"

"Yes, and I should probably apologize to him in advance for all of the tongue-wagging it seemed to induce downtown." Gabi shook her head as she pictured all of the widened eyes and elbow-jabbing she'd seen as she'd puttered through Echo Lake.

Piper shrugged as she opened the door for Gabi. "Small town. Everybody knows what everybody else drives. And when a new hottie shows up in the Camp Echo limo, it's going to crank up the rumor mill. I'm sure I'll get an earful at Bellinis later."

"Well, as long as you paint me taller, blonder, and bustier, I'm good with the rumors. G'ahead and start a few."

Piper laughed. "Sorry, honey. You've been spotted. Your stats and prospects are already being debated up and down Main Street."

"Stop it." Gabi mock shivered. "You're scaring me." She started to open a yogurt, then swore as it spewed onto her shirt. "Okay, next question. Any idea where I can do laundry?"

"Luke will tell you he washes his clothes in the lake."

Gabi sighed. "I was afraid of that." Then she paused. "*Does* he?"

"No. He hates the feel of line-dried clothes. He takes his to the next town up. There's a decent Laundromat there. But I'll tell you what—if we work it right, maybe we can convince Luke to let you sneak out and come do it at my condo over the weekend."

"Condo? With walls? Indoor plumbing? Be still my heart."

Piper laughed. "I'd invite you for a sleepover so you could have a real bed, too, but I don't think Luke would forgive us for abandoning him with the girls for that long. But you *could* take an actual hot shower while your clothes are in the dryer."

"It's a deal. And also, I love you."

Gabi walked closer to the window, watching as Luke gave instructions to the girls, and with a minimum of grumbling, they carried them out. To her utter surprise, on the cement platform, there now lived a wooden framework that looked like it might, just might, turn into a bathroom.

Eve said something that made him laugh, and the way he tossed his head back and let that laugh out just grabbed at Gabi's heart. He pointed at Eve like she'd gotten him good, and Gabi put her hand to her chest as she watched Eve turn away, a small smile on her face.

Huh. He was getting to them. He was . . . *getting* them.

"He's good." Piper came up behind her, handing her a cup of tea.

"I . . . can see that. We might actually have a bathroom here before too long."

"Not what I meant."

Gabi nodded slowly. "I know. But here's what I can't figure out—how does a camp handyman get this . . . good?"

Piper looked at her, and Gabi saw a dozen different

answers cross her face before she shook her head the slightest bit.

"That's for him to tell, but . . . don't ask him yet."

"Why not?"

"Because." Piper looked out the window, watching Luke. "He won't answer you."

Chapter 12

Two days later, Gabi stepped out of the dining hall just after dawn, hands gratefully clutched around a mug of Luke's coffee. She walked down the pathway toward the beach, passing the bathroom shell, and as she'd expected . . . hoped . . . Luke sat in one of the chairs, his hands around his own coffee mug.

She stopped, studying him before he saw her. He had on his standard T-shirt and jeans combo, this time with a Red Sox hat turned backward, and she swallowed hard. She'd always thought she liked clean-shaven men best, but apparently she'd never spent much time with someone who rocked a five o'clock shadow quite so well.

"You going to stand there all morning, or come sit down?" He didn't move a muscle besides his mouth—just kept sipping his coffee and staring out at the lake.

She took a deep breath, heading to the empty chair and sitting down beside him. "Thanks for making coffee."

"Can't start my day without it. Noticed you can't, either."

"No, I can't. And I think you've already converted me to your brand."

"No-brainer." He shrugged, smiling. "Girls a little tired?"

"More exhausted than I've ever seen them, yes."

"Amazing what a couple of days of hard labor can do, hm?"

She sipped her coffee, not sure how to answer. Yes, working them till they were bone tired every day was an effective way to prevent them from having the energy to bother getting into trouble, but her worry was that she wasn't sure it was one that would stick with them after they were done here at Camp Echo. Dorm life at Briarwood was hardly comparable. As soon as they were back there, she was afraid they'd fall back into the same routines, the same lulls, the same petty conflicts.

He looked over. "You don't agree?"

"I agree that it's working currently."

"But you don't think it will continue to?"

"Have you ever heard of the honeymoon period, Luke?"

He smiled. "Enlighten me."

"This is all new—the setting, the work . . . you." Gabi waved a vague hand. "Even though they hate the manual labor, they're doing what you're asking, but I'm not confident that this will continue long term. The bathroom is a serious carrot you're holding in your hand, but once that's up and done, I don't know whether this cooperation thing will continue. Challenging authority is what these girls do best. They're bound to crack."

He nodded. "Huh. So I'm not a miracle worker who's converted them all in a week flat? Damn."

"Fine." She had to smile. "So you're not delusional."

"Not usually. So what do you suggest we do?"

"I suggest we don't take our eyes off them for a

minute. They have an escapist history . . . but I guess you know that."

He looked out at the lake, then back at the forest edging into the camp's central area. "Gabi, they do know how dangerous it could be to take off from here, right?"

"They must."

"Do they? Really?"

She sighed. "I don't know. I would hope so. I'd hope they'd be petrified to try it, but these are the girls who made exceptionally stupid decisions together not too long ago. Not sure I trust their groupthink."

"Okay." He nodded, thoughtful. "I have an idea. Let's get ahead of them, then. Maybe we'll take a construction break today. How's a hike sound?"

Gabi cringed, picturing every single muscle in her body still screaming in protest from the work of the past couple of days. It was mortifying how out of shape she'd let herself become, sitting in her little dorm apartment all winter long.

"Honestly? Sounds like *ow* right now."

He laughed. "Hikes are good for loosening up sore muscles."

"How's a hike going to convince the girls not to take off in the dead of night?"

"Easy. I'm going to spend a lot of time pointing out all the signs of all the wildlife that roams through here in the dark."

Gabi shivered, and he laughed again.

"Also, I think it'd be a good idea to teach them some basic survival skills, so if they get some cockeyed notion to go off by themselves, at least they won't die . . . as quickly, anyway."

"That's comforting, Luke."

He shrugged. "Not saying they will or won't—take off, I mean, not die—but they've got a history, and we've got a responsibility. If they bolt on our watch, whose head's it gonna be on?" He paused, looking intently at her. "I have a feeling, based on your presence here, you already know how *that* goes down."

"See that?" Three hours later, Luke pulled up short and pointed at a tree, making all of the girls grumble. They'd been hiking for two hours already, and even Gabi was tiring of the endless encyclopedia of wilderness information Luke was doling out.

Her head was spinning with the parade of don't-eat-this and do-eat-this and don't-burn-this and do-drink-this items in Luke's repertoire, and though she was pretty impressed with his knowledge, she was afraid if push came to shove, she'd stare at every single one of these plants and not be able to remember which one could sustain her and which one could likely kill her.

"What are we looking at?" Madison sighed, adjusting her backpack straps. Luke had insisted they all carry these old army-surplus bags, loaded with water and granola bars and flashlights and matches, among other things. They were heavy, even though he'd said they were only going out for a few hours, and the girls were starting to grumble.

"See those marks up there?"

Gabi looked up at the thin, vertical stripes, but she had no more idea what they were than the girls did. Luke stood on a log to reach up and touch the stripes, rubbing his fingers together after he stepped down.

"Fresh." He smiled. "That's bear."

Waverly's eyes suddenly darted around, and she pulled in closer to the group. "What do you mean, that's bear?"

"Claw marks, and the sap's still running out of them. Probably came by this morning."

"It *is* this morning," Madison screech-whispered.

"Yep." Luke looked around casually, like he wasn't at all bothered that they were sharing the woods with a creature that could pummel them with one paw and eat them for lunch. "Probably has cubs, too. Bears generally stay out of your way if they smell you first, but if you ever get between a mama and her cubs, you better say your prayers."

Gabi gulped, looking around for little bundles of fur.

"Don't worry." He smiled. "You four walk like a pack of elephants. She'll have taken her babies well out of our way by now. But just good to know they're out here. If you see one, don't run. Just back away slowly, like you're not interested in hanging out today, and hope for the best."

Wow, he really was pouring it on thick here. He wanted to scare the girls into staying at camp? Well, score one for him. He'd now scared *her* into peeing her pants before leaving the tent to use the outhouse.

"You ladies ever seen a moose?" His eyes were bright, amused, but the girls were anything *but* amused.

"How about we head back to camp?" Eve suggested. "You know, in case the bear is still around."

"Nah. We brought lunch. I know a good spot." Luke started forward, then stopped dead and put his arms out, scaring every single one of them. He looked at the ground in front of his feet. "Well, would you look at that."

"What?" Sam narrowed her eyes, gripping her backpack straps. "What is it?"

"Can't tell for sure. Scat. Lynx or catamount."

Gabi felt her eyes go wide. Lynx? Catamount? In these woods less than half a mile from the tent? Their next project was going to be a sleeping cabin with walls and windows and a damn door.

"What is scat?" Eve whispered.

"Poop. Big cat." He studied it. "Probably yesterday. Last night, maybe. They move around at night, mostly."

He looked back at the girls. "Lots of action out here at night. Not all of them are big enough to take down a human, but some are. Make sure you don't give 'em a reason, okay? Some of them don't actually require one."

Gabi turned backward, pretending to gaze behind her so the girls wouldn't see her smile. She would *now* be willing to bet not one of them would consider taking off from camp. Bears? Moose? Lynx and catamount? Yeah, there was no way these girls were even going to sleep tonight, let alone stage an escape.

Score one for Luke.

An hour later, after an epic climb that Gabi would definitely be feeling in her thighs for days to come, the six of them were seated on a rocky outcropping at the top of the world. At the top of Echo Lake, Vermont, at least. Directly in front of them, far below, was the lake, shimmering in the noontime sunlight, and Gabi was pretty sure she'd never seen anything quite so beautiful in her life.

A breeze wafted over the tops of the trees and cooled her heated face as she drank from her water bottle, then wiped it across her forehead. The girls were splayed out over the rock, moaning and groaning instead of enjoying the view, but she could care less. If they didn't want to take advantage of their hard work by looking around, that was their problem.

"Anybody want some chocolate?" Luke waved a couple of Hershey bars in the air, and the girls all snapped upright, making Gabi laugh.

Waverly practically drooled. "You have chocolate?"

"It's good energy food for a hike like this." He tossed the bars toward them. "Split 'em up. Don't forget to drink your water. Long hike down."

Twenty minutes later, the girls had finished their lunches and were each leaning on their backpacks, practically asleep. Luke winked at Gabi, then banged a metal spoon on his metal bowl, making all four girls jump practically out of their own skins.

"Question—how many of you think you could find your way back to camp if you needed to right now?"

All four girls raised their hands slowly, like they weren't at all sure they could, but didn't dare admit it.

"Really?" Luke's eyebrows hiked upward. "So you all paid close attention to the twists and turns we took all the way up?"

Madison rolled her eyes. "No. We were following you."

"Yes." He pointed at her like she'd given exactly the right answer. "So, second question—what if I fall off this cliff right now? Or what if I trip and conk my head on a rock on the way back down? Think you could find your way *then*?"

Gabi's stomach felt suddenly cold as she realized she, too, had merely followed his lead all the way up the mountain, not even trying to keep track of landmarks, turns, or anything in the world that would help them get back to camp if something happened to Luke.

Shit. He was going to make them find their way back to camp. She could feel it.

He paused, letting all of them come to that same realization, and then he grinned. "I'm not going to make you find your way back. Not this time, anyway."

Gabi felt her shoulders fall in relief as she watched the girls' faces relax. Next time, she promised herself. Next time she'd mentally mark every tree, every rock, every blade of grass. How had she not thought to at least make an attempt at doing so this time?

"Here's the thing," Luke continued. "No matter how many people you're with, you have to keep your eyes open, your ears open, your brain open. The woods are beautiful, and this mountain is one of the most amazing places on Earth, but you *have* to pay attention, or you could end up dead."

"Dead? What else is *out* here?" Waverly's eyes widened. "Gabi? Do our parents know about *this*?"

"He's exaggerating." Gabi tried to send him a warning with her eyes, but Luke either wasn't paying attention, or didn't care.

"He's not." His voice was firm. "One of the first rules of survival is to respect your environment, and that means you need to understand *all* of the possible dangers, and you need to know how to keep yourself safe. That includes always knowing how to get home if you need to. It also includes knowing what to do if you *can't* find your way back. That's what we're going to talk about this afternoon."

Gabi looked at the girls, and she had to hand it to Luke. He sure had their attention *now*. Even Madison had her arms folded on her knees, eyes glued to him as he started demonstrating how to clear a space for a fire, then had them dump out their backpacks so he could show them what to do with each of the items he'd insisted they put in there.

Two hours later, they had a crackling fire, a makeshift shelter, and four dirty girls who each glowed with an inner sense of accomplishment. They'd hauled branches, they'd chopped down pine boughs, and they'd identified three different plants whose stems could be eaten. They'd learned to filter water from the stream that cascaded over nearby rocks, and to wait until it was safe to drink. They'd learned to mark a trail if they got lost, and how to read a compass. And they'd learned that the fastest way to get *any* of those things done was to work together.

As Gabi watched them gather up their things and stuff them into their backpacks, she felt a tiny glow of possibility take hold. For an entire school year, the only thing these four girls had agreed on was that they despised each other. But now, after only a week at Camp Echo, they were actually working together.

She turned to gather her own pack, rolling her eyes as she did so. *Yes, Gabi. The world is now solved. One bathroom and one hike, and we're good to go.*

"You okay?" Luke's voice interrupted her inner diatribe as he came up behind her.

"Sure. Yeah. Of course." She pulled up a smile and turned his way.

He raised one eyebrow. "That was convincing."

"I know." She shook her head, stuffing things into her pack. "Sorry. I was just kicking myself for getting all excited about how well they've been working together for the past couple of hours."

"Why would you kick yourself about it?"

"Because it's not real. It's temporary. It's them being out of their element and under different supervision . . . temporarily."

"Ah." He nodded. "And you're convinced none of these cooperation skills could possibly transfer to their Briarwood lives?"

"I'm sure they *could*. But I'm just as sure they won't make it happen."

"I'm not."

She paused to look at him as he watched the girls put out the fire, covering the coals with dirt and water, just like he'd taught them.

"I appreciate your optimism, Luke, as misplaced as it might be."

He half smiled, like he found her more amusing than the herd of girls he'd shepherded up the mountain.

"Well, misplaced optimism or not, it's been a good day, right?"

"Yes." She'd allow him that. "It's definitely been a good day."

"An-nd they're definitely too scared now to take off at night, right? So it'll be a good night, as well?"

"Definitely possible." She rolled her eyes. "Are you going to say something about one-day-at-a-time being a camp mantra now?"

"I wasn't." He shrugged. "But I could. We've made some baby steps here, Gabi. And that's something. Don't discount it. There's a long month ahead. Plenty of time for us to see what more we can do."

"We?" She heard the word come out before she could stop it.

He turned toward her. "Or you. I'm not jumping in on your job here. Just offering to help, when you need it."

"Okay."

"But if you're ready to dismiss me, I'll just head on down the mountain and wait for you guys at camp." He grinned.

"Not funny, Luke."

"See? You do need me. At least a little."

He turned, and as hard as she tried, she couldn't stop herself from letting her eyes travel his body.

Oh, she needed him, all right.

She just didn't *want* to, dammit.

Chapter 13

The next morning, Gabi and the girls slogged into the dining hall at seven o'clock, having been jogged out of bed by a bugle Luke had unearthed from God-knows-where. Gabi was not amused, but less amused were the girls, who still thought they should get to sleep in at least on the weekends.

"Good morning, ladies!" Luke called from the kitchen. "Bright eyed and bushy tailed, I see!"

Gabi looked at him, and before she could stop herself, swallowed hard. Clad in his customary cargo shorts and a dark blue T-shirt, with his hair still damp from the shower, he stood at a big griddle, spatula in one hand and coffee mug in the other. Yes, it was a summer camp dining hall, but it was such a sweet domestic picture that Gabi had to blink hard to shut down the thoughts it triggered.

The girls slithered onto picnic table benches and put their heads down on the table, groaning about the early hour, while Gabi made her way to the coffeemaker.

"A bugle? Really?"

Luke grinned. "Forgot I had that old thing."

"Could you please forget again?"

"Nah. The girls kept getting up later every day. Had to nip it in the bud. We've got a lot to do today."

Gabi took a long sip of her coffee. "It's the weekend, Luke. Do you ever give it a rest?"

"Nope. Saturday's just as good a day to work as any other. No way that project list will get done on five-day weeks, especially if we keep taking time out for hikes and stuff."

"The hike was your idea, mister."

"Yep. And it was a *good* idea." He pointed to the girls. "Look at these exhausted young ladies. I love it!"

Waverly raised her head, but just barely. "Gabi? Are you paying him to be this annoying?"

"Nope." Luke grinned. "I come by it naturally. Now, let's all eat some breakfast so we can head out and finish up that bathroom. If all goes well, I suspect we might, just might, be able to get this thing done today."

"Really?" Madison raised her head. "Seriously?"

"Depends on how you ladies do, but it's definitely possible. Leach field and septic tank are all set. All you girls need to do is the above-ground part of the job."

Gabi saw Sam crack a smile as she slid off the picnic table bench and headed for the plates. "I'd love for the rest of Briarwood to know the true way to your heart is a flushing toilet, princess."

"Shut up, Sam." Madison rolled her eyes and got up as well, followed by Waverly.

Gabi sighed. "An-nd we're back."

"Nah." Luke sipped his coffee. "Leave it to me."

"That phrase should really, really scare me."

He turned off the griddle and tossed the spatula into the soapy sink. "Piper said you need to do some laundry? And that you don't care to use the lake? Which I can hardly believe?"

Gabi smiled. "Yes. We have *piles* of laundry. And no, I have no desire to wash clothing in the lake. Piper said I could use her washer and dryer this morning, but that would mean leaving the girls with you."

"And you're not sure that's a good idea?"

"Well . . . I'm more afraid that it's an incredible imposition."

"You afraid for them? Or for me?"

She laughed. "Little bit of both, maybe?"

"Understandable." He shrugged, pointing out the window to where the bathroom stood framed on its cement pad. "I've got eyes enough to watch them, and Oliver's here to call 911 if somebody slices off a finger. We're good to go."

Gabi took a deep breath. "Do you *try* to be like this?"

"Nope." Luke winked. "We're fine. Go do laundry. Have lunch in town. Take a break, Gabi. I imagine you don't get too many of those."

The tone of his voice was sweet, caring . . . almost affectionate, and Gabi wasn't sure how to react. One week ago he'd stood beside the van with his arms crossed, obviously wishing he could turn them right around and send them back to Briarwood, and today? He was practically ordering her to go do something nice for herself while he did her job.

"Are you sure? I still have a thing about power tools. Just saying."

He patted her shoulder gently. "I know you're paid to be a worrywart, but I officially give you permission to stop. They won't get hurt. And if they do, we have hospitals."

"Luke."

"Go, Gabi. We'll be fine, and just think—tonight? You'll have a bathroom."

She turned toward her little crew, but before she could

open her mouth to give them the list of dos and don'ts for while she was gone, Sam put up a hand to stop her.

"We know. Just go."

Luke laughed, then covered his mouth. "Sorry."

"Fine." She smiled. "I'm gone. I'll expect running water when I get back, girls."

They mock saluted as she headed out the door, but she stopped on the third step. With a sigh, she headed back up the stairs and poked her head through the door.

"Luke? Any chance you could tell me where Piper lives?"

"I never thought a hot shower could feel so good." Gabi walked into Piper's living room, toweling her hair off. "Thank you so much."

"You're so welcome." Piper handed her a cup of coffee. "Come sit on my deck. I have a whole two hours off, and I intend to spend it sitting on my butt beside the river."

Gabi laughed. Piper's condo was in a riverfront building that had housed a tiny mill, long ago. Its walls were aged brick, and sturdy wooden beams outlined the tall ceilings. The river-facing wall was almost entirely glass, and with the French doors open, the cascading water made a soothing, hypnotic sound.

They settled on lounge chairs, and Gabi let her head fall back, eyes closed. Yes, the camp cots were more comfortable than the plywood floor of the tent, but still. Cots left a lot to be desired. She was pretty sure, given ten straight minutes, she could fall asleep right here on Piper's chair.

She opened her eyes, lest she do exactly that. "I don't know how you ever *leave* your house, Piper."

"I know." Piper nodded. "Someday Noah and I will

build a log cabin on a hill, but for now, this is pretty perfect."

"It'd be hard to give up, even for a house on the hill."

"Well, we almost had a house on the lake, right next to Camp Echo, but that went up in a poof of regulatory smoke."

"Oh, no. What happened?"

Piper set down her mug. "When Noah moved here, he and Luke had this grand plan to buy the property next to the camp. They were going to turn it into a corporate team-building type of place, where leadership teams would come and find their Zen by doing all of these high-risk activities and stuff."

"Sounds intriguing." Gabi sipped her coffee, picturing Luke working with corporate clients the way he'd been leading her girls the past few days.

"It was. Or it would have been. They were *this* close to signing the paperwork last spring when a title search turned up something screwy. Long story short, they lost their loan, and after a lot of legal wrangling, the property ended up in a nature conservatorship of some sort. Can't ever be developed."

"And now my rich-chicks' school has bought Luke's camp property." Gabi nodded, things suddenly becoming clearer. "He's not having a very good year, is he?"

"That would be putting it mildly."

"Does he really think Briarwood aims to turn Camp Echo into a little lakeside paradise for the rich and richer?"

Piper raised her eyebrows. "You don't?"

"No. Why would they? We, I mean? It's an investment property, as far as I can tell."

"Exactly. And how much return on that investment do you think they'll get if they continue to cater to underprivileged kids?"

"I'm sure it's not about . . . profit." *Was it?*

"Does Briarwood do a lot of other community-support types of things? Because if you do, that might be something Luke would really like to hear. Might make him believe things are remotely on the up and up here."

Gabi nodded. "Of course we do." She'd sat through enough board meetings where a hundred dollars was approved for the food bank, or fifty bucks went to the homeless shelter, but she cringed internally when she pictured Priscilla asking—*every* damn time—whether Briarwood would get public credit for the donation.

Then she pictured Laura, the board chair, gaveling Priscilla.

And really? Was fifty dollars here or there really making a difference in anyone's universe? Gabi knew the size of their endowment. It was crowed in every annual report. But what did that money actually get used for? Priscilla's salary? Renovations on a dorm that didn't need them? A BMW van, for goodness' sake?

When she'd first heard last week about the purchase of Camp Echo, she'd entertained momentary hope that finally this endowment was being used to actually serve a needy population . . . that Briarwood was finally embracing a role as a steward of a community that needed one.

That *was* what they were doing here. It had to be.

She took a deep breath. "I had no involvement in the purchase, obviously, but I guess I'd like to think my school is acting in good faith."

Piper looked at her sidelong. "I don't want to insult your school, Gabi, but have you seen the list of projects they gave Luke? It doesn't look like they have *any* intention of keeping things running the way they've always been run."

"I've only seen a list that Luke showed the girls one day when they were prioritizing projects, but it had silly stuff on it like a TV lounge and a performance stage. It was just a joke list he printed up so they'd all agree that a bathroom was top priority."

Piper looked out at the river, and Gabi could tell she was trying to choose her next words carefully. "That wasn't a joke list, Gabi."

"What?" Her stomach jumped. No way. "It had to have been."

"That's the list they presented Luke with when they did the site visit in May . . . the same site visit where they told him they were shutting the place down for the summer."

"Oh, no." Gabi's head spun as she pictured a bunch of suits walking the camp property with Luke, then handing him that ridiculous list as they tried not to make eye contact with each other, lest he smell a rat.

"So you can see why he'd be worried."

"I'm—this can't be—I don't know what to think. Couldn't it be possible that they're just trying to improve the property? Bring it up to the standard of others in the area?"

"With a performance stage? A workout facility?" Piper's eyebrows were heading higher up her forehead, and Gabi didn't know what to say to bring them back down. It didn't look good. It really, really didn't look good.

She lifted her coffee cup to her lips, staring at the cascading water. Was Piper right? Was *Luke* right? Was Briarwood turning this decrepit—yet gorgeous—little property into some sort of sparkly girls' camp, without being honest with Oliver and Luke?

Her voice was unsteady as she replied. "I'm not sure that's automatically damning, though I can see why it would have Luke's and Oliver's hackles up. But boys use stages and workout rooms, too. Maybe they're really trying to improve the place."

"It's possible."

"But not likely." Gabi nodded slowly. "I can hear that loud and clear in your tone."

Piper shrugged. "I just call it as I see it. And what I see doesn't look good for Oliver and Luke, which makes it really hard to sit back and watch it happen."

"How long have they been at this? How long's the camp been here?"

"Thirty years."

Gabi felt her eyebrows fly upward. "Seriously?"

"Yup. Oliver used to be a victims' advocate in the court system. After a few years, he figured he could do kids more good by trying to intercept them before they *got* to the court system, so he applied for a slew of grants, and dumped every last cent into buying this piece of property. He ran it as a normal camp for a lot of years while he built it up, and then as time went on, he narrowed the focus so it catered to at-risk boys, mostly teenagers."

Gabi blew out a breath, picturing kindly old Oliver spending his entire salary—which, like any public servant who did the most important work in the universe, was probably dismal—building a getaway for boys who so desperately needed one. She pictured Sam and Eve, who'd probably never had a chance to attend a camp before this lousy summer, and wondered how different they might be if they'd been given the chance to come somewhere like Camp Echo when they were younger.

"So really what you're saying, Piper, is that my school has come in like a stereotypical corporate shmuck, and is railroading a man whose entire life has been focused on creating a safe, structured camp for kids who probably have very little of either of those qualities in their day-to-day lives?"

Piper put up both hands, palms up. "I'm not sure I said it quite that strongly."

"Shit."

Piper's eyes widened, and then she laughed. "I've never heard you swear."

"You've only known me for a week."

"But still. Unexpected."

"Even rich bitches swear, Piper."

"Hey." Her hands went up again, placating this time. "I *never* said that."

Gabi closed her eyes, shaking her head. "I'm sorry. I don't even know where that came from."

"Maybe from constantly dealing with people assuming you *are*? Rich and bitchy, I mean?"

"Well, I'd be glad to show them my bank balance. It'd at least end the rich part of the equation."

"You're not bitchy, Gabi. Or if you are, you cover it well."

Gabi looked down, scraping the last of her nail polish from her thumbnail. "Seems like Luke had the girls and I pegged well before we got here, and now I'm stuck fighting his assumptions, because of what he thinks my school is doing to his camp."

"Can you really blame him? I mean, no offense, but really?"

"No." Gabi sighed. "I guess not."

"He's just going by experience, Gabi. And to his credit, he does seem to be trying to put it aside, at least. He *is* helping you."

"He is." Gabi nodded. "He definitely is, and on one hand I'd love to just be grateful and thankful. But on the other hand, I can't figure out if he's doing it because he really does want to help, or because he's afraid if he *doesn't* help, he'll be mounting a search party for my runaway girls within a week."

"I imagine it's a little bit of both."

Gabi smiled. "Thanks. That was the part where you were supposed to weave a little platitude to make me feel better."

"Oh." Piper laughed. "Sorry. Missed it."

"He walks around that camp like he owns the place, and he and Oliver have way more of a partner-ish sort of relationship than a director-to-handyman one. He's got survival skills, and he can teach them." She paused. "And he's frighteningly intuitive about my girls. It doesn't quite compute. He plays at being this uneducated handyman, but I'm not buying it."

"You don't think camp handymen come with the power to understand teenage females?"

Gabi snorted. "Does *anyone* come with that power?"

"Good point."

"Did he go to college?"

Piper sighed, but continued smiling. "Are you here to do laundry? Or play Twenty Questions about the hot handyman?"

"I'm not—no." Gabi felt her cheeks flush. "I'm just curious, that's all. And he doesn't like to talk about himself, at least to me."

"Give him time. He's kind of a grumpy old cuss, for a man so young. He'll warm up eventually."

"How long does this process generally take?"

"Well, a week ago, Luke was dead sure you were a princess getting brought down a peg for the summer, so that has to enter in."

"I'm not a prin— Never mind." Gabi took a deep breath, knowing Piper couldn't possibly have any idea how deeply her words cut, and why. "I'm not the stereotype he has in his head. I'm really not."

Piper smiled. "Might not be my place to say so, but I think he's already figuring that out." She shrugged. "And if it matters, Luke's got a pretty finely tuned bullshit meter, so if he still thought you were rich-bitch material, you wouldn't be getting the time of day from him, let alone help with the girls."

"Um, thank you? I think?"

"Give it time, Gabi. I have a feeling you'll be surprised by what both you *and* your girls could learn from Luke."

Chapter 14

"Ceremonial flush?" Gabi laughed as she handed garbage bags of clean clothes to the girls, who'd jumped up from the picnic table as the Briarwood van had emerged from the leafy driveway into the tiny parking lot.

Sam smiled. "Apparently it's a thing."

"Yeah." Eve piped up. "When you complete a plumbing project, after it passes inspection, you do a ceremonial flush."

"And Luke made you wait till I got back to have this little ceremony?" Gabi laughed as she closed the van doors. "Gosh, I'm honored."

Madison rolled her eyes. "Yeah, that's quite an honor, Gabi. You should be so proud."

"Oh, but I am." Gabi squeezed Madison's shoulder. "A flushing toilet is nothing to sneeze at here. We're just one step from the Ritz now, girls."

"Right." Waverly half sneered, but couldn't help but let a smile sneak through it. "Come see, Gabi, so we can actually start using the thing."

The girls tromped down the pathway before her, setting their bags down outside the bathroom, which now had actual walls and a door. As the girls went inside,

Gabi walked around the outside, feeling her eyes widen as she ran her hand along the planks, pausing to admire a dead-even row of nails.

"Didn't think they could do it, did you?" Luke's voice, soft and deep, startled her from behind. He was close—too close—and the feel of his breath on her ear sent signals to all sorts of places that really didn't need to be awake right now, thank you very much.

"Um." Flustered, she turned around to face him, but when she caught his amused smile, words fled her brain.

"Um?" His smile grew, and his dimple appeared. "We've been working our asses off all day on this, and I get *um*?"

"Sorry. It's awesome! I can't believe they got it done. *You* got it done. You all got it done." She shook her head. Good Lord. It'd be helpful if some blood could return to her brain here.

"Hey, Gabi?" He—damn him—stepped six inches closer, and she found herself nose-to-pecs with his chest. She inhaled, expecting a mixture of sweat and man. He'd been working all day in the heat, after all. But what she smelled was soap, detergent, and was that aftershave? On a guy who didn't seem *to* shave? "Don't move."

He lifted his hands, deadly close to her body, and a slew of thoughts went careening through her brain while her feet stayed frozen to the ground. Then he slid both hands into her hair, gently, slowly. What was he *doing*?

"Spider in your hair," he finally said, stepping back, dangling a huge wolf spider from two fingers. Was it her imagination, or did his voice sound a little huskier than before?

Her hands flew to her hair as her eyes took in the huge black arachnid.

"Don't worry. They're ugly, but they're harmless." He

backed up another step, letting the spider go on a tree branch.

She shivered, but she knew it was more from his touch than from the fear of a spider building a nest in her damn curls.

"Thank you." Her voice was strangled, soft, and she swallowed hard, trying not to let him know just how strongly her body had reacted to his fingers skating gently through her hair.

"Welcome." His eyes met hers, then lowered to her lips, then closed as he blew out a breath and turned away. "Okay. Girls are waiting."

"Right. Girls. Yes."

Gabi shook her head as she followed him around the bathroom to the doorway. Could she *be* any more pathetic? Had she thought he was going to kiss her or something? *Why* would she think that?

She took a deep breath as they reached the doorway, pasting on a bright smile as he turned around to motion her inside.

"Your bathroom, Ms. O'Brien."

Gabi stepped inside, and her fake smile turned into a real one as she smelled the fresh lumber and saw four new stalls and an open area at the end, where the girls were standing.

"This will be the shower, eventually." Eve pointed at the walls of the open area.

"Look!" Sam bounced her eyebrows up and down as she swung a stall door open and closed. "Doors!"

"Heck with that!" Waverly pointed inside a stall. "Toilets!"

Gabi laughed at their expressions. "And you guys did all this? Seriously?"

"They did." Luke leaned against the door frame, arms crossed across the chest she'd almost reached out and touched just a minute ago. She wondered what it would feel like to slide her hands up inside that soft T-shirt, feel—

"Okay, girls." Sam pointed. "Places, please."

Gabi ripped her eyes away from Luke, but not before she caught a knowing arch to his eyebrows as he looked back at her. She shook her head, focusing on the girls as they each took up a position in a stall.

"Ready, set, flush!"

In unison, the four toilets flushed, and Gabi crossed her fingers, hoping everything actually worked. After how much effort they'd put in, she'd hate to see one of the pipes burst open, or see water come gurgling out of one of the bowls.

Each of the girls watched her own toilet, and Gabi would have laughed at their rapt attention had she not been just as invested in the process as they were. And then there was a collective whoop as they realized they'd done it.

"They work!" Eve's eyes went wide. "We actually did plumbing, and it worked!"

"Oh, goodie." Madison rolled her eyes for effect, but Gabi could see pride peeking through her bluster. "Now we're qualified to help Hank in the dorm."

"That's a great idea." Gabi nodded. "Hank could use some weekends off. And if you girls know how to handle this stuff now, maybe we could give him some time."

"Oh, no, you don't." Waverly wagged a finger. "What happens at camp stays at camp. *No one* will know we got excited about toilets, understand?" She turned a slow circle, pointing at each of the other girls, and Gabi and Luke laughed.

He pushed away from the door frame. "You *should* be excited. You worked hard, and now you have a set of flushing toilets. And if I'm not mistaken, I might have seen Gabi smuggle some ice cream into the freezer the other day. Anyone want some?"

The girls whooped and headed for the dining hall, but then Madison turned around, a glimmer of humor in her eyes.

"So now do we get to do a ceremonial burning of the outhouse?"

"Chow time!" At eight o'clock the next morning, Luke stacked pancakes on a plate, then set them on the counter with a platter of sausages.

The girls barely lifted their heads.

He raised his eyebrows. "We commence work in thirty minutes. You can do it with fuel on board, or without. Your choice. I don't care one way or the other."

Grumbling ensued, but all four of them pushed up from the table and came to fill their plates. Gabi watched as each of them took more food than she'd ever seen them eat at school, and she smiled as she realized they were hungry because they'd actually been burning calories doing something other than sniping at each other.

"Where's Piper this morning?" she asked Luke as she plucked a sausage link from the platter.

"She's too busy with work right now to give us weekends. I figured I'll do breakfast, the girls can get their own lunches, and maybe you could do dinner—if that works for you."

"Sure." She cringed. "As long as you like pasta."

He raised his eyebrows. "Not a cook?"

"I live at a boarding school where an executive chef prepares our meals. Not a lot of opportunity to learn, unfortunately." The words came out of her mouth before she had time to consider how they sounded, but it was too late to reel them back in.

He didn't take the bait, which she found odd, but somehow comforting. "What about when you were a kid? Didn't your parents ever teach you to cook anything?"

She shook her head. *Ha*. She wasn't sure the kitchen at any of her homes had ever been used by anyone but caterers.

"Um, no. I lived at Briarwood then, too."

Luke turned. "So have you ever *not* lived at Briarwood?"

"Briefly." She shrugged. "I went to Wellesley before I came back to work there, which—I know—sounds totally cliché."

"I didn't say it."

She raised her eyebrows. "You didn't have to. I could feel you thinking it."

He pasted a bored expression onto his face as he held out the spatula. "Pancake?"

"Just so we're clear"—she took the pancake—"I'm not some boarding-school princess who doesn't know how to tie her own shoes."

"I assume you've got shoes covered. We can work on the oversensitive piece next. And maybe we need to teach you how to cook while you're here, so you don't starve if the executive chef goes on vacation?"

"Very funny. I *can* actually cook enough to stay alive."

"What's your specialty?" He raised one eyebrow in challenge.

She shrugged uncomfortably. "I don't know that I have a . . . specialty, so much."

"All right. Say it's a chilly Sunday night in the fall. You've had a long weekend, and you just want a nice dinner. What would you cook yourself?"

"Lucky Charms. Isn't Sunday-night cereal a universal thing?"

"No, though I applaud your taste in breakfast-for-dinner." With his foot, he opened a cupboard under the griddle and pointed at a giant box of the cereal.

She laughed. "No way."

"Why do you sound so surprised?"

"Luke, you make your own granola." She shook her head. "I did *not* peg you for colored marshmallows."

"A guy's gotta have his weakness." He smiled, and her stomach did a flippy thing that scared her.

"Well, your coffee's becoming *my* weakness." *Yes, coffee.* "I had no idea camp coffee could taste so good."

"Camp coffee?" He put a hand to his chest like she'd stabbed him. "You think this is *camp* coffee?"

"It's not?"

"Oh, it hurts to hear you say that." He flipped the last pancake to the platter and shut off the griddle. Then he opened a cupboard near his head and pointed to a canister of coffee grounds she was used to seeing at the little grocery store near Briarwood. "*That* is camp coffee."

She nodded. "Does this mean you're sharing your own personal stash with me?"

"I am, and it's dwindling rapidly. You drink an impressive amount of coffee."

"I know. I'm sorry. Job hazard of raising teenagers."

He did that one-eyebrow-up thing. "Raising them?"

"These girls get dropped off on September first and picked up on June thirtieth, Luke. I don't know how it is at other boarding schools, because I've never experienced them, but at Briarwood, most of the dropping off and picking up isn't even done by the parents. Most of these girls go home for a week in December, but not all of them. They live at Briarwood. Twenty-four-seven, they live with me."

"Huh." He poured juice into two glasses and handed one to her. "I never really thought about it that way. Never pictured your population as particularly . . . needy."

"They are, Luke. Just not in the traditional sense of the word."

"Well"—Luke gathered his own plate and headed for the swinging door out to the dining area—"in my experience, money generally creates more problems than it solves."

She followed him to a table and sat down. "What *is* your experience? Because I get the distinct sense that you might rather have seen your camp go up in flames than see it bought by a hoity-toity boarding school."

He raised that damn eyebrow again. "Your words, not mine."

"Never mind. I get it."

He wasn't talking, and Piper'd said not to push him. As dead curious as she was about his history, for now, she'd stop asking. She rolled her eyes, biting into a pancake. It was crazy-good, especially followed by a bite of spicy sausage. She might just have to take him up on his offer to teach her to cook, if his pancakes were any indication of his abilities in the kitchen.

And if his abilities in the kitchen were any indication of his abilities . . . elsewhere . . .

"Good?"

She looked up to find Luke watching her, an amused expression on his face. She put her fork down, wondering just how quickly she'd inhaled the second pancake. Also wondering how well he could read her thoughts.

She swallowed hard. "The pancakes are delicious, yes. Thank you for cooking for us."

"Breakfast is *my* specialty." He winked, but she couldn't tell whether he'd intended a double entendre, or if she was just hearing one.

"So." She wiped her lips with a paper napkin and set her plate aside. "You said work commences in thirty minutes. What's your plan?"

"Showers."

She smiled widely. "Showers? Really?"

He laughed, rolling his eyes. "If I'd known this was the way to your heart . . ." Then he looked away, like he hadn't meant for those words to come out of his mouth.

"Actually, the way to my heart is a big cast-iron tub full of lavender-scented bubbles, but I'd happily make do with a camp shower at this point."

"Yeah, no tubs here." He pressed his lips together like he was trying to knock a vision out of his head. "And definitely no bubbles."

"Does this mean you're offering to keep supervising my monkeys?"

"God help me, but yes. I think I am."

Gabi laughed at the expression on his face, then felt a pang of guilt as she pictured the list of things he was *supposed* to be getting done right now.

"Are you sure you really have time to keep doing this? With them, I mean?"

"Why? You want them back?" He smiled. "Because just say the word."

"I just feel guilty. You have a huge list of stuff to get done. And before you say it, I know you don't necessarily *like* that list."

"I don't."

"An-nd you said it."

He shrugged. "It's true. But on that list is a new bathroom, with showers. So I'm still getting stuff done that needs doing. I'm just getting a little more help with it than I expected."

"Is that how you're seeing it?" Gabi pictured the pile of bent nails the girls had collected last night when they were done. There was no way this bathroom-building was going faster with her girls involved.

He took a deep breath. "It's all good, Gabi. Let's finish the bathroom, and then we can figure out the next steps, okay? I've *got* work, and they *need* work. Match made in heaven, yadda yadda. And you and me?" He waved his index finger back and forth between them. "We're not the worst team ever, right?"

Chapter 15

Four hours later, Gabi was about to dunk Luke and the girls *all* in the lake. All morning, he'd sat in a lawn chair outside the new bathroom. All morning, he'd sipped his coffee and read the newspaper. All morning, the girls had gotten closer and closer to killing each other.

He'd handed them the plumbing plans after breakfast, pointed them to the parts, and told them they needed to figure out how to plumb the shower. When Gabi had flipped out—just a little bit, mind you—about torches and soldering and the like, he'd given one of those long-suffering sighs he was so good at, and had then pointed at the pile of plastic parts.

"No metal. No fire."

"You're having them build a plastic shower?"

He'd put his hands up in the air, exasperated. "You prefer fire?"

So now an entire morning had gone by, and the girls were at each other's throats. Gabi'd taken a short walk just to get away from the sniping, but now she was back in the clearing, heading for Luke.

"How are they doing?"

A squawk from inside gave her all the answer she needed, and she winced.

He sipped his coffee nonchalantly. "It's alpha-dog day."

"What do you mean?"

"They're sick of working cooperatively. Today they're all trying to be in charge at the same time. It's not going well."

"Even Waverly?" Gabi felt her eyebrows rise.

"Nah. She's just trying to align herself with whoever's in charge at the moment. Tough morning for her—it keeps changing."

Gabi looked at him, the picture of relaxation. "You seem awfully amused by this. And unconcerned about your endless list of things that need doing."

He shrugged, looking back down at his newspaper. "It'll get done. This is important for them to work through."

She paused at his words. How did *he* know what needed working through? And why was he willing to give up his entire day to it, anyway?

She shook her head to clear it. "So how's the actual plumbing coming? Are they making *any* kind of progress?"

He looked up. "Desperate for that shower, aren't you?"

"Yes. And don't think it hasn't occurred to me that you must have a perfectly good one in your cabin, because you keep showing up just-showered-fresh, and it's driving me nuts."

She felt heat rise in her cheeks as the words came out, and she turned away. Yeah, it was driving her nuts, because when he came in with his hair all damp and his body smelling like the piney outdoors, all she wanted to do was touch the nape of his neck, where the dark waves met skin. All she wanted to do was press her body against his, to see if the muscles in his chest were as strong and solid as they looked. All she wanted—

"Gabi?" His amused voice broke into her totally inappropriate daydream. "You lusting after me? Or my shower?"

"I'm not lusting after any—"

Just then another shriek rose from inside, but this time it sounded like elation, then pounding feet.

The four girls poured out of the doorway, smiles on their faces. "Luke! We're ready! It's ready!"

He looked up. "You sure?"

"Yes! Turn on the water!"

Gabi smiled, their enthusiasm contagious. "You guys really figured it out?"

"Yup!" Eve wiped her hands on her shorts. "Piece of cake."

Luke pushed up from his chair, headed for the water shutoff. "All right. I'll turn it on. Just one question, though—I see some parts still lying here on the grass." He pointed down at three pieces of plastic. "You didn't need those?"

"No." Madison had a superior look. "We tweaked the design, and used less parts. That's allowed, right?"

"I guess we'll see, won't we?" He motioned them back into the little building. "Okay. Let's turn this baby on!"

After they'd gone inside, Gabi sidled up to him. In a low voice, she whispered, "Are those missing parts going to be an issue?"

He looked up at her, his hand on the valve, a sly grin on his face. "You're about to find out."

He twisted the valve to its left, and there was a pause, then a chorus of screeches. These ones, however, were not the happy kind.

"Turn it off!"

"It's flooding!"

"Oh, no!"

"Madisonnnnnnn!"

Gabi couldn't help but laugh as the girls came stumbling out of the bathroom, soaked to the skin, their hair hanging in dripping ropes. Luke stood beside the valve, which he shut off as soon as Madison emerged, the last of the crew.

He walked calmly to his chair and picked up his coffee, then opened the newspaper back up. When nobody moved, he looked up.

"So . . . obviously something's not right. Try again. And maybe use all of the parts this time. Designs exist for a reason, girls."

After they'd picked up the extra pieces and headed—muttering—back into the bathroom, Gabi took a deep breath and plucked his newspaper out of his hands, forcing him to look at her.

"Did you know it was going to be a failure?"

"Yep."

"So why did you let them continue?"

He raised his eyebrows. "Because that's how you learn."

"By failing?"

"Sometimes."

She narrowed her eyes. "I'm not sure I approve of your methods, Luke. Don't you think you should help them now?"

"Nope."

"You're willing to sacrifice this entire day to this project?"

"Yep."

Oh. My. God. She was going to strangle him with a string of his own "nopes" and "yeps."

"Gabriela, let me ask you this—when they step into that shower tomorrow, will they enjoy it more if *they* figure it out? Or if I go in and bail them out?"

"I don't honestly think they'd care, at this point. They just want a shower."

"Well, if I go help them right now, then they leave the project thinking they failed. If they battle it for the afternoon and win, then they've succeeded at something today."

"They succeed at things *every* day, Luke. Who exactly do you think you're dealing with here?"

He paused, and she got the distinct feeling she'd hit another nerve. Then he plucked the newspaper back out of her hand and took a deep breath, meeting her eyes.

"I think I know exactly who I'm dealing with here."

"Okay, we're ready for inspection." Sam's voice was muted as she came out of the bathroom to fetch Luke two hours later.

Ten times that day, he'd been tempted to leave the girls on their own and go tackle his own projects, but fear of them taking off had kept him glued to the perimeter of the bathroom. The girls might seem focused, but they were also sly enough that they'd slipped through Gabi's supervision once. He'd be damned if it would happen again, this time on his watch. Not when he'd worked this hard to gain even a modicum of her trust.

So he'd sat there and pretended to read, for hours on end. He'd listened as the girls had grappled for control inside the bathroom. After Gabi had headed up to the dining hall to start making dinner, he'd smiled as they'd insulted each other with words that would have made even his most hardened students blush.

And then it had gotten quiet. Blessedly quiet. For a

minute, he'd worried that they'd headed out a window and down to the lake, but then he'd heard tinkering, and then the oddest sound of all. One of the girls had giggled, and then another, and before long, it had sounded like all four of them had succumbed.

That had been a half hour ago.

And now Sam was fetching him to check over their work. He crossed his fingers that they'd done it right this time, but not just because their mistake had made such an unholy mess the first time. Something deep down made him want them to succeed at this task, both to prove to themselves that they could do it, and to prove to Gabi that he hadn't been nuts to make them try.

"Use all the parts?" He didn't get up.

"Every single one, yes." She nodded. "Turns out, when you look at the plans right side up, things make more sense."

"Funny how that works. Though I'm not exactly sure how four people your age could possibly not notice it was upside down in the first place."

"Luke, no offense, but we don't do a lot of plumbing at Briarwood."

He pushed out of his chair. "All right. Let me see how you did."

He walked into the bathroom, where the other three girls leaned against the new stalls. They looked tired and hot and sticky, but also triumphant. Good.

He looked at the piping they'd run, checked the connections, tapped on a few things for effect, then nodded.

"Looks good. All right. You guys stand here. I'll go turn it on."

Eve scooted out the door. "Oh, hell, no."

"What's the matter, Eve? Don't trust your own handiwork?"

"I trust my own handiwork just fine. It's *other* people's handiwork I'm not so crazy about."

"Well, you all worked together on this one." Luke shrugged. "So I say you all stand right there outside that shower stall and see what happens when I turn on the water this time."

Eve rolled her eyes, but she headed back into the bathroom to wait with the others. Luke walked around to the back of the building and turned on the valve, bracing himself for the sound of sputtering water, but the only sound that greeted him was silence.

He smiled. They'd actually done it.

"Nothing's happening." Waverly's voice was nervous through the window.

"That's good," he answered. "Try the handles now."

He heard shuffling, then metal on metal as one of the girls turned on the faucet. Then there was a satisfying splash as the shower started.

"Oh, my God! It worked!" Eve shouted.

Madison and Waverly squealed, but then Luke heard Sam's voice. "Um, problem."

"What?" the other girls said in unison.

"It's cold."

Luke smiled as the girls realized that they had indeed plumbed a shower, but not one with actual hot water.

"Luke?" Madison emerged from the building, hands on her hips. "Did you just design us a cold shower?"

"Nope." He smiled, and he knew they were going to want to kill him. "Today was shower-building 101. Tomorrow, we add heat."

"Are. You. *Kidding?*" Sam's eyes looked like they were about to spin out of her head. "There's no *heat*?"

"Well, let me ask you this—did it occur to any of *you* that you had no heat source?"

Waverly scrunched her eyebrows together. "What do you mean?"

"Water doesn't heat itself, girls. Look." He waved at the faucets. "You want hot water, you need to have a way to make it hot. Tomorrow, we install a water heater."

Sam flopped on the grass, her arm slung over her eyes. "I don't care. I hate plumbing. I hate this place. I hate water. And I definitely hate—you."

Luke laughed. "Good. We're right on schedule."

A little while later, Gabi looked out the huge windows of the dining hall to see the girls trooping down to the water, Luke in tow. All except Sam were in their bathing suits. Apparently the heat had gotten to them enough that they finally didn't care just how frigid the lake water was.

She wiped her hands on a dish towel, dinner prep finally finished. Two hours ago, Luke had pointed to the menu on the huge fridge, then pointed to the ingredients. "Let me know if you need help," he'd said.

Not a chance, she'd thought. *No way am I going to admit that I don't have a clue what to do with six chicken breasts, six potatoes, and a bunch of salad ingredients sitting in the fridge.*

But she'd figured it out. The chicken was in the oven, a green salad was in the refrigerator, and she'd even made brownies. From a boxed mix, but still. Who said she had no domestic skills?

She headed out the screen door and down to the shore, smiling as she saw Madison, Waverly, and Eve dare each other to jump off the dock. Sam watched from the sand as they held hands and counted to three five times before one of them—Gabi couldn't tell who—finally dragged the other two into the water. When they bobbed to the surface, letting out the requisite squeals, Sam shook her head.

"Idiots," Sam muttered as Gabi sat down beside her in the sand.

"You don't want to join them?"

"Do I *ever* want to join them?"

Gabi sighed. "Not by choice, no. But it's really hot. You don't want to cool off?"

"Ha." Sam sent a glare at Luke, who was fiddling with something over by the equipment shed. "If I want to cool off, I'll just go use our brand-new shower. It's very—refreshing."

He smiled tolerantly. "Cold shower's better than no shower, right?"

"Cold shower?" Gabi was confused. "Why do we have a *cold* shower?"

"Girls forgot a heat source."

"Girls didn't *know* about heat sources," Sam shot back.

He shrugged. "They do now."

Sam growled, which made Gabi laugh.

"It's not funny, Gabi."

"I know. I'm sorry. I'm not laughing about the situation. Laughing about you growling at Luke."

"Well, then you would have been in hysterics if you'd heard me earlier. I might have taught him some new curse words."

Gabi felt her mouth go tight. "I don't think that's exactly the goal here, Sam."

"Yeah, well, a hot shower was the goal here, and we didn't get that, either." Sam tossed a pebble toward the end of her toe, missing widely.

"Hey, Sam! You coming in this time?" Madison beckoned from the water.

"Nah, I'm good."

"Oh, come on, Sam." Waverly popped up beside Madison. "You never swim."

"You're not afraid of the water, are you?" Madison tipped her head, and Gabi was struck by how clearly she resembled the meanest of the mean girls in the movie they'd watched in the dorm last month.

Sam drew her knees up to her chest. "Not afraid. Just don't feel like swimming."

"But you *never* feel like swimming." Waverly smiled like a Cheshire cat, and an alarm pinged in Gabi's gut. "Come on, Sam. Just come in with us."

"No." Sam shook her head. "Go find a turtle to torment or something. Leave me be."

Madison took three steps toward shore, like a piranha going in for the kill. "Oh, Sam. I really think you need to come swim with us."

One second later, Gabi jumped in surprise as she saw Eve streak around behind Sam. Then, in an obviously rehearsed motion, Madison and Waverly sprinted out of the water, grabbing Sam's legs just as Eve slid her hands under Sam's armpits and lifted her out of the sand.

Sam screeched like Gabi'd never heard before, and her arms and legs flailed in the air as the girls carried her down the dock.

"Going swimming with the fishes, Sammy!" Madison sang. "You've avoided it long enough."

"Stop. It. Right. Now!" Sam squawked, and the sound got Gabi's alarms clanging at full volume. "Put me down!"

"Girls!" Gabi yelled. Sam didn't look pissed. She looked terrified. "Girls! Put her down!"

But either they didn't hear her, or they ignored her, because five seconds later, with a mighty heave, they tossed her off the end of the dock. There was an enormous splash, and the girls ran back up the dock toward shore, laughing wildly.

Gabi jumped up, scanning the water. Out of the corner of her eye, she saw Luke moving quickly down the lawn toward her. Time seemed to freeze as she watched the spot where Sam had landed, and she silently willed her to stop joking around and come back up.

But ten seconds later, her annoyance turned to terror as the surface of the water stayed unbroken.

Sam was down there . . . and she *wasn't* coming back up.

Chapter 16

Gabi sprinted to the water's edge, flinging herself in a shallow dive just as Luke ran for the dock. She covered the distance to where the girls had tossed Sam in a matter of seconds, but it felt like minutes as she cut through the frigid water.

When she got to the end of the dock, she paused to tread water and get her bearings, then dove under. The water was as clear as glass, but hellishly deep, and her hand went to her throat when she saw Sam's blond hair ten feet down, farther away than she thought the girls had flung her. The girl's arms were flailing, and as Gabi headed toward her, she could see Luke circling around to come up behind her.

As soon as she got close enough to touch Sam, she reached out to pull on her arm, lungs burning. But with surprising strength, Sam streaked both arms toward Gabi and grabbed her neck, holding on so tightly that Gabi panicked. Oh, holy hell! Sam was pulling her downward, and Gabi didn't have the strength to kick them both to the surface.

She tried to lift Sam's arms from around her neck, but couldn't get them loose, and Gabi felt chills rush to her head as her own arms seemed to lose power. Oh,

God. Where was Luke? Sam was going to drown them both!

An eternity later, she felt his body close around hers from behind, then felt a painful tug on her hair as he pried Sam's hands loose. He gave Sam a push backward, then sent Gabi toward the surface with a mighty heave. As she floated upward, she watched as if behind a kaleidoscope lens as Luke circled around behind Sam, clamped his arm around her middle, and shot toward the surface with the girl, who'd gone suddenly, frighteningly limp.

Gabi broke through the surface of the water and gulped air, flailing as she tried to convince strength to return to her limbs. One second later, Luke's head broke through, then Sam's.

"You okay?" he huffed. She nodded, not trusting her voice. "Can you make it up onto the dock?"

"Yes." She had no idea where the strength came from, but she grabbed hold of the dock pilings and hauled herself up to the planks, then reached down to help Luke lift Sam up. Madison, Waverly, and Eve stood on the dock, stock-still, their eyes wide with fear.

"Go call nine-one-one! Now!" Gabi yelled, and after a momentary freeze, the three of them sprinted back up the dock toward the admin cottage.

As soon as they had Sam on the dock, Luke pulled himself out of the water and kneeled next to her, tipping her on her side and clapping her back as Oliver jumped onto the dock from shore.

"C'mon, Sam. Spit it out. The fish need the water, not you."

No response.

"Sam, honey." Gabi leaned close to her ear. "Come on. You're gonna be okay. Everything's okay now. Come on. Everything's going to be okay."

She heard the babble-panic in her own voice, and she knew Oliver and Luke heard it, too. *Dammit.* How had she never known Sam couldn't swim?

Luke continued to thump Sam's back while Oliver held the phone to his ear, but she still wasn't responding.

"She wasn't down for that long." Gabi looked at Luke. "How could she—"

"Probably panicked and inhaled when she hit the water. Got a lungful of lake." His voice was calm, but he looked at his watch, then at the parking lot, then back at Sam's face. The alarms went to full-on panic in her stomach as she realized he might be timing Sam's chances here.

She leaned closer to her ear. "Listen, Alexandra Marie. If you don't spit out that water—"

Just then Sam's entire body heaved, and she spit out an absolute gush of water. Then she coughed and gagged and emptied the rest of her stomach over the side of the dock.

"Oh, my God. Oh, my God." Gabi pulled Sam's head onto her lap. "It's okay. You're okay." She stroked the girl's hair as Sam took some sobbing, hitched breaths. "You're all right now. It's okay, Sam."

"Ambulance is coming." Oliver nodded toward the woods, and Gabi could hear a siren, but it sounded a long way off still.

Luke took Sam's feet and rubbed them hard, probably doing some sort of emergency treatment Gabi had no knowledge of.

"You still have all your toes. Phew." He leaned over so he could see her face. "Camp legend has it that if you go below the ten-foot mark, the lake monster eats your toes."

No response from Sam as she lay there, which was

far more worrisome to Gabi than if she'd hauled off and sworn at Luke for treating her like a five-year-old. Even *more* worrisome than that was the fact that she *was* lying still, allowing herself to be comforted. The Sam she knew *never* let anybody touch her.

Gabi looked at Luke, who took Sam's wrist and checked her pulse as his eyes traded silent messages with Oliver's. "Let's get a heat blanket on her, just in case."

Oliver turned and quick-stepped toward the office while Luke wrapped his hands around Sam's feet. Gabi swallowed hard as she watched him.

"Is she hypothermic?"

He shook his head. "Shouldn't be. She wasn't in there long enough. But she's shivering like crazy. Probably a combination of cold and adrenaline dump, but better to be safe than sorry."

Gabi stroked Sam's spiky blond hair back from her forehead, trying to corral her own adrenaline. What would she have done if Luke hadn't been there? Would she have had the strength to pull Sam out of the water? Would she have even gotten to her in time? Would she have even known the signs of early hypothermia so she could have helped treat it before the ambulance arrived?

She hated that the answer might have been no—to all of those questions.

And as she watched Luke calmly take over, tucking the blanket around Sam, then gently wiping her face with the towel Oliver brought, Gabi was struck by an overwhelming urge to—to what? Hug him in abject relief? She didn't even know. What she *did* know was that the irritated, standoffish man she'd met when she'd gotten out of the van a week ago didn't seem to be anything like the one she was looking at right now.

Luke leaned over Sam again. "Hey, Snarkasaurus—is it true your real name's Alexandra?"

Sam shook her head, then coughed out more water before she buried herself in the blanket. "I have no idea what you're talking about."

Luke stood in the darkened dining hall just after midnight, looking out the windows at the moonlit lake. He was still too amped up to sleep, and he imagined he wasn't the only one, so he'd wandered down the pathway to see if maybe Gabi was in her favorite beach chair. She and Sam had returned from the hospital hours ago, but besides a quick stop in the admin cottage to say they were back and Sam was okay, she hadn't emerged from the tent yet. The girls had gone to bed at nine, and since then, he'd been pacing and cursing and dying to talk to her.

He'd sat down to wait, hoping against hope that she'd come out. At eleven o'clock, he'd told himself he'd only wait until eleven-thirty. At eleven-thirty, he'd decided he could wait till midnight. At midnight, he'd decided . . . ah, hell. He had no idea what he'd decided.

A movement on the pathway caught his eye, and as he watched, Gabi emerged from the woods and headed for the beach. A strange feeling gripped his gut as he saw her wrap her arms around her midsection like she was trying to hold herself together.

The sudden realization that *he* had a strong urge to be the one holding her like that made him pause a minute longer before heading down to join her. Finally, he closed the screen door quietly behind him and walked down the pathway, stopping when he was twenty feet shy of where she stood in the sand. For a week now, he'd watched her go toe to toe with this little crew, and he'd been impressed with the inner strength that kept her sane. But right now, it looked like the steel had left her spine. She looked sad and defeated . . . and like she could really, really use a—what? Friend? Ally? Long, hot kiss to make it all fade away?

He shook his head. She needed A and B. *He* was the one who'd started thinking too much about C.

"You okay?" he finally asked, trying to keep his voice quiet so he didn't scare her.

She paused before she turned, and he tried not to notice she was swiping her sleeve across her eyes. *Shit.* He did not do tears.

"I'm okay." She turned, and the tears were gone, but they'd left her eyes red, and left tracks down her exhausted cheeks. It was all he could do not to cover the ground between them in two steps and take her in his arms.

"How's Sam?"

"Doctors said she's physically fine." She tipped her head. "Might be a long trip back for the nonphysical end of things."

He took a step toward her. "I can't believe she doesn't know how to swim."

"Yeah, well, surprise surprise." Gabi sniffed, then blinked hard as she tightened her arms around herself. He wasn't sure whether it was the tears pooling in her eyes, or the way she looked like she was afraid she'd snap apart in the middle that did him in, but before he could think better of it, he closed the distance between them and pulled her close.

"Hey. It was a tough scene, Gabi. You did great."

She took a shuddering breath against his chest, and he realized she might be about to lose it completely. She might dissolve right here in his arms—tears and sobbing and fear and hysteria—and he was going to be stuck, because what kind of asshole opened the door and then slammed it shut?

But for the first time in his life, it didn't actually scare him. For whatever crazy reason, he just wanted to stand right here and hold her in his arms until she didn't need him to.

"I'm sorry," she mumbled against his chest. "I'm not—I don't usually do . . . this."

"It's okay. Losing it's a pretty standard reaction when somebody almost drowns on your watch." Her shoulders shook as she took another breath, and he pulled her tighter. "Hey. It's okay. She's okay now."

"She could have died, Luke."

"She didn't."

"By the grace of God . . . and you. I can't stop thinking what might have happened if you hadn't been there."

"You'd have figured it out, Gabi. You'd have saved her." He said the words he thought she needed to hear, but knew she would see through them. Neither of them knew what might have happened. Gabi couldn't weigh more than a hundred and thirty pounds soaking wet, and Sam wasn't a tiny twig. It would have taken all Gabi had—and more—to get that girl off her neck and out of the water.

"I'm not so sure, Luke. I'm really not, and that scares me."

"I know." He reached up to stroke her hair, finding it even smoother and softer than he'd realized when he'd plucked out the stupid spider. "And I know you'll see through whatever platitudes I can come up with right now, so I'll stop."

"Okay." She looked up at him, tears in her eyes. "I just keep seeing her in the water, below me, out of reach. I don't dare close my eyes, because that vision's going to haunt me forever. I don't think there's any way I'm going to sleep tonight."

Her voice was shaky and raw with fear, and in another life, Luke might have offered himself—his body, his bed—as a comfort. He'd have done that, if he didn't care so much about what the next morning would look like.

But this was Gabi. Granted, he'd had precious little time to get to know her, but he was one hundred percent sure she wasn't the kind of girl who did the casual, trauma-induced hookup thing. And he wasn't anymore, either. Someday maybe he'd be ready to go all in with somebody. But until then, he wasn't going *anywhere*.

But then she looked up into his eyes for a long moment, then at his lips. And *damn*. He knew he could kiss her right now—somehow knew she'd let him. But he also knew she'd regret it. She was vulnerable and exhausted, and he'd be a total ass to take advantage of it.

She closed her eyes, breaking the moment. Then she leaned her forehead against his chest, like she didn't want to pull away.

"I just can't believe none of us knew. I mean, she never went in the water. Never. How did I not even *think* of it? I just assumed she was being obstinate. Or that she was just trying to make sure she never again did *anything* that the other three do. I still can't believe I didn't know."

"Kids are good at hiding what they don't want us to know. You know that. It's not your fault. She never told you."

"I know, but Jesus, Luke. I'm usually not this obtuse. How didn't I even wonder? It never even crossed my mind. I mean, who gets to this age and doesn't know how to swim? It just didn't—didn't even occur to me."

He stroked her hair back from her face. "Stop beating yourself up, Gabi. Some of this is on her, you know. She should have told you."

"Right." Gabi rolled her eyes. "Because that wouldn't have been embarrassing at all for her to do."

He put his hands on her shoulders and looked straight into her eyes, willing her to stop blaming herself for what had happened.

"The important thing here is how we move forward, right? What's done is done. We can't go back. We can't undo it. But we can get to the bottom of what's eating at these girls so that the next three weeks can be less of a disaster."

"Or . . . I can take them back to Briarwood." She bit her lip, looking off toward the dock, and he knew she must have been running that possibility through her head for hours now.

"Yeah, you could."

She snapped her eyes back to his, like she'd hoped he'd argue, not agree, and he almost smiled. *Good.* She didn't really think that was the right solution.

"Or you could stick it out here, and we could work together to make things better."

"Says the camp handyman saddled with a bunch of hooligans trying to drown each other." She shook her head. "Why do you even *want* to help at this point? We have turned your summer completely upside down. I can't imagine there's any sight you'd like better right now than our taillights disappearing down that driveway."

He laughed quietly. "The thought has crossed my mind."

"So why, Luke? Why *do* you care about making this work?"

He took a deep breath, stalling for time. *Why, indeed?* Then he pulled her close again, hugging her tightly. Was it about the kids?

Or was it about Gabi?

Chapter 17

The next morning, after a solemn, quiet breakfast, Luke gathered the girls together at a circle of logs with a huge bonfire pit in the center. As Gabi looked around, she could imagine a normal summer here at Camp Echo, filled with crackling fires, campfire songs, and kids laughing as their marshmallows dropped into the flames.

This morning, though, there was no fire, no singing, and definitely no laughter. The girls were all quiet, wary . . . scared. Gabi'd woken up this morning no more convinced that they should stay here than she had been last night, but after torturing herself for two hours with the pros and cons, she'd decided she needed to give Luke a chance, at least for another day.

He hadn't answered her question last night—had just turned her around and walked her to the tent, like he was afraid she might lose her way if he left her to do it alone. And at the tent, he'd leaned in and kissed her softly on the forehead, and that damn kiss had just about undone her. It'd been sweet and kind and oh-so-tender, and her lack of sleep this morning had just as much to do with the promise of that kiss as it had to do with her fear of going to sleep and having drowning nightmares.

"All right." Luke sat down on one of the logs, and as

she looked at the concert T-shirt he had on, she tried not to remember what it had felt like to have her cheek against that chest last night. Tried not to think about how his arms had settled around her like they belonged there. Tried not to remember how badly she'd wanted him to *really* kiss her, even though it would have been spectacularly ill-advised, given the scared, emotional wreck she'd been at the time.

She wondered if he'd wanted to kiss *her*.

Eve and Waverly sat on one log, Sam on another, and Madison on a third, and every single one of them looked like they were about to face a firing squad. Sam had her knees pulled up under her too-large sweatshirt, the picture of defensiveness and fear. Madison, on the other hand, had her legs crossed, arms crossed, and if she could have gotten her eyes to cross and stick there, she might just have done it for effect.

"Let's talk about yesterday." Luke looked at each of them. "Because I know it's *exactly* what you all want to do this morning."

A snort came from one of them, but Gabi wasn't sure who.

"We had no idea." Eve's voice was quiet, pained. "Really."

"It was just in fun," Waverly chimed in, her voice shaky. It occurred to Gabi that the girl had probably been up all night, worrying about what would happen this morning . . . wondering if she'd be called to task for her own actions, even though they'd been directed by Madison. "We never meant to hurt you, Sam."

Luke nodded. "I think we've established that this was an accident. You can each make your apologies to Sam in your own way, and I really hope that you do. It might not have been personal, but I'm sure it *felt* personal, and you really need to make sure you deal with that part."

He took a deep breath, scanning each of their faces. "She told you to stop, and you didn't. That's on you three."

Madison uncrossed her arms. "We didn't know it was because she couldn't swim. We just thought she didn't want to get dumped into the lake."

"And that's on her." Luke shifted his eyes to Sam, who Gabi knew would never meet them with her own. Her head was down, and she was picking at her fingernails. "Sam? Did you know you couldn't swim?"

She looked up, not even bothering to disguise her sneer. "Do I really need to answer that?"

"You never told anyone?"

She shook her head. "It was nobody's business. I stayed out of the water. It wasn't an issue till Madison decided to drown me."

"I didn't—" Madison stood up, angry spots of color in her cheeks. "I was trying to dunk you, not drown you. Jesus, Sam."

"Girls." Gabriela's voice was sharp. "This isn't helping."

"Okay, okay." Luke made placating motions with his hands. "Simmer down. I think it's fair to say that nobody here intended for what happened to . . . happen. I'm sure it rocked all of you, no matter how big and strong you think you are. Give yourself permission to freak out a little, okay?"

Gabi had expected them to be obstinate, pissy, snarky—like they'd been since they'd gotten here. Instead, the prevailing emotion she saw in their eyes right now was . . . fear. And that's what told her they hadn't meant to hurt Sam—they really hadn't known she couldn't swim.

She took a deep breath, relieved. Throughout the night, she'd lain awake, eaten alive by the thought that maybe Madison *had* known . . . that maybe, in some convoluted, serious lapse in judgment, she'd engineered the scene on purpose, not really believing the worst could possibly happen.

Luke let the silence linger—on purpose, she knew. Age-old technique and all. But the girls didn't say anything more. He wasn't getting anything else out of them.

"I believe you," he finally said, and he noticed their shoulders visibly relax. "I don't think anybody here really meant to hurt anybody else. But here's the thing. *She* knew she couldn't swim. She knew why she'd been sitting on shore for a week now. She just didn't choose to share that with anyone. And look what happened."

"Oh, my God." Sam's eyes widened. "You're pinning this on *me*?"

"I'm not pinning it on anybody. Every single one of you has some ownership of what happened, though." He pointed at Sam. "You didn't share something really, really important." Then he swept his hand across the other three. "And you didn't listen when your friend was clearly terrified."

"Friend." Sam snorted. "Yeah, that's the word we use here."

Gabi sighed, wishing Sam could drop the untouchable act just for a few minutes. But after what had happened, her walls were up higher than ever. No way was Luke going to get her to be cooperative this morning.

"I get it, Sam." He nodded. "And if I was in your shoes, I'd be hard-pressed to use the word right now, too. What happened was scary. You're not likely to get it out of your head for a long, long time."

"Thank you, Dr. Freud."

"Sam—" Gabi warned, but Luke put up a gentle hand to stop her.

"You know what? Maybe you guys will never be friends." He shrugged. "And that's okay. Totally fine. But you *do* have to figure out how to live together and work together . . . and not kill each other—literally *or* figuratively—so that's what we're going to work on, starting today."

Eve narrowed her eyes. "What does *that* mean?"

Waverly giggled, then clapped her hand across her mouth. The poor girl was a nervous wreck.

"The first thing we're going to do is start working as a team. A real team. Not the kind that snips and snipes and annoys the hell out of each other whenever possible."

"But—" Eve piped up.

"No buts. You guys are exceptionally good at pissing each other off whenever possible. I imagine it's your pattern at Briarwood, and I also imagine it's a huge contributor to why you ended up here in the first place. But here's the thing. If you don't break this pattern, you're going to go *back* to Briarwood doing the same thing, and from what I understand, every single one of you is one tiny step away from being expelled." He stopped, scanning their faces. "Anybody anxious for that to happen?"

Gabi honestly figured a couple of them might raise their hands at this point, but nobody did. *Huh.*

"Good." He rubbed his hands together. "We've got a lot of work to do, and the first thing we're going to tackle is the very thing that got us into yesterday's situation."

Madison looked up suspiciously. "What do you mean?"

"I mean . . . Sam's going to learn to swim."

"What?" Sam looked like she might just flee the clearing and take her chances with the bears.

"You heard me. It's camp policy, actually, so my

hands are tied. If we discover that a camper isn't confident in the water, it's our job to make sure that gets fixed. What I *do* know, after all these years, is that it's never the camper's fault that he or she hasn't been taught to swim. It's their grown-ups' fault for never making sure they *got* taught."

Gabi cocked her head, listening to his words. She loved how he was taking the blame squarely off from Sam's shoulders, but couldn't tell if Sam was buying it yet.

He continued. "So, Sam, whether you were ever given the opportunity to learn or not, the fact is, somebody failed you. And I'm really pretty ticked off at that person right now. Or those persons—I don't know who's responsible." He ducked his head toward her, subtly forcing her to engage. "We won't fail you, Sam. You will not leave here without knowing to swim. And once you do, you will no longer have to be afraid of the water, okay?"

Sam looked up at him, a mixture of terror and—was that hope?—in her eyes.

Madison raised her eyebrows. "Who's going to teach her?"

Luke looked at each of them in turn. "We'll figure that out."

"Oh, hell, no." Sam unfolded herself from her log and stood up. "I'm not taking swimming lessons from them. No way."

"Sam?" He said it softly, but Gabi knew nobody in the circle would miss the tone. *Don't you dare leave,* it said.

Sam rolled her eyes, but shoved her hands in her shorts pockets, leaning against a tree, making sure he knew she'd leave whenever she damn well pleased, thank you very much.

Gabi loved that Luke let her have the win on that one.

That night, Gabi pulled the tent flap closed behind her, then zipped up her sweatshirt. She couldn't sleep, and she was sick of lying on her cot wondering what every snuffle and scratch outside the tent was. She'd spent the day practically tethered to the girls as they'd finished painting the bathroom and installing the water heater with Luke, and though they'd been generally cooperative, she still didn't know whether she'd made the right call, not putting them all in the van and heading back to Briarwood.

The vision of the hard-hat signs tacked to the dorm doors was the main thing that had kept her from doing just that, she was afraid.

But the bigger thing that had stopped her from begging Oliver for her battery was the fact that if they went back now, having solved *nothing,* they'd drive back through those school gates, settle back into their previous patterns, and probably end up expelled before October.

It would be the end of the scholarship program at Briarwood. It would be the end of the road for Eve and Sam. They'd go back to what passed for their dismal homes, and then . . . Gabi took a deep breath. Then, who knew what? Would they graduate? Or would they fall into the same statistical traps that held so many of their peers hostage?

But as much as she worried about the two of them, she couldn't help but stew about Madison and Waverly, as well. The two of them had grown up privileged, had gotten away with minor incidents all year, and thanks to Priscilla and the entire board at Briarwood, had essentially gotten away with an actual crime just weeks ago, since the police had never been involved. So what had they learned if Gabi failed here this summer?

They'd learned that money would pave the way, would cover their tracks, would absolve them of responsibility, while they lived by the mantra that rules applied only to other people.

Just like Garrett.

Gabi pictured her older brother, blond and gorgeous, full of himself and untouchable, and she shivered. He'd been a boarding-school brat just like her, but unlike her, he'd spent most of his boarding-school years getting into one sort of trouble or another. Usually it was minor stuff—typical stupid pranks—but other times, Gabi knew her own father had slid proverbial cash under proverbial tables in order to ensure that one headmaster or another would turn a blind eye to Garrett's little crimes.

Once she'd figured it out, she'd been disgusted. What was Garrett learning if Dad constantly used money to cover up his transgressions? And as she got older, she knew that what he was *learning* was that he *wasn't* responsible for his actions . . . that no matter what he did, Dad would bail him out, because it was better than weathering the inevitable scandal that might accompany the truth getting out. Dad's political platform—ironically enough—was founded on the ideals of honesty and transparency. A wayward son threatened that, so the wayward son was sent on a constant stream of faraway, low-profile excursions to keep him far from the spotlight.

Countries with looser laws were a favorite destination.

Yes, if normal societal rules had governed her brother's upbringing—and the night that still made bile rise in Gabi's throat—he'd be rotting in a cell right now, exactly where he belonged. Instead, he was probably traveling the Mediterranean on some friend's ginormous cruise boat, still untouchable, still using Dad's money as if he'd earned it himself as he blazed a trail through a bevy of fashion models and starlets. Gabi shuddered, wondering if any of *them* had seen his dark side . . . if Dad was still paying new people for their silence.

Gabi pictured her friend Nora, tears coursing down her face as she'd refused to talk to the police. Then she pictured herself packing her suitcase with shaking hands that same Christmas night, buying a bus ticket to Boston, and calling her mother hours later to let her know she was safe.

And to let her know she would never be home again.

She'd returned the checks her father had sent her, the ones that came with notes begging her to think about family, keep her mouth shut . . . make sure Nora did the same.

Her reward had been a clean, swift cut. *Our family's not good enough for you? Then our money isn't, either.* And her trust fund had been reallocated to Garrett.

She'd sat out the next semester at Wellesley, working two different part-time jobs and applying for scholarships, and when she'd finally entered the brick buildings again, under her own power, she'd done so with a clarity of purpose she hadn't let go of since.

Yes, she had a responsibility to open up opportunities for girls like Sam and Eve, but just as importantly, she couldn't let Madison and Waverly—or any of the other girls at Briarwood—grow up thinking they were untouchable. She couldn't turn them out into the world thinking there was a different set of laws created for those who could pay for protection. She couldn't—she

wouldn't—let them *ever* get away with hurting someone again, whether it was intentional or not.

Because if she didn't do *her* job, she'd be allowing
two more Garretts to wreak havoc on the world. And
people like Sam and Eve would be victims like Nora.

She turned on the flashlight and did a sweep of the
clearing, but didn't see any scary sets of eyes in the
bushes, so she set off down the pathway toward Luke's
cabin. It was eleven o'clock—definitely too late to visit
someone without notice—but Gabi couldn't lie in that
tent any longer without talking to him.

As she crested the rise, she saw his log cabin nestled
against the steep hillside, warm lights glowing from its
windows. The cabin had a stone chimney gracing the
right side, and a wide front porch with a swing and two
Adirondack chairs. The door was open, and she could
see Luke through the screen, moving about a little
kitchen area in just his shorts.

She swallowed hard, watching him even while she
chided herself for doing so. How pathetic was it to be
standing outside in the dark, ogling a man who didn't
know she was there?

As she watched, he got two beers out of his fridge.
Oh, no. He had company. Gabi was standing outside his
cabin like a peeping Tom, and he was entertaining a
woman.

She started to turn back down the pathway, but
stopped when she saw him pull a shirt over his head,
grab a metal mixing bowl and the beers, and push open
the door onto his screened porch. He set the beers down
on a table between the Adirondack chairs, then stood
up and looked like he was staring directly at her.

She instinctively backed up, even though there was
no way he could see her, right? Then his hand came up,

and suddenly she couldn't see at all, because a painfully bright light was shining directly in her eyes.

Well. Apparently he could see her just fine.

"Out for a stroll, Gabi?" He moved the light down her body and away from her, and she could hear the amusement in his tone. *Great.*

She walked toward him, stopping when she was just inside the light cast by the porch lanterns. "Sorry. The girls are zonked, but I couldn't sleep. Just thought I'd take a walk."

"After the hike I took you on the other day? You're willing to chance it out here at night?"

"Really, really couldn't sleep. And I figured most of your warnings were for effect." She motioned to the drinks on the porch. "I'm sorry. I didn't mean to disturb you when you have company."

"I don't have company."

"But—two drinks." She shook her head. It wasn't her business. "Never mind."

"Gabi, I saw you come over the hill. Figured you were either sleepwalking, or you needed some company." He narrowed his eyes like he was trying to zoom in on her face. "And if you're sleepwalking, you're awfully lucid."

She looked up at him, wishing she didn't feel so damn vulnerable right now. It made it hard to sort out whether she'd have found him just as gorgeous, just as warm, just as sweet if she was in a normal state of mind . . . on her own turf.

He motioned to the porch. "I have your favorite kind of chair here. Want to sit and have a beer with me? I'd offer wine, but I don't drink the stuff."

When she didn't move, he continued, "I could use the company. All I've got here is the four-legged variety." As she started up the steps, he opened the screen door, and two little white balls of fluff tumbled out and zoomed her way.

She laughed when she got to the top step and found herself unable to walk as the two tiny dogs threaded themselves around her feet.

"Down, killers." Luke scooped one dog with each hand, letting Gabi pass through the door. "Sorry about that. We don't get a lot of company."

"They're adorable." Gabi reached out to pet one of them, and was promptly rewarded with a lick to her chin. "Aww. Hi, little one." She looked at Luke. "How come we see so little of them?"

"My friends Josie and Ethan run a special home in town for kids who are dealing with cancer. Josie comes and kidnaps the dogs all the time to go hang out with the kids."

"That is so cool. So they're like therapy dogs?"

"Not officially. They're just small and sweet and love kids." He shrugged. "It works."

"Can I hold one?"

"Be my guest." He handed her a dog, who squirmed in her arms, desperate to deliver more kisses. She sat down, giggling, as the tiny thing burrowed its head into her neck and licked her ear.

"I'm sorry. You can put her down." Luke reached for the dog, but Gabi laughed.

"Oh, she's fine." She settled the dog in her lap, where it promptly turned three circles and lay down, looking up at her with big brown eyes. "I have to say, I totally would have pictured you with a Saint Bernard or something."

"Thank you. I think. I did used to own a respectable-sized dog. Just putting that out there." Luke handed her a beer, motioning to the popcorn. "I don't know what you drink. Hope this works."

"I live in a dorm with fifty girls. I usually *don't* drink, though they give me ample reasons to take up the sport."

He clinked the top of his bottle with hers. "Then this oughtta taste really good."

She put the bottle to her mouth, trying not to notice his eyes on her lips as she took a long draw.

"Good?" He smiled.

"Almost as good as your coffee, yes." She popped a piece of popcorn into her mouth. "And I haven't had popcorn in forever. Thank you."

"So . . . what really brings you out into the wilds at this hour, braving life and limb?" He set down his beer, full attention on her. "I suspect there's more to it than sleeplessness."

She took another sip, trying to choose her words carefully. After trying and discarding multiple possibilities, she took a deep breath and looked him directly in the eyes.

"I think . . . I want to give you the girls."

Chapter 18

The words that came out of Gabriela's mouth couldn't have surprised Luke more. Or Gabriela, he guessed. When he'd seen the beam of her flashlight come over the rise, his stomach had jumped hopefully. Was she lonely? Had she been replaying their almost-kiss on the beach in *her* head all day, too? Had she spent last night restlessly wishing she could sleep . . . like he had?

Or had she spent it wishing she had a reason *not* to spend the night sleeping?

He cleared his throat. "I'm not sure I follow. And also, that's a really frightening proposition. Just saying."

She took another sip of her beer, and he struggled to tear his eyes away from her lush lips as they cradled the bottle. Oh, to taste those lips.

He shook his head. *Jesus.*

"I've been thinking about what you said that first day we came—when you asked if I wanted to bring the same girls back to Briarwood, or different ones."

He nodded. He'd said something of the sort, yeah. Funny that she'd been noodling on it since then, though.

"I need to bring back different ones, Luke. I need to bring back girls who aren't going to fall back into the same patterns they had before they left. I need to bring back girls who will have the confidence to pave their own way and stop spending so much energy fighting everything, just for the sake of the fight. I need these four girls to get along, set an example for others, and maybe even like each other."

He felt his eyebrows hike upward. "That's kind of a tall order. You've only got three weeks left."

"I know. That's why I'm here, abjectly begging for help."

"Which I'm guessing is not something you do often? Or easily?"

A shadow of a smile passed over her face as she took another swallow. "Bingo."

Luke nodded thoughtfully. The situation with Sam had scared Gabi silly, obviously . . . so much so that one day later, she was here on his porch, drinking his beer, asking for his help—*real* help this time, not babysitting. It had to be killing her.

Despite the fact that not so long ago, he'd half hoped to see the taillights of the BMW van heading to the highway, he found himself nodding. Hell, as much as her four charges were certifiable pains in his ass, he couldn't help but want to make their time here at Echo worth the trouble they'd put everyone through.

He could definitely help. But he needed to do it in a way that didn't make Gabi feel like she'd failed first. He could practically feel the vulnerability radiating from her as she made quick work of the Sam Adams he'd handed her, and the last thing he wanted to do was make it worse.

"I might have some ideas," he finally said. "But you'd really have to trust me."

She paused, her bottle halfway to her mouth. "I know, and that scares me."

"And I'd need your help. There's no way I'd take these four on without it."

"So I can't bribe Oliver into unlocking my battery in the morning and taking off for a hotel for the next three weeks while you work your magic?"

"No."

"Dammit."

"I'll do it under one condition."

She smiled. "You know how I feel about conditions."

"But you're more desperate now than ever. It's my opportunity."

"Fine." She rolled her eyes. "What's your condition?"

"That you help me convince the Briarwood board not to go through with their plan to decimate this camp."

Gabi swallowed hard. "Just that?"

"Yeah." He nodded. "Just that."

"You do realize that you're asking a person who got sent to the wilds *by* that very board. Not sure my kind of influence is what you're after here."

"Well, I haven't had any luck finding us a Daddy Warbucks bailout, so I'm going to the trenches here. You're my inside girl."

Gabi sighed. "There is only one person on that board who has ever even given me the time of day."

"Great. Start with her." He stopped his beer halfway to his mouth. "Who *is* her?"

"Laura Beringer."

He nodded slowly. "Met her in April. She seemed . . . strangely normal, compared to the rest of them."

"She is." Gabi laughed quietly. "She's also the only one who dares to smile in meetings, not afraid to risk people thinking she's human, even though I'm pretty sure she's practically made of money."

"Even better. *Definitely* contact her."

Gabi sipped her beer, then nodded. "Okay. I accept your condition. I'll try to get hold of Laura."

"Good." He nodded. "Now, want to know what I'd do with your girls, going forward?"

"Absolutely."

He nodded, his wheels turning as he took a swig of his beer. "Okay, here's what I think. The work-crew stuff is working. They're learning new skills, they're working together even when they don't want to, and they're too busy to get into trouble while they're doing it."

"Agreed, but I still fear it's not going to last. Look what happened yesterday."

"I know." He nodded slowly, the perfect plan taking shape. It was nothing new or rocket-science-like, at least to him, but this is what he'd been doing with kids for years. But maybe it'd be new to her, and it *certainly* would be new to the girls. "Have you heard of challenge by choice?"

"Of course I have." She raised her eyebrows.

"What if we have the girls do work-type stuff in the mornings, and we design a course of challenges for the afternoons?"

"What kinds of challenges?"

He shrugged. "We could do almost anything. We've got a lake, a mountain, acres of forest . . ."

He watched as she turned the thought over in her brain and probably examined it from fifty angles, and he knew she wasn't immediately convinced.

"How much choice would you give them? I mean, could they just opt out of the whole thing? Because that would be a bust."

"I've rarely seen it work out that way. Peer pressure is a beautiful thing when you use it for good."

She raised her eyebrows. "And you know how to make them use it for good?"

"I can certainly try."

"And the challenge-by-choice stuff? You know how it works?"

"I know how it works, yes." He sighed, finally ready to shed the handyman cloak. "I've been the assistant director of this camp for six years now, and was *supposed* to take over as director this year."

She nodded like she'd known it all along. "So why the charade?"

"Because." He took a drink. "I figured if you thought I was just a hammer-and-wrench guy, you wouldn't look to me for help."

"Even though you started offering advice less than two hours after we arrived? Good plan."

"I know. Sorry. I overstepped."

She shrugged. "You were right."

"I know."

She laughed, rolling her eyes. "And also, incredibly modest."

"It's a skill." He raised his eyebrows. "And no one forced you to take my advice."

"True. But I did, and it worked, and guess what? Your own plan to stay disengaged backfired, because now I think you *do* have a clue, and now I *am* asking for help."

"I knew it was a bad idea."

She looked out at the dark woods, thoughtful for a moment. "So since you're suddenly being all honest, what do you do during the school year?"

"I'm a school psychologist. Over-degreed, underpaid—the whole cliché—just like you."

"You have a psych degree? Seriously?" Her eyes widened.

"Thank you for not looking completely, utterly shocked or anything."

She laughed. "It just makes *so* much sense now. *You* make so much sense now."

"Okay? Explain?"

She shook her head like she was hugely relieved, but he couldn't tell yet just what she was relieved *about*.

"You're just . . . really good with them. And in my lowest moments—of which there have been quite a few since we got here—I was really, really ticked off that you were doing a better job with my girls than I was."

"But now it's okay because I actually have a degree?"

"Maybe?" She wrinkled her nose. "Is that terrible?"

"Do *you* think it is?"

"Oh, don't even try that psych-speak thing on me. I don't care how many degrees you have. It won't work."

"You sure about that?" He smiled, sensing he had her off balance now.

"Yes. Maybe. Depends." She narrowed her eyes. "How many degrees *do* you have?"

"Three. Education, outdoor recreation, and a master's in adolescent counseling."

"Holy crap."

He laughed out loud as she deflated back into her chair and took another swig of her beer. "I didn't realize this would be such a shock."

"Well, hello. We roll up a week ago and you introduce yourself as Luke Magellan, camp handyman. And you're all handy . . . and man-ish."

He smiled, watching color rise to her cheeks as she checked to see how much of her beer she'd drunk. Looked like Gabriela O'Brien was a lightweight.

"Define 'man-ish.'"

Gabi rolled her eyes. "You know—all walking around with your big muscles and your five o'clock shadow and your perfect-fit jeans." She swallowed. "Delete that last part. I haven't noticed your . . . jeans."

"But the rest of the package is . . . man-ish?" He grinned.

"I *definitely* haven't noticed your pack— Oh, God." She buried her head in her hand as she handed her beer toward him. "Please cut me off."

He laughed. "Gabi, you've barely had half a beer."

"I know. So imagine the possibilities of me finishing that."

He was silent, doing exactly that as he watched her sitting in the candlelight, completely, beautifully flustered. Her skin had already turned golden in the sun of the past week, and her hair was streaked with lighter strands. Her sweatshirt didn't quite cover the tank top and yoga pants she'd probably worn to bed, and she looked ridiculously comfortable . . . and dead sexy.

"All right," he said, trying to momentarily ease her mind by pretending to change the topic. "So what do *you* know about challenge by choice?"

She looked up, and he couldn't tell whether she was relieved or disappointed by his redirection. Looking into her eyes, he'd bet on disappointed. *Good.*

"Just the basics, I guess." She pulled up her knees, curling her arms around her legs.

He paused for a long moment, trying to gauge his next move . . . trying to gather up the courage, really, which was a little hard to admit.

"Want to practice?" he finally asked.

"In the dead of night in the middle of the woods?" Her eyebrows flew upward. "No. Definitely not."

"But you don't even know what the challenge is."

"I don't think I need to. I did enough of these things in college."

"You've never had a Luke Magellan–inspired Echo Lake challenge, though."

"True." She rolled her eyes, smiling. "Fine. What's the challenge?"

"I challenge you . . . to kiss me."

Oh, hell. He'd put it out there.

Now her eyes opened for real. *"What?"*

"We're just—you know—practicing the concept. I imagine it's been a while since you've done it, right?"

"Um, kissing?" She shook her head. "I'm not—*what*?"

He laughed softly as her cheeks grew pink. "I meant the challenge thing, not the kissing. And it's challenge by choice, Gabi. I challenge you to kiss me. You get to choose whether you do."

He held his gaze steady, but inside, his head was churning. What the hell was he *doing*? Yeah, it was almost midnight, and he was a red-blooded male with a gorgeous female within arm's reach, but still. Gabi was out of here in a few weeks' time. Why was he looking to start something tonight?

Was he looking to start something tonight? Or had it just been way too long?

To his surprise, without breaking eye contact, Gabi uncurled her legs and stood up slowly, moving gracefully around the little coffee table to where he sat. He swallowed hard as she put both hands on the arms of his chair, leaning down so she was just delicious inches from his face. He tried to keep his eyes glued to hers so they wouldn't travel to where her tank top gaped, giving him a dead-gorgeous view of creamy curves, but apparently he slipped, because suddenly he felt her finger under his chin, lifting it.

Her eyes were amused as she moved closer, then slid her lips close to his ear, speaking in a whisper.

"I reject your challenge, Luke."

Chapter 19

Luke shook his head quickly. "What? You can't—*what*?"

She pulled back, but didn't lift her hands from his chair. He struggled to keep his eyes north of her neck, but dammit, he was pretty sure she was torturing him on purpose.

"I said I reject your challenge. You said I had a choice, right?"

"But—why—Gabi, seriously. You come walking over like you're about to drag me to bed . . . and then you say you reject the challenge? Not nice."

She smiled. "Not trying to be nice. Maybe I have my own challenge in mind."

"Oh?" God, he was dying to reach out and pull her onto his lap. Dying to let his hands slide off her clothes and touch all of that silky smooth skin. Dying to lift her up and take her inside, the future implications be damned. "What's *your* challenge?"

She tipped her head. "I'm an old-fashioned girl, Luke. Maybe I want *you* to kiss *me* first."

He smiled, relieved, sliding his hands into her hair. "But I don't have to?"

"Nope. You can reject mine just as easily as I rejected yours."

He laughed, sliding one hand around the back of her neck as he brushed wisps of hair from her forehead. He pulled her gently forward, watched her eyelids flutter closed.

"Ah, hell, sweetheart. I *definitely* accept your challenge."

And then his lips were on hers, and holy hell, it was like he'd never kissed a woman before. The zinging energy that flew directly from their lips downward had him shifting in the chair after only a few seconds, like he was in frigging junior high. She was tentative, sweet, and oh, so soft, and she tasted like strawberries and Sam Adams. Her hair fell around his face, and it was all he could do not to imagine it fanning over him in bed.

He gave her a gentle tug, and then she was nestled against him, one hand on his chest while the other slid slowly up his jawline and into his hair. And all the while, their tongues danced a slow, sweet rhythm as he tightened his arm around her, pressing her close.

It had been a long, long time since he'd been able to completely shut down all of his sensors and just live in a moment, but Gabriela gave him no choice. There was no way to think about anything *but* her as she whimpered softly when he pulled her closer. No way to imagine anything but slipping those clothes over her head and cupping her ass as he lifted her to his mouth.

Would she stop him?

They kissed for what felt like hours, until he could feel his pulse ratcheting up to meet the birdlike one he felt just under the skin on her delicate, sweet-smelling neck. He slid his hand under the hem of her tank top, meeting impossibly soft, silky skin. As his thumb grazed her curves—good Lord, no bra—she made a low, contented sound that went straight to his nether regions, and he knew if they didn't stop soon, he wasn't going to want to stop at all.

Oh, who was he kidding? He *already* didn't want to stop. He had no idea where the woman had learned to kiss, but Jesus, she was going to do him in here, and he was going to be loath to prevent her from doing so.

Her fingers played in his thick hair, a heaven-sent erotic massage as she broke the kiss and pulled his head to her neck. He planted soft kisses along her collarbone and up to her ear, tracing it with his tongue, making her gasp and tighten her hands on his head.

With one hand, he slid the strap of her tank top aside, kissing a trail over her shoulder as his fingers slipped down her arm and onto her thigh. He could hear her breaths coming faster, could feel her pulse racing under his lips . . . knew there was no way making love to her would be anything but frigging spectacular.

And then one of the dogs yipped and moved to the edge of the porch, quickly joined by the other one. Gabi jumped, pushing her shirt back to rights as she pulled away from him. Luke swore internally as he grabbed for the flashlight. The dogs, even though they were small, weren't barkers. If they were yipping, they'd seen or heard something in the woods. And there were four teenagers in a tent in those woods.

"Gabi?" A tentative voice came from just outside the light of the porch, making Luke swing his flashlight her way.

Make that three teenagers.

Gabi stood up quickly, almost losing her balance. Her cheeks were dead pink, as was her neck, and her hair was mussed from his hands, but she did her best to be all business as she turned to Sam.

"What's up, Sam? Everything okay?"

"Um, yeah. Just woke up and saw you were gone, and you didn't come back. Figured I'd better make sure you hadn't been eaten by a bear." She shrugged, crossing her arms. "But I guess . . . well, that wasn't exactly the issue. Never mind. Carry on. Forget I was here."

Gabi looked back at Luke, her eyes wide, but he didn't know what she wanted him to do. Clearly they'd been caught. Even if Sam hadn't seen them kissing, she'd only have to take one look at Gabi right now to know they'd been *this* close to taking things inside.

"Hey, Sam?" Gabi cleared her throat. "I wouldn't mind if maybe we could keep this—you know—between us."

Sam smirked, but Luke noticed it didn't have quite the venom of a week ago. "You want to offer me something for my silence?"

"No. I'm just asking, one woman to another."

Sam was silent for a long moment, but finally nodded. "Fine. I saw nothing, but if you *do* get mauled by a bear on the way back to the tent tonight, I want it on record that at least one of us gave enough of a shit to check on you."

"Y'know, you can put that thing on backwards six times, and it's still not gonna fit." Oliver shook his head as he put his hands on his hips early the next morning. "Where's your head today?"

Luke looked up from the outboard motor he'd been trying to repair, then sighed as he set it down and wiped his hands on a rag.

"My head's fine," he growled, then put up an apologetic hand. "Sorry. Not a lot of sleep last night."

"Ah." Oliver turned to the workbench, but not before

Luke saw him smile. "Wouldn't have anything to do with a woman, would it?"

Ha. It had every-damn-thing to do with a woman, and that woman was currently in the water, doing dock-to-raft laps, even though the air temp was still hovering below seventy degrees. She'd forgone her morning coffee in favor of a penguin plunge, which left him wondering exactly how much sleep *she'd* gotten after she'd followed Sam back to their tent last night.

"Why does everyone always assume a bad mood or sleepless night is about a woman?"

"Because usually it is." Oliver shrugged. "And I might have seen one wandering your way last night, long after she should have been asleep."

"Oh."

"In my defense, I wasn't looking . . . well, any more than I've had one eye out that window for thirty years now. Old habits and all."

"Well, then, you must have seen her come back *down* that pathway an hour later, right?"

"Nope. Went to sleep. Figured you could handle her."

Luke sighed, watching her touch the raft and head back toward the dock. She picked up speed, her strokes long and fluid, and he wondered if she was half as conflicted this morning as he was.

"I don't know, Oliver. 'Handle' might be a strong word."

"Well, I imagine she didn't head your way looking to borrow a cup of sugar." His eyebrows were up as he turned toward Luke. "Freak you out, did she? Not exactly the type you'd expect to show up at your door at midnight?"

"She's not the type I'd expect to show up at my door *anytime,* if she wasn't trapped here with us."

"And that's what's got you all discombobulated this morning?"

"Maybe."

Hell, yes.

Oliver shrugged again. "Might not be my place to notice, but all things being equal, I gotta say, she seems genuine. She could have come in here with a lot more bluster and a lot less class, and she didn't. Somebody pulled a big-ass snow job on her with this assignment, and she hasn't taken off yet."

"Well, that's because we're holding her van hostage."

"Bullshit. She knows she can have that battery anytime she asks. It's not her we're trying to keep from leaving."

"I know."

"She hasn't been too proud to ask for help, either. I think that says a lot."

Luke rolled his eyes. "Pretty sure that says she's completely, utterly desperate."

"Not that you have a pool-boy complex or anything."

"A pool-boy—*what*?"

"Complex."

Luke sighed. "I heard you. I just don't know what you mean."

Oliver reached for a metal stool and sat down. "Luke, we've known each other a long time, right?"

Oh, boy. In the scheme of conversational openings, this one never ended well. "Yeah. A really long time."

"So you'll excuse me for knowing a lot more about you than you're probably comfortable with, right?"

"Nope."

Oliver nodded, smiling. "Good. Then you'll also excuse me for being more than a little pissed that you don't think you could possibly measure up to a woman like Gabi."

"It's not about measuring up."

"No?" Oliver sent his eyebrows upward. "Then what is it?"

"It's about—hell, I don't know. It's about the fact that this isn't reality, you know? She's here for four weeks, I'm here for—well, I don't even know, given Briarwood's plans. We're from completely different worlds, Oliver, and I'm pretty sure neither of us has any plans to change that anytime soon."

"That's a weak argument. Just saying."

"No it's not, and you know it. It's reality. She's here because she's stuck here, not because she would have ever chosen a summer like this."

"So it's Stockholm syndrome? You're going with the theory that the captive is falling for the captor, because he's the best thing on the menu?"

"She's not fall—she's *not* a captive. Jesus, Oliver." He rolled his eyes, trying to refocus his attention on the motor.

"Hey." Oliver's voice commanded attention, and Luke's head snapped up, just like it had the night Oliver had bailed him out of that stupid drunk-tank cell. "You're not the going-nowhere kid you tried so hard to be fifteen years ago. You're not some sort of carbon copy of the loser father who never showed up to raise his son. You've made a life for yourself, and it's a damn good one. You're making a difference, and the right woman is going to see that. I have a feeling a good woman is *already* seeing it."

"She knows nothing about me, Oliver."

"And you think her feelings would change if she knew you spent your early days bouncing around from foster home to foster home? Think she'd find you less attractive if she knew you'd spent years fighting anybody who pissed you off, just because you didn't know what else *to* do?"

"Yeah, I do." Luke nodded, his jaw set hard. "Because that kid's still boiling inside, and that kid will never get over getting left behind when his mother's rich new boyfriend thought she'd be more attractive with fewer little truants in tow. So yeah, I'm all reformed adult and all, but there's still a lot of anger there, and it's firmly directed at a lot of people who deserve it . . . people who reside in the same circles as Gabi does."

Oliver was silent for so long that Luke thought maybe he was finished speaking. But then he sighed carefully.

"What happened to your sister isn't Gabi's fault, Luke."

Chapter 20

Half an hour later, Gabi toweled off her hair in the new bathroom, feeling refreshed and tortured at the same time. She'd tossed and turned for most of the night, and had decided as dawn broke outside the tent that if she didn't start the day with an arctic swim, there wasn't going to be enough coffee in the universe to wake her up.

On one hand, she was filled with zingy, delicious energy as she thought back to last night. On the other, she was filled with what-the-*hell*-were-you-thinking pain. She hadn't gone to Luke's cabin with any intention of having things end the way they had, but omigod, once he'd issued his little challenge, there'd been *nothing* she could do to stop herself from slinking over to his chair and kissing him like a complete hussy.

Not that he hadn't returned the favor. And not that he hadn't been the one to suggest it in the first place, but seriously. She knew better. Yes, she'd been lusting after him practically since she'd opened the van door almost two weeks ago, but really? A midnight walk to an almost-stranger's cabin was ticking off the first of the fall-fast-fall-hard-fall-stupid boxes. And as much as she knew better than to ever walk that pathway again after dark, it was the *only* thing she could think about doing right now.

She'd been kissed before. She'd even been kissed well. But she'd *never* been kissed like Luke Magellan had kissed her . . . like his only mission was to make sure she never, ever wanted to stop.

Would they have stopped had Sam not appeared? That question had tortured her into the wee hours, and as she looked in the mirror to see feverishly pink cheeks, she had a pretty strong feeling she knew the answer, if the decision had been left to her.

It was a good damn thing Sam *had* showed up.

She brushed her teeth, desperate for her early-morning routine to still the grasshoppers in her gut. What would she say to Luke this morning? How would he look at her? Was he having regrets?

Or was he reliving their moments like she was, unable to shake them from his brain, either?

She sighed. Here she was, staring down her thirtieth birthday, and yet she felt like a thirteen-year-old with a summer-camp crush. And as much as she wished she could head out for a hike, or just hide in her tent, or maybe even grab a paddle and disappear for the day in a canoe, she had to face the day.

And that meant she had to face Luke.

She took a deep breath, bundled up her swimsuit and towel, and headed out the door, only to run smack into the very person she'd been hoping to avoid for at least a little bit longer.

"Oof!" she huffed as she slammed into him.

He grabbed her upper arms, steadying her, an amused smile on his face, but distance in his eyes. Dammit.

"Little distracted this morning, Gabi?"

She felt her cheeks go red. "Just didn't expect anyone to be skulking outside the bathroom door, thank you."

"I wasn't skulking. I was walking *by* the bathroom when you barreled through the door."

"I did not barrel. I *do* not barrel."

"Fine." He rolled his eyes as he slid his hands free. "You were the epitome of grace. I apologize for suggesting otherwise."

"Thank you."

"Did you have a nice swim?" He pointed at her beach towel.

"Yup. But does this lake ever get above freezing? Just curious?"

"It's usually tolerable by late August, yes."

"Fantastic. We'll be gone by then."

The words fell out of her mouth before she considered their implication, in relation to their time together last night, and she didn't think it was her imagination that his mouth tightened as she spoke.

"I know, Gabi." He shook his head. "I know."

"Are you . . . regretting your challenge?" She forced the words out, sensing a chill in his tone, needing to know where she stood before the girls got up and she had to face Sam's accusatory face.

He ran a hand through his hair, not meeting her eyes. "Yes and no."

"That's helpful."

"Are *you* regretting it?" He looked at her finally.

"Well, I am right now, since it looks like you'd rather have a poker to the eye than spend one more minute in my presence."

He smiled sadly. "Not true. I'm just—I don't know. I think maybe we weren't necessarily thinking clearly."

"Ah." She fought the tremble that almost immediately

hit her chin. Even at age almost-thirty, rejection still sucked.

"It's not you, Gabi."

"Omigod, are you serious? Did you just say that?"

He closed his eyes. "Sorry. I know."

"Okay. Well." She took a deep breath, looked around, not knowing what to say. "I should . . . go." Then a nervous laugh burbled out. "But I can't . . . go. There's nowhere *to* go. I'm stuck. You're stuck. We're . . . stuck. This is stupid."

"You're babbling."

"No shit, Sherlock."

He reached up to touch her face, and she tried to back up, but couldn't. "It's really, really not you."

"And yet, after one kiss?"

"After one kiss, I didn't sleep a wink, okay? Does that make you feel better?" He pulled his hand back, sighing as he stared out at the water. "I don't do . . . this, Gabi."

She tipped her head. "By *this,* you mean—"

"I don't do the casual thing. And as much as I could easily have taken you inside last night and kept you awake all night—as much as I *wanted* to—we both know that in the end, we'd just be making an epic mistake."

"Oh." Gabi crossed her arms. "Well, gosh, when you put it that way."

"That's not—bad word choice—sorry." He shook his head, reaching for her, but she backed out of reach.

"No, really." She put up a hand, and dammit, she could feel tears prick behind her eyes. No way could she let him see that. "I've never been someone's epic mistake. Not really interested in changing that, so thank you."

"Gabi, that's not what I meant. I just mean—shit. I

don't know what I mean right now. You've got my head tied up in knots."

"If it's any consolation, I didn't go to your cabin last night with some sort of evil plan to seduce you."

"I know. I'm . . . sorry. And I'm not sorry." He sighed. "I just don't want you to have regrets."

"Me? Or *you*?"

"I don't want either of us to have regrets, but I assume you're the one who'd be more likely to suffer them, okay?"

"Why?"

"Because be honest, Gabi." He swept his arm around the woodsy area. "I'm sorry I issued a stupid challenge. This isn't really your world, slumming at a rustic camp. And I imagine it's not really your habit to go slumming with camp employees, either."

Gabi felt her eyes go wide. One hand crossed her middle, while the other went to her throat. Had he really just said that?

The psychology major in her suspected what he might be doing here—striking out and disengaging first, before she had a chance to do it herself—but knowing it and hearing it aimed directly at her were two very different things.

"I see." Her voice was quiet as she nodded slowly.

"It's just—listen. We've got, what, only weeks left here? And then you go back to your Briarwood life, right? This camp thing isn't your reality, and I'm a little old to be someone's summer-camp romance. I'm definitely too old to be someone's one-night stand."

"Because you think that's all you could be?"

"I don't know. But I *do* know you're tired, you're vulnerable, you're scared, and you're so far out of your normal element that you're kissing a practical stranger."

He crossed his arms, and she felt cold envelop her.

"I don't want you to end up resenting me because I took advantage of that."

"Luke! Help! Help me!" Katrina's voice pierced the night air as flames crackled. "Get me out!"

Luke looked up at the second-floor window where his little sister screamed, eyes widening when he saw flames licking out of the window in the next bedroom. There was no time. No time.

There was no ladder, either, and the tree next to the house was too far away. But maybe, if he prayed hard enough and stretched far enough, he could climb it and get her to jump to him. He'd catch her. He knew he would. Yeah, he was a no-good sixteen-year-old, but he could at least do that.

He started climbing the tree, her screams getting louder and louder. But for every branch he conquered, another seemed to grow, and no matter how long he flailed, and how high he climbed, he couldn't get closer.

The flames got hotter, licked at the tree, caught, and now he could only see little Katrina through fire. He climbed faster, felt his breaths coming shorter and harder, but still, he couldn't get to her.

"Trina! Hold on! I'm coming! Jump for the tree!" he called, but his voice was hoarse, and her screams were getting softer as smoke filled the air.

"Don't breathe in! Jump, Trina! Jump!" The grass was soft. Maybe she'd break a leg or something, but at least she wouldn't be dead.

He kept climbing, kept climbing, kept climbing, but the tree mocked him. Branches popped out of nowhere, thrusting themselves in his face as he went hand over hand, struggling upward.

And then there was no sound but the flames, and he panicked.

"Trina! Trina!"

"Luke. Luke, honey." He felt his shoulder being jostled gently the next morning. "Luke, wake up. It's okay. You're okay. Just a dream."

Piper's voice stabbed at him from outside the dream, and he opened one bleary eye, completely discombobulated to see her hovering over his couch.

"You okay?" Her voice was soft, concerned, as he struggled to shake the dream and sit up. "What was it this time?"

"Fire." His voice shook, and he cleared his throat. He hated the fire dream the most of all of them. That damn tree with its branches, the smoke, the crackle of flames. He rubbed his eyes with the heels of his hands. "Damn. What time is it?"

"Six. I just came to drop off some cinnamon buns from Mama B. She said you hadn't been in to get any in a week, and she was concerned you were melting away to nothing."

He tried to smile, tried to force the dream back into submission. "Thank you."

"Hey, Luke?"

He shook his head. "Please don't ask me if I think I should see somebody about this. I *am* a somebody, and there's nothing that will stop the dreams."

They'd been suddenly worse since Sam's incident, and it didn't take a psychologist to figure the reasons for *that* one out. Plus, the more exhausted he was, the more vulnerable to them he seemed to be. And right now, he was dead tired.

After he and Gabi had parted at the bathroom yesterday morning, Luke had spent the entire day feeling
like a complete shmuck for accusing her of slumming.
He'd seen the words hit hard, but they'd already done
their damage before he could pull them back. He'd
reached for her, and she'd put up a hand, walking toward
the tent like she couldn't possibly be in his presence for
one more moment.

She'd taken the girls, despite the plans they'd made,
and had steered clear of him all day. At nine o'clock,
she'd headed into the tent, and despite his hope that
maybe she'd appear on the pathway . . . that maybe he'd
figure out how to apologize by the time she did, she'd
never appeared.

He was an idiot to have said what he did, and he was
ashamed of himself for purposely hurting her. He just
hadn't figured out what to do about it yet.

"What about Josie? Maybe she could help?" Piper's
voice brought him back to the present.

"No. I don't need—I don't want help. Someday they'll
go away. Or they won't, and that's my cross to bear. I
deserve it. I couldn't save her, Piper, and I was the only
one left in her life who gave a damn enough to try.
There's no therapist who'll ever be able to exorcise that
demon."

Chapter 21

An hour later, Gabi folded herself into her favorite Adirondack chair, pulling up her knees and zipping her sweatshirt around her. The usual morning mist was just lifting from the lake, and the usual loons were making their usual last calls, but this morning, it didn't relax her. Instead, it all made her even edgier than she'd woken up feeling.

Yesterday, Gabi had taken the girls up to the garden after breakfast, knowing she needed to steer clear of Luke at all costs. They'd hoed, they'd raked, and they'd whined, but by the end of the day, that garden had been almost ready for planting.

So much for turning the girls over to him. One day later, here she was, trying to figure out how to get through the rest of their time here without things being completely awkward.

His words from yesterday still haunted her, and as much as she wanted to be furious at him, she was more mystified. She knew damn well he'd enjoyed that kiss as much as she had. And she knew *damn* well that neither of them had been anxious to back off when Sam had shown up and thrown a proverbial bucket of ice over the scene.

But yesterday morning, for whatever reason, he'd tossed his own bucket, and she had no idea what to do about it except to stay away from him as much as possible until she figured it out. Meanwhile, she kept torturing herself by replaying the scene in her mind. And as much as she tried to convince herself she'd made a big fat mistake in kissing him in the first place, she knew that if she got a do-over, she'd probably do it again in a heartbeat.

She closed her eyes, reliving the most perfect half hour she'd ever spent—his hands tenderly roaming, his lips turning her into a quivering wreck, his tongue gentle and demanding at the same time.

"Morning."

Gabi's eyes popped open as Luke's voice preceded the smell of fresh-brewed coffee. He set a mug down on the arm of her chair, then sat heavily in the matching one. She looked at him quickly, not sure whether to be relieved or amused that he looked like . . . well, hell. If he knew what she'd just been thinking, it'd be even worse, she was sure.

"Are you all right, Luke?"

"Yep." He took a healthy glug of his coffee, wincing as it went down. "Nope."

She wasn't sure what to say to that, so she opted to sip her coffee and wait him out instead. Why was he here? Bringing coffee, even?

Yes, it had sort of become their habit, but still. Awkward.

"I need to apologize, Gabi." He still didn't look at her.

"For?"

"One—for kissing you, and two—for making you feel like shit about it."

"Oh. Just that."

He looked at her sidelong. "Yeah, just that. I'm sorry. I didn't mean to make you feel like . . . well, however you ended up feeling. I am a certifiable schmuck."

Gabi took a deep breath. "How I ended up *feeling,* Luke, is that because I arrived in a BMW van, you've somehow got it in your head that I must act and think in a prescribed manner that couldn't possibly end up working in your favor."

"I know."

"Do you have any idea what my annual income is?"

"No, and it's none of my business. Also, it's completely irrelevant."

"I don't think it is." She took another sip of her coffee, mostly as a delay tactic. "Because it's all I *do* make. I'm not putting in time at a cushy private school so I can feel good about my contribution to society, then move on to spend the rest of my years chairing fundraisers and pretending to give a hoot about popular causes I know nothing about."

"I know that."

"Do you? How could you?" She felt her cheeks heat up. "I really don't think you do, actually. I think you've got it in your head that because I grew up coddled, I couldn't possibly have a brain cell in my head devoted to anything besides myself."

"Gabi—"

"I work at Briarwood, Luke, because I *hate* how entitlement turns out the kinds of people you hate. I *hate* that schools like mine pamper rich kids and sweep their transgressions under expensive Oriental carpets. I *hate* that kids like Madison and Waverly grow up thinking the world is there *for* them, not the other way around. The reason I'm there is to challenge that entire system, and it pisses me off to no end that I've been doing that for eight years now, and yet the moment I step off campus, the *first* thing you believe is that I'm just another rich bitch putting in her time."

He pressed his lips together like she'd hit a tender nerve. "I don't think any such thing, Gabi."

She barreled forward, even though she knew she should probably stop. She wasn't even sure where all of these words were coming from. "Do you have any idea how hard I fought to get those two scholarships approved? How many meetings I had to attend? How much research I had to do in order to prove to the board that having *two* strangers in our midst wasn't going to ruin the entire reputation of my stellar, snobbish school? Do you have any idea how hard I've worked to try to expand that program? To make the case that we should be spending our endowment money on our students, instead of new science buildings and a raise for Priscilla?"

"No." His word was simple and quiet.

"No. You don't. That's right. And yet you stand there yesterday, after sharing what—I'm sorry—was probably the best damn kiss of my entire life, and you accuse me of *slumming*?"

"I—"

"I don't slum, Luke. I don't fall for people based on their economic level or their résumés. I most certainly don't kiss people I wouldn't want to see the next morning. And I have never done the hookup thing. Ever. I don't. I won't. I kissed you because I like you. I kissed you because you looked so flipping gorgeous sitting there in the moonlight that I couldn't *resist* kissing you. And I *kept* kissing you because I liked it. I liked *you*. It had nothing to do with vulnerability or fear or any of the other things you threw at me."

"Gabriela?"

Gabi took a breath, trying to corral her racing thoughts. "What?"

"Stop talking." His voice was gruff and pained at the same time as he stood up and reached for her hands.

Before she could think better of it, she let him pull her out of her chair, and before she could react, he'd hauled her against his body, holding her close as he found her lips with his. This kiss had none of the gentle, languishing energy of two nights ago. *This* kiss was powerful, commanding, hot.

His hands wandered downward over her jean shorts as he kissed her, and as he cupped her, he pulled her tightly against his body, leaving her with no doubt that she wasn't the only one feeling the heat.

Minutes later, after both of them were a little breathless, he pulled back, sliding one hand deliciously upward to cradle her jaw. His eyes skated over her eyes, her nose, her lips, and as if he couldn't resist doing so, he kissed her again. This time it *was* gentle, like she was made of the thinnest glass and he was afraid to shatter her.

And when he pulled back, his eyes were dark, but his smile grew slowly as he tucked her hair behind her ears, then slid his arms around her, bringing her against his chest. He laughed softly, and she could feel him shaking his head gently, his chin moving on top of her head.

"Apparently I like you, too, Gabriela. Didn't mean to. Didn't *want* to. But damn, woman. You're going to be the death of me."

"Whatcha doing?" Two hours later, after the girls had scattered to brush their teeth and tidy up the tent, Gabi walked toward the admin cottage, where Luke had what looked like six miles of rope lying scattered on the grass.

"Laying bait."

Gabi felt her eyebrows go upward. "For *what*? What are you hoping to catch?"

"Relax." He laughed. "Didn't mean it literally. Thought I might see if the girls might be interested in learning a little rock climbing."

"Rock climbing?" Gabi swallowed. "Like on cliffs? That sort of thing?"

He shrugged casually. "Yep."

"Um, no. They're not. Interested, I mean."

"Had a feeling you'd say that."

"Luke, they're not ready for something like that. I mean, I know we talked about doing some challenge-type stuff, but I didn't think you meant *this*. This is potentially dangerous."

He stopped coiling a bright green rope, a half-smile on his face. "Waking up in the morning is potentially dangerous, Gabi. Rock climbing with perfectly good safety equipment is not."

"But—cliffs."

He winked, holding his thumb and index fingers an inch apart. "Just little ones."

"Not funny."

"Let's just see what happens, okay? They may not even take the bait."

She put one hand on her hip. "But you're pretty sure they will, aren't you?"

He laughed. "They totally will."

Half an hour later, Gabi sat at the picnic table watching the girls finger the ropes, intrigued by the colors and textures. Luke stood casually winding up different lengths of rope and using complicated-looking knots to bind them.

Sam spoke first. "So you use these for rock climbing?"

"Yep."

Waverly held up a fluorescent one. "I never would have pictured you using a hot-pink rope, Luke."

He shrugged. "One of my favorites."

"Where do you actually go?" Eve asked. "To do the rock climbing?"

Luke pointed across the lake at Kizilla Mountain, which Gabi thought looked much bigger now that she was imagining her girls hanging off its sides.

"Good cliffs over there."

Sam raised her eyebrows. "You usually take camp kids to do it?"

"Yeah. Took a whole crew last summer. We made an overnight out of it. Hiked up, climbed, did some rappelling." Luke shrugged like it was no big deal. "Fun stuff."

"Can *we* do it?" Eve asked, running a blue rope through her fingers.

Luke made a derisive snorting sound. "Hell, no."

Gabi felt her eyes go wide. What? Hadn't he laid out these ropes exactly for this purpose—to get the girls intrigued and wanting to try it?

"Why not?"

"First, because we have too much to do here. Second, because there's way too much to it. You have to learn knots, and how to build body harnesses, and how to rappel and hold for each other, and—" He made a motion that dismissed the entire idea, and Gabi almost laughed, now realizing what he was doing. When he shot her a warning look, she lifted her water bottle and took a sip, trying to tamp down her smile.

"We could learn." Sam put her hands on her hips. "You could teach us."

"Nah. We really don't have time."

"We have *weeks,* Luke."

"Exactly. *I* have only weeks left to get this camp whipped into shape. I showed you guys the project list. I don't have time to teach you this stuff. Sorry."

He turned away from them, setting a coiled rope on the picnic table. As he did, Sam motioned for the girls to pick up other ropes.

"Come on, Luke. Please? Just teach us one knot." She put up her eyebrows like *she* was playing *him,* and it was all Gabi could do not to laugh. "One knot'll take, like, five minutes, right?"

He sighed, then turned around, rolling his eyes. "Fine. One knot. But that's it. We've got work to do."

Twenty minutes later, all four girls were sitting in the grass, working their ropes into complicated configurations. Luke had shown them four different kinds of knots, and then handed Gabi a length of rope, as well.

"Want to try?"

"Oh, absolutely." She smiled as she took the rope, speaking almost in a whisper. "You're good, Luke."

He shrugged modestly. "Nah. They're just not always as complicated as we make them out to be."

He walked around the grassy area checking knots, nodding here and there while he gently pointed out mistakes, and despite the fact that she was supposed to be tying her rope, Gabi couldn't unglue her eyes from him.

He crouched down beside Madison to help her untangle one of her knots, and Gabi felt herself staring at the way his T-shirt pulled tight against his back. She took a deep breath, trying to look at anything but him, and her eyes landed squarely on Sam, whose eyebrows were arched.

Sam looked at Luke, then back at Gabi, and she shook

her head, a frown touching the corners of her lips as she returned her focus to the rope in her lap.

Later that afternoon, Gabi was up in the garden with Madison, Eve, and Waverly when she heard splashing from down below, and immediately panicked. She and Luke had split up the girls this afternoon in an attempt to tackle more jobs, and the sound of the water sent her adrenaline coursing.

Was it Sam? How could it *possibly* be Sam?

She ran to the edge of the grassy area and peered down through the trees, praying nothing bad had happened. She heard another splash, then saw a ball of white fur, and she laughed. Luke's dogs were playing in the water, and—wait—*was* that Sam?

It was. And she was *in* the water. Still in a T-shirt and shorts, even though Gabi'd bought her a swimsuit before they'd left school, but she was in. The. Water.

Gabi put her hand to her mouth as she watched Sam wade up to her waist, giggling as the dogs circled her. Luke stood only a few feet away in the water, tossing little sticks to the dogs when they came toward him.

After a few minutes, she saw Luke talking to Sam, but was too far away to make out what he was saying. Then he motioned toward the dock, and picked up a couple of tools he'd put there. He handed her something and pointed, and before Gabi knew it, Sam was holding the dock steady, handing tools to Luke as he ducked under to fix something.

Gabi felt her forehead furrow. Sam didn't even look scared right now. She'd avoided the beach area at all cost since they'd arrived, except when she'd pseudo-bathed in water barely over her knees, but now she was waist-deep in water, working on the dock with Luke.

Was this another one of his baiting exercises? Was he getting her into the water under the guise of helping him? Had he already decided that getting her to agree to swimming lessons was a useless venture? Was he using a back-door approach that—so far—looked like it might actually be working?

Then she crossed her arms carefully, thinking back to his words this morning, the way his hands had splayed across her ribs, inching slowly, achingly higher the other night.

Was he baiting *her,* too?

Chapter 22

Just before dinner, Gabi was in the kitchen helping Piper when she heard giggles coming from behind the admin cottage. Pausing with a potato half peeled, she looked up at Piper, who'd paused as well.

Piper cocked her head. "That's an odd sound from this crew."

"I know," Gabi answered, setting down the potato and wiping her hands. "I'm not sure it's a good one."

She walked quickly through the dining area and pushed open the screen door, heading for where she'd heard the laughter. When she came around the corner of the cottage, she stopped fast, her eyes widening at the sight. Hanging from the trees were all four girls, tied into rope harnesses Luke must have taught them to make themselves.

Piper came up behind her, laughing when she caught sight of the girls. "Well, this is different."

"He's tied my students to trees." Gabi tried to make her voice sound imperious, but when all four girls broke into laughter at once, she stopped bothering.

"They're only three feet off the ground," Piper pointed out.

"Yes, but . . . trees. They look like monkeys."

Just then, Luke tossed a beach ball into the air. "Score is three to two. Go!"

The girls scrambled to get hold of the ball and toss or kick it to—well, she had no idea what the goal was, but *they* seemed to know. They bounced and swung and grabbed the ball, aiming it at each other and cheering randomly. A minute later, they all dissolved in laughter when Madison got her foot caught in her rope and spun in two full circles before she was able to get it freed.

As Luke held Madison's rope steady, he seemed to realize for the first time that Gabi and Piper were there.

"Hey, ladies. Want to play?"

Piper stepped forward. "Calvinball? You bet I do."

"Gabriela?" Luke reached down for a rope. "Remember the harness I showed you?"

She crossed her arms. She was *not* getting tied to a tree. No way, no how. "Yes, I remember. And no, I don't want to play, but thank you."

"Oh, come on. It's fun." Piper's fingers flailed as she tied her rope into a series of knots that would probably keep *her* from executing an embarrassing splat, but Gabi was far less convinced of her *own* knot-tying skills.

Sam tipped back in her harness, to the point where Gabi started to reach for her so she didn't topple out and land on her head.

"Come on, Gabi," she said. "Let Luke tie you up. It'll be fun."

Gabi's eyes flew to Sam's, but the imp had already fixed her gaze elsewhere. Luke's shoulders were shaking, however, as he knotted a rope.

"You know what?" Gabi lifted her chin. "Fine. I will."

Waverly and Eve smiled, but Madison assumed her trademark bored face, even though she'd been laughing just minutes ago.

"Come here." Luke motioned to her, his eyebrows up, and Gabi struggled to keep her mind focused on an innocent game of Calvinball, whatever the hell that turned out to be. She walked the ten steps to him, then stepped into the harness he'd fashioned. He drew the ropes up her legs, and she swallowed hard as his fingers skated slowly upward.

His eyes met hers, and in that moment, she knew that he knew *exactly* what he was doing, torturing her. She narrowed her eyes, but he just smiled. He spun her around and checked the knots, then took the end of her rope and climbed up one of the pine trees.

"Climb up on that stump and I'll tie you up," he called from above her.

She was going to kill him.

She stepped up onto the stump, then felt the rope pull hard as he looped it around a thick branch and tied it securely. She hoped.

"Okay, test it."

She pulled with her hands and it didn't give. "I think it's fine."

"Just jump, Gabi." Sam rolled her eyes. "You'll fall, like, two feet if you dump."

She held on to the ropes tightly, sure she was about to make a spectacular flop, but to her surprise, instead she sailed a few feet one way, then swung backward. It was kind of like flying.

"See? No crash and burn." Luke smiled from above her, then caught Piper's rope when she tossed it up to him.

After he'd tied Piper in, he climbed back down the tree, and Gabi couldn't help but think about the range of muscles it took to scale a tree without looking like it was taking any effort at all. She also couldn't help but think about what those muscles would look like with less clothes on, but shook her head before *that* distraction did her in.

One minute later, the ball was bouncing, the girls were laughing, and Gabi and Piper were right in the thick of things. Before long, Gabi's stomach and cheeks hurt from laughing, and an hour later, when Luke called the game in favor of Eve and Waverly, Gabi'd forgotten why she ever thought his baiting technique was a bad idea in the first place.

The girls had learned to tie their ropes, they'd learned to make their own harnesses, and they'd spent a couple of hours getting comfortable with hanging in them . . . all without realizing Luke had very clear goals for what seemed like just a silly game.

As Piper disappeared into the dining hall with the girls, Gabi finished untying her knots and coiling her rope.

"Have fun?" Luke raised his eyebrows, obviously already knowing the answer.

"None." She shook her head. "Clearly."

"Want to help me get this stuff put away in the shed?" Again with the eyebrows. "Girls will be busy for a bit."

Gabi felt her cheeks flush, so she turned to grab a few ropes before he could see how easily she blushed.

"You know what I love?" His voice was low and close to her ear, and shivers enveloped her whole body as he spoke.

She swallowed nervously. "What?"

"I love that your face doesn't let you hide your feelings. You're like an open book, Gabriela."

"That is not at all comforting." She stepped away from him. "Has no one ever told you that a woman prefers to be a mystery?"

He shook his head. "Mystery is overrated. I like you just the way you are." He leaned toward her, and she automatically closed her eyes, already longing for his kiss.

But just then, a shriek from the dining hall had Gabi springing away from him and sprinting up the hill, Luke hot on her heels. When they banged open the screen door, they stopped fast.

First they saw the girls huddled together on top of a table.

Then they saw the bear cub.

Chapter 23

"Luke?" Gabi's voice was low and panicky as he pushed her behind him and scanned the room. The cub was up on the service counter, but he couldn't see a mama bear. With all of the screaming they'd just heard, he'd find it hard to believe she was still in the building, but unfortunately, he found it *harder* to believe she'd have left her cub behind.

"There's a tranquilizer gun in the admin cottage." He spoke in a low murmur to Gabi, whose eyes were wide as she looked from the cub to the girls and back again. "Go get it in case we need it."

"I can't leave them," she whispered back.

"You have to." He sidled by her, opening the door. "Go. I'll take care of them."

"Oh, God." She whimpered as she backed out the door, then sprinted toward Oliver's office. Luke watched her go, then turned to Piper and the girls.

"Okay, ladies." He spoke in a quiet voice, not looking at the bear cub. "Step down backwards and back toward me slowly. Don't look at the bear, and don't make any sudden movements."

The girls stayed frozen on top of the table, apparently under some delusion they were safer there. He sighed.

Maybe later, they'd have a little talk about how high bears could climb.

"I don't know where mama bear is, girls, and I don't want to find out. We need to get out of here in case she's still here."

He wished he could see into the kitchen, but the half-wall service area was blocking his vision. He'd seen this particular mama and her cub a couple of times this summer, but never this close to camp. And *never* inside a building.

He scanned the windows, looking for dark fur moving in the trees. If she wasn't in the dining hall, then he was damn sure she wasn't far away. At this moment, he didn't know if it was safer to have the girls stay inside or send them out.

Just as Gabi came flying up the steps carrying the gun, there was a tremendous crash in the kitchen, and the question was answered. He took the gun and cocked it, aiming toward the noise. He was trained to use it, but damn, he'd never wanted to.

Not moving his arms, he motioned with his chin for the girls to head for the door behind him.

"Now. Go. Head for Oliver's office and stay there until I come get you."

They stayed frozen.

"Go!"

Finally, logic seemed to overcome terror, and they eased down from the table and backed out the door, taking off at a dead run for the admin cottage once they were clear of the steps. Luke let his eyes bounce from the cub to the cottage until he was sure everyone was inside.

"Gabi. You, too. Go. Mama bear's in the kitchen. This might not be pretty."

"I can't leave."

"Why not?"

"Because I'm scared of papa bear."

Luke almost chuckled, but then realized she was serious. She had no idea how the whole bear thing worked—no idea that papa was probably nowhere close to here.

"There's no male. Just these two."

"So he's not sitting by the kitchen door, sharpening his claws in preparation for a nice, juicy housemother?"

"No. But once mama bear gets done pilfering the kitchen and decides to make a break for the woods, I don't know which way she'll go. I'd prefer you're not between her and an exit, okay?"

Gabi slid farther behind him. "Luke? Remember when you showed us those claw marks on that first hike?"

"Yep."

"I really hoped you were joking."

"Gabi? *Now* can we go back to Briarwood?" Eve whispered as they crowded to look out the admin cottage windows. "Pretty sure our parents didn't okay *this*."

Gabi didn't answer, her eyes trained on the dining hall. Luke was still in there, and Oliver had left the cottage with two pistols. "One shoots blanks," he'd said as he sidled out the door. "Just to scare them away."

Piper squinted. "See anything come out yet?"

They both jumped as they heard a shot, and then two bundles of fur bounded out the kitchen door, headed for the woods at a dead run.

Waverly closed her eyes, huddled in the corner. "Can't believe we saw a bear. Can't believe we have bears. Can't believe Pritch-bitch wants us to get eaten by bears."

Her words somehow broke the tension inside the cottage, and one by one, the girls started giggling. Gabi resisted joining in, but when even Sam fell victim to the contagious laughter, she felt herself give in as well. A minute later, when Luke showed up at the door, he looked from one to another of them, shaking his head.

"What in the world is so funny?"

"Bears." Sam snorted, then laughed harder.

Luke's eyes widened as he looked at Gabi, who put her hand over her mouth, clamping her lips shut. "Sorry. Just a little nervous terror here."

"That's a big mama bear. Glad none of you went in the *back* door." He leaned against the doorjamb, scanning all of them again. "Speaking of doors, there is an *unholy* mess in that kitchen, and the *reason* there's an unholy mess is because *someone* left the door unlocked. I'm gonna let you guys figure out who that someone was, and then that person can get busy with a broom."

The girls looked at each other. "Wasn't me," claimed Madison.

"Me, neither," said Waverly.

"Not me." Eve shook her head.

"Definitely not me." Sam smiled. "I was in a tree."

"Oh, no." Piper's eyes widened as she looked at Gabi. And in that moment, Gabi pictured dropping a potato peeler to go see what the laughter was about outside the dining hall. She cringed as she looked at Luke.

"It was us."

"You?" His eyes went wide.

Piper raised her hand. "Us. Crap. Sorry, Luke. I never thought—I mean, we were right there behind the admin cottage. That's pretty bold, isn't it? For them to come in when we were so close?"

"Yeah, it is. They're getting bolder all the time. I don't like it." He sighed. "Really? You two?"

"Sorry." Both Piper and Gabi spoke at the same time. Then Gabi stood up from the desk where she'd been leaning. "I'll get it all cleaned up. And I'll pay for whatever damage they caused. I'm so sorry, Luke. I just didn't think."

She could feel the girls' eyes bouncing between her and Luke, wondering how he was going to react. Sam's arms crept across her stomach, while Eve stepped back, and Gabi swore internally. If he got angry right now . . . if he made these two girls feel scared of *him* in addition to the damn bears, whatever fledgling feelings she had for him were going right out the window.

But instead of getting mad, he smiled. And then he laughed, and she saw the girls eyeing each other like they weren't sure what to think.

"Well, girls. Looks like Piper and Gabi have some work to do, unless anyone here feels like chipping in to help." He raised his eyebrows. "I might be able to make it worth your while."

Madison looked around. "No offense, Luke, but I'm pretty sure there isn't enough money in the world to make me want to clean up bear slobber."

"I'm not talking about money," he said, holding up six tickets like they were million-dollar lottery winners.

The girls perked up immediately. "What are those for?" Sam asked.

"Snowflake Village. It's a theme park just a couple of miles away. My friends run the place, and they dropped off some tickets in case I thought you all deserved an evening away from our little paradise here."

Eve's eyes narrowed like she didn't quite trust him. "What *kind* of theme park?"

"The kind with rides and bad-for-you food and Christmas music piped in 365 days a year."

"Good rides?" Sam piped up. "Or little-kid ones?"

"Both." He smiled. "So if you're hankering for a tea-cup or merry-go-round, Sam, you're all set."

"Very funny."

"You asked." He put the tickets back in his pocket. "So what do you think? Evening at Snowflake Village worth a little extra elbow grease?"

The girls looked at each other like it still might turn out to be a trick, then seemed to decide it was worth the risk to find out. Sam grabbed for the door handle.

"Come on, minions," she ordered. "Let's do this, so we can actually leave this joint."

As the girls headed out the door, Luke moved to stand closer to Gabi, making her feel torn between backing up from his heat . . . or melting into it.

"Just a quick question?" Gabi put up a finger as she reached for a roll of paper towels in the supply closet. "How likely is it that mama bear and baby bear will make another appearance?"

He raised an eyebrow. "You want the comforting answer? Or the truth?"

Two hours later, Luke and Gabi were strolling through the courtyard of Snowflake Village, which was ablaze with thousands of tiny white lights strung from tree to tree. Sunset was still a long way off, but under the tinkling music of the rides and the speakers high in the pines, Luke could hear peepers and tree frogs warming up for their nightly chorus.

It had taken the girls a remarkably short time to put the kitchen back in order, most especially because Gabi and Piper had hardly let them do any of the work. When he'd argued, they'd both pointed to the door.

"We caused this," Piper'd said.

"We'll clean it up." Gabi'd finished.

But now they were here, and he'd finally convinced Gabi to let the girls go off exploring on their own, pretty sure there'd be little risk of them heading for the hills. Ethan, Molly, and Josie ran a fun, but tight, ship here at Snowflake Village, and if any of the girls tried to make an escape, the security guys would alert Ethan before they got even ten feet from the park's borders.

"Thanks for returning the van battery." Gabi leaned into him slightly, and he fought the urge to slide his arm across her shoulders in a possessive move he had no idea how she'd react to. "And for driving us into town. You're right—I don't think my driver's license covers the skill it takes to get the van around that curve by the river."

"The battery return is just temporary. I figured you could all use something to think about besides bears, but I'm still under orders to keep you under lock and key, don't forget."

"Oh, I couldn't if I wanted to." She rolled her eyes. "This place smells ridiculously good, by the way. I haven't been to an amusement park in—well, actually, you know what? I don't think I've *ever* been to one."

"How is that possible?" He knew *he'd* never been to one as a kid, but as a foster kid bouncing around from one poverty-stricken family to another—until the last one, that is—that was no surprise.

She shrugged. "It just wasn't . . . done, I guess?"

"Because?" He braced for some sort of classist statement she wouldn't necessarily mean to make, then hated himself for doing so.

"I don't know. I think Mom was always afraid to go to one."

"Why?"

"Not sure." She shrugged. "Maybe she was afraid she'd actually enjoy it."

"Well, that *would* have been terrible." Before he could

think better of it, he took her hand. "But since she robbed you of the experience, apparently it falls to me to help you discover all the joys of the American theme park, Christmas edition."

Gabi laughed, and he was relieved that she didn't take back her hand. "Where should we start?"

"Fried dough," he said, without hesitation. "Because if you don't have fried dough with maple syrup before you leave this property, I'll have failed you miserably."

"Sounds delicious. What else?"

He squeezed her hand. "Onion rings, hot dogs, and a creemee, but not necessarily in that order. And rides. *All* the rides." He paused, putting up a finger. "On second thought, maybe rides *before* food, if you're a newbie at this."

She nodded. "I appreciate that." Then she pulled out a park map, pointing at the far northwest corner. "How about we start here and work our way back to the food? If you keep me busy enough, I won't have time to freak out about the bears coming back for a midnight snack."

Luke's mind immediately cycled through a *lot* of ways he could keep her busy for the next two hours, but he swallowed hard, pasting a smile on his face as they set off toward the log ride.

Half an hour later, a little breathless from the roller coaster, Luke handed Gabi into a sleigh, and they settled in for a ride around the park on raised rails. After covering at least a mile of pathways and five different rides already, Luke was ready for a break, and he'd always loved this ride. It was peaceful as it creaked along thirty feet above the park, winding in and out of the trees.

"Wow." Gabi peered over the side. "Coolest ride ever."

He smiled. "Better than the roller coaster?"

"Slower than the roller coaster." She held her stomach, grinning as she turned to him. "Which we definitely need to do again before we leave, even though I'm not sure it's a good idea at all."

Luke laughed. "I thought you were going to break my fingers on that last loop."

"Well, next time, I'll know it's coming."

"Hey, Gabi?"

"Yup?"

"I might be mistaken, but I think I've made a theme-park convert out of you in a half hour flat."

"Possibly true." She paused, and her face got serious. "But now we have a problem. We're just humming slowly along here, and I'm not fearing for my life . . . which makes me—you know—start thinking that when we head back to camp, I *will* be fearing for my life, and those of my students."

Luke nodded, not at all anxious to let her know how nervous *he* was about the bears making a return visit.

"We'll move you guys into the dining hall tonight."

"Where the bears already broke in?" Her eyes went wide.

"It's better than a tent. Oliver's reinforcing the doors while we're gone. There are plenty of other places they can find food more easily. They'll move on." She didn't look remotely reassured, so he added, "They probably already have."

"Can they get in the windows?"

"Nope. Too high off the ground. I'm sure it'll be fine. As long as we stay secured, she'll forget about the place eventually. Oliver's pistol should have scared her plenty, too."

"Are you going to leave me with *that* tonight?"

"No, but I'll let the dogs stay with you."

Her eyebrows went up as her jaw dropped. "You're

going to leave Puff-n-Fluff to protect us? At ten pounds of raging fury each?"

He laughed at the expression on her face. "You'd be surprised at the damage they can do."

"Luke, that bear's *ears* are bigger than your little cuties."

"Are you insulting my dogs?"

"No!" She laughed, and he realized he could quite happily listen to the sound of it all night long. "I love your dogs. I just don't know that they bring the right . . . skills to the job."

"They don't need to *eat* the bear. They just need to scare her away."

"And you think they can do that?"

"Yep." He looked over at her, and he could tell from her expression that she wasn't quite sure whether he was kidding. In her eyes, he could see humor, but it was clouded by real fear. "I'm sorry. I'm not trying to make light of the situation. Really not. But it's just the reality of where we are. Bears live here, too, and we can't leave snacks lying out for them and expect them not to take advantage of it. But the fact that one bear got in and made herself at home doesn't mean we're doomed. We'll be fine. We just need to be careful."

"Is it always like this, though? Don't you worry about the boys, usually? I can't believe none of them has ever snuck a chocolate bar into his backpack."

Luke shook his head. "No, it hasn't always been like this. These woods have a lot more people moving through them in the past three years since a couple of touring outfits opened up. They're doing a lot of marketing in NYC and Boston, and it's drawing a boatload of tourists who don't—I don't know—understand, I guess is the right word. Then there are the city folks who buy up wilderness parcels so they can cut down trees and build ugly monstrosities they call summer homes. The bears have less space, the humans give bears more access to food, and it all trains the bears to associate humans with free lunch. It's not good for anybody, most especially the bears."

"Do they ever get aggressive?"

"The tourists? Oh, definitely."

"Luke."

He winked. "The bears we have around here only get aggressive if you get between a mama and her cub. So don't do that."

"Not a problem. If you're looking for me for the rest of the summer, I will be in the admin cottage. With the doors firmly locked."

He smiled as they rounded a bend in the tracks, and sparkling water filled the space downhill through the trees. "And there's the view that might convince you never to leave Echo Lake."

"Ha. Us never leaving Echo Lake is probably your worst nightmare right now."

He shrugged slowly, realizing that her never leaving was the exact *opposite* of a nightmare right now. It was sobering at the same time as it left an unfamiliar zing traveling up his spine.

He smiled. "You never know. Maybe I'm coming around."

Chapter 24

They rode in silence for a couple of minutes as Luke watched Gabi take in the sights and sounds of the park below her. At one point, she spotted the girls, and she relaxed against him, as if putting her eyes on them had reassured her that they were indeed still roaming the park.

"So . . . now that I have you trapped up here . . ." He waggled his eyebrows, and she immediately blushed.

"In the scheme of opening lines, that one's kind of alarming, just so you know."

He smiled. "Sorry. I have no evil plans for you, I promise. It's just nice to have you all to myself for a few minutes."

"Yeah." She smiled up at him. "This is pretty okay."

"So I've been wondering something." He swallowed, half hating himself for asking the question that had been eating at him for days. On one hand, he really wanted to hear the answer. On the other, he feared he already knew what it was. "Where do you see yourself, say, in ten years?"

She pulled away from him, her face thoughtful. "That's kind of a big question. And . . . I don't know. I don't think I've ever gotten quite that far."

"What's your dream? Is that easier?"

She shook her head, smiling. "My dream. Hm." Then she took a deep breath and clasped her hands together. "Promise not to tell?"

"I promise."

"I want to be a ball girl for the Patriots."

He laughed out loud. "Come on. That was a serious question."

"And that was a serious answer."

"You want to be a ball girl."

"Yup." She looked very pleased with herself. "Now you. What's *your* dream, Luke?"

He took a deep breath, shaking his head. "Pretty sure I don't like how you play this game, sweetheart."

"I don't play games. You asked a question, and I answered it. What were you expecting me to say—initiate world peace or something?"

"Absolutely. Finding a cure for cancer was right up there, too."

"Good to know. I'll save that one for next time we play."

He reached out for her hand, and was relieved when she let him take it. "I'm serious, Gabriela. I want to know you better."

She looked into his eyes like she was trying to assess whether he actually meant it, and must have finally decided he did.

"Okay. Sorry. I just feel like . . . we barely know each other. It's kind of weird to head into superpersonal territory like hopes and dreams and all that."

"Should we stick with the speed-dating variety, then? I could ask you what your first pet's name was."

"I never had a pet, really."

"Not even a token designer dog?"

"No." She frowned, studying him for a long moment like she didn't appreciate the tone of his question. He didn't blame her, damn it all. Why had he asked that? "You?"

Ha. Right. A pet would have been tough to fit into the garbage bag he got to take when he changed foster homes.

"Not till I was an adult. Just Duke. And now—what did you call them? Puff-n-Fluff?"

She laughed. "We *have* to name those dogs. Why don't you ask the girls for help?"

"Because they'd suggest things like Justin and Selena, or Kim and Kanye, or some other sort of dorky social reference I'm too old to get, and then the dogs would be stuck."

"You don't place a lot of trust in my girls yet, do you?"

He raised his eyebrows. "Should I?"

Gabi sat back in the seat, studying him with that gaze that made him feel like she was peeling him back, layer by layer . . . but doing it so gently that it didn't hurt. "My turn for a question. What made you do this job, Luke? How did you decide this is where you belonged?"

He studied her right back, thoughts churning in his head. What should he tell her? What *could* he tell her? What would he tell her if he thought they had a chance for this relationship to go beyond a summer fling? What would he tell her . . . if it didn't?

He didn't know.

"I have a lot of reasons, Gabriela. We've got a broken system, and I have the power to try to fix it—at least my little piece of it. So that's what I do. The guys that come through Camp Echo aren't guys who are brought up thinking they have a lot going for them. Oliver and I? We think they do. So we try to help them get there."

She took a deep breath, tipping her head, still examining him. "Well, I haven't seen you work with your usual clientele, but if you're half as good with them as you are with my girls, then I bow to your talent."

"Oh, really?" He took in her cheeky smile and rolled his eyes.

"Seriously. I'd actually love to see you work with your normal crew. I think I could learn a ton from both you and Oliver."

Luke felt his heart sink at her words, because if all went as he and Oliver figured it was going to, then they'd probably already had their last summer as a team. He shook his head. Now was not the time or place.

He cleared his throat, emotion clogging it for a second. "Oliver's the best. Incomparable, actually. And he gives all the credit to his gut. If he thinks a kid deserves a chance, he does everything he can to get him that chance."

"How'd you ever meet him, anyway?"

Luke paused, looking into her eyes. Then he barreled forward before he could stop himself.

"I *was* one of those kids he decided deserved a chance."

"Let go, Eve." The next day, Luke stood at the bottom of a small rock face, belaying for Eve as she tried her first climb. Gabi stood five feet away, trying not to wring her hands too obviously. Luke had been convinced the girls were ready for this. Gabi was not.

They'd camped out in the dining hall last night, and even though Gabi'd known they were safe, she'd barely slept. Knowing Luke was just outside in a little pup tent hadn't helped, either. In fact, it'd just made things worse, because all she'd wanted to do was get up and go to him, bears be damned.

"What do you mean, let go?" Eve held on to the rock like it might stage an escape if she didn't keep her grip tight enough. "I thought the object was to stay *on* the rock?"

"It is. But it's important to feel what happens when you let go, too."

She looked down at him, over her shoulder. "No offense, Luke, but you said we were climbing, not splatting."

"There will be no splatting." He pointed to the rope, which was clipped securely to the harness he had on. "I've got you."

"Hey, Luke?" She turned back to the rock, but made absolutely no move to let go. "Pretty sure you still don't actually like us. Why would I trust you?"

Gabi saw him smile. "Good question. Two answers. One—you're growing on me, and two—I've had the opportunity to drop way more annoying kids off from a rock, and I've never given in to the urge. I think you're safe. Plus, our insurance would go through the roof."

"Very funny." Eve turned her head to look over the other shoulder. "Gabi?"

Luke raised his eyebrows, and she knew he was silently asking Gabi to support what he was doing here, even though he knew she wasn't completely on board with it. Gabi scanned the ropes, saw the tension in his wrists as he tried to play everything casual . . . saw the way he balanced his body so it was crazy-stable.

She had to trust him.

"It's okay, Eve. You need to let go. Do what Luke says."

Luke nodded at her. "Fall off the rock, Eve. Just let go with your fingers and fall back a little."

Gabi watched Eve's fingers tighten, then saw her take a couple of deep breaths. Then, like she knew she'd chicken out if she didn't go big, she pushed herself away from the rock. She let out a timid squeak as she found herself suddenly hanging in midair, but then looked down at Luke, who held her completely steady.

"I didn't fall."

He shrugged. "Nope."

"Huh." She looked over at Gabi and winked. "Maybe he *does* like us."

Luke laughed. "Don't push it. Get back on your rock."

Eve clambered back onto the rock face and found finger holds, and five minutes later, she'd reached the top of the fifteen-foot mini-cliff. She stood up, grinning, and Gabi had to laugh at the pride she saw on her face.

"I *own* this rock!" Eve shouted, and Luke nodded calmly, adjusting his grip on her rope.

"Yep. And now you get to come back down."

"Down?" Her grin faded. "But I—you never said we had to go back down. There's a perfectly good path right there. I can walk down to you guys."

"Remember when we did the rappelling yesterday off from the admin building roof?"

Gabi felt her stomach jump. When had he done *that*?

He looked up at Eve. "Come on down. Same as the building, just rock. Hold on to the rope, bounce on your toes, and I'll feed the rope out to you. Trust me."

Eve growled as she sat down and turned around to face the rock, fumbling with her rope. "You know what, Luke? I never hated those words before, but I sure do now."

Luke glanced at Gabi, smiling. "It's okay. You're not the only one."

"A-plus, Sam. You're doing it. You're totally doing it." That afternoon, Gabi heard Luke's voice as she looked up from the letter she'd been trying to compose to Laura

Beringer, the chairwoman of the Briarwood board. She'd been sitting in the dining hall for an hour now, searching for just the right combination of words—respectful, but pleading—that might make Laura change her mind about the future of Camp Echo . . . and in turn, lead the other board members to change theirs. So far, she had six crumpled pages at her feet, and she growled in frustration as she crumpled yet another one and stood up to walk to the window.

Luke had Sam in the water, floating on her back, and the girl wasn't flailing, or scared, or exhibiting any of the emotions Gabi would have expected. The puppies cavorted around her in the water, but even their splashing didn't seem to panic her.

"He's got her, Gabi." Oliver's soft voice came up behind her, and she looked back to smile at him. He pointed to the thinning hair on his head. "I got a lot of gray hairs over the years, but none of them came from him. You can trust him with your girls."

"I know." She nodded, but didn't uncross her arms.

As Gabi watched, Sam rolled over in the water, as graceless as a baby seal, but not slipping under. As Luke walked beside her, she dog-paddled to the end of the dock, then turned around and paddled back to where the water was up to her knees.

Gabi put her hand to her mouth as she felt tears in her eyes. She was—swimming! Clumsily and slowly, but . . . swimming! As she watched, Sam leaped out of the water and gave two giant fist pumps. "I totally rocked that, Luke."

"You totally did." He smiled, and Gabi melted. She'd never once seen Sam grin so widely, and her own chest ached with pride as she watched Sam do a little victory dance.

After they both toweled off, Luke started to walk

away from Sam, doing the forced-casual thing Gabi'd learned was sort of his MO. But Sam grabbed his arm before he took two steps.

"Luke?"

"Yeah, mermaid?"

Sam smiled. "Thanks for helping me."

"Eh, it was nothing." Luke shrugged. "You helped yourself. You had it in you all along. I just watched."

Oliver touched Gabi's shoulder as he turned to go. "Told you."

Gabi clasped her hands under her chin as she watched Sam hug Luke, then run up the beach, heading for the tent. Luke sat down on the dock, looking suddenly ragged, like he hadn't been nearly so convinced of her abilities as he'd let on.

As Gabi watched him brush the water out of his hair and close his eyes to the sun that bathed his body in a glorious light that made him look even more like an Adonis, she had a sudden, painful, beautiful realization.

She wanted him—wanted *all* of him—and it scared her to her very core.

Chapter 25

"That is not a word." Gabi took a sip of her beer and pointed to the Scrabble board later that night. "Define it."

It was eleven o'clock, the girls were long asleep in the dining hall, and she was sitting on Luke's porch with letter tiles in her lap. The bear hadn't made a reappearance since its kitchen foray, but they'd made a mutual decision to keep the girls behind locked doors until they were sure mama bear wasn't an issue. Luke had brought down the dogs again just as everyone was settling in for the night, and as much as Gabi knew the little puffballs wouldn't be able to defend anyone from more than a rogue mosquito, it was still comforting to know their little ears would warn them of danger.

But right now it was quiet except for the crickets and a pair of loons out on the lake. Luke had pulled out Scrabble after she'd admitted a weakness for men who played board games, and as they'd set up tiles, her zapping nerves had decreased to a low hum.

Luke raised his eyebrows. "Seriously? You're challenging me?"

"Absolutely. You feed me your favorite beer and give me the comfy chair, and then you do those eyes . . . and that half-smile thing. You think you're toying with me, but I'm onto you."

"That so?" His smile was lazy, inviting, oh-so-flipping-hot. "And what is it you think I might do if you let your guard down?"

She felt her face flame as possibilities flew through her mind. "Um, cheat?"

"I don't cheat."

"Okay. What . . . *would* you do?"

"I don't know." He studied her. "But has anyone ever told you you're cute when you're flustered?"

"No." She rolled her eyes. "And what makes you think I'm flustered?"

"You're blushing, which I find incredibly . . . cute. You're also cute when you're annoyed. Cute when you're downright mad. Cute when you're overthinking. Cute when you show up in the dining hall in the morning with one side of your hair all mashed down and the other side sticking out."

He laughed as she automatically reached for her head. "I'm not sure how you are when you're in your normal element, but I'm finding I like the out-of-her-element Gabriela. Like her a lot."

"Well, I could use a few more element-appropriate skills."

"I do kind of have those wrapped up." He winked, holding up a bruised thumb. "For instance, my skill with hammers."

"Well, you do have . . . *some* skills." She smiled. "Like, for instance, pancake making. You are excellent with the pancakes."

"Comforting." He sipped his beer. "Anything else?"

"Absolutely. You're aces with rope tying."

"Aces?" He smiled. "Seriously?"

She pointed to the Scrabble board. "And you can . . . spell. I assume. Not tonight, but usually."

"Vital life skill. Thank you." He nodded at the board. "And that is, too, a word."

She looked at his face, let her eyes trace his jawline, his lips, the eyes full of heat. Then she swallowed hard. "You wear a Red Sox T-shirt really, really well."

He tipped his head. "Well, there's a skill I never realized was a thing."

"Oh, it's a thing. It's most definitely a thing."

She pushed herself up, and like a hummingbird to sugar water, stepped toward his chair. "You also take *off* a Red Sox T-shirt really, really well."

"Is that so?" He set down his beer, full concentration on her.

"Yes. I might have maybe seen you do it once or twice. It might have been a problem."

He reached out one finger and slowly hooked the elastic waist of her skirt, pulling her ever so slightly toward him.

"What kind of a problem, Gabriela?"

She let him pull her, let herself fall slowly toward him as his other hand came up to caress her cheek.

"Um . . . the kind of problem that makes concentration a little challenging?" Her voice faded to a whisper as his fingertips touched her earlobe and she leaned her face into his hand.

"Sounds kind of serious."

"It—is."

"What should we do about it?" He slid his fingers ever so slowly along the waistband of her wispy skirt, and she took a sharp breath as he pulled her even closer. There was no way she'd be able to resist him tonight, even if she wanted to.

"I think . . . maybe we go inside?" Her voice was breathy, shaky as she swallowed.

He pulled back. "Is that what you want to do?"

"I—yes. No. Yes? I don't know?"

He paused, smiling again. "One thing I've never put you down for is indecisive, Gabriela." Then he kissed her softly, making her sigh quietly. "Easy question, sweetheart—do you want me? Because I have to tell you, there is nothing in the world I want more than you right now."

"Oh. God." Her words left her lips just as he kissed her again, then stood up, holding her hand firmly as he swung open the cabin door and led her into the warmly lit space.

Gabi smiled as she got her first glimpse of his home. Warm pine walls glowed in the low lamplight from two end tables, and a futon-style couch separated the living room from the kitchen area.

"Wow," she said, as she spun around slowly. "I love it. It's so rustic and charming and warm." She narrowed her eyes. "And neat. Are you always this tidy?"

"Depends. Is that a requirement on your perfect-man checklist?"

She laughed. "I don't have a checklist."

"You should. How will you ever know when you've found him?"

"I'm hoping my well-scarred gut, along with my brain, will help me out with that, thanks. And if I did have a checklist, tidiness wouldn't be on it. I'm too much of a slob to make that fair."

He reached out and braced his hands on her hips, making her shiver in anticipation. "All right. Let's make you a list. What *would* be on it?"

"Let's see." She looked up, pretending to ponder. "I'm really a tall-dark-and-handsome sort of girl, as cliché as that is."

He nodded, pointing at his hair. "I've got the tall and dark covered. You'll have to look elsewhere for the handsome part."

Gabi laughed, taking in his gorgeous eyes, the perfect five o'clock stubble, the mouth that promised to make tonight one she'd never forget.

"Yes, I've been meaning to talk to you about the homeliness thing."

He rolled his eyes. "What else would be on your list?"

"Really? We're doing this? You want me to draw a picture of my perfect man for you?"

"Yes. Because for some reason—and I'll be really clear here, this has never happened before—I feel like I need to know."

"Oh." Gabi bit her lip, feeling the weight of his words hit her way down low. A slow smile crept over her face. "Okay. I want a man who can make me take myself less seriously."

"Easy," he nodded. "What else?"

"Someone who's dead sexy, but doesn't flaunt it."

"I'm a total nerd. Got that one covered."

She laughed. "Someone who's not afraid to fight coons and skunks and bears, should the need arise."

"Hm." He tipped his head thoughtfully. "Gonna be hard to find one of those outside this general area."

"Someone willing to share his secret stash of coffee, even though I drink more than the average air traffic controller."

"You *do* drink a lot of coffee."

"I do." She nodded, pausing. "But you know what's really tops on the list, if—you know—there was a list?"

"I'm dying to know."

She took a deep breath. "I need somebody who can sweep me off my proverbial feet and make me feel like . . . the only person in the world. I need the guy who'll swoop in when things are at their worst, kiss me silly, and make me feel like together, we can face anything. I need the guy who isn't afraid to be romantic and sweet and self-deprecating, all while he rocks a sexy smile and a deadly five o'clock shadow." She put up a finger. "The stubble thing's a new addition, by the way. Never liked that before."

"Honored." He smiled, but didn't say more.

"This is totally ridiculous, and you can freely say so, because I'm already admitting it . . . but I want the rom-com ending, Luke. I want to take the journey and earn my happy ending, but I *want* that happy ending, and I'd prefer to find it before I'm a million years old."

Oh, God. Had she just said that? Had she just practically set her ticking clock right on the table beside them like a huge flipping red flag? Had she even known she was *harboring* the damn clock?

"Sorry." She started to pull back, knowing she'd just handed him the nails to the coffin of this fledgling relationship, such as it was. "That was *way* too much information."

He smiled softly, reaching one hand up to slide it along her jaw while the other arm pulled her closer.

"It was definitely a lot of information. But it wasn't the kind that scares me."

"Sure."

"I'm serious." He propped up her chin, forcing her to look into his eyes. "It might have, were you another woman, another place, another time . . . but . . . it doesn't." His eyes crinkled at the corners as he searched her face. "It really just . . . doesn't."

And then his lips were on hers, and his arms were around her, pulling her close—but not nearly close enough—and she heard herself whimper as his hands slid downward and cupped her rear, lifting her against his body.

He walked them through a wide pine door into his bedroom, and before she had time to do more than register soft lights and that soapy, woodsy smell that was so him, he was lowering her gently onto the bed.

His tongue tangled with hers as he slid his hands under her shirt, groaning when he popped the buttons through their holes and found her lacy bra underneath.

"So beautiful," he whispered as he pulled upward, tracing his fingers along the seams, then unhooking the front clasp and letting the cups slide slowly apart. She saw his pupils darken as he looked at her, as he took her in his hands, stroking his thumbs across her nipples.

And then he kissed her, harder this time, more insistent, before letting his lips trail down her neck, along her collarbone, to where his fingers played. She moaned as his lips touched her most sensitive spots, and she fisted her hands in his hair as he sucked gently, then moved to the other side, torturing her with his tongue.

Her body arched, aching for more, and his answered. He slid his hands up her thighs, under her silky skirt, meeting the elastic of her panties, and he groaned as he traced the lacy edges with his fingertips. She squirmed as he caressed her through the silk, then reached for him as he slid them slowly down her legs.

"Not yet, sweetheart," he said, his voice low and almost playful. He pulled her gently toward the edge of the bed, using warm, sure hands to part her legs as he kneeled on the carpet. "Not yet."

Chapter 26

Early the next afternoon, Gabi stood in the window of the dining hall, watching a completely chaotic scene unfold on the water as she tried to keep her eyes open. Luke had the girls out in kayaks, but this time, they were playing a game of bumper boats that had them spinning and crashing and flipping over.

She'd known him long enough to know that the game had purpose, and she recognized that every time they got dumped, they got practice getting out of the kayaks, flipping them back over, and getting back in, but there were moments when she wished they were maybe at a municipal pool, with six lifeguards at the ready. As deliciously tired as she was, there was no way *she'd* be able to stage a rescue this afternoon.

"Ah. Bumper boats." Piper came up next to her. "My favorite. Girls, too, it sounds like."

Gabi nodded. "Pretty sure they haven't laughed this hard since they got here."

"He knows his stuff, that's for sure."

"I know. But I have to say—I wish his *stuff* could be a little less dangerous at times."

"You know they're in, like, four feet of water, right? And have life jackets on?"

"Yes, but every time one of those boats flips, my whole stomach does, too. What if somebody gets stuck upside down?"

"Then he'll help her." Piper shrugged. "You know, if I didn't know better, I'd guess you actually love these girls just a little."

"Don't tell them. It'll weaken my authority."

Piper smiled back. "How about Luke? Falling for *him* yet? For real?"

"Nope. He's awful. Ugly, too, as I'm sure you've noticed."

Piper laughed out loud. "I'll take that as a yes."

"Don't tell him, either."

Oh, she was falling for him, all right. Hook, line, sinker, and the whole damn fishing boat. After what she could only describe as a magical night in his cabin—in his *bed*—she'd woken at dawn, and since then, had been cycling the night through her head on high speed, then slo-mo.

He'd been generous. He'd been impossibly sweet. He'd been more than impossibly hot, and had she mentioned generous?

God, her body shivered, just thinking of the things he'd done with his hands, his lips, his tongue.

But this morning, in the light of day, she'd already started to freak out about the entire thing, because magic was awesome, but it wasn't reality. And the reality was that their time together was temporary, though they'd both claimed to each other that they didn't *do* temporary. So getting in deep with this man who made every cell in her body vibrate for him? It was bound to be a disaster in the end, when they both came to their senses.

She really hated how logic and reality bumped off fantasy rom-com every time.

"Huh." Piper sipped her lemonade. "Not sure if

you've noticed that your face is a complete giveaway, but given the shade of pink you just turned, I'm pretty much dead sure you guys have done the deed."

"Piper!"

"Busted. When did it happen?"

Gabi didn't answer, which only made Piper laugh again. "Rocked your world, didn't he?"

Gabi sighed. There was no way she was going to avoid this conversation, apparently. "Yes. He did. And I have absolutely no idea what to do about it."

Piper shrugged. "Well, if it was me, I guess I'd probably have him do it again." She raised her eyebrows. "But maybe I'm less complicated than you."

"I doubt it."

"So what's the problem? You like him, he likes you, the sex was out of this world, and he's the best catch in the land now that Noah's officially off the market." She winked. "Seems like a no-brainer to me."

"Well, there's the small matter of me leaving in a couple of weeks—I mean, for one thing." Gabi put up her hands like it was a rather obvious issue.

"Ah. The old summer-romance problem."

"I had no intention of *having* a summer romance. Or *any* romance." Gabi shook her head. "I didn't mean for this to happen."

"So now you're not talking to him? Because that's logical and everything?"

"I'm not . . . not talking to him." Gabi cringed, knowing full well she'd been avoiding him all day.

Piper nodded slowly, her eyes on the water. "You want some advice?"

"Depends what it is."

"Stop being afraid of Luke. He's a good guy. A really, really good guy." Piper's voice got serious. "He doesn't sleep with people, Gabi. It's like some kind of ironclad code with him. He'll flirt and he'll kiss and he'll rock the dinner-and-a-movie scene with the best of them, but he doesn't bring anyone home. Ever."

"So you did the deed, and now she won't talk to you?" Noah took a slug of his beer later that night. "That's gotta hurt."

"Funny." Luke rolled his eyes. "Rack 'em."

Desperate to get away from camp, where Gabriela seemed to be doing everything possible to avoid him, Luke had dragged Noah out for a couple of games of pool at Cooper's new place downtown. The bar area up front was hopping, but tonight, the pool tables out back were quiet. Everybody was out on the riverside patio drinking and flirting and making plans to hook up for the night.

Or maybe they were just drinking. In his frustrated state, he could be superimposing the rest.

Noah got the balls corralled in the triangle, then lifted it and hung it on the wall as Luke lined up his first shot.

Noah tapped on the table. "Just a quick question for you."

Luke closed his eyes, hands on the cue stick. "Does it have something to do with why I pick rich women who have no intention of giving up their golden palaces to be with me? Because if you were going to ask *that* question, I might have to hurt you."

"Nope. That one didn't enter my mind."

Luke took his shot. Missed. "So what's your question?"

"Give me a minute." Noah ducked out of range. "I have to think of another one."

Luke rolled his eyes. "I think she's just scared."

"Why?"

"I don't know." Luke took a deep breath. "I have a feeling this was not in the playbook for her summer."

"And she's a woman who really likes a playbook?"

"Pretty sure, yes." He took a slug of his own beer while Noah lined up a shot. "Also pretty sure she realized she's on borrowed time, and then she's outta here. I imagine she's not the type who likes to leave strings hanging behind her."

"Huh." Noah took his shot. Nailed it, as usual. Playing pool in bars around the world for almost ten years had given him an unfair advantage. "So what are you going to do about it?"

"Do about what?" Piper sidled over, picking up a cue stick. "Can I play the winner?"

Noah smiled. "No. You clean my clock every time. Play Luke after I smoke him."

"Oh, no way." Luke shook his head. "She's all yours."

"Damn right." Noah slung an arm around Piper's shoulders, kissing her soundly on the lips.

Luke looked away. Just last night he'd shared the same sort of kiss with Gabriela, only—if he had to be honest—it wasn't the same at all. Noah and Piper's relationship was rock solid, born of long years loving each other from afar, then finally getting smart and finding each other again.

Luke and Gabriela's relationship, on the other hand, was—well, what was it, really? Anything? A series of hot kisses that had led to the most passionate night of his life, yes, but a relationship? Even he wasn't stupid enough to believe one night gave him any right to feel like he was due a commitment. Maybe *he* didn't go in lightly, but he guessed maybe he didn't know Gabriela enough to know whether *she* did.

He sighed. Oh, who was he kidding? He knew damn

well she didn't, either . . . which was why the poor woman was suddenly running scared.

"So what were you talking about when I barged in?" Piper backed away from Noah and lifted her beer to her lips.

"Nothing," Luke replied.

"Gabi," Noah said at the same time.

"Oh, really?" Piper raised her eyebrows. "And how's it going with her?"

Luke rolled his eyes. "Like you don't already know. I saw you two talking up in the dining hall this morning. I'm sure she told you everything."

"Because we're girls and that's what we do, you mean?" Piper's eyebrows went even higher. "Maybe we were talking about the latest in aerospace-engineering research, or that new drug for multiple sclerosis, or—heck, I don't know—weighing the international-relations records of the presidential candidates."

Luke laughed. "Fine. Sorry. Just thought *maybe* you were talking about . . . things."

Piper took another sip. "Well, we were. But we *could* have been talking about all that other stuff."

"Of course."

Noah finished his shot. "So did she happen to talk about why she slept with Luke, but now won't talk to him?"

She shook her head. "No-o, not really."

Luke shot, missed, swore. "Jesus, Piper. I have no idea what happened, and every time I tried to get near her today, she invented some reason to be elsewhere. I know it was good—*we* were good. I know it's not that. But I don't know *what* it is, and it's driving me nuts."

Piper scanned his face, a tiny smile bending the corners of her mouth. "Huh."

"Don't *huh* me, Piper."

She elbowed Noah. "You see what I'm seeing, right?"

"Oh, hell, yeah." Noah grinned.

Luke looked from one of them to the other. "You know, sometimes I hate you both."

"I think she's scared, Luke." Piper bit her bottom lip. "And I think she's not sure what to do about it."

"Want some advice?" Noah asked.

"From you? Nope."

Noah laughed. "Sure you do. Here's what I'd do if I were you."

"Oh, boy." Luke picked up his cue and set it on its end.

"Do you happen to remember a guy who came around a couple of years ago, trying not to stay? And then he reconnected with this fireball Italian girl and couldn't get her out of his head? And *then* he moved here, even though it meant giving up his entire career and everything he knew?"

Piper elbowed Noah. "Hey."

Luke shook his head again, rolling his eyes. "Doesn't sound familiar."

"Uh-huh." Noah thwacked him on the back of the head. "Well, that's my advice."

"That was *not* advice."

"Sure it was." Noah lined up a shot, sank three balls, and set his cue stick down. "Just do what Piper did to me. Make her want to stay, Luke. Simple."

Chapter 27

Simple, his ass. Later that night, Luke closed the truck door as quietly as possible, not wanting to disturb Gabi and the girls. In truth, he *really* wanted to disturb her. He wanted to march into the dining hall, take her by the hand, and pull her to his cabin so he could show her that last night had meant more than she could possibly believe.

But that wouldn't be fair. The least he could do was wait till morning, when both of them would have had a night's sleep and clear heads to work with. With a sigh, he set off up the pathway toward his cabin, but just as he reached the admin cottage, he pulled up short.

Ah, hell. Gabriela was sitting in an Adirondack chair, her knees pulled up to her chest, staring out at the moonlit lake. He looked up the pathway toward the dining hall where the girls were hopefully sleeping, and nobody was stirring. Was Gabi having trouble sleeping?

Was it because of him?

He took a moment to watch her, and wished he didn't ache so badly to touch her. She had on his Red Sox T-shirt and her own yoga pants, and her hair was pulled up into a ponytail that made her look like she was barely twenty. Her feet were bare, flip-flops on the sand, and in the moonlight, her face looked dreamy and tired and—he squinted to see better—teary.

Was *that* because of him?

He stood still for a long minute, debating whether to let her know he was there. Clearly, she thought she was having a private moment out here on the beach. But before he could convince himself to make the intelligent decision and go back to his cabin, his feet were on the move, and they were heading directly for Gabriela. When he was about ten feet away, he saw her shoulders tense as she heard him coming, but she didn't turn around.

After a beat, she said, "I wondered if you were going to stop lurking in the shadows and come talk to me."

He chuckled. This was a good sign—her actually talking to him. "I wasn't lurking. I don't lurk."

"Did you have a good evening in town?"

He stood a few feet away from her, not wanting to spook her. "It was . . . fine. Got my butt whipped at pool."

"Noah?"

"Piper, actually. But Noah, too." He shrugged. "I pretty much suck at pool."

She laughed softly. "Well, I guess it's good you have some fallback skills."

"Mind if I sit?" He pointed to the other chair.

"Sure." She nodded. "I was kind of hoping to talk to you, anyway, actually."

"Well, that's a relief." He smiled. "I wondered if we were going to get back to that part."

"I know. I'm . . . sorry."

"Are you okay?"

She sighed, looking back out at the lake, her eyebrows furrowed. "I'm not sure, really. I think . . . I think I kind of dove in the deep end last night, and it turns out . . .

I'm not so sure I'm all that good at swimming right now."

"What does *that* mean?"

Gabriela sighed. "I don't even know. I'm just . . . petrified that maybe I'm more in love with the idea of *being* in love than I am really *falling* in love." She shook her head. "That makes no sense. And also, it's the kind of statement that should make you run. Fast. Sorry."

His gut fell. *Shit.* "It makes *some* sense."

"I don't want to hurt you, Luke." She pulled her arms closer around her. "I'm just in this—I don't know—weird space. You start creeping toward thirty, and you go to five weddings every summer, and suddenly you feel like the happily-ever-after boat's leaving, and you're going to be doing a life sentence on a deserted island with your pile of romance novels and your ten yowling cats."

"Every woman's greatest fear?"

"You'd be surprised."

He paused. "I have a question for you, and you can answer it, or not. Your choice, but   a part of me needs to know." He ran a frustrated hand through his hair, not even sure he should put the question out there at this point. "And another part of me *doesn't* want to know."

She looked at him sidelong. "If it's about the sex, last night was hands down the best night of my life."

He half choked on a laugh. "Um, no. That wasn't it."

"Oh." Her face immediately went crimson. "Should have let you finish. Obviously."

"I just—I can't help but wonder if it's *me* who has you running scared? Or if someone who came before me set you up to—I don't know—not trust that last night was . . . real." He put up his hands. "No pressure to answer, because that's *way* personal, but everything was . . . amazing, and then? I feel like you're sort of slamming the door before we even have a chance to figure out what we've got here."

"I know, and I'm so sorry." She blew a slow breath through her lips, but didn't look at him. "I probably should have warned you I'm an over-analyzer. Also, I'm pretty good at the whole pessimism thing. It's not healthy, but it's me."

"I imagine you have reasons. I mean, I can't pretend to know how you grew up, but—"

"Do you have any idea what my net worth is, Luke?"

He shook his head. *What?* "Of course not."

"I have three hundred dollars in the bank, Luke. Not three hundred thousand, not three hundred million. Three hundred dollars." She raised her eyebrows. "How I grew up is moot."

"No trust fund? No pot of gold?" Luke smiled, almost embarrassed by how happy it made him that Gabriela *didn't* come with either of those.

"Were you hoping?" Her eyebrows arched menacingly, making him laugh.

"Absolutely not. I'd be far more thrilled to know you were destitute."

"Well, good news. I'm pretty darn close. I had a trust fund, and it was a really nice one, but it . . . went away."

"What happened?"

She paused. "Long story. I chose integrity and friendship over family, and . . . family didn't like that choice. So, that was the end of the O'Brien Fund for me. In the end, kissing that money good-bye was probably the best thing that's ever happened to me. Made me have to grow up and be an adult. But at least I got to do it on my own terms."

"Wow."

She tossed a pebble toward the water. "My last boyfriend did not say *wow*. He tried to convince me that maybe it wasn't too late to make good with my family, see if I could get back into their good graces." She shivered. "But by that time, I'd kind of embraced the whole black-sheep thing. He wasn't amused. I'm pretty sure he had plans for my money already. And oddly enough, he broke up with me exactly one week after he realized I was not, in fact, the O'Brien heiress. Shocker."

Luke laughed. He couldn't help it. Gabriela as a black sheep was just such a funny image, when he sat looking at the most beautiful woman he'd ever met.

"It's not funny."

"It's *sort* of funny." He touched her arm. "I mean, come on. Idiot whoever-he-is thinks he's found the proverbial pot of gold, and then—dum-dum-*dum*—learns she's no empty-headed glamour girl with a loaded bank account, so he ditches her and goes looking for a new heiress? It's like a rom-com in the making."

"It's so not! Have you ever *seen* a rom-com? There's romance . . . and comedy!"

"Well, here's the thing." He raised his eyebrows. "That's the part that comes *next*. First you have to have the disastrous setup so the heroine can truly appreciate the *real* hero when he comes along."

"Ah, is that how it goes?"

Luke saw a smile start to take over her face, so he kept rolling. "Absolutely."

"So what happens next?"

"Well"—he pretended to ponder—"generally, we'd see a few minutes of clips that give a glimpse into her life. The audience would fall in love with her quirky smile and her terrible taste in flip-flops, for instance."

Gabriela looked down at her sandals, then narrowed her eyes at him, but didn't speak.

"We'd see her at work, maybe, doing good things for

needy people—like, say, obnoxious teenaged girls at a private school, though that one's kind of a cliché."

"Of course. So overdone."

"Shh."

"Sorry." She smiled, waving her hand. "Woman dumped, terrible flip-flops, obnoxious teens. Carry on."

He mock sighed. "Thank you. So *then,* something happens to throw this heroine off the path she thought she was on, and ka-bam. She ends up somewhere she never expected to be."

"Like, say, a summer camp for boys? Which has no boys? Or . . . camp?"

"Exactly. But it's all okay, because in the next scene, she meets the incredibly hot, also-not-rich, fantasy-inducing camp handyman-slash-director." He waggled his eyebrows. "You follow me?"

She laughed. "It's a complex plot."

"So then they fall in love, she moves to Echo Lake—I mean, the hero's hometown—and they live happily ever after."

"Ah." Her smiled faded. "Just like that, huh?"

"Well, there's usually the part where all seems lost, and the audience is supposed to believe they'll never, ever find their way back to each other, but somehow, it always works out. But we could totally skip that part. It's super-cheesy anyway."

She smiled again. "How many of these have you watched? You've got the formula down pretty well."

"Ten." He rolled his eyes. "Piper, Josie, and Molly made all of us guys do a chick-flick marathon one weekend last winter when we got snowed in."

"Pure hell?"

"Really was."

Gabriela was silent for a long moment. "Are you ever tempted to do something different, Luke?"

He looked at her, but in her face, couldn't read why she was asking the question, or what answer she hoped to hear. Was she hoping for verification that his commitment here at Camp Echo was ironclad? Was she hoping to hear that he'd ditch it all in a second for the right woman? He really didn't know, but he suspected she wouldn't believe the latter, even if it was true.

Which it wasn't . . . he didn't think.

"No, Gabriela. I'm not tempted to do anything different. Oliver's handing his legacy over to me, and I don't take that lightly. What Briarwood will do with this property is something I can't predict right now. But I've got a job to do, and it's a job I'm passionate about. There's nothing I'd rather be doing."

She nodded slowly. "I think that's very admirable."

"But?"

"No but." She shook her head.

"What about you?" He braced himself for her answer. What if she, too, said she'd never leave *her* current position? Where would that leave them . . . if there was to even *be* a them?

She shook her head again. "I don't know. Sometimes I feel like I'm banging my head against ivy-covered walls wherever I go. The endowment fund at Briarwood is embarrassing. There's so much money sitting there earning *more* money, and it makes me crazy. We could be educating *fifty* needy kids a year on that money."

She sighed. "I don't know. I'm just starting to wonder if I'm maybe . . . on the wrong path altogether. Maybe that's why I'm so impressed that you seem to have figured it out. I'm trying, but no matter where I turn, Briarwood is still an insular, connected place . . . and they're *really* not interested in making sure the other ninety-nine percent of the population breaks into their club. It makes me really angry, to tell you the truth. I haven't even been battling it for long, in the scheme of things, but in three years of trying to funnel money to kids who really, actually need it, I've managed a grand total of two scholarships. Two."

Luke put his hand on her arm. "You're doing the right thing, Gabriela, by trying. That's all you can do sometimes."

"Luke?" She took his hand, her voice soft, but didn't look at him. "You said Oliver decided you were a kid worth helping, way back when. Were you—"

"In the system? Yeah. Ten homes in seven years. And it was no more fun than anybody makes out. I know there are probably hordes of foster parents who are in it for the good of children, and who do a bang-up job raising them." He shook his head. "But I didn't have the opportunity to meet those types in my travels."

"I'm so sorry."

He took a deep breath, expecting the slicing pain that pity usually invoked, but to his surprise, it didn't happen. Maybe because what he saw in Gabriela's eyes was sadness, not pity.

"How old were you when you met Oliver?"

"Sixteen. Old enough to be deemed a lost cause by a whole hell of a lot of people, and I'd given them plenty of reasons to think so. He just didn't put up with the bullshit, and he saw through all of the posturing. He dragged me here to Camp Echo, put me to work, got me through school, and I'll be grateful to him till my dying day."

She smiled sadly. "I want to be Oliver when I grow up."

"Well, you've got a pretty good start, don't you think? You can't boil the ocean, Gabriela. You have to start somewhere, right?"

"I know. I just wish there was a way to do . . . more."

He nodded slowly. "Are you committed to staying at Briarwood?" He half held his breath for her answer, hating himself for hoping it might be no.

She tipped her head, frowning. "I think—it's all I know, really. I grew up there, I taught there, and now I'm a . . . whatever I am. And someday I could move into a position where I could actually enact some change, you know?"

"Ever think you could make a bigger impact with needier kids?"

"Yes and no. Maybe." She sighed. "But you know what? My kids are just as needy—just in a different way."

"I know."

"My parents shipped me off to my first boarding school in kindergarten, Luke. I didn't even know they *made* boarding schools for kids that young."

"Are you serious?"

She nodded. "I went home for Christmas, and the first summer. After that, I was at camps every summer. When I was ten, I scratched a line in my bed for each day I saw my parents that whole year. Guess how many lines I ended up with?"

"Twelve." Once a month, he figured. A terrible figure, but he was guessing low on purpose.

"Two."

His eyes widened. "No way."

She nodded. "Not kidding. Dad's secretary dropped me off at Briarwood in August, and Mom's secretary picked me up in June and brought me to camp. I saw them on Christmas Eve and Christmas Day. The day after Christmas, they left for a cruise, and I stayed home with the nanny until it was time to come back to Briarwood."

"Wow, I'm really sorry, Gabriela. I had no idea."

Luke felt guilty for assuming her life had been just one candy-coated, gold-plated carnival ride up till now.

She shrugged. "It is what it is, right? It's not like I got dropped off on church steps in the dead of winter. I mean, I had everything I needed, and Briarwood's an excellent school. I turned out okay."

Luke looked out onto the dead-calm lake, lit by an almost-full moon. He had a feeling Gabriela could well use a distraction right now, and he had the perfect idea. "Hey. Feel like an adventure?"

Her eyebrows went upward. "What kind of adventure?"

"The kayaking-at-midnight-under-a-full-moon kind."

She pulled her knees closer to her body. "I don't know. I've never even been in a kayak in the daylight. And this lake is deep."

"Well, despite what you saw when the girls played bumper boats, it's actually not that easy to tip them over. Promise."

She glanced toward the dining hall. "I don't know, Luke. We shouldn't leave the girls."

"Oliver's right in his cabin. He'll hear anything that needs hearing, and the dogs are with them. The girls know to go to him if they can't find us, right?"

"Yes, but—"

He stood up and reached out a hand. "Come on, Gabriela. It'll be fun. Trust me."

He saw Gabriela glance down, just as she always did when he said those words. At the beginning of the summer, it had kind of amused him that she so obviously distrusted him.

But now? Now it hurt. And he needed to fix it.

Chapter 28

Half an hour later, Gabi paused her paddle and looked up at the sky, marveling at the thousands of stars sprinkled around the moon.

"Gorgeous, huh?" Luke's kayak slid up beside hers, bumping softly.

"Indescribable." She sighed. "I think we get so busy looking around that we forget to look up."

"That's why I love to teach the astronomy stuff. Kids eat it up. Even your jaded, we're way too old-for-this girls liked it the other night."

"Yeah, they did, actually. Of course, maybe they paid attention because they're plotting their escape, and you showed them how to navigate by the stars. Totally putting that on you if they bolt."

"Gotcha. But I'm pretty sure they aren't going anywhere. If I had to hazard a guess, I'd say they might actually even like it here now."

"Well, we *have* improved the facilities substantially."

He laughed. "Touché. True. You know, if I had to hazard *another* guess, I'd say you might kind of like it here, too."

"Oh, see, now you're pushing it." Gabi smiled as she dipped her paddle in the water and pushed smoothly away from him, knowing instinctively that he'd follow. She made quiet splashes on the water as her boat glided silently toward the tiny island he'd pointed out just offshore. Luke had been right. She loved it.

"You *don't* like it here?" He came up alongside her, just far enough away so that their paddles didn't clash.

"Well, there are *some* things I like about—here."

"The hot camp director, right? I mean, that one's totally obvious."

"Yes." She nodded. "Oliver is definitely dreamy."

Luke paused his paddle, then dipped it in the water with a twist of his wrist, sending droplets flying toward her.

She laughed and tried to do the same thing back at him, but only managed to get her boat tipping from side to side, so she grabbed the edges with her hands before she went completely over.

"Huh." Luke circled her playfully in his kayak. "Looks like somebody could have used a few more games of bumper boat."

"I didn't have *any* games of bumper boat! And don't you dare bump my boat." Gabi laughed as she tried to spin around fast enough to keep track of him as he paddled.

In the moonlight, he looked like a cross between an impish teenager . . . and a Greek god. His smile was pure playfulness, but his body? She ached to feel it against hers again.

"So." He finally stopped circling and paddled up beside her. "About that rom-com."

She smiled. "What *about* that rom-com?"

"I think you're officially at the part where it's okay to fall for the hot camp director." He put up a finger. "The one that's not Oliver."

Gabi laughed. "Sounds kind of dangerous."

Sounds incredibly dangerous. Hot, scary, awesomely dangerous.

"It could be—I'll give you that." He paddled slowly beside her. "There's the very real danger that we could fall madly in love and end up holed up in my cabin playing endless games of Scrabble."

She laughed out loud. "Scrabble?"

"Or variations on the game. I can be flexible if it's not your thing." He shrugged. "I have Monopoly."

Looking at his fake-earnest face, it was all Gabi could do not to kiss him right there in the middle of the lake.

"Luke, I'm pretty sure if I were to hole up in your cabin, Scrabble wouldn't be the first thing I'd be thinking of doing."

He stopped paddling. "What *would* be the first thing you'd want to do?"

Gabi started to fling another quip his way, but something made her stop. She knew *exactly* what she'd want to do, and it scared her silly at the same time it exhilarated her.

"I don't know, Luke."

He seemed to sense her pulling inside herself, because he set his paddle gently on her boat, pulling her closer.

"Do you need some help thinking of some ideas?"

"No-o. I'm having more trouble *not* constantly thinking of ideas."

"So why don't you look happier about it?"

"Because, Luke." She sighed. "It scares me."

"What part?"

"*All* the parts."

"Why?"

His voice was soft, and was she hearing pain because *she* was feeling it? Or because *he* was?

She took a deep breath and let it out slowly, unsure of how to express what she was feeling. Hell, she couldn't even figure *out* what she was feeling, let alone put it into words. How was she going to tell him what was going on in her head when it was so damn confusing even to her?

She had no idea.

"Luke, I—I kind of suck at this sort of thing."

He smiled. "I might beg to differ."

"That's because you barely know me."

"I think I know you better than you'd like to admit."

"That might be true. And just so you know, that doesn't make it less frightening."

Luke took her hand in his, and she was torn between chills and heat as his thumb stroked her fingers. "I'm not your ex. I'm not like anyone else you've ever been with. I guarantee that."

"I know you're not like—anyone else. I know that."

"So is it possible I might be worth a chance?"

She sighed. "Luke, this is what I do. I fall fast, I fall hard . . . but unfortunately, I also fall dumb. I have seriously flawed radar."

"Can I repeat the part about *I'm not like them*?"

"You can repeat it till you're blue in the face, but I'm well-conditioned at this point not to hear you. I know it's not fair. Believe me, Luke. I wish I wasn't this way. I so, so do, because none of it's fair to you. I never should have let things go as far as I did, but God, I just couldn't help it."

"And that should tell you something, shouldn't it? Like, maybe instead of trying to deliver cheesy breakup lines you don't really mean, you could maybe just let me kiss you right now?"

"Oh, definitely not."

He chuckled. "Because that would be awful?"

"Terrible. The worst."

He grinned and put a hand to his chest like she'd stabbed him. "I'm hurt."

"I just . . . can't, Luke. You deserve somebody who can go all in, and that's not me right now. There's just too much going on, and too much baggage that's not nearly far enough away in the rearview mirror. It wouldn't be fair to you. And seriously? We've only got two weeks left, and then I'm gone and you're here. There's no realistic way we can make it work."

She saw his jaw harden, and felt immediately guilty. Dammit, she didn't know *what* she was saying.

He looked at her, scanning her face, landing on her lips, her eyes, her hair . . . back to her lips.

"I'll tell you what," he finally said.

"What?" Her voice was a whisper.

"You kiss me once. Right here, right now, out on this lake in the moonlight . . . and *then* you tell me we can't make this work."

"No." Her voice shook as his thumb caressed the palm of her hand in slow, slow circles. "There will be no kissing."

"One kiss, Gabriela." He raised his eyebrows. "One kiss, and if after that kiss, you tell me you don't think we have something worth at least exploring here, then I will stop asking."

She tried not to look into his eyes, knowing how dangerous it was to do so. But even in the moonlight, their deep emerald green just made her want to melt, not paddle away from him.

And as if he sensed it, he reached up, using his fingers to trace her jaw, pulling her closer, closer . . . and then his lips were on hers, and she couldn't pull away.

Hours later, her kayak hit the sandy shore with a swoosh and a bump, and Gabi did her best to look remotely graceful pushing herself out of it. She was pretty sure she failed. Luke, on the other hand, popped out of his boat and into the shallow water without looking like he'd first had to speak firmly to *his* limbs about cooperating.

Once they'd pulled their boats up onto shore and slid their paddles into the rack, Luke turned to her, a lazy smile on his face. He put his arms around her, then turned her around and pulled her back against his body. With his chin resting on her head, he pointed toward Kizilla Mountain.

"Looks like you kept me up all night, sweetheart. Now we get to watch the sunrise."

Gabi sighed, sinking back against him, loving the way his body heated hers . . . loving the mixture of hard planes and taut muscle. If it weren't for the fact that four girls would be waking up within the next hour expecting to be entertained, she'd be perfectly happy to stay like this, with his arms wrapped around her, all day, reliving the hours they'd just spend paddling the perimeter of the lake, lost in conversation until he'd pointed at the Camp Echo dock light and her heart had sunk, realizing they were back . . . realizing that their magical, completely unexpected night had come to an end.

She smiled, exhausted but elated. Maybe they really *could* figure out how to make things work between them. Maybe, if they both wanted it badly enough. If they wanted each *other* enough.

She sighed happily. "I love the sunrise here."

"Oh, good. I'm putting that on the list."

"What list is that?"

"The list of all the reasons why you should eventually realize you actually want to live here in Echo Lake."

"Not that we're rushing things. At all."

"I said 'eventually.' That was my out."

She rolled her eyes.

"I see you rolling your eyes, missy." He squeezed her

ribs, making her laugh. "And less than an hour ago, you agreed to give us a chance."

"A chance is different from deciding to move here. Much, much different." She turned around in his arms, sliding her fingers up to trace his five o'clock shadow. "We barely know each other, Luke. That's our reality, whether you're in the mood to admit it or not."

His face went serious. "I know it is, Gabriela. I know it is, and yet somehow I feel like I've known you forever. I don't pretend to get it, but there it is. And really, I'm finding it pretty impossible to ignore *this*."

On the last word, he leaned closer and kissed her softly—just a whisper of butterfly wings, really—and yet the kiss almost melted her knees.

He pulled away, running the backs of his fingers over her cheek as he searched her eyes. "I know the girls will be up soon, or I'd be pulling you back to my cabin right now. But promise me you'll come tonight, Gabriela. Please?"

Gabi swallowed carefully, knowing that if she did that, then there was absolutely no going back. She was already head over heels, and if she fell into his bed one more time . . . if she woke up under his downy-soft quilt that smelled like the firs on Kizilla Mountain, she'd be lost. Totally, beautifully, unforgivably lost.

"Will you come?" His thumb caressed her bottom lip, and it was all she could do to take a deep breath and slide free of his arms.

"I'll come."

He pulled her back to him, squeezing her tightly. "I can't wait." Then he turned around and steered her toward the pathway. "Think you can grab an hour of sleep before they wake up?"

Gabi knew she was far too amped up to sleep at this point, even if the girls *were* still zonked. But she nodded.

"I'll try. Will we see you at breakfast?"

He shook his head. "Heck, no. I'm exhausted. I'm sleeping till noon."

Gabi laughed as she headed down the path, and was still smiling as she opened the screen door of the dining hall and crept toward her cot, determined to at least lie down and close her eyes till the girls stirred.

Just as she was about to slide into her sleeping bag, she did her customary scan of the girls' cots, automatically counting bodies and heads. There were four of each, so she smiled and pulled her ponytail loose, suddenly deliciously tired as she laid her head on her pillow.

Even two days later, she wouldn't be sure what it was that made her sit back up. She wouldn't be sure what it was about one cot that pinged her radar. She wouldn't even be sure why she slid back out of her sleeping bag to take a closer look.

But what she *would* be sure of was the sight that greeted her when she flipped back Sam's sleeping bag.

Chapter 29

"What do you mean, she's gone?" Luke's eyes went wide when he came to his door five minutes later. Gabi had sprinted to his cabin in full-on panic mode, and she was breathing hard.

"Gone, Luke. She's gone. She was there when I left at ten and went down to the beach. I *know* she was there. I checked the bathroom, I checked the admin cottage, and I checked the van. She's not here."

"So she snuck out when we were on the lake." He ran a worried hand through his hair as he slid on his hiking boots. "Did you tell Oliver yet?"

"No." Gabi felt her voice reach a panicky tone. "I came to you first."

"Where are the other girls?"

"They're freaking out in the dining hall. I told them not to dare move till we figured out what to do."

"Okay." He headed to a closet and pulled out a backpack that looked fully packed. He slung it onto his back and motioned Gabi back out the door. "She left sometime between ten and five, so she's got some lead time on us. Do you have any idea whether she would have headed for the woods or the road?"

"None. *God*." Gabi stumbled to keep up with him as

he strode toward the admin cottage. "What if she did something like last time? What if she hiked out to the road? Hitchhiked? She could be *anywhere* right now."

He turned to her, gripping her shoulders. "Listen. Freaking out is not going to help us. We need to figure out which direction she went. And to do that, we need to look for clues. Go to the tent and see if she took anything. Grill the girls to see if anybody knows anything. Anything at all."

In any other situation or on any other day, Gabi would resent him telling her what to do, but in her panicky state of mind, it was actually comforting to have orders to follow. She had a feeling he knew that. Thus, the tone. Stacking a night devoid of sleep on top of the terror of finding Sam's cot empty was seriously compromising her linear thinking.

"What are *you* going to do?"

"I'm going to call the police."

"Oh, God." Gabi put a hand to her throat. He must be worried. She'd hoped for him to be stoic and reassuring and promise they'd find her by breakfast. But his first move was to call the police?

"Does that mean—"

"It doesn't mean I don't think we'll find her half a mile from here in the woods. It just means I'm following protocol and doing what you do in this sort of situation. It's a big forest, a big lake."

"Oh, God. The lake. I—oh God, Luke. She wouldn't have gone in the lake, would she?" Gabi pictured her blond head slipping under the water that horrible day. She could swim now, sort of, but still. In a panic, would she be okay?

"We would have seen her, Gabriela. No, she didn't go in the water."

"Okay. All right. Okay." Gabi spun around, heading for the dining hall. "I'll go talk to the girls."

"Tell them to get their survival packs ready."

"*What?*" Her jaw dropped. "We can't send them out to look. Are you crazy?"

"We're not *sending* them. We're taking them with us. It'll take the search-and-rescue crew an hour or so to mobilize. Between the five of us, we can cover a lot of ground in that time. Chances are good we'll find her before they even get here."

Fifteen minutes later, Gabi and the girls shouldered their packs, sliding water bottles into the slots on one side and granola bars into stuff sacks on the other. The girls were somber, scared, and their silence was far more frightening than if they'd been squealing or squabbling. They all claimed not to have a clue where Sam had gone, or when she'd left. Nobody had heard a thing.

While they waited for Luke to finish briefing the state trooper who'd pulled into the yard five minutes ago, Gabi looked around the dining hall one more time. Sam had taken her own survival pack, and as far as Gabi could tell, she'd filled it with exactly the items Luke had taught them all to pack if they were heading out into the forest for an unknown amount of time.

"She said nothing? To anybody?" Gabi scanned their faces, desperate for an eye twitch or a nervous gesture that would tell her somebody knew something . . . anything. But not one of them moved a muscle.

"Can *any* of you think of *anything* that might have set her off yesterday? Did something happen? Did one of *you* say something? Anything?" Gabi put up her hands. "Free pass here, guys. I don't care what it was, or who said what. We need to know. If there's something that'll help us figure out where she went, we have to know."

All three girls shook their heads, and as much as she was grasping for a glimmer of hope that one of them was holding on to a little nugget of information that would help, none of them spoke.

Dammit.

Just then, Luke hustled down the path, clipping a radio to the strap of his backpack. "All right. Let's do this."

The girls froze for a moment, not sure what "let's do this" was going to entail. Then Luke pointed to Eve.

"What do we look for first?"

"Clues at the departure spot." She rattled off the answer automatically, and he smiled.

"Exactly. So what do we know?" He pointed at Madison.

"She packed her survival pack. Food and water. The spare sleeping bag."

"Good." He nodded. "Waverly? Any other observations?"

Waverly scanned the clearing, then looked like she'd just realized something. "She took the dogs." She smiled. "Luke, she took the dogs!"

Gabi looked at Luke, who nodded thoughtfully as he slid his own water bottle into its slot. How had she not noticed the dogs were missing?

"Well," he finally said, "that's actually good news."

"Because?"

"Because the dogs will actually slow her down. When they get tired, they'll just sit their little butts down and refuse to keep going. She'll have to wait."

"So that's good, then." Gabi took a deep breath. "She won't have gone as far, maybe."

"Maybe. Unless she's carrying them, which she might totally do. But that'll add almost twenty pounds to her load, so that'll slow her down, too." Luke looked at each of the girls. "Last call for any information anyone's holding out on us. No repercussions, no blame. But if there's anything at all, we need to know. And we need to know it now."

He waited. And waited. He pinned his eyes on Eve, then Waverly, then Madison, and back again. None of them offered up anything, and Gabi was ready to push them all up the trail to get moving, but he just stood there, hands on his hips, the picture of I-can-wait-all-day-here.

What was he doing? They were wasting valuable time! Every minute they stood here in this clearing was another minute of Sam moving farther away from them. If they wanted to find her before the search-and-rescue team got involved, they needed to move. Now.

She widened her eyes at him, but he shook his head almost imperceptibly, then kept staring at the girls.

Gabi stared as well. What was he seeing that she wasn't? What energy was he picking up on that made him stand stock still and try to draw them out? Was he just bluffing?

He totally had to be bluffing.

And then Eve took a quick, catchy breath, and before she could turn around to catch them, two tears streamed down her cheeks. Gabi's eyes widened as she looked at her, but Luke put a hand out toward Gabi, subtle and low—*don't push*—so she stood still, waiting.

Madison and Waverly turned toward Eve, their mouths open. Madison was the one to finally speak. "What the hell, Eve? What's going on?"

Eve swallowed and wiped her eyes, taking a deep breath. She looked at Gabi, then at Luke, biting her lip, then blowing out the breath slowly. Finally, when Gabi was just about at her breaking point, Eve spoke.

"She doesn't want to go back to Briarwood." She took a shaky breath. "Said she'd rather take her chances with the bears than go back."

Gabi felt her jaw drop at the same second her knees turned to melted wax. *What?*

"What are you talking about? I've never seen her so happy as she's been the past couple of weeks. I don't underst—" Gabi shook her head, her eyes wide. "Why would she do this?"

Eve crossed her arms. "Because *this* is about to end. That's why. In two weeks, we'll be back on campus as the resident scholarship girls." She put up a hand. "And don't go all wide-eyed like you think you kept that a big secret. Seriously, Gabi. Everybody knew it the minute we arrived."

"They did not." Gabi wished her voice sounded stronger as she argued.

Madison blew out a breath. "Yeah, we did." Waverly nodded in agreement, looking worriedly from Gabi to Luke.

"Okay." Gabi's mind spun. "Right now, that's neither here nor there. Which way was she heading?"

"We don't know," Eve replied. "And that's the truth. I caught her packing the other night, but I didn't know if she'd actually do it."

"And you didn't *tell* anyone?"

"I think the answer to that's kind of obvious right now." She pulled her arms closer to her body. "I mean, given the situation."

"Nobody saw her leave?"

All three of them shook their heads.

Luke shifted his backpack. "All right. Then we need to assume she's got at least five hours on us. We need to move. Now." He headed for the trail they'd always used for their hikes, walking at a fast clip.

"How do you know she went this way?" Gabi struggled to keep pace.

"I don't. But if she was in a hurry to put some distance between herself and camp, she'd take the route she knew."

"But wouldn't she assume we'd assume that?"

"Depends how desperate she was when she left. And I'm figuring she was pretty desperate, if she took off at that hour into these woods." He turned to see if the girls were keeping up. "What are we looking for, girls?"

"Tracks," Madison offered. "Hers and the dogs'."

"Good. Waverly? What else?"

"Broken bushes, trampled grass, maybe a piece of her hair caught on something?"

"Yup. Eve? Anything else?"

"Dog poo."

The other girls let out tension giggles, and Luke laughed. "Perfect. Use your eyes, use your ears, and—now that she's suggested it—use your noses."

When they were twenty minutes away from camp, the trail forked, so Luke stopped short to look for evidence of which way Sam had gone. He leaned down to check for tracks, but didn't immediately indicate one route or the other. Gabi and the girls took sips of their water, waiting for direction. Finally, he pointed to the right, so they started walking that way. Two minutes later, he put a hand out to stop them.

He shook his head, looking down at the hard-packed path. "Little imp. I thought so."

"What?" Gabi followed his gaze, but couldn't see anything helpful.

"Look right here." He bent his knees and pointed at a faint imprint in the dirt. "There's her track." Then he pointed at the edge of the trail. "And there's one of the dogs."

"Okay?"

"Well, Sam's feet are aiming this way." He pointed down the trail. "And the dog's feet are heading back toward camp."

"What does that mean?"

He shook his head. "It means that she came this way to trick us, then backed up on her own tracks and headed down the other fork. But apparently she wasn't thinking about the dog tracks giving her away." He made a spinning motion with his index finger. "Turn around. Back to the fork, and we'll take the other trail this time."

They all turned around and walk-jogged back to the spot where the trail split. This time they headed down the left fork, but it was five minutes before Eve spotted any evidence of Sam traveling that way.

Gabi shivered. "I can't believe she was out here in the dark. She must have been terrified."

Her chest hurt as she thought about Sam trucking along this trail in the pitch-black night, with only the pups for company. What had she been thinking? What was she planning on *doing,* for God's sake? Gabi prayed that she was safe, and as the sun rose higher in the sky, baking the dew from the leaves and grass, she felt physically ill that this had happened on her watch.

On her watch. *Right.* All *she'd* been paying attention to last night was Luke.

His radio clicked, and he pulled it from his chest as Oliver checked in.

"Any luck out there?"

"Negative," Luke replied. "but we're on her trail. Tracks are a couple of hours old, so she's got a good jump on us."

"Okay. Team's gathering here in the parking lot. You think we should send somebody in from Webster Road? See if we can intercept?"

Gabi watched as Luke checked a map and nodded, giving Oliver GPS coordinates and a bunch of other numbers and directions Gabi didn't understand. Then he clicked off and started walking again. The girls were still oddly silent behind them.

"You've done this before, haven't you?" Gabi asked.

"Yep."

Luke turned and headed up the trail at an even faster clip, the girls right on his heels, and she realized she needed to catch up or be bear bait. She tightened her straps and took a deep breath, scanning both sides of the trail before she started. Something caught her eye through a tangle of bushes—a path of trampled grass that angled out of sight into the woods.

She looked up the trail, but Luke and the girls were already out of sight. Should she just check it out quickly and then catch up to them? She'd hate to call them back if what she was looking at was just a deer path, because they'd lose valuable time getting to Sam.

"Gabriela?" Luke's voice startled her from the top of the rise.

"I found something," she called. "Maybe."

He motioned to the girls, who appeared over the rise, one by one, and they all came back down the hill toward her. When he reached where Gabi was standing, she pointed at the grass.

"I don't know if it's a person path or something else, but it looks like something came through here not long ago, right?"

He squinted, then squatted down and separated blades of grass, but after doing that for a few seconds, he shook his head.

"I don't see any animal tracks, and that ground's soft enough that I'd see prints. It's possible she veered off and came this way."

"On purpose?"

He looked mystified. "I don't think so. The trail gets harder to see right about here. She definitely could have gotten confused and thought she was headed in the right direction by going this way." He nodded. "Let's check it out."

He slapped a reflective arrow on the tall pine right next to them, then motioned for them all to follow him. For the next half hour, they did just that, starting and stopping and changing direction until they'd ended up doing what felt like a complete circle. They were no longer on the trail, so all five of them fanned out, looking for any sign that Sam or the dogs had come through here.

Just as Gabi was about to suggest she'd been wrong about the path through the grass, Luke put up a hand, and they all stopped moving at once.

"Listen."

Gabi froze in place, desperate to hear whatever he was hearing. They stayed still for an entire minute, but she didn't dare move, as his hand was still in the air, waiting.

Then she heard it.

A yip. A tiny, faraway yip.

Her eyes widened as she looked at the girls, who were suddenly smiling. "Is that them?" she whispered. "Do you recognize the bark?"

Luke tipped his head, but frowned. "I don't know. Could be the search dogs are out by now."

"Would they be this far out already?"

"Maybe. Maybe not." He cupped a hand to his ear. "Valley makes it impossible to tell where the sound's coming from. Bounces off the rock walls like a damn pinball machine."

The girls waited in silence as he spun slowly on one

heel, trying to pinpoint where the yips were originating, and after a few seconds, he finally seemed to decide. He stuck another reflective arrow to a tree, pointing due north, and then called in their coordinates to Oliver.

After they'd done the requisite check-in, he clipped the radio back on his pack, and looked at the girls.

"How's everybody doing?" They all nodded. "We okay to keep going? Because if not, one half of us can rest here for a bit while the others keep going."

"No way," Eve said. "Nobody's resting till we find Sam."

Luke looked at the other two. "You guys agree? You're good?"

"We're good," Madison said. "Let's roll."

Ten minutes later, after clambering over a series of rock walls that had demarcated a long-ago property line, they paused to catch their breath and listen for the barking. For a long moment, they heard nothing but the birds, but then, just as Gabi feared they'd headed in the completely wrong direction, they heard another yip. This time, it was louder. Oh, thank God. They *were* getting closer.

The faint bark spurred them all forward, and they moved in silence broken only by their labored breaths as they half walked, half slid down the side of a deep gully and up the other side. When they got to the top and paused to listen again, Gabi looked at her watch. They'd been out here for a long time already, and she couldn't tell if they really were any closer to Sam than they'd been when they started. Was she moving just as fast as they were?

"I don't hear anything," she whispered to Luke as the girls uncapped their water bottles.

He sighed, staring intently in the direction of where they thought the last yips had come from. Then he spun slowly in place, and she could see his eyes darting left to right, left to right, looking for any evidence that Sam had come through here.

Madison wiped her forehead. "Is it weird that we haven't seen any prints or anything? How do we know we're really on the right track?"

Luke shook his head. "Not weird. She could have walked a path ten feet to the left or right of us, heading the same direction, and we wouldn't necessarily pick up on her trail. That's why search teams fan out the way they do. But we have a target sound, which is better than I expected we'd have. We just need to figure out where the damn thing is coming from."

He looked around one more time, and Gabi felt her stomach clench as she noticed the tightness in his jaw. He was conveying a confidence he didn't feel—she could tell—so he didn't freak the girls out.

He motioned them forward. "Come on. Let's stay on our heading, and eventually we'll meet up with the team coming in from the west."

Madison shook her head. "We'll find her first. We have to."

Half an hour later, they'd traversed another wide gully, scrambling up the far side by holding on to trees and each other. Gabi couldn't imagine Sam managing the climb by herself, especially without leaving evidence. The five of *them* had churned up leaves, pine needles, and rocks on their way up the hill. If they somehow ended up lost, the search team would have no problem figuring out which way *they'd* gone.

Of course, the fact that Luke kept slapping those arrows on trees every fifty feet would probably help, too. She caught up to him as they jogged down a steep grade toward a stream. "What's with the arrows? Are you afraid we might get lost, too?"

"No." He shook his head. "Just trying to help Sam find *us* if she's decided to start looking."

"Oh." Gabi swallowed. "That's a good idea."

"Shh." He put a finger to his lips.

"But—"

He put his hand lightly against her mouth. "Listen. Shh." He pointed a little to the left of where they were heading. "They're barking again."

Gabi felt her face break into a wide smile as she realized what he was hearing. It was definitely the dogs, and oh God, they were so close now.

The girls stood up straighter, new energy pouring into their exhausted legs, as they heard it, too.

Waverly's eyes widened. "They sound like they're just over that hill."

"They might be," Luke answered. "I hope to God they are. But remember—sound does funny things in these woods. Here's what we're going to do: we'll walk a hundred steps, and then we'll stop and listen. We're close, and I don't want to get stupid at this point and walk right by her."

He pointed in the direction it seemed like the yips were coming from, sending the girls ahead to count their steps, while he hung back with Gabi.

When they were out of hearing range, he turned to her, and this time, his face was registering a completely different emotion that made her chest jump.

"What's wrong?" Her voice shook.

"I don't know"—he blew out a careful breath—"but I think we'd better be prepared. Those dogs don't bark."

"You're scaring me, Luke."

"Not trying to. Just trying to prepare you. They wouldn't be barking unless there was something wrong. They're just not barkers."

"So why are we standing here?" Gabi clutched her stomach. "Oh, God, Luke. What if—"

He shook his head, putting up a hand. "Don't play the *what if* game. There are way too many of them out here. You'll make yourself crazy. But here's the plan—when I think we're close enough to finding her, I'm going to send you and the girls in another direction and I'm going to go check things out."

"No! You can't send us off. She's *my* kid."

"Gabi." He put both hands on her shoulders. "Listen to me. If something bad *has* happened, then you don't want the other girls to come across her first. Believe me."

"Luke—" Gabi felt tears threaten.

He squeezed her shoulders. "Let's pray for the best, okay? Something big enough to hurt her probably would have done in the dogs first."

Gabi's eyes widened. "So it's actually a good sign that they're barking."

"Let's go with that." He turned around. "Come on."

Ten minutes later, the barking was getting steadily louder, and all five of them were walking faster, knowing they were catching up to Sam. They had to be. Gabi tried not to think about how quickly they *were* catching up at this point, since it seemed pretty obvious that the girl was no longer moving forward.

They just needed to find out why.

Just then, Luke put a hand up to stop them, and he looked at Gabi long and hard before crouching down to the ground and sweeping pine needles with his fingers. She took a deep breath and let it out slowly. That was his signal. He thought he knew where she was.

She was torn between elation and terror.

Luke pointed at the ground. "I think I see a track. And another one. Looks like she might have veered off here." As he pointed down a hill that opened into a clearing to their right, Gabi found herself looking left, wondering what he'd seen that had triggered him to send them in a different direction. The dogs had gone quiet, and she saw nothing physical that would indicate they were right on top of her.

Then she looked up.

And saw thin vertical stripes on the huge pine next to them, sap still dripping from them.

Chapter 30

"Okay, you guys head for that clearing, but freeze when you get to the edge of it. Gabi will be right behind you. I need to go find a tree."

The girls rolled their eyes at his code for having to pee, but it did the trick. They immediately turned and headed down the hill, leaving Gabi and Luke alone. He quickly unclipped his radio and handed it to Gabi.

"If I don't signal you within fifteen minutes, just press this button to talk, and Oliver will be on the other end."

"Wh-what should I tell him?"

Luke pulled out a map and pointed to a spot. "Give him these coordinates right here, and he'll send one of the teams your way to get you out of the woods."

"But what about you?"

"I'll be fine. When the team gets to you, send them up to this spot. I'll leave an obvious trail so they can follow me to her."

He unholstered a pistol she didn't even know he'd brought, and her hand flew to her mouth.

"Oh, God."

"Do *not* freak out right now, Gabriela. Freaking out is the worst thing you can do."

"Okay. I know." She fought to control her racing pulse. "I'm trying. I'm sorry."

He turned her shoulders. "I'll whistle when it's okay to come back. Go. Catch up to the girls. And if you get into any trouble, use this." He handed her an air horn. "And the radio."

"Okay. All right." She clipped the radio to her own backpack, and slid the air horn into a loop of fabric. "Go find her."

As she stumbled down the hill, her vision clouded by a stream of tears, the entire summer flashed through her brain, as well as vivid scenes from the school year. She'd plucked Sam out of a hellish foster home, but what had she thrown her into? A boarding school where the girls treated her like shit, and then a camp where she continued to struggle, and now what? Things were so bad for her that she'd fled in the middle of the night into a strange forest.

That had been preferable to the life she was living.

Gabi took a catchy breath, realizing that in her zeal to provide an opportunity to Sam and Eve, maybe she'd called it completely wrong. She'd had some idealized, rose-colored vision of how it would go—like a Hallmark movie where the two girls were plucked out of obscurity by a caring, devoted woman, and went on to have beautiful, successful lives because of her efforts.

Bullshit.

Eve and Sam had stuck out like sore thumbs from the day they'd walked onto the Briarwood campus, despite their new school uniforms and materials Gabi had purchased for them so they *wouldn't* look and feel different.

But uniforms couldn't cover up the scars of lives like theirs. New notebooks couldn't mask the fact that they'd never owned a book in their lives. And Ralph Lauren bedding couldn't make up for the fact that they'd both spent most of their lives not even knowing whether their current bed would last through the next month.

Dammit, maybe she'd been totally wrong. Maybe by bringing them to Briarwood, she'd only made things worse for them. The thought was sobering, and terrifying. She'd built her entire career on this drive to bring more opportunities to those who deserved them, and yet her first try was going up in smoke.

Literally.

She wrinkled her nose as she sniffed the air. Wait— she *did* smell smoke. Someone had built a fire. Could it be Sam?

"Smoke!" The girls came running back up the hill, pointing at the spot where they'd left Luke. "It's coming from up there!"

She wiped her eyes quickly so they wouldn't know she'd been crying, then put out a hand to stop them.

"Hold on a second. Luke hasn't signaled us yet."

"Signaled?" Madison looked perturbed. "He had to *pee.*"

"Right." Gabi nodded like she'd forgotten. "And we don't really want to walk up on him, right?"

Madison growled. "But we see smoke! It could be Sam! She was always the best one at starting fires." She stepped from foot to foot, itching to go past Gabi. "Come on. We have to go check it out."

Just then, they heard a piercing whistle coming from the same direction as the smoke. Luke!

"Is that the signal?" Eve's eyes widened. "Can we go?"

"Yes!" Gabi practically pushed them by her. "Go! Go! I think he found her!"

Five minutes later, they emerged into a tiny clearing and broke into a run when they saw Sam lying on the grass against her backpack. Luke stood right next to her, digging into his own backpack, and when Sam spotted the girls sprinting toward her, she smiled wider than Gabi had ever seen her.

Eve, Madison, and Waverly slid their backpacks off and fell down on the ground beside Sam, hugging her while Gabi watched. She met Luke's eyes, and he gave her a tiny thumbs-up. She turned away and blinked hard, trying not to let the relieved tears flow. Sam was okay. She was really okay.

"Gabriela, I need the radio." Luke reached out for it, then called in their coordinates as he checked his compass, then the map.

Madison looked up. "This would be an awful lot easier if you could use a cell phone up here."

"Nah. Cell phones are for sissies. I got this." He turned away, walking a few steps toward the woods as he talked to Oliver.

"He's such a dinosaur," Madison grumbled.

"He has a GPS, Madison." Gabi winked. "He's just playing you."

Madison narrowed her eyes as she watched Luke walk away. "Figures."

Gabi crouched down beside Sam, touching her hand as the dogs jumped up to kiss her cheeks with their cold noses. The poor girl had dirt everywhere, and for the first time, Gabi noticed her right boot was off and her ankle looked huge. Before she could formulate the best way to start talking with Sam, the teenager saved her the trouble.

"Gabi, do you remember that day back in June when you came up to the lounge to deliver our doom?"

Gabi's eyebrows went upward. "Yes?"

"And remember how you admitted you were plotting our murders?"

"I don't think I ever admitted that, really." Gabi smiled. "Considering, maybe. But definitely not plotting."

"Well, I was just thinking that the murderous feeling you had then is probably *nothing* compared to the one you have right now."

"Not true." Gabi shook her head. "I'm just glad you're okay."

"Gabi?" Sam's eyebrows matched her own. "You are a seriously sucky liar."

"True, but I'm not lying right now. I've been far more worried than mad this whole time."

Eve nodded. "It's true, actually. She didn't even threaten to leave you out here for the bears once."

"Thank you, Eve." Gabi rolled her eyes. "See? I even let them call a search team."

"What?" Sam's eyes looked suddenly frightened. "Oh, God. I'm in so much trouble. I was *already* in so much trouble. But now?" She laid her head back on her backpack, closing her eyes. "I'm dead."

"Actually, you're not." Madison pointed to her. "Disgusting and dirty, but definitely not dead. What the hell happened, Sam? Why did you take off without telling us?"

Sam kept her eyes closed for a long moment, then opened them. "I don't even know where to start."

Luke came back over just then, clipping the radio back to his pack and pulling out a med kit. He pointed to Sam's ankle and raised his eyebrows.

"Okay, team. What do we have here?"

All three girls leaned over to view her purple, swollen ankle. It was at least sprained badly, maybe broken. Gabi glanced at Sam's eyes. The girl had to be in some serious pain.

Waverly tipped forward onto her knees. "She's got a

sprain or a break. We need to splint and wrap it, and somehow we're going to need to carry her out of the woods, because there's no *way* this girl can walk on this foot."

"Good," Luke replied, handing her a med kit. "Go to it."

"Me?" Her eyes widened.

"Yup." He shrugged. "You diagnosed the problem, you get to direct the treatment. Eve and Madison? Do what she asks."

Gabi watched as a glow came over Waverly's face. Then she turned to Madison, and probably for the first time in her life, gave *her* a command. Madison, probably for the first time in *her* life, merely nodded and did exactly as Waverly directed.

As Gabi watched, she felt Luke's eyes on her, but when she looked up to meet them, he suddenly got busy with the map.

"We're about two miles in from the road right now," he finally said. "We're going to need to do a carry."

Sam's eyes widened. "You're going to carry me out of here?"

"You have a better suggestion? Feel like walking on that ankle?"

Sam winced. "No."

"Then we're carrying."

"Okay," she whispered. Then, as Gabi watched her, huge tears started dripping down her cheeks toward her ears. She closed her eyes, wincing as Waverly picked up her ankle to wrap tape around it. "I'm so sorry."

"Why did you take off, Sam?" Luke's voice was conversational, nonconfrontational, like they were just sitting around the campfire discussing why someone's favorite food was spaghetti instead of steak.

"I—don't think I can explain it right now."

"It'd be really helpful if you could, because guess what? A hell of a lot of people are going to be asking."

"I was—scared."

"More scared than heading out into the woods in the middle of the night was likely to make you?"

She nodded miserably. "Yeah."

"Why, Sam? What in the world were you scared of?"

She shook her head, looking at the girls, and Luke seemed to understand at the same moment Gabi did. He cleared his throat and put his hand on Waverly's shoulder.

"Okay, team. Let's give the ankle a break for a minute. We need to make a litter for her. You remember what we need?"

Eve nodded. "We're really going to make one?"

"Unless you want to carry her piggyback, yeah. We're going to make one." He pointed at the edge of the clearing. "That looks like a good spot there. Take my hatchet and see what you can find."

Gabi's eyes widened, but Luke put up a hand. "Gabriela, if you say anything about sharp objects right now, I might just leave *you* out here."

Gabi buttoned her lip, suitably chagrined. As the girls headed away from them, Luke positioned himself at Sam's ankle and resumed the splinting job Waverly had started. He wound tape around and around her foot and calf without speaking, and Gabi waited him out, not even really knowing why she did.

Finally, he looked up at Sam. "What got you this scared, mermaid?"

At his use of the affectionate term, Sam's face completely crumbled, and tears poured out of her eyes. Gabi crouched down and took her in her arms as the girl sobbed. For two full minutes, her tiny body shook, until it finally seemed she was empty. She wiped her nose on her sleeve, then crashed back onto her backpack.

She looked from Gabi to Luke and back again, then took a deep, pained breath.

"I'm pregnant."

Chapter 31

Three hours later, Gabi parted the curtain to Sam's emergency room cubicle, still unsure of what she was going to say to her. She'd just finished talking with the doctor, who'd pointed out a fracture on her X-ray, and had then showed Gabi some lab results.

She sat down carefully on a stool, waiting for Sam to meet her eyes. When it appeared she wasn't going to, Gabi decided to start with the obvious.

"Looks like your ankle's actually broken. He's going to send someone in to put on an air cast sort of thing in a few minutes. It's too swollen for a real one right now, so we'll have to handle that when we get back to Briarwood."

"Okay." Sam's voice was almost a whisper, and it broke Gabi's heart to see her lying so small in the ER bed, her arms crossed like it was her against the entire, big-bad world.

"I have some other news, too." Gabi waited a beat, and finally Sam looked at her. "You're not pregnant, Sam."

Sam nodded slowly. "I know."

Gabi tipped her head. "What do you mean, you know?"

"Because I've never—y'know. Never mind." She shook her head. "It'd be a miracle, okay?"

"Then why did you tell us you were?"

Sam pulled her arms tighter to her body, and Gabi saw her chin start to quiver. What in the *world* was going on?

"Sam, honey. You've gotta tell me what's happening, or I can't help you. I *want* to help you. I've been trying to help you since I read your application a year and a half ago. But honey, you've got to be honest with me. Why did you say you were pregnant?"

"Because." Sam took a deep breath, closing her eyes. "Because my epic escape failed miserably. I was out of options. I . . . wanted to be expelled, Gabi."

"What?"

"I hate it at Briarwood. Hate it worse than where I was. I don't belong there, I have no friends, the teachers look at me like I'm going to steal their precious pencils, and I just—hate it, okay? I've been trying to get expelled for months, but you keep covering for me and giving me more chances. I know you're trying to help, but please, Gabi, just let Pritch-bitch expel me, would you?"

Gabi sat back, shocked. "What do you mean, you've been trying to get expelled for months?"

Sam looked at her like she was dense. "Smoking in my room? Feeding the lab rats Pop Rocks? The Ex-Lax? After a certain number of those incidents, I should have been put up before the disciplinary board. And they could have decided I didn't belong." She hugged one knee to her chest. "Because that would have been news and all."

"But . . ."

"I know you were trying to do what was best. I get it. But Gabi, even you can see that letting me come to Briarwood was a mistake. I am so not a Briarwood girl, and I never, ever wanted to be, anyway."

"I was just trying to give you opportunities, Sam."
Gabi felt her voice falter. She'd known Sam wasn't
happy, but clearly she'd had no idea just *how* unhappy
she'd been.

"I know. But honestly? I don't think I want that kind.
I just want to go back."

"To the home you were in when I came to get you?"
Gabi felt her eyebrows hike upward. She couldn't help it.

Sam shrugged. "It wasn't so bad. Not nearly as bad
as some of the others, anyway."

"Sam, I can't guarantee *where* you'd end up if I
brought you back. It could be much, much worse than
what you left."

"I know. But at least I'd fit in, you know? I'd be watching my back for the things I understand. Briarwood?
That's something I'll never understand."

"The first year is always a little rough somewhere
new, honey," Gabi pleaded. "I'm sure this fall will be
easier, don't you think?"

Sam leveled a frustrated look her way, then pointed
at her ankle. "If I thought that, would I have taken off
and gotten myself into *this* situation?"

Gabi looked at the ankle, which was now an angry
purple color under the swelling. She shivered when she
thought of Sam lying in that clearing by herself, alone
and scared.

As much as she hated to see a parallel, it reminded
her of when she was seven. She'd never forget when the
housemother at her dorm had fetched her from her bedroom to the hallway phone three days after her birthday
because her mother was on the other end of the line.
"Happy birthday, darling," she'd said, and even at that
age, Gabi had known better than to remind Mother that
she'd missed it. She'd just been happy to hear her voice,
late or not.

And when she'd thanked her mother for the stuffed giraffe and drawing set and new dresses, Mother had sounded mystified. Two minutes later, Mother had given her signature "ta-ta!" and hung up. Ten minutes later, the housemother had come out into the hallway and lifted a tearful Gabi to her shoulder. She'd taken her into her own apartment and given her hot cocoa and Oreos, then let her watch a birthday cartoon.

When she got back to her own room, Gabi'd stuck the giraffe and dresses under the bed, and she'd given the drawing set to her roommate. The two Oreos she'd slid into her pocket, however, stayed tucked under her pillow until they were a pile of crumbles.

She took a deep breath and looked at the emergency room floor for a long moment, then back up at Sam. "So taking off and heading for Pendleton? Your idea?"

"Um, hello." Sam rolled her eyes. "*You* weren't letting me get booted. I had to take it up a notch, out of your jurisdiction."

"Oh, God." Gabi held her stomach. "I'd pinned this all on Madison. And it was you? You're the one who got *them* to go?"

"Yeah, because it was really hard." She shook her head. "I said the word 'boys,' and Madison said, 'Shotgun!'"

"You wanted out of Briarwood so badly that you did—that?" Gabi felt sick.

"In my defense, I drove really slowly. I never thought we'd get to Pendleton before you caught up to us. I figured Kacey would narc before we left the parking lot."

"Were you hoping?"

"Heck, yes. I really didn't want to drive all that way."

"Did it ever occur to you to just—I don't know— maybe *talk* to me about it? *Tell* me how miserable you were? I mean, really? Was all of this really necessary?"

Sam looked down at her blanket, picking at nonexistent pills. "I didn't know what to say. I figured it'd be easier for you in the long run if I just turned out to be impossible . . . not ungrateful."

"So you set out to be impossible."

"Yeah. And I had a good run for a while there. But you're so damn tolerant, Gabi. It's frustrating as hell."

Gabi felt a laugh sputter out. "I'm really sorry."

"So . . ." Sam's face grew serious. "What happens now?"

Gabi took a deep breath. Damn if she knew. "What are you *hoping* happens now?"

"It's not obvious?"

"I'm not taking you back to Boston, Sam. I won't. You deserve a better life than you were living." Gabi shook her head fiercely. "You can fight me till you're blue in the face, but I'm not giving up on you."

Sam raised her eyebrows. "I'm not some sort of pity project, Gabi. You don't actually get to decide that."

"Oh, yes I do."

"No. You really don't." Gabi watched a spark come into Sam's eyes, and she almost backed up in response. "If you won't let me go back to Boston, then I'll just keep trying to get there the hard way. You know I will."

"Stop it, Sam. There are other choices. We can figure this out."

Sam shook her head. "I'm done figuring. Next time I leave, I just need to make sure I don't get caught."

"Hey." Luke settled into the Adirondack chair beside Gabriela on the beach later that evening, not missing the defeat in her eyes as he did. "You okay?"

She sighed, her shoulders slumped. "Well, I won't lie. I've had better days."

"Yeah." He handed her a beer. "Me, too."

She looked at him, and he physically felt the pain in her eyes. "Thank you for all you did today."

"It was a team effort. You should be damn proud of your girls."

"I am. I don't think any of them knew they had the . . . strength they used today. I sure didn't."

Luke nodded. "Hard to believe these are the same four girls who could barely stand each other when they got here."

"I know."

"How's Sam doing now?"

"I honestly don't know how she is. We still have a lot to talk about. Obviously." Gabriela sighed, pulling her knees up to her chest in that way that made him want to pick her up and comfort her like she'd probably been comforting Sam for the past few hours. Who *did* comfort her when she needed it?

"How's—the baby?" He already knew the ankle was good and broken. She'd managed to avoid all of the creatures of the night, and had walked for miles without GPS or any knowledge of the terrain, but eventually, she'd been felled by a stupid rock when she'd jumped over the stream and landed badly. He still couldn't believe how far she'd walked on it before she'd given up, but he imagined fear and adrenaline had kept her going until she'd found a clearing that had seemed safer than being in the deep woods.

Gabi shook her head miserably. "There's no baby, Luke."

"Did she lose it?"

"No. There never was one."

"But—"

"I know. And believe me, if I could make sense of— anything—right now, I'd have an explanation. But I don't." She put her hand to her forehead like she needed to physically hold it up, and again he ached to somehow comfort her, but he sensed an invisible, electric fence between them. "She was hoping . . . if I believed she was pregnant, I'd have no choice but to tell Pritchard, who'd have no choice but to expel her."

"That's pretty extreme."

"She was desperate. Her pranks hadn't gotten her booted. Stealing the van and heading off in the middle of the night hadn't gotten her booted. Her escape had failed. I guess it was the best she could come up with in a pinch. She hates it at Briarwood, Luke. Hates it so badly that she'd rather head back to foster care." She sighed. "How do you do this?"

"Do . . . what?"

"Work with kids like her? This is your thing. This is the kind of kid you see all the time. It must break your heart ten times a day. It's breaking mine ten times an hour here, and I am dying here because I can't fix her. How . . . *how* do you do it?"

He looked at her, stripped completely bare of any armor she'd come with, tears in her eyes and the weight of the world on her shoulders, and he slid the heel of his hand over his chest, disturbed by an actual, physical ache. He felt his eyebrows furrow as he realized it came . . . from her—from her vulnerability, from her trust, from her belief that he had some sort of wisdom to impart, even at her lowest point.

"I had a little sister." The words were out before he could run them through his head and be sure he was ready to deliver them, and it shocked him. Only Oliver, Piper, and Noah knew this story, and it had taken him a hell of a long time to tell.

"Had?"

"In foster care. Not by blood, but we were together for almost six years—got moved five different times together. It was as close as I ever came to having a real sibling."

"What happened?"

He took a deep breath. "Our last place was a crap deal. Got assigned to a house in the suburbs. Three bedrooms, two-and-a-half baths, garage, the works. When we drove up, I was old enough to know better than to hope it'd work out, but she was blown away by the pool, the dog, her own room. She was sure this was it—that if she was good enough, they'd adopt her."

He looked at Gabi, who had her thumbnail between her lips, her eyes firmly on him. In her face he read concern, interest . . . but not pity, and that's what made him continue.

"Turns out the house made a pretty picture from the outside. It even looked okay when you stepped in. But they were into some really bad shit, and Trina was so desperate to fit in and stay that she fell under the spell of the stuff they were cooking in the basement, and before too long, she was hooked."

"Oh, Luke."

"So I did what I knew how to do. I acted out, tried to get us kicked out so I could get her out of there before it got worse. Randall—the father—kept talking about how pretty she was . . . how sweet . . . and I knew it was only a matter of time." Luke felt his hands ball into fists. "We ran once, together, but he found us before we got far enough away, and he promised not to turn us in if Trina behaved."

He took another breath, the rest of the story hurting worse as it banged to get out of his head.

"I knew what Trina *behaving* was going to mean,

even if she didn't, but I'd been such a rotten shit for so long that nobody at social services believed a word I said about any of it. I stayed so I could keep an eye on her, but things just kept getting worse. She was losing weight, getting that wild-eyed look, and I knew an OD was on the menu, just as much as the other crap was. Around the same time, Randall figured out I was onto him, and he got me booted. Just me.

"I raged and called my social worker ten times a day, and finally they sent somebody out to investigate, but surprise, surprise, Trina said everything was fine and I was a nut job. By that time she was so hooked there was no way she'd risk cutting off her supplier. So I did the only thing I could think of—I tried to bust into the house in the middle of the night to get her to come with me."

He stopped, remembering the scene—the pleading, the crying, and eventually, the shouting. Randall had called the police, and Luke had been yanked off the porch in cuffs as Trina'd sobbed. He'd landed in the drunk tank downtown, completely sober, and had been contemplating options for ending it all when Oliver had shown up.

As he told the story, Gabi's jaw dropped, and he watched her carefully, desperate to know what she was thinking . . . desperate to know if she understood. When he finished, he blew out a long breath, staring out at the lake.

"That's why I'm here, Gabi. And that's why I'll never leave willingly. I can't *not* do this. I can't *not* hope I make enough of a difference for some desperate kid to make this all worthwhile. I couldn't save Trina, but I can do my damndest to help save somebody else. Or a hell of a lot of somebody elses. I don't have a choice. And if Briarwood does close us down, then I'll have to find another way to do it. I'll just be doing it with Oliver's en-

tire life on my conscience, because I guarantee you this
will kill him."

"What happened to Trina?" Gabi's voice was shaky.

Luke steepled his fingers in front of his face, thumbs
under his chin. "She OD'd a week later."

Chapter 32

"Hey, Gabi. How are you doing?" Piper banged through the back door of the dining hall early the next morning carrying three shopping bags stuffed with food, and Gabi immediately felt guilty, because they wouldn't be here to eat it.

"Jury's out, I think." Gabi tried to smile as she helped lift the bags to the counter, but after spending the night flipping and flopping on her cot, her exhaustion was getting the better of her.

Piper peered over the service counter. "Where are the girls?"

"Up in the garden, believe it or not."

"At seven in the morning? They doing penance for yesterday's epic getaway-gone-wrong?"

"No. Not really. I don't think so, anyway. It's going to be hellishly hot, and weeding's apparently on the agenda, so they wanted to get done before the sun gets any higher."

"Wow." Piper nodded as she started emptying the grocery bags. "That's kind of . . . initiative-ish."

Gabi wrinkled her nose, smiling. "I know." Then she felt her face grow serious as Piper took three giant trays of eggs out of one bag. "I wish I'd known you were going shopping this morning."

"Why? Did you need something?"

"No." She blew out a breath. "I would have told you maybe not to worry about it. I had a long talk with Luke last night, after everything settled back down, and . . . it looks like I'm going to head back to Briarwood with the girls this afternoon."

"What?" Piper's eyebrows flew upward, and Gabi knew she'd better come up with an explanation that made sense before she faced Luke. The truth was, she didn't know if she *had* one. As he'd told her about his foster sister last night, she'd been struck not only by the story, but by the purity of purpose that drove him here at Camp Echo.

She didn't have that.

Well, she'd *thought* she'd had it—*thought* she'd been doing her best to change lives, but the events of the past twenty-four hours had her questioning everything.

Everything except *one* thing.

Being here at camp for any longer was a recipe for disaster. If it wasn't her girls getting into trouble, it was her heart, and *that* had left her so distracted that she hadn't even noticed Sam taking off last night.

She needed to go back to Briarwood and get her head on straight, get the girls back to an environment she understood, even if she didn't like or respect it all that much at this point.

And maybe, with time—and distance—she'd be able to figure out what to do about Luke.

She took a deep breath. "It seems like the best option right now."

"Does *Luke* think it's the best option?"

Gabi suddenly found a crack in the countertop that

needed her attention. "Um, he doesn't actually . . . know."

Piper stopped unpacking bags, instead leaning against the counter and appraising Gabi. "Are you scared they'll run again? Or someone else, I guess? Guess Sam's not going too far at this point."

"Yes and no. I don't know." Gabi blew out a breath. "That's what's killing me."

"What's killing you?" Luke's voice preceded him into the kitchen. Looking wary, he matched Piper's pose against the long counter.

Piper raised her eyebrows at Gabi. *Are you going to tell him?*

"Not sure I know where to start," Gabi finally replied, feeling like the ultimate coward.

"She was just telling me that they're leaving today." Piper turned to open the fridge. "She was wishing I hadn't gone grocery shopping, because apparently they won't be eating all of this food."

Luke was silent for a long moment, appraising Gabi with his arms crossed. Then, "Leaving." He let the word drop between them, and guilt clawed at her throat.

"I think I forgot something in the car." Piper grabbed her keys. "Be back in a bit."

They both watched her go, then Luke turned to Gabi. "What the hell?"

"I . . . I talked to one of the deans yesterday. Our dorm is done. We can go back. So . . . I feel like, given everything, that's what we need to do."

"Because?"

"Because everything!" She put up her hands. "I mean, seriously! We had to call out mountain rescue on one of my girls, Luke."

"So you're going to give up and go back?"

She sighed. "My girls are a walking disaster, and we

have turned your lives upside down for three weeks already. I thought we were making progress . . . was starting to think maybe this hadn't been such a horrible idea after all . . . and then Sam. I mean, seriously. I can't risk them making another plan."

"So you'll bring them back to the hallowed halls of Briarwood, where you can keep them safe?"

"Yes."

"Because there, things like hotwired vans and unlicensed trips to neighboring states never happen?"

"Put your eyebrows back down, all right? I'm well aware of what got us here, but being here didn't . . . solve anything. If anything, it just made it all worse."

"How?"

Gabi felt her eyes go wide. "Have you *seen* Sam this morning? Air cast? Crutches?"

"That didn't happen because she was here, Gabi."

"What can that possibly mean? Of course it happened because she's here."

"Why did she take off?"

"Because she hates Briarwood so much that she was willing to risk life, limb, and bears to get expelled, that's why."

"So why would you bring her back there?"

"Because I need to figure out what to do—with her, with Eve, with . . . me. And I can't do that here."

"Why not?"

She sighed. *Because, idiot. You're the reason I wasn't there for her when she got desperate enough to take off. You're the reason I feel like complete shit about my own skills after watching you make such huge strides with my girls in such a short time. You're the reason I can't walk in a straight line, because all I do is look for you.*

"We just . . . can't be here."

He nodded slowly. "So let me see if I understand. For

the past, what—three years?—you worked your ass off to get a scholarship program approved, despite every board member but one being against it. And although you'd rather have fifty—a hundred—girls there with help, you know you can at least do well by these two." He paused. "How'm I doing?"

She rolled her eyes.

"So then they come, and you firmly believe they'll embrace the opportunity, realize what they've missed, realize what you've given them, and be happy. Grateful, even."

"I'm not looking for gratitude, Luke."

He put up a hand. "Not what I meant. You envisioned pulling these two girls out of their hellish situations, setting them up for a better life, and having it work out, right?"

"Well, yes. That was the whole point of the program. Why wouldn't I?"

"You would. And that's why, when it doesn't seem to *be* working out, you're sitting here, blaming yourself, wondering what the hell you could have done differently to *make* it work out."

"Yes."

"I hate to tell you, but you can't."

"Can't what?"

"Make it work out. You're not that good."

She swallowed. "Thanks. Really."

"Nobody's that good, Gabi." He shook his head. "I'm not that good, Oliver's not that good. Nobody. This isn't something you can engineer with a handpicked roommate list, or three weeks at a summer camp."

"Clearly."

"But *four* weeks could make all the difference."

Gabi sighed, shaking her head. "Because that extra week has some sort of special power?"

"Maybe." He shrugged. "You never know when the magic will happen, and here's the thing. We tapped that magic yesterday."

"We were on a search-and-rescue mission yesterday." She ground the words out.

"Exactly. And those three girls doing the searching? They weren't doing it because we assigned them to it. They were doing it because they gave a shit about Sam. They carried her out of the woods on a litter they made themselves because they gave a shit about her. They maneuvered her up the hill to the garden an hour ago because they gave a shit. And they will bring her back down. Because they give. A. Shit."

Gabi felt her eyebrows furrow as she heard the invisible periods punctuating his sentence. "It was an emergency. They didn't have a choice. It doesn't mean any of that will translate once we leave Echo Lake."

"Wrong." He shook his head firmly. "It's *exactly* the kind of thing that will translate. These four have survived a really unique experience here. It will bond them, whether they like it or not. This summer will be etched into their memory banks forever, and the fact that some really shitty stuff happened isn't necessarily a bad thing. Trauma bonding is some of the strongest stuff out there."

"Great." She laughed bitterly. "I've trauma-bonded my crew. The board will be thrilled."

"They were scared out of their minds, Gabi. But they weren't scared of you. They weren't scared of me. They weren't scared of the elements. They were scared *for* someone, and I have a feeling that's not something that happens lightly. Not for any of them."

"I . . . I don't know." Her voice was almost a whisper, and her head was swirling.

"I *do* know." He stepped toward her, putting a gentle

finger under her chin. "Gabriela, don't make a decision today. Don't leave."

His touch on her skin, the intensity of his eyes on hers, the heat of his body so close to hers made Gabi want to melt into him, feel his arms close around her, lay her cheek against his soft T-shirt. And that scared her just as much as anything else right now, because she could easily lose herself in this. In him. And whether it happened today, or it happened one week from now, she *would* leave, and the shattered little pieces of her heart would leave a trail behind her as she fled.

It would be easier to do it before she had a chance to fall for him any harder than she already had.

He pulled away as if he could read her thoughts clearly, and she shivered as a tiny chill crept up her spine.

"You're going, aren't you?"

She took a deep, shaky breath, knowing she hated the answer more than he could possibly believe.

"It's the only choice, Luke."

"What about us, Gabriela? Are you leaving *us,* too? Before we even have a chance to figure out what—us— even could be?"

She closed her eyes, searching for the words that would hurt the least to hear . . . and deliver.

"I'm not making this decision lightly, Luke."

"If you say 'it's not you, it's me' right now, I'm throwing you in the lake. Fair warning." She could feel the effort he was exerting, trying to keep his voice light, but tension crept into his jaw, his shoulders . . . the hands tightening on his own arms as he kept them crossed.

"But it *is* me. Luke, be serious. I'm Briarwood born and bred, and I don't know *how* to do anything different. Pretty sure the last twenty-four hours makes that really, really clear."

He shrugged. "So learn. You've been doing that all summer."

"I just—I don't know if I *want* to do anything different." Her voice faded. "I'm sorry."

"Well." He nodded slowly, stepping backward. "I guess that's a different problem, then."

Chapter 33

That afternoon, Gabi tossed the last sleeping bag into the back of the van, then closed the door firmly. The girls were milling around, strangely silent, as Gabi traced her finger down her checklist one last time.

"Okay, looks like that's it." She slid the clipboard into the driver's seat and turned toward Piper, who was standing quietly next to the van.

Piper raised her eyebrows. "You sure about this?"

"Not at all." Gabi tried to smile. "But I need to get everyone back on our own soil and try to figure out what to do next."

Piper glanced toward Luke's cabin, her eyes concerned. "You sure you don't want to talk to him before you go?"

Gabi sighed, trying not to let her eyes travel to the cabin porch, where she and Luke had shared their first kiss. She tried not to look at the windows, tried not to wonder whether he was watching her leave.

"We . . . said our good-byes earlier," she finally said.

Just then, Oliver came barreling out of the admin cottage, his eyes wide. "Don't get in the van just yet, Gabi."

"Why?"

He pointed down the long driveway. "Because there's a car headed our way. Looks like we're about to get a surprise visit from the Briarwood Express."

Alarms buzzed in Gabi's stomach. "What does *that* mean?"

"I don't know. Ike just called from the garage. Said a lady in city duds just filled up. Said she was heading this way."

"That could be anyone . . . couldn't it?" Even as she asked, the alarms picked up speed.

Oliver nodded. "Could be, except that this particular *anyone* is driving a Briarwood town car."

Gabi's stomach sank. It had to be Priscilla. And Priscilla had to have heard about Sam. But already? How?

Just then, they all turned as they heard wheels on gravel, and as she looked down the long driveway, a black town car inched its way toward them. Its windshield caught the morning sunlight, so she couldn't see who was driving until the car pulled to a stop beside the Briarwood van.

"That old codger at the gas station warned you I was coming, didn't he?" A cackly voice emerged from the open window, and Gabi felt her face break into a huge smile as she moved to open the car door.

"Laura?"

"One and the same. Help me out of here, would you? It's been a long drive. Not sure all my bones are still in the right place."

Gabi laughed as the Briarwood board chair hauled herself out of the car, leaning heavily on both Gabi and Oliver, who'd stepped closer to help.

Laura finally stood up straight, shaking them both off as she grabbed a cane from the passenger seat. It was encrusted with pink crystals that matched the band on her hat.

"There. Guess I'm in working order after all. That's a relief."

"What are you doing all the way up here?" Gabi asked. Despite her multiple attempts to sit down and write Laura, like she'd promised Luke she'd do, she'd yet to put the right words together, so the visit was completely out of the blue.

"I'm on a mission. Official inspection."

"Oh." Gabi's stomach dropped as she glanced over Laura's head at Oliver. Given the expression on Oliver's face, this inspection was definitely a surprise. She couldn't imagine what Luke's would look like when he found out. "What kind of inspection?"

"Well, I'm given to understand that there's a list of projects under way in order to shipshape this little camp, so I'm here to check on progress."

"Oh."

Gabi felt her shoulders sink at Laura's words. All this time, she'd been hoping there'd been some sort of misunderstanding—that the list was a fabrication of some sort, even though she'd seen it with her own eyes. All this time, she'd been hoping her school wasn't, in fact, going to be responsible for the demise of a program that had made a difference in the lives of so many deserving kids.

But no.

Apparently the list was real, her school *was* responsible, and now its longest-serving board member was here to verify that the t's were getting crossed and the i's were getting dotted.

Laura smiled, patting Gabi's arm. "Don't look so scared." She turned to the girls. "Have we had a good summer, ladies?"

The girls mumbled and nodded politely, but didn't offer up any stories, thank God.

Laura pretended to do a head count. "Looks like you're all still in one piece." She leaned around Madison in order to see Sam better. "Well, most of you, anyway. What happened? Camp director teaching you MMA fighting or something?"

The girls giggled nervously, and Sam shook her head. "Nah. Got in a fight with a bear. But he looks much worse than I do right now."

Laura laughed, full-bodied and stronger than Gabi would have predicted for a woman her age. "Well, any Briarwood girl who's up for taking on a bear after just three weeks at camp is a girl I want on my team." She winked at Gabi. "And any housemother who helps to get her there? I'll take her, too."

Gabi smiled tightly. "Only the best for Briarwood." She said the phrase automatically—an oft-repeated mantra she'd internalized throughout her childhood.

Laura waved her off. "All right, who's going to give me a tour? And where is Luke? I've got some questions."

An hour later, Laura had oohed and aahed her way through a tour of the camp, even insisting on trying out one of the cots in the tent. She'd marveled at the bathroom, tested the hot water spray in the shower, and despite Gabi's arguments, had hiked all the way up to the garden to see the girls' seedlings. The farther they'd walked, the bigger her smile had grown, and Gabi had found herself viewing the camp through new eyes.

They really *had* done a lot of work over the past few weeks, despite the rocky start. Fresh paint covered the sheds and admin cottage, fresh gravel was spread in the parking lot, and the girls had repaired and painted the dock all by themselves over the weekend.

They'd even used power tools, and Gabi hadn't freaked out about it, thank you very much.

But through it all, Gabi had felt like she was handing Laura the nails to Camp Echo's coffin. Every time Laura gushed over the new showers or exclaimed about how much better the buildings looked, Gabi winced. Because each of those repairs brought this camp closer to being operational under the Briarwood umbrella, and that meant that Oliver and Luke would be out of jobs . . . and robbed of a mission both of them had dedicated their lives to.

Throughout the tour, Luke had stayed away, and Gabi didn't blame him. Gabi had tried to defend Briarwood all summer, not believing the board would really do what Luke firmly believed they would, and now they'd sent a board member up to inspect the place. Sure, she was friendly, and sure, she seemed really focused on making sure the girls knew how grateful she was for their hard work, but the undercurrent of Briarwood's real plan ran strong in Gabi's head. . . . and in Laura's questions.

But now the tour was done, and Gabi knew it was her last chance to plead Luke and Oliver's case. If she didn't act now, then it was practically guaranteed that this idyllic shoreline would be home to a bunch of twittering teenaged girls next year—ones who could easily afford to be a hundred other places.

"Laura? Could I please talk with you before you meet with the guys?"

"Absolutely, my dear." Laura put a hand on her arm. "Girls, how about you take a break for the rest of the afternoon? Get your suits on and go swimming."

The girls paused, looking toward Gabi for permission, which half surprised her, even while it warmed her heart a little bit.

"Go ahead." She smiled. "You've earned it."

They scooted up the pathway as Gabi led Laura to her favorite Adirondack chairs and held her arm while the older woman sank into one.

"Gosh," Laura said. "I'd forgotten just how beautiful it is up here."

"You've been here before?"

"Oh, yes. We came up last year to tour the place." She winked. "Had to know what I was getting for my money."

"Your money?" Gabi tipped her head. "*You're* the anonymous donor who funded this?"

"Not *so* anonymous, I'm afraid."

"I had no idea."

Laura smiled. "You weren't supposed to."

"Is it . . . would it be all right to ask you a really pointed question?"

"Sounds like the best kind."

Gabi took a deep breath. "I apologize if this is out of line. But I have to know—what are Briarwood's plans for this property, really?"

Laura was silent for a long moment, and that silence told Gabi everything she needed to know. So instead of waiting for Laura to compose what she imagined was supposed to feel like a comforting line of bullshit, Gabi barged ahead.

"Laura, I've seen the project list, and I have some serious reservations about what I think is happening here."

"Oh?"

"Yes." She took a deep breath. "This camp—I think this camp was perfect just the way it was . . . before we came."

"How so?"

"Because it served the right people, Laura. Oliver and

Luke have dedicated their entire adult lives to this place, and their work is the kind that's pure, and good, and self-less. I have no idea what either of them makes for money, but I have a very strong feeling that whatever it is, it gets poured right back into this camp. Do you know how many boys have come through here in the past five years?"

"How many?"

Gabi paused, seeing a trace of amusement on Laura's face. Seriously? She thought this was funny? Gabi rattled off the figure Oliver had given her last week, and Laura's eyes widened appreciatively, though she didn't speak.

"Briarwood doesn't need to extend its seasons, Laura. Our girls have plenty of options, plenty of other camps that are designed for exactly what their families are looking for. This is not that place."

"But it could be, don't you agree? It could be so much more."

Gabi suppressed a sigh. "Of course it could be. It's beautiful, it's quiet, and it's surrounded by wilderness that's awe-inspiring and frightening at the same time. It's the perfect location . . . for exactly what it's always been. There are hundreds of kids who came through here, Laura, and those kids didn't *have* other opportunities. There *was* no other camp for them. They're foster kids, needy kids, last-stop-before-court kids, and Luke and Oliver made it their mission to turn things around for them, to give them a place where they could learn to believe people actually cared about them."

"And you don't think Briarwood girls deserve the same?"

"Of course they do. But they don't need it *here*. Places like this just don't exist all over the country, and places like this should be reserved for exactly who they were designed for."

"I see." Laura nodded, but Gabi couldn't read her expression.

"I'm sorry if I overstepped." She clasped her hands in front of her. "But the longer I've been here, the more I've seen Luke work with the girls, the more convinced I am that the mission of this place needs to stay intact."

"And you don't think Briarwood intends to do that?"

Gabi took a deep breath, picturing Luke's damning project list. "No. I don't."

Laura nodded again, slowly. "I don't, either."

An hour later, Gabi pushed open the screen door of the dining hall to find Laura, Oliver, and Luke already seated at one of the picnic tables. She'd sent the girls to unpack the van, since it was now too late to head back to Briarwood, even if she'd dared. Laura had asked her what had felt like a hundred more questions—and Gabi had countered with her own, but when Laura had finally motioned for Gabi to help her out of her chair, Gabi knew the woman had had her fill.

And even though she'd boldly agreed that she didn't believe Briarwood was fully on the up-and-up, Laura had still lauded the property, the potential, the benefits they could extract for the right population of kids.

It just wasn't the same population Gabi thought needed them now.

She took a deep breath and stepped toward the table, where Laura had a pile of thick folders in front of her. Gabi felt her stomach sink as she imagined what might be lurking inside that stack of papers.

"Oh, good. You're all here. Come sit, my dear." Laura motioned Gabi to sit beside her on the picnic bench. "I'm not going to beat around the bush here, mostly because I'm too old to waste the time, but also because it drives me crazy when people do." She took a breath. "I have some things to go over with all three of you."

Gabi swallowed, looking at Luke for the first time since she'd entered the building. His eyes were shuttered, though, barely registering her presence.

Ouch.

Not that she deserved any different.

Laura took a deep breath. "Oliver and Luke, I know you've been up here working really hard on the project list you were given at the beginning of the summer, and I know I speak for the board when I express my deep gratitude for all of that work."

Oh, no. Gabi dug the fingernails of one hand into the palm of her other. Laura was about to dismiss both of them, and she'd invited Gabi in for the show.

"Now," Laura continued, "it all looks wonderful . . . but unfortunately, I'm going to have to ask you to cease and desist on that list, effective immediately."

Luke's head snapped up, and Gabi knew he'd come to the same realization as she had. "What do you mean?"

"I mean just what I said. Whatever you haven't gotten to on that list is hereby officially canceled."

Oliver tipped his head, his mouth in a tight line. "Are you speaking for the board?"

Laura was silent for a long moment. "The board is . . . in flux at the moment."

"What's going on, Laura?" Gabi tried to pull her hands apart before she drew blood. "Has something happened at Briarwood?"

"No. Nothing's changed at Briarwood." She shook her head. "And that's exactly the problem. I was informed by my attorneys eight weeks ago that the Briarwood board has decided to take Camp Echo in a new direction. They have their reasons, and I understand them, whether or not I agree with them."

Luke sighed. "What new direction?"

"They've decided they'd like to use the camp as an outreach of the school itself, to give families an opportunity to have their children be under the Briarwood umbrella throughout the entire year, rather than just the school year."

Gabi looked at Luke, and this time he met her eyes. It was exactly what he'd said, and she couldn't be more ashamed of her employer right now. How dare they? Apparently her words of an hour ago had fallen on deaf ears.

Laura cleared her throat. "However, all is not lost."

"Laura." Oliver sighed. "If they sent you up here to offer us a severance check and a wave, I have to tell you, I won't go willingly."

"There's no severance check."

Gabi watched Luke's jaw tense. He looked straight ahead, out the window toward the beach, and she could only imagine the thoughts screaming through his head. It was his worst nightmare, and Gabi sat there as a representative of the entity that was causing it.

"Gentlemen, before I tell you the rest, I do want to let you know that Gabi did her level best this afternoon to convince me that Camp Echo's mission should not be derailed . . . that the population you served up until this year is exactly the population this property *should* be serving . . . and that the two of you as a team are the right people to be directing this place."

Gabi took a careful breath, trying to be thankful that Laura was trying to extract her from blame. But it didn't feel any better knowing the result was going to be the same.

Laura nodded. "And I have to say, I agree with her on many of those points."

She did?

Gabi's head came up, and she darted a glance at Luke, but his eyes were still locked on the window.

Laura opened her folder, pulling out three fat packets of stapled papers and handing one to each of them. "One question for you all before we look at this—how old do you think I am?"

All three of them looked directly at her, and Gabi almost nervous-laughed at the expressions on Oliver's and Luke's faces.

Oliver shook his head. "It wouldn't be gentlemanly to answer that question, Laura, and I'm sure Luke would agree with me."

Luke nodded, his eyebrows pulled together as he studied her.

"Well, I'll tell you, then." Laura smiled. "Eighty-eight. Which is a nice round figure, don't you think?"

No one answered.

"Here's what's so nice about that age—it takes a lot to get here, and when you are worth what I'm worth, it takes a lot of *attorneys* to get here. I've got the best of the best, and now?" She winked. "Now I've got a little surprise."

Chapter 34

Surprise? Gabi looked down at the papers in her hand. A surprise couldn't be bad, right? Had Laura figured out a way to keep Oliver and Luke employed, even though the board was ready to turn this into an all-girls' camp?

But would they even *want* to be here if that happened?

Laura took a deep breath, lifting her own packet. "Here's the thing. It was my financial gift that bought this property, on the recommendation of one of those attorneys. I had heard of Camp Echo, and he convinced me that there wasn't another venture in New England more deserving of my investment. I did my research—though none of you probably even knew I *was* doing so—and the more I learned, the more I came to agree with him."

Gabi could practically feel Luke's wheels turning, wondering who this attorney was . . . and where Laura was going with this.

"I managed this bequest through Briarwood, because I truly wanted to believe that we could do better work for more children, and I was assured that the camp would be updated, staffed, and reopened next summer. I believe that's all under way, so that makes me happy." She tapped on the folders. "What *doesn't* make me happy is that this board took that vote eight weeks ago. What makes me even *less* happy is that I suspected that's exactly what they *would* do."

"But—" Gabi shook her head slowly. If she'd known, why had she funneled the donation through Briarwood? Why not just do it outright, if she suspected they'd rejigger it in the end?

Laura put up both index fingers, stopping her. "I bought this property, and I donated it to Briarwood, but I didn't give it freely. My attorneys wrote in a provision requiring that any change in purpose or mission be approved by me. We were sure they'd balk, but they approved it." She shrugged. "Obviously they were anxious to get their hands on the land, and I imagine they see me as the old, doddering fool who either didn't understand the legalese, or who wouldn't notice if they buried the mission changes in a pile of other things that came up for blanket approval at that meeting."

She arched her eyebrows. "I noticed. And I did *not* approve of the changes. An-nd, since we were unable to come to an agreement, the original bequest requires that the property be moved into a trust administered by my attorneys and myself."

"Wha—" Gabi felt her mouth fall open as a tiny glimmer of hope took hold. "So Briarwood no longer owns the property?"

Laura smiled. "I have very, very good lawyers."

Luke set down the papers he hadn't yet looked at, but Gabi couldn't tell from his face whether he thought Laura's news was positive, or just more of the same garbage.

"So what does this mean?" he asked.

"Well, that's why I'm here. I have some ideas, but before I finalize them, I want your input—all three of you. You're the ones who built the place, live here, and have seen it work. I want to hear what you have to say."

Gabi backed up on the bench, putting up her hands. "I've only been here for a few weeks, Laura. I can't possibly participate. I shouldn't."

"Wrong." Laura's voice was so strong that it made all three of them jump. "Why do you think you're here, Gabriela?"

"Huh?" Gabi blinked, knowing full well that Laura had been in the board meeting where Gabi's summer had gone up in smoke. She'd even voted, presumably. Why was she asking?

"Um . . ." she stammered. "I'm here because my girls got into hot water and this was the board's solution."

"Wrong again." Laura smiled, gentling her tone. "You're here because I've been watching you for years, and I love your spunk and your spirit and your heart . . . and I wanted you to fall in love with Echo Lake. I knew damn well what this board was going to do—that's why I made sure the provisions were written into the agreement in the first place. But a small part of me wanted to give them a chance to prove me wrong."

She sighed. "They didn't. So I sent you here."

"*You* sent me here?"

"Yes." Laura smiled like she was quite entertained with herself. "I'm quite good at influencing others when I put my mind to it. I just have to know their triggers. Since Priscilla Pritchard's particular trigger is misery, I suggested Camp Echo as a consequence to the girls' little escapade, but I made sure it sounded ever so much worse than it really is." Laura winked. "She went for it like a dog for a steak."

"Shocker." Gabi frowned, trying to connect Laura's dots. "But why did you want *me* to fall in love with Echo Lake?"

"Well, this is the best part." Laura crossed her hands over her chest like she could barely contain her excitement. "I have a plan, my dear. And God willing, you'll be part of it."

"A plan?" Gabi darted her eyes around the table, a distinct hum taking over her gut. It was the ninety percent fear, ten percent excitement type of hum, and she crossed her arms, swearing everyone else could hear it.

"A plan." Laura smiled as she slid more papers out of her folder. "I'd like to build a school."

Luke coughed. "A school?'

"A school." She nodded firmly. "A charter school, fully funded by my ridiculous wealth, aimed at the kids you most think could benefit from an Echo Lake–style education."

Luke tipped his head suspiciously. "What kind of kids?"

"That would be for you to decide."

"Me." The word fell softly, like he wasn't comprehending. Good, because neither was Gabi.

"Well, you and Gabriela, with input from Oliver."

"What?" Gabi shook her head. "But . . . Briarwood. My job—what?"

Laura smiled and patted her shoulder. "I'm sorry. I've had this idea running around in my head for two years now. I need to remember that nobody else here has a clue I've even *had* an idea." She took a deep breath. "Let me start from the beginning."

Oliver nodded, but a smile was busy taking over his face. "I think that would be advisable."

Laura stood up, walking to the windows. "Here's what I imagine—a school, right here on the shores of Echo Lake, where just the right kids live with just the right mentors. We find them, we meet them where they're at, and we care for them, educate them, and provide a safe haven so they can grow into successful, productive adults."

She turned her gaze toward them. "Oliver, you created this place. Luke, you've dedicated your own life to it. And Gabriela, you *need* this place. And selfishly, *I* need this place. I need to feel like the money my father left me is doing more than supporting a wealthy school full of wealthy girls who already have lives full of opportunity. I want this money to support those who don't have those advantages." She paused. "I want it to be used for the kids everyone else has forgotten. Because *those* are the ones who need it, and those are the ones who most deserve it."

Gabi looked at Luke, whose eyebrows had steadily hiked up his forehead as Laura had spoken. She still couldn't tell whether he thought she was for real.

"So this school . . ." His voice still held a healthy level of suspicion. "What do you envision, in concrete terms?"

Laura smiled, like she knew she'd hooked him, at least a little bit. "Well, on the physical end, I envision *some* building, just to make this a place suitable for year-round education. So, student cabins, a weatherproof dining hall, and some sort of indoor classroom space." She put up a finger. "But I assure you, I don't want this place to become an indoor-classroom type of school."

"What *do* you want it to become?"

"I don't want it to *become* anything. I want it to go back to exactly what it was last summer, and the summer before that, and the one fifteen years ago. You have a system that already works. You have teaching methods that already work. You have materials that already work." She shrugged her shoulders. "You *know* how to educate these kids, Luke. I wouldn't presume to change anything you already do. I just want to give you the funding to make it less painful, and to make it possible for you to do it for more kids."

Then she turned to Gabi. "And you, Gabriela, are hungry to do more, to *be* more than you can ever be at an insular, pretentious school like Briarwood. You've worked your proverbial ass off to make things change there, and what have you been able to accomplish?" She raised her eyebrows as Gabi slowly shook her head. "I *know* you're not happy with the board. And I know you have a huge heart that wants to do more. This is the perfect opportunity. You and Luke, overseen by Oliver, can create a school you can both be proud of."

Gabi swallowed. Holy . . . cow.

"Now, obviously we'd have a lot of details to work out, and you'll need some time to think it over, but I'm ready and willing to open up my account as soon as the three of you sign on the dotted line. We could be ready to open next June. Salaries will be negotiated between you and me, and I promise they'll be more than fair. My accountants are looking into all of that necessary-but-boring stuff like insurance and retirement and the like, but I am determined to have all three of you join me on this mission, and I'll do whatever I have to do to make it happen."

She stopped, looking from Gabi to Luke to Oliver, and then she laughed. "Oh, if you three could only see your faces right now."

"Well." Oliver shifted on the bench. "You do come in like a tornado-on-steroids, Miss Laura. It might take a little digestion time for us."

"Take all the time you need." She sat down, tapping her folders. "But I'd love an answer in the next two days."

Late that night, Gabi sat in her favorite Adirondack chair by the lake, running the meeting with Laura through her mind. It was all so much to take in, and she hadn't quite figured out how to process it yet.

When she heard Luke's footsteps stop about ten feet

behind her, she sat stock-still, wondering if he had come to find her.

He folded himself into a chair. "Wow, hm?"

"That would be an understatement." Gabi tossed a pebble from the pile she had in her lap. It made a satisfying *plink* when it hit the water.

"You think her plan's got legs?"

She nodded. "Oh, I think it's got a *lot* of legs. But it's also huge and risky and completely frightening."

"Which parts?"

"*All* of the parts. She's talking about turning Camp Echo into a year-round charter school, and she wants *us* to run it. You and me. It's complete and utter insanity."

"Or brilliance. She wants the school to serve the kind of kids we've always had here, but with her financing the operation, we'd be able to have them year-round."

"I know." She sighed. "I'm completely boggled by it all."

He looked out at the moonlit lake. "Which part really scares you the most?"

Gabi was silent for a long moment. "I'm not even sure, Luke. And I'm so low on sleep and high on adrenaline that I can't even think straight right now. I don't know how to process it."

"I know." He nodded. "I get it. It's a lot easier for me. I get to stay right where I want to be, working with kids I totally get, living in a town I'm already in love with. I wouldn't be giving up anything. It's a totally different ballgame for you."

"It is. Briarwood's kind of all I've ever known." She cringed. "And don't think I'm not fully aware of how pathetic that is."

"It's not pathetic, Gabriela. You grew up there, you loved it, and you went back there to try to make a difference. Hardly pathetic."

"Thank you," she whispered. "It sure feels it, though.

You know, for years, I had no idea she was anything but a smiling face at board meetings. I'd get up there at the head of the big conference table and make some plea for something I thought was worth pleading for, and she'd always be at the other end, smiling away like she thought it was the best idea since sliced bread."

"It probably was."

"Thank you." She rolled her eyes. "I always just figured she was like that with everyone."

"Well, apparently she wasn't. She had your number, and she was making plans."

She turned toward Luke, putting her hands over her stomach to try to quell the hive of bees that seemed to be trying to bash their way through her skin. "What do you really think of her plan? Do *you* truly think it has legs?"

"Hell, yes. I think it's exactly what this area needs . . . and a lot of areas within driving distance. Opening up this school will give us the opportunity to target kids like Sam and Eve—get them out of their current situations, but give them the kind of education that'll feed their souls, rather than sticking them where they can never belong." He put up his hands. "And I'm not saying that in judgment. I'm just repeating what you said to me."

"I know." Gabi sighed. "I just—I can't fathom how it would all work. It's so huge."

"It is. But when you look at the expertise you, Oliver, and I bring to the table, it's three pretty damn good brains. I don't get the sense that Laura makes stupid decisions, and she's got this one planned out to the finest detail. The woman's practically made of money, it sounds like, but she's trying to do good things with it. We'd be insane not to take her up on this."

He reached for her hand, and she let him take it. As

his skin touched hers, she felt the buzzing subside, and she took a deep breath, letting it out slowly.

"Gabriela, this could be your chance to make the kind of difference you've been wanting to make for all these years. This is your chance to give fifty, a hundred, two hundred kids a better life . . . in just one year. No fighting the Pritch-bitches of the world. No watching trust funds grow while kids go hungry. You could be right here, with us, making every day count. Think about how that would feel."

His voice was soft but convincing, and Gabi felt herself caving little by little as he talked, but she still couldn't quell the nerves zapping every inch of her body.

On the surface, it seemed like the perfect solution. She'd get to do great things, she'd get to live in a place that belonged on postcards. She'd get to . . . be with him. Every day. Maybe every night. It seemed almost too perfect to be true.

And that was exactly why she knew she needed to step back, take some time to think it through, and not jump in with both feet before she'd thoroughly considered all of the angles.

"Please don't hate me," she finally said, "but I can't say yes to this. Not right now. Not yet."

He sighed. "Because?"

"Because I need to think, Luke. This is huge with a capital *H*. This would be me upending my entire existence on a chance that things might work out here. This would be me leaving behind any sense of stability I still have. Me leaving everything I know in the rearview mirror. I can't turn that sort of decision around in twenty-four hours, as idealistic as this whole project sounds. I just . . . can't."

"Understood." He nodded slowly, pulling his hand back. "How long do you think you might need?"

"I have no idea. I need to go back to Briarwood, settle the girls back in, and take some time for myself so I can think it through. I just—I don't honestly know how long that might take. I'm sorry."

"Okay," he said, and she couldn't help but see the hurt expression in his eyes as he turned away.

"It's not just the school we're talking about here." Gabi's voice cracked as she spoke, and she tried to swallow the emotion so it wasn't so damn obvious.

"I know, Gabriela. And I guess I was looking at that as falling firmly in the pros column, rather than the cons." He tapped his fist quietly on the arm of the chair. "But maybe I'm the only one seeing it that way."

"You're not. I mean—" She put her head back against the chair, blowing out a long breath. "We've known each other for a whole three weeks. That's it. And now we're talking about tying our professional futures together in a pretty tight way. And maybe that'd be all fine and wonderful if our personal lives were similarly entwined. But good God, Luke. That's a lot of togetherness, even for the most solid couples. And we're not even—"

"A couple?" He raised his eyebrows.

"Well . . . *yes*. We're . . . I don't even *know* what we are, at this point." She closed her eyes, on one hand, longing to slide onto his lap and have him tell her everything was going to work out beautifully . . . and on the other hand, thinking maybe she should run to the end of the dock and dive in, hoping for the cold water to slice some sense into her.

"Or what you want us to be? If anything?" His voice was level, but Gabi could feel him forcing the casual tone.

"Yes. No." She cringed. "This is the problem. I don't know. And it's not fair to skulk around here for the next week trying to figure that out. I don't think I can."

"Because it's impossible to think straight when you're in my presence?" He lifted his eyebrows. "What with all the handy-ish, man-ish vibes and all?"

Gabi smiled, grateful that he was trying so hard to keep this lighter than it really was. But he was dead right. If she *didn't* leave right now, she'd make her decision—whichever way she went—for all the wrong reasons.

And for once in her damn life, she wasn't going to complete the fall-fast-fall-hard cycle with an epic fall-stupid.

"I have to go, Luke. I'm not saying I won't be back. I just . . . have to go."

Chapter 35

The next afternoon, an hour into the trip back home to Briarwood, Gabi glanced in the rearview mirror and saw the same sight she'd been looking at for the entire trip so far—four girls looking out separate windows, all with their arms crossed. It mirrored the way they'd looked on their way *to* Camp Echo, but this time, the crossed arms were *her* fault, not Pricilla Pritchard's. As furious as these four had been to come to Camp Echo in the first place, they were far angrier about leaving.

And somehow it'd be easier to take, if she herself hadn't been tempted to turn around ten times already. All she wanted right now was to be in Luke's arms, Luke's cabin, Luke's . . . *life,* but she'd promised herself a time-out somewhere far away from Echo Lake so she could think clearly, and as much as it was killing her to drive south right now, she knew she was doing the right thing.

Definitely.

Pretty sure.

Definitely.

"I still don't understand why we need to go back early." Madison glared at Gabi. "Is Sam even supposed to be up and around yet?"

"She's on crutches, Madison. She's fine. I explained it this morning. The dorm is ready, Oliver and Luke still have a million things to do back at camp, and we were in the way. You guys have served a long enough sentence. There's no reason to keep hanging out there when we could be out of their hair and back at school. We'll get the jump on the other students, you know? Get there early and have a little down time."

Despite her manufactured chipper tone, the argument fell just as flat as she knew it would, dammit.

Waverly spoke up. "Did *Luke* say we were in the way?"

Gabi sighed. "No."

"Then why are we leaving?" Eve sat up straighter. "Don't bullshit us, Gabi. Did you and Luke have a fight? Is that why we have to go?"

"No. Luke and I aren't—no. He has nothing to do with this."

"Right." Madison rolled her eyes. "He's just the best thing that's happened to us *or* you in, like, ever. But we definitely shouldn't stay and be happy about it. Yes, let's go back to a deserted campus and hang out being mortally bored for the summer while we wait for the rest of the princesses to show up."

Sam snorted. "Says the princess of the princesses."

Gabi braced for Madison's reply, realizing that only an hour away from Camp Echo, the girls were already reverting to their pre-camp relationship. The weight of dismal failure that had been sitting in her stomach since yesterday sank even further.

"Yeah, well, maybe being a princess is overrated," Madison replied, making Gabi's eyebrows fly upward.

Sam turned to look at her. "This mean you're going to actually act like who you *are* this year, instead of putting on the rich-bitch cloak when you leave your bedroom?"

Again Gabi braced herself, but Madison just smiled. "I will if you will."

"Right. Like I have one."

"You have your own. But you're actually not nearly as angry and standoffish as you wanted us all to think."

"Don't let it get out." Sam rolled her eyes.

Waverly tapped Gabi's seat. "Just because they're getting along now doesn't mean we're not still royally ticked that you're bringing us back early. Just so you know."

"Noted. Thank you."

An hour later, the girls begged for a bathroom break, so Gabi pulled into a rest area. Sam didn't want to navigate with her crutches, so Madison stayed with her while Gabi and the other two went inside. There was free coffee on the hospitality counter, so Gabi filled up a cup and stirred in creamer while she waited for Waverly and Eve to come out of the restroom.

She wandered the tiny building, picking up random brochures, trying to quell the faint nausea creeping up her throat every time she thought of Luke.

But she was doing the right thing. Space and time were important here. She had to make the right decision, for the right reasons, and she couldn't do it at Camp Echo, where her eyes were trained to look for his soft T-shirts and jeans . . . where her ears listened for his whistle even when she wasn't trying to . . . where her skin ached for his gentle, gorgeous, perfect touch so damn hard.

Finally, when she'd drunk almost half of her coffee, the girls emerged.

"You guys okay?" Gabi scanned their faces, worried something about lunch hadn't agreed with them.

"Fine. We're good. Let's roll." Eve pointed at the doorway.

When they got into the van, Madison leaned over Gabi's seat, putting her hand on Gabi's arm so she couldn't put the key into the ignition.

"Are you sure about this? Because we could still go back. I'm betting Luke could find us enough work to keep us busy for the next week, and maybe the two of you could work out whatever happened between you."

"Madison, there is nothing—"

"No offense, Gabi, but save it." Waverly leaned over as well. "We know you guys—you know—hung out."

"We're just friends." Gabi felt her face heat up.

Sam snorted. "Friends with ben—"

"No." Gabi put her hand up. "Don't even say it. Don't even go there. I do *not* do that."

"But . . . you did." Madison did her best cringe-face. "More than once."

Gabi felt her cheeks go scarlet. "Honestly, this is none of your business."

Eve stood up in her own seat, leaning onto the one in front of her. "Actually, it kind of is."

"How do you figure?"

"Well, we earned ourselves a ticket to a free four-week camp. We *got* a three-week camp. You still owe us a week."

"Fine. I'll pitch you a tent at Briarwood."

"We want to go back, Gabi," Waverly said. "Please?"

"No. Absolutely not. It's time to move forward and get ready for the new year."

Eve flopped back into her seat. "This sucks."

Waverly mirrored her actions, crossing her arms. "Totally."

Madison sat back down. "Fine. But when you dry up like a raisin and become an old bitty spinster—or whatever they call those—don't blame us. We tried."

Gabi put the key in the ignition. "Noted. I will accept

full blame." She turned the key to start the van, but instead of the purr of the engine, all she heard was a click. She turned the key again, and again, click.

She knew that sound. It was an awful lot like the sound the van had made when Luke had removed the battery.

"Girls?" She looked in the rearview mirror, but four innocent faces met her eyes. "Anyone know what's wrong with the van?"

All four of them shook their heads, but Gabi felt dread fill her gut as she popped the hood and got out of the van. She walked around to the front and lifted the hood, then sighed and closed her eyes when she saw the empty space where the battery was supposed to be.

She counted to twenty, then let the hood drop back down. She walked calmly to the door and slid back into the seat, and she sat there for a full minute without speaking. Finally, she looked into the rearview mirror, where again, four innocent faces greeted her.

Then Sam grinned. "This guy—he just came right over and stole it while you were in the bathroom."

"Yup," Madison agreed. "I saw it with my own eyes. Nothing we could do to stop him."

Gabi's eyes shifted to Waverly and Eve. "And the ten minutes it took *you two* to *pee*?"

Eve shrugged. "Bad fish for lunch."

"You had peanut butter sandwiches."

"Bad peanut butter," Waverly said, smiling.

Gabi took a deep breath. "Where's the battery?"

"Gone." Madison pointed toward the ramp that went back onto the highway. "A garbage truck pulled in beside us. It was kind of—you know—fate."

"You *threw* the *battery*—" Gabi took another breath and blew it out slowly. "Why? Why did you do this?"

The girls were silent for a long moment, until Sam finally leaned forward. "Because you're being a moron."

"Excuse me?"

"You're totally, completely, sickeningly in love with Luke, but you won't let yourself admit it. So we're helping."

"How is this helping?" Gabi felt her voice rise an octave.

"Well, we figure the worst thing that could possibly happen to you is find yourself in a situation where you're helpless and need a rescue." Madison shrugged. "So we arranged the situation. And now we'll arrange the rescue."

She pulled out her phone and punched a couple of buttons before Gabi grabbed it. "Don't you dare call him."

"She doesn't need to." Sam held up her phone, an impish look on her face. "I texted him an hour ago with the plan. He's on his way."

Chapter 36

"You can stop laughing anytime now, Luke." An hour later, Gabi crossed her arms as he slammed the hood of the van back down, a brand-new battery now in place.

"I'm sorry." He grinned. "I really just can't. I mean, come on. They took out the battery and tossed it in the back of a garbage truck? That takes some serious balls."

"We could have been stuck here for hours."

He held up his phone. "Looks like they thought that part through. You couldn't have even been in White River before I got Sam's text. These girls are planners, Gabi."

She rolled her eyes. "And once again, I'm apologizing for them. I'm so sorry you had to drive all the way down here."

"I'm not." Before she could think about resisting, Luke reached out and braced his hands on her hips. "I am *thrilled* that your closest associates are a bunch of scheming teenagers. I'm *thrilled* that they know how to disable a car and call for a rescue. But the thing I'm most thrilled about is that after only three weeks, they knew they could call *me,* and they knew I would come."

She rolled her eyes and sighed. "I know."

Luke raised his eyebrows, leaning down so she was

forced to fall into those damn smoky emerald eyes of his.

"Gabriela, I know you're the queen of I-don't-need-no-knight-in-shining-armor in my life, but in actuality, everybody needs one. Even, y'know, your average hot camp director. Or, say, codirector of the forthcoming Echo Lake Charter School."

Gabi felt a bubble of laughter sneak out. She couldn't help it. With his hands circling her hips, and that dimple taunting her as he looked at her, all she wanted to do was close the inches between them and feel his arms pull her close.

He tipped her chin up with two fingers. "Guess what just occurred to me?"

"I can't imagine."

"You know how we were talking about how you want the rom-com?"

"I never agreed to that. I just want the happily-ever-after *ending*."

He bounced his eyebrows playfully. "Well, we've just now had the whole all-is-lost moment, and you did the dramatic run-for-the-hills thing, but you had to careen to a halt because your impish crew of teenagers decided to do your thinking for you, knowing that in your heart, you *do* belong with the guy from Echo Lake." He put both hands in the air dramatically. "We've done it! We made a rom-com!"

Gabi laughed. She couldn't help it. "So what comes next, hot camp director?"

"Oh, the next part's easy." He smiled. "We do a kiss full of silent promises while we ignore the fact that we're in a highway rest area, and the cameras pan out to show an idyllic Vermont scene, complete with a big white van making a U-turn and heading back to Echo Lake, where the audience knows it's just a matter of time before the hero will convince the heroine to follow her heart and stay."

"It's that easy, hm?" Gabi smiled, but her butterflies were in full flight.

Luke's face grew serious. "No. It's not easy at all. It'll be hard work, and we'll have fits and starts, and we might even argue once or twice. But dammit, Gabriela, this is real. You know it's real, and I know it's real." He leaned down, and before she could think to back up, he kissed her softly. "Come back to Echo Lake, Gabi. Come back, and we can build something amazing."

Gabi looked up at him—at eyes that heated her from the inside, lips that whispered the perfect words, and she knew she really *didn't* have a choice. She knew that somewhere not so deep inside, she was secretly thrilled that the girls had taken it upon themselves to disable their ride home, in hopes that they could go back to the very spot they'd dreaded just three weeks ago.

She knew she had to go back. She had to give this a chance, because if what she felt for Luke *wasn't* real, then . . . nothing was. She would hate herself forever if she didn't give this an honest shot.

She nodded slowly, watching his face break into a grin as she did. "I think I'm completely, utterly nuts to say yes."

"That's fine." He squeezed her tightly. "I can deal with completely, utterly nuts."

"Are you sure about this?" She blew out a breath. "Really, really sure?"

Luke brought both of his hands up to hold her face— so gently she felt like delicate crystal. "I've never been more sure of anything in my life, sweetheart. If there was a minister in the next car, I'd totally ask him to marry us right here, right now."

"Good God, Luke." She laughed nervously.

"But it's okay that you're not there yet." He winked. "I can totally wait another week or two."

"That's . . . very generous of you."

He slid one hand into her hair as the other encircled her waist, a mysterious smile on his face. "So are you ready?"

"For?" she breathed.

He cocked his head and rolled his eyes to the right. "I think our little matchmakers are waiting for the end."

"The end?"

"Of the movie. The big kiss. The swelling music." He shook his head. "You know."

Gabi smiled, reaching up to link her fingers around his neck, feeling like nothing had ever been more right.

"Okay," she whispered. "Kiss full of promise. I'm ready."

He touched her lips with his—softly, sweetly, like they were alone . . . like cars weren't whooshing by on an interstate just beyond the grassy median. And she melted into him like four teens hadn't whooped and clapped the moment their lips met.

He pulled back, smiling. "I love you, Gabriela. And that's not for rom-com effect. That's . . . from my heart."

Gabi laughed, the butterflies settling down for the first time since he'd driven into the rest area in his beat-up old truck that somehow was exactly perfect for him.

"You know what?" She shook her head like she could hardly believe what she was about to say. "It turns out . . . I love you, too."

Epilogue

"Oh, Gabi. It's perfect." Piper's eyes got all watery as she did a circle around Gabi, pulling gently at the layers of white satin. "It's so . . . you."

Gabi looked in the mirrors, twisting left and right to see how the wedding gown looked from all angles. It was stunning. Absolutely stunning.

Laura stood up from the fancy wingback chair in the corner, and Gabi's hand went to her mouth as she saw the tears in the older woman's eyes.

"Oh, Gabriela." She circled slowly, touching the pearls, the lace, the satin. "I never thought I'd be so proud as I was the moment you agreed to wear my dress. But seeing you in it right now? I'm just bursting. You look . . . so beautiful."

Gabi reached out to hug her. "Thank you for saying so. And for asking me to wear your dress. You can't possibly know how much it means."

"Well, I do claim some responsibility for this wedding, so it seemed only appropriate." Laura smiled. "And I hope you'll have a marriage as long and as happy as mine was. I never had a daughter to pass this along to." Laura hugged her tightly. "Thank you for wearing it."

Piper wiped her eyes with a tissue, then shook her head like she was pulling herself together.

"Hannah just texted from the salon. She's on her way."

Gabi smiled, picturing the blond bombshell that ran Hannah's Hair Palace. She operated at two speeds—fast and super-fast, and over the past year, she'd become one of Gabi's closest friends. For the first time in—well, ever, Gabi actually *had* a circle of friends she could picture keeping for longer than a semester, and she marveled at the fact that she'd never considered that Luke might come with a prepackaged group of people he was more than willing to share.

An hour later, Hannah turned her toward the mirror, and Gabi gasped. Her hair was pulled back in a gentle updo, with strands left loose to frame her face. Hannah had done her makeup, as well, and Gabi felt like she'd just stepped out of a magazine.

"You guys!" Her eyes welled up. "I look like a . . . bride!"

Piper, in a dark blue strapless bridesmaid dress that matched Hannah's, dabbed at her eyes. "That you do, my dear. Luke is going to *flip* when he sees you."

The subtle bell on the bridal salon door rang, and Laura looked at her silver watch. "Now, who could that possibly be?"

Piper went to the door, and Gabi fluffed out her dress in the mirror, wishing she was already walking up the aisle. She smiled as Piper returned with a box, a mystified look on her face.

"What is it?" Gabi asked.

"I don't know." Piper handed it to her.

Gabi looked down, and her smile turned into a contented sigh as she saw Luke's handwriting. She opened the box, then laughed out loud when she realized what was inside.

"What's in there?" Hannah crowded close, then laughed as well. "DVDs?"

Piper peered over her other shoulder. "Good Lord, there are, like, twenty of them. Has Luke not heard of video streaming?"

Gabi just smiled as she picked up one of the movies and turned it to see the cover. *"Pretty Woman."* She put it back in, picked up another. *"Sleepless in Seattle."* Her smile grew bigger as she pulled out rom-com after rom-com. *"Dirty Dancing, Love Actually, The Proposal."*

She put a hand to her mouth. "How in the world did I ever doubt this man?"

Piper laughed. "Is he promising to actually *watch* those with you? Because that would pretty much seal the deal. I mean—you know—besides the whole wedding ring and dress and everything."

"Oh, you'd better believe it." Gabi finished pulling the movies out of the box, then reached in to find a creamy envelope lettered in gold.

"Why'd he put a copy of your wedding invitation in there?" Hannah asked.

"I . . . don't know." Gabi smiled as she opened it, then sank down onto the antique settee behind her as she read the words he'd printed inside the card.

Piper sat down beside her. "What does it say?"

Gabi laughed quietly, then wiped her eyes. "It says, 'When you realize you want to spend the rest of your life with somebody, you want the rest of your life to start as soon as possible. *When Harry Met Sally,* 1989.'"

"Aww. He stole a rom-com line?"

"He totally did."

Laura pulled the curtains aside. "I believe our ride is here, ladies. Gabi? Are you ready to go meet your groom?"

Gabi looked out at the white limo, then at Luke's words, and then back at the three women who, one year ago, she'd barely known, and her face broke into a huge grin.

"I've never been more ready for anything."

Piper held the door for her as she walked out of the bridal salon, then tip-tapped on her heels over to the limo, kissing the driver full on the lips.

"At your service, ma'am." Noah smiled and bowed as he helped Gabi's dress follow her into the limo. "I'm in charge of making sure the bride doesn't head for the hills before the wedding. Apparently it's a thing."

He closed the door and walked around to the driver's seat, and fifteen minutes later, the limo was bouncing down the dirt road toward Camp Echo. As they pulled closer, Gabi could see car after car parked at the edge of the dirt road, and she felt the flutter of nerves.

"Who invited all of these people?" Her voice was shaky, and Piper took her hand.

"You did. And they all said yes."

Finally the limo parked, and Noah opened the door and helped each of them out. He put one arm out for Piper and one for Laura, and they disappeared up the pathway toward the dining hall, which looked like it was lit with a hundred thousand twinkling white lights. In the autumn evening darkness, the entire camp looked magical.

The new school buildings peeked over the hilltop behind Luke's cabin, all freshly constructed with logs from the surrounding forest. In just two weeks, the first fifty students would arrive, and Gabi and Luke had both been running from dawn till dusk to make it happen.

But tonight? Tonight was about them.

"Well, Ms. O'Brien." Oliver's voice came from behind her. "May I escort you to your wedding?"

Gabi turned toward him, but instead of holding out an elbow for her arm, he held both hands wide. She laughed and leaped into his arms, almost toppling him over.

"I can't believe you guys did this. Look at this place!"

Lights covered the cottages, the remodeled administration building, and were even strung down the dock. She pointed at the Adirondack chairs by the beach, which were glowing with pink bulbs.

"Look at the chairs!"

Oliver smiled. "We had a little help with the decorating."

Gabi spun. "I can't believe you did this all this afternoon. I wasn't even gone for four hours!"

"Well, when you hire the best . . ." A familiar voice came from behind the limo, and Gabi's face felt like it might actually crack as Sam stepped into the light. "We might be girlish and pretty, but we're workhorses, right, Oliver?"

Gabi smiled as she pulled Sam into her arms. "Thank you, Sam. It looks unbelievable."

"Well, I had a little help." Sam pointed to another car. "Come on, girls. Show your ugly faces."

The door opened, and Gabi squeaked as Eve, Waverly, and Madison stepped out, and suddenly she felt tears flying down her cheeks, probably ruining Hannah's careful makeup job as she hugged each of them.

"I can't believe you guys are here!" Gabi turned to Sam. "How—"

Sam grinned. "Well, since not all of them can be lucky enough to live here now, like I do, we went to get them."

"Who did?"

"Me and Luke. This morning."

Gabi put her hand to her chest. "So he wasn't in town doing errands . . . obviously."

"Nope. Halfway to Massachusetts before you even woke up." Sam squeezed her hand. "He knew you'd want them here."

Waverly smiled, adjusting her dress. "We *are* kind of the reason you're getting married in the first place. If we'd never gotten in trouble, you'd never have met the man of your dreams."

"Yeah." Madison smiled. "You're welcome, Gabi. And look what we did."

She pointed behind Oliver, where Luke's dogs sat quietly, little blue bows around their necks. Gabi laughed when she saw the ring boxes attached to their collars.

"You added Puff-n-Fluff to my bridal party?"

Sam smiled as she grabbed their leashes. "It seemed apt."

Oliver motioned toward the dining hall. "Ladies? I think we've got some people waiting, and a very anxious groom."

Gabi took a deep breath, looking up the pathway, lit with even more white lights. The girls and dogs headed toward the building, and once they heard the door close, Oliver crooked his arm and held out his elbow for Gabi.

"Shall we go meet your groom, Gabriela?"

She took his arm, dabbing quickly at her eyes as she felt a huge smile take over her face. "Absolutely, Oliver. Let's go meet my groom."

At midnight, Gabi stood on the dock under the twinkling white lights, her back nestled against Luke.

"Are you happy, Gabriela?" His voice was soft in her ear, and shivers cascaded down her entire body.

"I'm happier than I ever knew anybody *could* be." She turned, smiling. "And you?"

"I'm feeling like the luckiest guy on Earth, yeah." He kissed her softly, brushing her loose tendrils of hair back with gentle fingers.

She pulled back a tiny bit. "So is this the part of the rom-com where you deliver the super-cheesy romantic line, and then we fade to black?"

"Absolutely."

"Okay." She smiled. "I'm ready."

"Okay." He nodded, letting his eyes dart back and forth like he was thinking. "Um, okay. Ooh—nobody puts Baby in a corner?"

She laughed. "Um . . ."

"You complete me? You had me at hello?" He cringed. "Anything there?"

"Mm, no-o."

"Oh, I've got it. Best one ever."

"I can't wait."

He laced his fingers with hers, pulling her close. "Say you love me, Gabriela."

"You love me, Gabriela." She bit her lip, then squeaked as he tickled her. "Okay, okay. I love you."

He took a deep breath, like he was about to utter the single most epic rom-com line in history, then slid his hands up to cradle her jaw. He looked into her eyes, so serious that her breath caught.

Then, with his eyes crinkling at the corners, he whispered, "Ditto."

Don't miss the first two novels in this
heartwarming series by bestselling author
Maggie McGinnis

Forever This Time

Heart Like Mine

From St. Martin's Paperbacks